**Praise for** *The Excali...*
*The Oak C...*

A delight to read. (Doyle's) tale of the sword is convincing and realistic. It reads like an epic movie.

—June Stevenson
former editor *United Church Observer*

It's a fun read, almost cinematic in scope with one accelerating scene after another… (There's) rich atmosphere in the rough and tumble of the good guys, the Welsh monastery and the Welsh Valleys, and the lagoons of modern day Venice. Look forward to the sequel

—Bruce Rogers
former host CBC Radio

What a great read! The plot is thick and surprising. I'm a picky reader and this one is as good as Tom Clancy!

—Dr. Doug Davis
Eastern Illinois University

Barrie Doyle has woven a distant past with a very dangerous present. Mystery, adventure and sacrifice planted in ancient times causes a frightening modern conflict. You're going to enjoy this book. It is a fresh telling of one of the great myths of western culture.

Coleman Luck
—Hollywood Screenwriter
TV producer, (*The Equalizer*)
and author (*Angel Fall*)

This action packed tale will leave you breathless and reading until the wee hours of the morning, wondering what happens next!

—Robert White
host FaithFM

(It) reminds me of Ken Follett. Fast paced. Deep local colour, plausible characters and a unique story line. A satisfying and illuminating read.

—Kirk Vanderzande

# The Lucifer Scroll

# The Lucifer Scroll

Springwater Public Library

## Barrie Doyle

Book Two - The Oak Grove Conspiracies

## THE LUCIFER SCROLL
Copyright © 2016 by Barrie Doyle

All rights reserved. Neither this publication nor any part of this publication may be reproduced or transmitted in any form or by any means, electronic or mechanical, including photocopying, recording or any information storage and retrieval system, without permission in writing from the author.

This is a work of fiction. Names, characters, places and incidents either are the product of the author's imagination or are used fictitiously, and any resemblance to actual persons, living or dead, businesses, companies, events, or locales is entirely coincidental.

Printed in Canada

ISBN: 978-1-4866-0620-7

Word Alive Press
131 Cordite Road, Winnipeg, MB R3W 1S1
www.wordalivepress.ca

Library and Archives Canada Cataloguing in Publication

Doyle, Barrie, 1946-, author
    The Lucifer scroll / Barrie Doyle.

(The oak grove conspiracies)
Issued in print and electronic formats.
ISBN 978-1-4866-0620-7 (pbk.).--ISBN 978-1-4866-0621-4 (pdf).--
ISBN 978-1-4866-0622-1 (html).--ISBN 978-1-4866-0623-8 (epub)

    I. Title.

PS8607.O9885L83 2016         C813'.6         C2014-905682-6
                                             C2014-905683-4

*For Joshua and Kaleb*
*who have both taught me the values of*
*courage, compassion, patience and strength.*

## Glossary and Locations

| | |
|---|---|
| **Alban Hefin** | Druid midsummer festival |
| **Anglesey** | Island in North Wales |
| **Anschluss** | Nazi takeover of Austria, March 1938 |
| **Bach** | Welsh expression, similar to "friend" or "mate" |
| **Bore Da** | "good day", "hello" (Welsh) |
| **Bundesarkiv** | German State Archives |
| **Caddesi** | "Zyaa-dess-si" Street (Turkish) |
| **Cami** | "Zya-me"; Mosque (Turkish |
| **Cariad** | car-ee-add; darling, sweetheart (Welsh) |
| **Castell y Draig** | Dragon Castle |
| **Die Heilige Lanze** | "The Holy Lance" (German) |
| **Diolch yn fawre** | Dee-olk in vower; thank you very much (Welsh) |
| **Duw Duw** | dew-dew; Welsh expression of surprise or amazement |
| **Enoninu** | historic district in Istanbul, Turkey |
| **Gila** | mountain range in New Mexico, USA |
| **Gorsedd** | Gor-seth; meeting or council (Welsh) |
| **Guvnor** | British slang for "boss", or "chief" |
| **Iachy da** | Ya-kee-da; Cheers (as a greeting) (Welsh) |
| **Istanbul** | Largest city in Turkey; formerly known as Constantinople |
| **Jeton** | Zj-e-ton; Istanbul transit token |
| **Koblenz** | city in Germany; home of state archives |
| **Optio** | Roman army rank; second-in-command to Centurion |
| **RPG** | rocket-propelled grenade |
| **Oberfuhrer** | Nazi rank equivalent to Brigadier |
| **Resolven** | town in Vale of Neath, South Wales near Swansea |
| **Sakel** | sa-keel; idiot (Turkish) |
| **Samhein** | So-ween; Druid celebration at halloween |
| **Schloss** | Shh-loss; castle (German) |
| **Sidhe** | "see-th-e"; mythical fairy-like being of Celtic and druid legends |
| **Sturmbanfuhrer** | Nazi rank equivalent to Major |
| **Sultanahmet** | historic district in Istanbul, Turkey |

| | |
|---|---|
| **Tara** | Historic site in Ireland; the place where ancient Irish kings were crowned; sacred site to Druids |
| **Telly** | British slang for television |
| **Uni** | British slang for university |
| **Wicklow** | County in Ireland; on coast of Irish sea just south of Dublin |
| **Yns Mons** | Ancient Welsh name for Anglesey in North Wales |
| **Zell am See** | town in Austria |

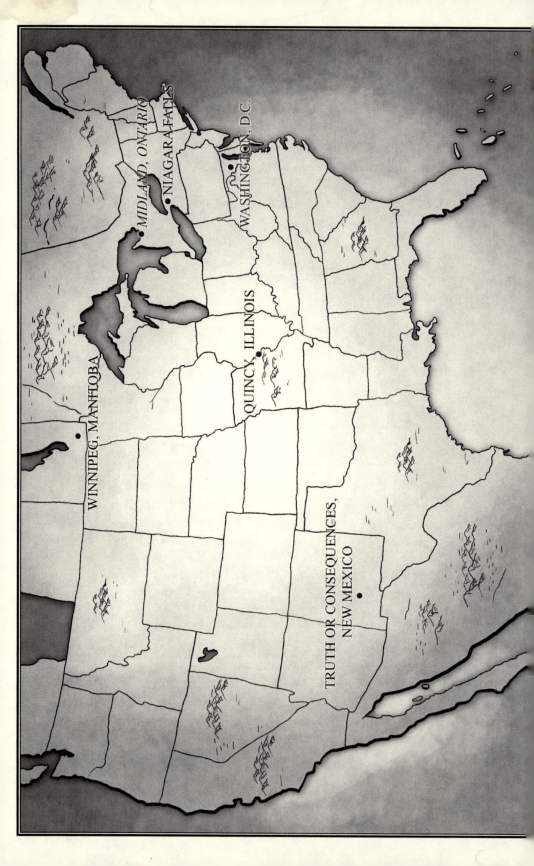

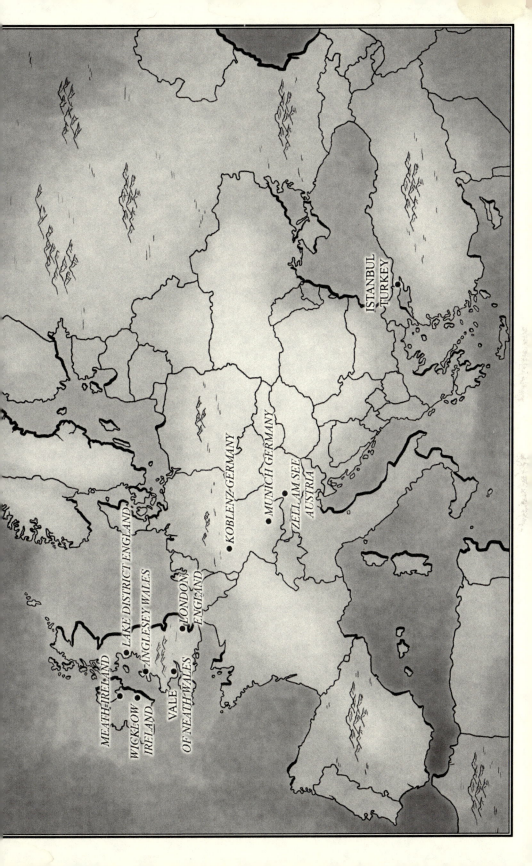

And I suppose I must go alone if I am to do that and save The Shire. But I feel very small, and very uprooted, and, well, desperate. The Enemy is so strong and terrible.

> Frodo Baggins,
> "Lord of the Rings· Fellowship of the Ring"

Yet such is oft the course of deeds that move the wheels of the world· small hands do them because they must, while the eyes of the great are elsewhere.

> Master Elrond
> "Lord of the Rings· Fellowship of the Ring"

# Prologue

### The shores of the Dead Sea, AD 34

It was the same every night. He dreaded the visitations. He wrapped his arms around his still muscular knees, squatting in the dirt and rocking back and forth in his rocky cave high above the Salt Sea.

Marcus Lucinius Janus, former Centurion of the Tenth Fretensis Legion howled his frustration. His ragged tunic was ripped and covered in filth—his own as well as that of the animals that had inhabited the cave before him. Cominius Centra Bestia, his Optio, stood at the cave entrance, his shining helmet and armor in sharp contrast with Lucinius' misery and dirt.

"It begins again this night." Bestia's words were as much a comment as a question.

Lucinius mutely nodded, tears flowing down his cheeks "I cannot fight any longer. This is my punishment for executing the Nazarene." Spittle dripped down his grizzled face that had not seen a blade for days. The standards of cleanliness for Legionnaires did not apply now, not since he'd left the garrison fourteen nights ago, renouncing his legion post and surviving as a beggar on his lonely trek from Jerusalem to the Salt Sea.

He confided only in Bestia his Optio, the second in command, and one of his few friends in the Legion. Bestia did not judge but only nodded when Lucinius told him of the misery of the night demons. When he could take it no longer, after months of fighting the visitations, he told Bestia of his plan to disappear from Jerusalem in the hopes that removing himself from the site where he had commanded the crucifixion of the Nazarene would stay the hauntings.

"You will be hunted down as a deserter and executed, Marcus." Bestia calmly told him when he heard the desperate plan.

"Better that than these horrible dreams."

"You obeyed Pilate's orders. You prevented revolt in the city."

"I did. And I have had the night demons each night since. They get stronger and more terrible until my mind feels like it must explode." His fist grabbed his tunic and ripped it open, exposing his scarred and bloody chest, the scrapes and scratches of his nails covering deeper, fresh scars. It was Bestia's plan to run to the Salt Sea. It was Bestia who helped him find the lonely, hidden lair.

Lucinius stared at his Optio standing coolly at the cave entrance, scarlet cape swirling in the hot winds that scoured the hillside. "I cannot escape, not even when I try to kill myself. Look!"

More tears coursed down his face as he jumped up, drew his gladius and dug it deeply across his body. Blood spurted out, staining his tunic yet again and dripping into the dirt at his feet. He screamed again towards the cave entrance. "Each night I slice my wrists, open my chest, or pierce my gut with my sword. And each day I wake up, scarred but healed again. The Nazarene was a magician. He must be the one who heals me each night. They said he was a healer. It must be him. I cannot live in the city. I cannot carry out my duties. I am a madman driven from all that I have known."

He dropped to his knees, tears and blood mixing and flowing to the ground. "No relief. No relief, Bestia," he wept.

Unmoved, Bestia watched his senior officer. "There is relief Marcus. Do as the night demons command." His voice seemed to deepen and change in the gloomy cave.

Lucinius turned and looked at his Optio. The face was the same, but there was a darkness about Bestia' face, a darkness that had little to do with the falling light and deepening shadows. It was a deeper, blacker darkness that oozed out of Bestia inner being.

"I have the materials. I have the tools. Do as the voices say Lucinius. Write the letter."

*The Lucifer Scroll*

He stepped forward and pointed to Lucinius' mutilated body. As he did, the blood pouring out of the deep wound across Lucinius' chest suddenly stopped flowing. The sliced flesh began to scar before his eyes. Lucinius fell on his back, staring at the soldier before him.

"Who are you," Lucinius croaked. "You are not Bestia."

"What does it matter who I am? Do as the voice commands Lucinius. Write the words you hear in your head. Write it in this scroll." The velvety voice had a deep hollow sound coming from depths beyond the human body.

Bestia stepped forward, put a hand under Lucinius' elbow and pulled him erect.

"Obey the voice Lucinius. The torment will be over soon."

## Constantinople, May 29 1453

The stench of burning flesh was stronger now and it stung in his nostrils. Father Manfred scurried through the narrow back alleys of the great city, grasping his muddy black robe, struggling but failing to keep the hem out of the offal and dirt. He flung himself around a corner beckoning to his servant. "Come. Hurry. Keep the light before my feet." There was a fear deep in his belly that had little to do with the siege.

The servant, a lithe young lad clothed in a dirty grey-white tunic rushed up beside the portly priest, breathing heavily and thrusting the light ahead so they could see their way down the dark hill. As they crossed over one street Father Manfred quickly glanced over his right shoulder. On the hill above Galata and across the Golden Horn he could see the myriad of lights that marked the encampment of the Ottoman army. Even in the dawning light they flickered.

For nearly two months the city had resisted the young Sultan Mehmet. Yet the city was battered and besieged. Fires started by flaming arrows devastated parts of the city close to the Horn. It was the flesh of those killed in the attacks and then burned in the fires that he could smell. He raised a soiled cloth to cover his face and kept running.

Rumors said the Emperor made overtures to the Hungarians and they were raising an army to come and throw the thrice-damned Muhammedans back. Rumors also said the Emperor had boldly refused Mehmet's demand that he surrender the city. But then, the priest shook his head even as he ran, this was Constantinople a city built on rumors; always had been, always would be.

Breathless and a pain stitching his side, he plunged down yet another street. God help me, he thought, I've got to get to the church!

Father Manfred had not expected yesterday's order that all the city's priests and religious leaders attend St. Sofia cathedral, that magnificent jewel of the empire. Nor that the service would last all night. He'd attended reluctantly. The time for praying was surely long gone. God had not answered yet; it was unlikely he would now.

Inside the glorious domed structure the Patriarch urged them to pray for Emperor Constantine XI and victory over the pestilence that was the Muhammedans. The service droned on through the night praying and beseeching God for a miracle. The scent of burned incense and the chanting of the brethren initially hid reality but as dawn approached even the least delicate noses could smell the burning wood and flesh; the most sensitive ears rang with the cries and screams of battle.

As artfully and quietly as he could, Manfred had grabbed his servant and shuffled his way through the host of clerics, finally slipping out a side door. In the dim dawn light he raced as fast as his stubby legs could manage, past the Great Palace and the ancient Hippodrome then laboring up another of the many hills that marked the golden city.

He saw lights above Galata moving steadily downhill. The Ottomans were on the march and a new attack at the Golden Horn was underway.

As they had for the past months, the Ottomans attacked the great walls of the city that encircled and protected the land side. For a thousand years those walls protected them from land attack and the Bosporus and Golden Horn protected the city from sea assaults. Only the Frankish Crusaders two hundred and fifty years before had captured the city. Even then, with all the raping and looting, at least they had been Christians and not pagans, he considered.

But the walls were old. They'd been breached, shorn up and breached again in a never-ending struggle since that day in early April when Mehmet's armies first appeared.

He ran, pushing and shoving his way down the Messe and through the Forum of Theodora to the Amastrianon. When he got to that square he leaned on one of the walls breathless, bent double. After a few deep breaths he struggled to run again, aware that he was running towards the battle, for his church lay in a district near the great walls and the Marmora Sea. It was ironic Father Manfred thought, since he was quite comfortable with the fact that he considered himself a coward. He much preferred the ceremony and quietness of his normal Constantinople life. Not for him the desire for danger, blood and suffering that was the norm for most men. As daylight increased he was barely aware that his servant had himself slipped away, deserting the priest as they ran toward the walls.

The dawn was now pierced with the unearthly screeches and moans from the Muhammadan hordes. A priestly friend told him earlier that it was what the Ottomans considered music. The squeals of their instruments were backed by the sudden enormous thundering bangs of the god-forsaken cannons from the mouth of hell that Mehmet aimed at the city walls.

Eighty thousand Muhammedans against the seven thousand commanded by the Emperor; It should have been a slaughter, but the ancient walls stood firm against all odds. Manfred questioned how much longer the walls and the Emperor's depleted ranks could continue to defend against the never-ending plague of Ottomans. For all the prayers that filled the cathedral this day, he could not throw off the blackness that engulfed him. This day smelled and sounded bad, as if the very pit of hell was opening.

A troop of Varangian Guards dashed past, axes and swords in hand, headed for the wall. Horns and trumpets now blared and in the distance he could hear the shouts and chants from the Ottomans accompanied by the defiant cries of the Emperor's defenders.

His only thought was to get to the church as he punched and pushed his way through the panic-stricken hordes, finally opting for the lesser used back alleys and streets. At last he crossed over a small square and dashed into the dark, cool sanctuary, slamming the church door behind him and dropping a heavy cross beam in place to bar the door against unwelcome visitors. He doubled over a rough wooden bench, gasping for air.

In the coolness of the Church of St. Theodor Martyr, he allowed himself a moment. Slowly his breath returned and his gasping subsided. He clutched his side again and stumbled towards the altar.

Sweet Jesu's blood, he muttered to himself gripping the altar, please give the army strength. He reached down and tried to shift the finely carved stone altar. Too late, he'd regretted his decision in March to send the scroll to Baldric. As soon as he knew what it contained he should have destroyed it. But greed and curiosity had silenced the voice in his heart.

He knelt at the altar and prayed. Was this the end of days, he wondered. Is this the day God would redeem us and damn all the others, including the foul Muhammedans, to the pit of hell? He continued to pray alone and in silence.

Finally he pulled himself upright, calmer now. One of his major faults he freely acknowledged was his tendency to panic and make hasty decisions. Perhaps this was one of them. Perhaps the city would not fall. Perhaps he should have destroyed the scroll. Perhaps.

He heard running behind him. Startled, he turned then relaxed as he saw his scribe Timotheus hurrying towards him.

"Father Manfred, They have breached the walls at Kerkoporta Gate. The Muhammedans are coming to kill us all." White-faced, Timotheus clutched at Manfred's sleeve. "Even now their flag is flying from the walls. The Varangarians are fighting hard, but the enemy is everywhere. The army is defeated. They say the Emperor was killed in the assault!"

Manfred heaved a deep sigh. He could do nothing now; it was out of his hands. Calmness swept over him. He made his decision and realized it had more to do with his cowardice than it had with any priestly or church concern. He would far rather face this present than the future catastrophe the scroll represented.

He looked deep into Timotheus' eyes. "I have not been a great priest to this congregation. Not even a good one." He shushed the young man's protests. "I have sinned mightily against God. The sins of pride and avarice in particular!" He reached down beside the altar once again. "Help me!"

Together they pushed and shifted the heavy marble altar. It moved slowly until a stone slab underneath was revealed. Manfred, gasping and wheezing, moved the stone and pulled out a leather pouch. He placed it on the altar.

"Many months ago, two merchants from the Holy Land passed this way. You remember them?" He continued as his acolyte nodded. "They brought me some goods; some special goods." Father Manfred wrung his hands together nervously. The screams and shouts seemed closer now.

"My brother Baldric provides sacred relics to the churches across the Holy Roman Empire as well as our own. I sometimes find such relics for him and pass them along. Those merchants brought me such a thing." He paused. "It was a scroll they said they traded for at a village near Jerusalem."

Manfred paced alongside the altar as Timotheus watched, puzzled that his master was speaking about events of months ago when death and destruction were circling in on them.

"I opened the scroll. It is in Latin, which is surprising since it came from the Holy Land. It was written by a Roman centurion. I read it." Manfred gulped and wiped his brow while he continued pacing up and down. "I should not have done so. My arrogance is my downfall and God will punish me this day." He picked up the leather pouch. "I copied some of it but could not finish. It is too horrifying, too ungodly." He hefted the pouch. "It is in here."

Timotheus waited, silent. Manfred took out the parchment, smoothed it out and read the document to himself once again. He shook his head in pain and disgust.

"Pride. Avarice," he spat the words out. "I am doomed to eternal damnation for not destroying that scroll."

The clamor in the streets outside grew. Dark grey wisps of smoke penetrated the damp coolness of the church. Outside they heard women and children crying in horror. They heard screams of agony and the clash of steel. The Muhammedans were getting closer.

"I know not what they will do when they get to the church." Manfred said hurriedly. "But we cannot wait." He shoved the manuscript back into the pouch, placed it in a small bronze box and laid the box under the stone slab once again. "This is my translation and my confession." He glanced up at Timotheus as if seeing him for the first time.

"I sent the scroll to my brother Baldric at Finsternisdorf in Germania." Manfred looked around wildly as he pushed the slab back into place. "You must get out of the city and go to him, tell him he must destroy the scroll for the world's sake. It is from the pit of hell itself."

Motioning to Timotheus, they slid the heavy altar back into place.

"Come." He dragged Timotheus into a back room. He sat quickly and scribbled on parchment, dusted it and sealed it. "Give this to Baldric and no one else. I have written instructions on how to find him and they are in the pouch." Manfred pulled a gold signet ring from his finger and thrust it into Timotheus' hands. Astounded, the young acolyte said nothing. The ring is my token. He will recognize it and know I sent you."

"I cannot promise you safety, my son. But you must now flee this place." He shook his head in sadness and resignation. "I doubt that any place is safe in this city now. The Muhammedans know only that they want to kill. But you know the back alleys and can slip unseen through many narrow places. You know this city."

"I will not leave you, Father," Timotheus interrupted, tears streaming down his face.

"You must." Manfred began pushing Timotheus towards a side door. "Ibrahim the merchant has one more place on one of his ships. He is in the harbor of Theodosius. He has safe passage from the Muhammedans to leave the city but it must be today."

Manfred slowly removed the golden cross and chain from around his neck. "This will be a sign to Ibrahim that you represent me. He is a fair man. He will give you value for this gold. Enough to pay for your passage with him and to Finsternisdorf. Sail with him to Nicaea. Wait until you get passage to Venice or Genoa then go overland from there."

"It is your letter Father. Go with Ibrahim yourself."

Manfred interrupted, his fingers pressed hard against Timotheus' mouth. "The Lord Jesus has shown me my sins are too great so I must send you."

He shook his head at Timotheus' continued protestations, steadily pushing him out the door. "Go to Finsternisdorf. But you must insist, nay demand, that of all the relics I have sent him, he must destroy this one. That must be his last gift to me."

He paused at the door, holding Timotheus by the arm. The shrieks of pain and terror were louder and closer now. Manfred suddenly pulled Timotheus to him and hugged him tightly.

"Go with God, my son and pray to the Holy Child for me. Go!" With one last shove he pushed Timotheus out. Manfred quickly closed the small door and barred it, then ran to his personal alcove and picked up yet another parchment. May God forgive me, he mumbled to himself, but this is my confession and may the one who reads this offer it in absolution. He jammed it into a small amphora then carefully tucked the earthen jar into a small alcove against the outer wall. He carefully sealed it with a square of marble he'd earlier cut to size. Satisfied, he rocked slightly on his heels then walked slowly over to the altar and knelt. He buried his white tonsured head and stubby unshaven face into his cupped hands and began to pray. In the background he heard the screams of agony creep ever closer. Yet, even then, the solitude and quiet of the cool church muted the clamor and cacophony of the disaster unwinding outside the doors. He looked up and smiled at the gold mosaic of Christ enthroned above the world, that overlooked the altar.

He buried his head in prayer again. The church door crashed open and still he did not look up.

"Manfred!"

At his name, Manfred turned and saw a dark hooded figure its features black against the bright light of the morning sun now streaming through the smashed door.

"You have something I want. I have travelled far through many lands searching for the scroll. You have it. I want it."

"I have no idea who you are sir, but I assure you I have nothing of yours. Ours is a poor church."

"The scroll. You have the scroll. It is from our Lord Cerrunos. Give it to me now." He stepped forward swiftly, grabbing Manfred by the throat and hissing into his face. "Give me the scroll."

Manfred saw cold black eyes stare through him. An icy shudder of fear ran down his spine. The weathered face, lined and scarred, was marked by a large black tattoo above the left eye and stretching back across his forehead and under the hood. Gasping, he shook his head, croaking his repeated denials.

The choke hold became tighter. Forgive me God for more sin, this time another lie, but I will not tell this monster what I know.

Outside the clamor of war increased, screams and cries flooded into the street before them. Time was running out. The figure spewed curses in his foreign tongue as he dropped Manfred onto the slab floor. As he dropped gasping, he heard the dark man muttering "Cerunnos has spoken. The scroll is his. As he commands."

Oblivious to the chaos outside the man drew a short sword and slowly and deliberately sliced through Manfred's throat. He flung Manfred's body to the stone slabs in front of the altar. Blood flowed across the floor and seeped into the cracks. He wiped the sword on Manfred's cloak then strode back down the nave and into the street unmindful of the pandemonium. At the remains of the door, he turned and addressed Manfred's body.

"Ta muid anseo. The Master has spoken."

# Chapter One

**Yns Mons (Anglesey), Wales**

In the near distance, clouds were rolling in off the cold grey waters of the Irish Sea. Night was falling and in the small white stone farmhouse, the men and women were slowly gathering. Little was said other than acknowledgements and greetings. The discussion would come later.

The cars that transported them to the remote site on Anglesey were quickly hidden away in out buildings as soon as they deposited their sole passenger. The drivers, as ordered, remained isolated in the barns with their vehicles. To ensure their obedience, armed guards stood at the doors.

In the tiny reception room and kitchen area some picked away at the plate of sandwiches and small Welsh cakes the farmer and his wife had provided. On a sideboard, bottles of whiskey, brandy and other liquors lay largely untouched. There was a palpable tension in the air that the assembled neither acknowledged nor attempted to lessen.

The back door opened slowly and a short, stooped man, silver haired and bearded walked through. He paused and merely said "It is time." At his words, each individual began robing themselves in shimmering silver-white cloaks, each boldly embroidered with varying designs and ancient symbols signifying the wearer's status and position in the group. As jackets and outer garments were discarded, prominent black dragon tattoos were visible on each of their forearms.

As night fell the group trudged out of the farmhouse, crossed the meadow and followed the old man into the woods surrounding the isolated farm. Their cloaks swirled and flapped as the winds picked up and as they climbed the forested hill before them. On the crest of the hill, they entered the ruins of their sacred Castell y Draig. Stepping over discarded and tumbled stone walls, he led them into a large enclosure, surrounded on all four sides by massive stone walls but opened to the wild skies above. The old inner courtyard still served the Druids well.

At his signal, each of the assembled thirteen sat on stone rubble that seemed randomly thrown about. Yet when the assemblage was complete, they formed a circle with the old man's seat positioned so that he loomed above the others.

"You know why we are here." His voice, though wavering held a surprising resonance and depth. "We have lost our Dragon Master. It is time to choose another."

"Why not you, revered one?" A woman's voice blurted out in the darkness.

"He has refused every time it was offered," another, deeper voice interrupted. "I think he fears the position and prefers others to take it."

Even above the wind, the collective gasp at the blunt and unexpected challenge was audible. It was followed by complete silence.

The old man rose. "You think I refuse out of fear, Brother Branok?" In the darkness a luminous sheen surrounded him. Its waver gone, the voice took on a deep cold velvety tone that seemed to come from somewhere other than his frail body. "Do you truly believe I fear any human, Branok of Cornwall? That I am bound by this feeble structure called a body?"

His voice oozed a silky resonance that sliced the darkness with warning. "I guide the Dragon Master. He or she does my will. Together we will lead to victory over the cursed Christians."

Branok jumped up. "Rhiannon and Wyndham also said they were leading us to victory. Now they are gone and their so-called victory is only thin air. Same in France. Is this how you guide old man?" His challenge reverberated around the stone walls. "I am ready to take the place of Dragon Master. But I will not be guided by you or any other. I am guided only by the gods."

Silence vibrated around the enclosure. The assembled group lacked even the will to draw a breath, so sudden was the challenge to their wise one. After a moment, the bearded man rose and seemed to gain in size and stature as he did. "You are not worthy to be in this Gorsedd. You are no longer needed."

The old man's icy voice penetrated the increasing buzz from the assembled Druids. Light blazed from his eyes as he simply pointed a finger at the Cornishman. "Be gone!"

The words had not even left his lips as Branok slumped suddenly to the ground, gripping his sides and uttering strangled gasps. Dark clouds rolled away and in the moonlight the group could see Branok's face frozen in a tortured grimace. His eyes stared unseeing at the sky.

The old man raised his arm to still the clamor. "Do not move!" His command rang across the courtyard. "We are called to select a new Dragon Master." He paused then stepped forward, staring at each individual. Each felt his arctic glare grip their bodies before he passed on to the next.

At the center of the ring he stopped and intoned a chant in a language none of them had heard before. His hands opened to the sky, his face lifted to the rolling, scudding sky. Moonlight bathed him. He chanted again, then fell silent.

"The gods have decided it should be Diarmuid of Ireland. Are there any who question this?"

Silence greeted his pronouncement. "You may all leave. Take the traitor Branok's body with you and dispose of it. You will all erase this night, save our decision, from your memories. Diarmuid you remain. We have much to discuss."

In silence, they began to move. Four of them picked up Branok's lifeless body and all of them stumbled their way through the ruins and into the woods below.

The old man beckoned Diarmuid to sit and waited patiently as the rest disappeared. When they were gone, he sat in front of the still silent Diarmuid. His claw-like fingers grasped both the Irishman's shoulders in a fierce vice like grip. His eyes sought and found Diarmuid's eyes and he began to croak a chant, drawing Diarmuid inexorably in.

I BEGAN MY SINGING

I BEGAN MY CHANTING

AT THE EDGE OF THE CIRCLE OF THE WORLD,

RESTING ON THE RIM

CALLING MY PEOPLE, CALLING THE POWERS

CIRCLING THE REALMS AND CALLING THEM MY OWN.

THE DRAGON'S CLAWS GRIP YOU, THEY EMBRACE YOUR BEING

UNDER HIS CLAWS MAY YOU WITHER

> Under his claws may you dry and drain
> The Dragon's claws embrace your being
> New blood they bring; new powers instill
> Wind winger; stallion of the skies, resting on the rim
> At the edge of the circle of the world
> Embraces you and take you for his own.

When he was done, the wizened old man let Diarmuid's shoulders go, but refused to release his eyes. He began to speak softly but powerfully and was still speaking as dawn began to break

### Arlington National Cemetery, Virginia

Stone Wallace stood beside the white engraved tombstone. It was a simple stone, like most of the others in the cemetery. His father's name, year of birth and death, army rank and his Purple Heart were listed. Nothing else. As he looked across the headstone in the near distance he admired the two monuments to the Challenger and Columbia space disasters and a tall cross memorializing those Americans who fought in World War One for Canada before the United States entered the war.

It was a quiet spot, punctuated only by rustling leaves as breezes filtered through the trees in the warm spring afternoon. Stone lifted his head as he heard a mournful bugle play 'Taps' at a funeral in another part of the cemetery hidden by manicured trees and hills. He stood staring at the gravestone, a myriad of thoughts and memories swirling around inside his head; memories of a happy boyhood cut short interspersed with vague recollections of a smiling woman and stern-faced man. As he stood there, Stone unconsciously ran his hand though his sandy-brown hair. All six feet of his trim frame was rigid as he wrestled with feelings of anger, grief, abandonment and anxiety. This was not the TV personality and travel writer the public knew. This was an intensely private and, until now, self-sufficient workaholic who blocked people from his life.

He'd not visited his father's grave since the funeral when Stone was only thirteen. His dad's Vietnam service made him eligible for Arlington but until now Stone had never wanted to return. His father's sudden death in a plane crash was followed several years later by his mother's losing fight with cancer. Each death coiled a hard shell around him even tighter. With no siblings or other immediate family, work rather than people, became his focus; his emotional sustenance. Pushing people away and building his armored shell became so ingrained he rarely realized how alone he really was. Few had penetrated his self-created shell. One who had, to a large extent, was Huw Griffiths. Another was Huw's daughter Mandy.

Huw's wounding and kidnapping by Druids last fall shook him deeply and Mandy had also begun to pierce his shell. When he almost lost Mandy in last fall's hunt for the sword Excalibur he realized that his feelings were fast moving from admiration to romantic. Her kidnapping by the Druid Dragon Master Rhiannon and the subsequent battle to save her had solidified his feelings. But the most powerful spear into his shields came from watching the profound impact of how Huw and Mandy's faith helped them handle times of extreme stress.

Locked in silent thoughts before the simple grave, Stone reflected "Huw, my old friend, you have no idea how much you mean to me. You've made me appreciate people and relationships and even got me thinking about God. You are why I'm here today to finally come to grips with losing Dad."

Stone gently flexed his arm and stretched down to place his hand on the stone. As he did he was startled to see splinters of the simple white cross disintegrate in front of him. Without thinking, he dropped to his knees and rolled to his right behind another stone.

My God, someone's shooting at me, he thought.

More fragments flew off his father's headstone and then the one in front of him. Stone jumped up and began running, weaving in and out of the headstones. He felt rather than heard the shots race by his head. They're using silencers, he thought. That means they're pros. And they want me.

He spun again, heading for two trees. He dared not stick his head out looking for the shooter but he panicked, realizing he was trapped. He frantically looked behind him. Another twenty yards and a clump of trees would offer better protection. Beyond them was one of the cemetery's roadways. Typically, there were people wandering down the roads taking in the beauty and history that was Arlington Cemetery. If he was lucky and made it that far, perhaps he could mingle with some of them and escape.

Another shot thunked into the tree trunk inches from his head. Now or never, he prayed, as he raced at full speed towards the clump, falling into their protection as more bullets threw up dirt and wood. He rolled down the slight incline, relieved to see a startled group of camera-laden tourists stare at him as he suddenly flopped onto the roadway.

"Sorry. Fell," he hastily explained.

He began to brush himself off hurriedly as he ran away from the crowd only to hear sudden cries of pain. He wheeled around and saw one man spread-eagled on the grass bleeding profusely. As the group screamed and scattered, a woman went down without a sound, blood and matter spraying from her head.

Stone dove behind a large leafy bush, desperate for any cover. As he did, a large black Suburban squealed to a halt beside him, the driver side rear passenger door opened and an African-American wearing dense aviator sunglasses, leaned out.

"Get in. Now, Mr. Wallace."

Stone froze behind the bush barely able to comprehend. He dimly heard sirens in the background.

"Chad Lawson sent us. Get in."

Stone scrambled to the back seat. As he did the front passenger window shattered from a shot. Ferociously, the man grabbed Stone by the back of his jacket and heaved him bodily into the vehicle. As he did, the Suburban burned rubber accelerating in reverse before spinning and racing off.

As they hurtled down the leafy pathway they heard the sirens draw closer. The vehicle slowed to a crawl. "Don't want to attract attention," the driver muttered. Seconds later, he pulled off to the side as police and ambulances raced past them. The Suburban picked up speed again, headed towards the cemetery's main entrance.

Panting with exertion and fear, Stone pulled himself upright onto the seat. "Chad sent you?"

The massive man beside him smiled and twisted sideways to face Stone. As he did, his slate grey suit jacket fell open enough for Stone to see he was also carrying a sizeable handgun in a shoulder holster. He stuck out his beefy hand.

"Leon Marshall, Mr. Wallace. Security Investigation Directorate. Chad was worried you'd still be targeted for reprisals from the Druids. Seems he was right. We've had you under surveillance for the past few months."

"SID has been following me? Flushing, Stone angrily demanded to talk to his friend, the police officer turned intelligence agent.

"We're taking you to him now, sir."

The Suburban easily fit into the traffic flow across the Arlington Memorial Bridge, past the glistening white Lincoln Memorial and weaved onto the westbound I-66 interstate highway. Angry and shaking from his intimate brush with death, Stone fumed silently while his rescuer kept careful watch out the sides and rear, watching for possible pursuers.

"Who were they? Who was shooting at me?"

Keeping his eyes on the surrounding lanes of the interstate, Leon merely shook his head.

"No idea, sir. Maybe Chad will know. We were told to keep you in sight at all times. I was watching from the knoll beyond the space memorials. When the shooting began we got to you as fast as we could. Thank God you headed for the roadway."

He touched his ear and Stone noticed a communications device. Leon listened intently for several minutes then quietly said, "Roger that. Get over to Ft. Myers and cadge a ride back to Chantilly."

He turned to Stone. "That was my partner at the cemetery. He couldn't ID the shooters and obviously they were using silencers." Leon paused slightly. "Two dead and one wounded on that roadway. No sign of the shooters. Our man identified himself to the cops when they showed, but other than that, very little information."

Ten minutes later they pulled into the basement parking garage of a small office building. Chad Lawson was waiting. He stood, arms folded across his muscular frame dressed as always in a casual golf shirt and trousers. His generally neat dark head of hair, one unruly lock still sticking upright, offset his worried deep set brown eyes. A two-day growth of stubble framed his face.

Without waiting for the SUV to fully stop, an angry Stone flung the door open.

"I've got questions for you pal, and you'd better have good answers!"

Two hours of explanations and promises later and Stone was still shaking His narrow escape at Arlington rattled him and in his mind's eye he still saw the dead and wounded sprawled over the roadway in the middle of that peaceful place. He shuddered again, rubbing his eyes and massaging his temple, trying to eliminate the vision.

Aware that Stone's anger was partly a reaction to the frightening events at the cemetery, Chad Lawson quietly explained why he'd been under surveillance.

"You were instrumental in the destruction of their plans, Stone. You destroyed Excalibur and blocked their plans to take over the Presidency. No way were they going to ignore it. It was obvious that you'd still be in their cross hairs. The Druids are never going to let you get away unscathed. Not in Britain and not here. Too many of them know of your involvement."

Calvin Tyler, SID's director sat silent through the session watching Stone and making quick notes on a pad in front of him. His bulky frame hunched over his desk as he peered owlishly at the two men from behind his oversized glasses. His bald head with white fringes and barely visible wire-framed glasses reminded Stone of a warmer, friendlier Dick Cheney. His suit jacket and shirt were rumpled as always. Staff at SID were convinced he slept in his suit every night. Finally, he stirred and leaned forward across his desk. "It's a good thing they don't know about your killing Damien Wyndham. If they ever find out you eliminated their chief conspirator and financial resource, well…." He trailed off, opening his arms expressively.

"What we don't know is why they moved all of a sudden. Why now?" Chad looked at Stone. "Have you done anything to stir up the hornet's nest?"

Stone unconsciously ran his hands through his hair again and shook his head. For more than an hour they grilled Stone, interspersing questions about who he'd spoken to, what articles he'd written and wondering if he'd inadvertently emailed anyone with information about Druid activities inside the USA. While the American Druid leader, former Senator and presidential candidate Liam Murphy was now a non-factor, Tyler told Stone he believed Murphy's cohorts were rooted deeper in the US government than he'd expected.

Halfway through the interrogation, a knock on the door interrupted them. At Tyler's acknowledgement a sharply-dressed woman stepped into the office and silently handed Tyler some sheets of paper. Tyler looked at it, grunted and nodded to the woman. "Helena Martinez, this is Stone Wallace. You can report in front of him.

She focused penetrating brown eyes on Stone then began, a slight Latino accent barely discernable in her clipped description. "Innocent victims," she said waving the papers. "One man from Missouri and a woman from South Carolina. A third victim is in serious condition in hospital but expected to recover. Casings at the scene and forensics indicate the shooters were using standard NATO ammunition and it appears they were shooting from some bushes two hundred yards or so away. It's early, but so far police can find no link between the victims. They were just visiting the cemetery. Obviously, as far as they know there is no known motive."

She stopped speaking and pierced Stone with a fixed gaze from her fiery brown eyes. "You were extremely lucky Mr. Wallace. One move the wrong way and your body would be draped over Arlington's grave stones as we speak."

Stone shifted uncomfortably under her steady gaze. "Call it luck or whatever you will, Miss Martinez, I just want to know who and why."

"As do we, Mr. Wallace. As do we!"

"Other than us and the shooters, does anyone know Stone was the target?" Chad broke in. "Can we somehow keep him out of the news reports?"

Tyler leaned back. "Thank God Leon got there when he did. In the confusion, if any of the witnesses saw him pull up and reverse out, they haven't mentioned it yet. And even if they did they'd probably think it was just someone trying to escape the shooting."

Silence enveloped the room as the trio considered the implications of the day's events. As Tyler thanked the woman and gestured for her to leave, Stone kept his eyes riveted on Tyler. "Bottom line is, you kept me under observation partly to ensure my safety but you were also hopeful that I would be bait to identify some more of the bad guys."

Both Tyler and Lawson had the grace to look shamefaced.

"The thought crossed my mind, I admit, Mr. Wallace, but the reality is that we never had a credible threat against you and we never identified anyone following you. Your phone lines at home and in your office are bug free." Again, Tyler's voice trailed off.

"You bugged me as well?" Stone yelled, arms flapping in the air in disbelief.

"We didn't bug you, Stone," Chad interrupted quickly. "But we did regular security sweeps to make sure they were completely clean and no one else was bugging you."

Tyler brought the session to an abrupt close. "We've got to get you out of here and out of sight until we can figure out why you've suddenly become target of the day. The safe house, Chad. Now."

Chad hustled Stone out of Tyler's office and stepped into an elevator that took them down below the sub-basement of the SID offices. Exiting, they walked quickly down a very long non-descript tunnel brightly lit with LED's. At the end of the tunnel, Chad placed his palm against a black sensor plate and put his right eye up to a retinal scanner, waited for the blinking green light, then led Stone through the silently opening door into another non-descript tunnel leading off to the right. A short distance later, they mounted a staircase. At the top, a door opened into a small office crammed with a desk, photocopier and file cabinets. In just six steps they were across the room and out into what was obviously a carpet showroom.

Chad grinned at Stone's confusion. "Part of our cover operation. This carpet store is about three blocks from the office building. It allows us to move in and out without prying eyes looking over our shoulders."

They nodded to the store staff, passed a couple of customers and walked casually out the automatic front door. Chad strode over to a white Mercedes Sprint van sitting in the strip mall's parking lot, gesturing to Stone to get in. As he did they heard a swoosh and looked on in horror as the store front exploded in a fireball. Instinctively, Chad pushed Stone into the van as bullets sprayed the back door and driver's side of the vehicle. In a second Chad was in, started and threw the vehicle in reverse, bouncing off the rear bumper of the car behind and screeching around other cars to the parking lot exit.

"Security breach! Security breach, at the store, dammit." Chad screamed repeatedly into his communicator as they spun onto the six lane road, bounced over the concrete median and hurtled down the highway.

Behind them, flames engulfed the store and several vehicles parked in front.

White faced and grim, Chad gripped the wheel. "They want you, Stone. God, they want you real bad."

# Chapter Two

### Istanbul, May

Professor Huw Griffiths hurried down the cobble path leading from the Archaeological Museum to Alemdar Caddesi as fast as his limping stocky body would allow. Turning right, he passed along the walls that marked Topkapi Palace and Gulhane Park. Although it was warm, he pulled his light nylon jacket tighter, trying to keep the rain out.

Lost in thought, he stepped around a concrete bollard only to hear the angry clanging of a bell as a white and blue multiple-car tram sped downhill towards him. He stepped back, waited, and then hurried across. Cars, trucks, cycles, motorbikes and the occasional overloaded handcart scurried up and down the street in typical Istanbul chaos intertwined with blissfully unaware pedestrians.

After just a few days he'd learned that the pedestrian's cardinal rule was 'avoid eye contact with drivers of any vehicle'. Everyone in Istanbul operated on this theory; if you don't make eye contact, it's the driver's responsibility to avoid you, ergo you will be safe.

Fine in theory, Huw grumbled to himself, but while his inbred survival instinct normally caused him to look carefully he still found himself dropping easily into the local mindset. He followed the cobbled road and tram tracks along Hudavendigar Caddesi's narrow sidewalks past the colorful souvenir stalls, carpet shops, ceramic and silk sellers, small hotels and countless eateries. More tram trains clanged by him, jammed to the hilt with residents and tourists alike. The cobbles glistened with rain, splashing as vehicles met the numerous puddles.

At the broader Ankarra Caddesi he turned right past the magnificent and ornate pink-trimmed Sirkeci train station, the final destination of the famed Orient Express. In front stretched the Golden Horn and beyond it, the Galata Tower in what was euphemistically called the 'new' or European Istanbul.

In the near distance he heard the mournful call to prayer from the minaret of Yeni Cami, the New Mosque, followed seconds later by more calls from nearby mosques creating an eerie reverberating effect that added to the noise and bustle of the vibrant city.

Now that he was not sheltered by buildings, strong winds roared off the Bosporus and up the Golden Horn driving the shower harder. Judiciously he crossed the street again, dodging the chaotic tangle of yellow taxis, buses and scooters. His temporary office was just a few hundred yards away now. It was all arranged by his good friend Dr. Enver Turel, at Istanbul University, as part of the enticement to bring Huw to Istanbul. The office had a wonderful view over the Horn and the bi- level Galata Bridge. To the side, just out one window, he could see the superb structure of the Suleymaniye, the Mosque of Suleiman the Magnificent. It was, Huw acknowledged, a worthy bribe—a nice office overlooking the Horn not to mention a decent sized hotel room in the Sultanahmet District.

Enver's expertise was in archaeology and there was little he did not know about the Byzantine city of Constantinople. Indeed Huw often teased him that he 'lived' in Constantinople only pausing briefly to eat and sleep in twenty first century Istanbul. He'd needed Huw's theological and historical expertise translating a pile of old documents recently found in the rubble and ruins of yet another Byzantine building unearthed by Istanbul's incessant construction boom.

When he learned that Huw was still recovering from an accident he waited, somewhat impatiently, because, as he'd told his superiors, Huw was the leading historical theologian in the world. His expertise was vital. All Enver knew was that Huw's accident happened in the United States. Because it didn't happen in Constantinople, the Turk, while commiserating and wishing him well, did not probe further. As long as Huw gave him a few days as soon as he was able, Enver was satisfied.

Huw jumped at the opportunity, eager to travel to Istanbul as soon as the doctors cleared him. In spite of a slight limp and stiffness, souvenirs of his run in with the Druids, Huw finally arrived at Ataturk Airport in May expecting to stay only a week revisiting a city that had once been the centre of the known world.

From the time Constantine chose the site as his capital, the city had grown in stature and influence as the Byzantine Empire grew. Huw found himself soothed and seduced by the history that oozed out of every crack of the bustling metropolis. He rejoiced in its Byzantine structures like the great city walls, the Hagia Sofia and the Basilica Cisterns through to the Ottoman buildings such as Topkapi Palace, the Grand Bazaar and the multitude of mosques great and small, old and new. The history reflected Istanbul's status as a city straddling two continents, eastern and western history and a multitude of religious faiths and practices.

It was a city made for Huw Griffiths even if he was only there to look at a few documents.

Two days into his assignment, he knew he had to stay.

And for the past three weeks he'd been pestering Enver and the powers-that-be at the museum, the city and the Ministry of Culture for permission to continue a dig at the long demolished small church of St. Theodor Martyr.

"There's nothing more at that dig Huw," Enver had protested that first evening, smoothing his huge thick black moustache subconsciously. His piercing brown eyes peered out at Huw underneath prominent black eyebrows. They'd argued long into the night when Huw first asked permission to further explore the site.

"The city only allowed me a few weeks to excavate the site. They're building a subway extension to link up with the new line under the Bosporus and they're already well behind schedule. They will not agree to further delays. I just wanted you to see and translate that document. As it is, everything has been stalled since December because of problems with the construction company. They won't tolerate more delay."

Huw protested. "Look you, Enver, this city always has to delay construction projects because of archaeological finds. This is just another one, boyo."

"No. Sorry, my old friend but St. Theodor Martyr is a minor church find, one of many. It's worth only a few weeks and we've used them. There is nothing there of importance that would persuade the city to allow an extension. I have other documents from other sites that need your attention." He could not resist a dig at his old friend. "If you had come earlier you would have had all the time you want."

Huw grimaced at the reminder.

"Look you. I'm not asking for a long delay. Just a few days beyond what you've already been allotted." Huw spread his hands in a gesture of supplication.

"I don't understand? What could a few days more possibly give you that we haven't already found?"

He offered Huw a glass cup of chai, the Turkish hot tea, and a slice of pistachio baklava. Ever hungry and willing to nibble, Huw obliged. After a sip he picked up a photocopy of one of the documents he'd translated.

"This is a fragment of a message written by the priest, a Father Manfred. You said you found this in a cracked amphora hidden behind one of the walls. He confesses that he traded in relics and hints at something important—he calls it ungodly—hidden under the altar. You haven't found the altar yet, have you Enver?"

The Turk shook his head. "How important can yet another fragment be? I researched him. Manfred was the priest when the Ottomans captured the city. He was probably writing about the likelihood of the city falling."

"Perhaps. But if we could find the church's altar, this fragment says there's a secret buried underneath. You know me Enver. Once I get something in my teeth, I must follow through to the conclusion if I can."

They argued for hours until finally, reluctantly, Enver agreed to seek an extension.

Now, three days later, they'd finally had a positive meeting with the officials at the museum. There were no guarantees yet, but the museum's director agreed to approach both the city and Culture Ministry officials for an extension to Enver's dig.

Huw crossed the plaza in front of the Spice Market. The rain was easing but the wind whipped across the open space. As he stepped inside he heard a voice call his name. Enver, short and pudgy though he was, was chasing across the plaza after him, his tie flapping in the stiff breeze.

"I thought we said goodbye at the museum, *bach*" Huw asked, as they approached the building that contained his office.

"We did, but the Director wanted a word with me before I could speak to you privately." He grabbed Huw by the elbow and pulled him into the building's tiny elevator. "Why do you have people following you everywhere?" he asked as the elevator rose slowly through the floors.

Amazed, Huw shrugged and shook his head staring at Enver with a puzzled look. "Get on with you, I've no idea boyo. Are there really?"

Enver nodded. "I've noticed for several days that there are two or three men who trail you wherever you go. One is waiting outside the doors to this building even now. He followed you from the museum. They track you everywhere; from this office to the university to the museum to the dig site. Everywhere. Always the same ones." Enver pushed the stop button and the elevator shuddered to a stop. "Is there something you're not telling me old friend? Is there something I should know?"

Again Huw shook his head. His face blanched. "I honestly have no idea, unless they're Turkish police or security. Even so, why would they follow me?"

"Pah! These men are not Turkish, I can tell you that. Yesterday I sent one of my students to ask one if he needed help on our campus. The man shook his head and said in English that he didn't speak Turkish. My student called him some filthy names in Turkish, but the man did not even react. No, he is not Turkish."

"I'm at a loss then. I know no reason why anyone should be following me."

Enver stared at Huw for a moment or two, shrugged and then pushed the up button again. Crankily, the elevator sputtered to a start and climbed slowly to the fourth floor.

"I appreciate your concern Enver, but are you perhaps over reacting to coincidence?"

"This city may be called Istanbul now, my old friend, but it is still Constantinople; still the city of intrigue. This is a place where one keeps one's own counsel and watches one's way."

As Huw got out and walked down the hall towards his office Enver gripped his elbow and added one more piece of advice. "Be careful what you say in this office and who you speak to on the telephone. Same at your hotel. Those men did not look like friends."

### Wicklow Mountains, Ireland

From the bow window, Diarmuid Callaghan could revel in the views of the Wicklow Mountains glimpsed through the tall trees that concealed his home. If he stood up and walked over to the main living room window, he looked out over the green fertile farms towards the Celtic Sea. But he did neither. Instead, he sat at the gleaming black Yamaha baby grand and began softly playing some of his beloved jazz. It was a ritual with him. Always, after a tiring drive from Dublin to his isolated retreat, he unwound at the piano.

His mind was racing. So much had happened these past few months. The original plan to revolutionize the west was in ashes. Across the Atlantic, his friend and fellow Druid leader Liam Murphy abruptly pulled out of the American Presidential race a week before the election for 'personal' reasons. Callaghan's contacts, however, confirmed Fitzpatrick was in fact in custody, languishing incommunicado at an isolated compound in New Mexico

Closer to home, the movement's financial benefactor, billionaire Damien Wyndham had disappeared—either imprisoned without trial or, most likely, dead. The former Dragon Master, Rhiannon, was most definitely dead, buried by rocks and boulders in the mysterious destruction of her Welsh headquarters. Worse, the disaster was intensified by the shambles in Brittany when French security forces raid disbanded and scattered the French Druid conspirators killing their leader Andre Tonnerre and wounding others including his own brother Declan.

And all traces of Excalibur, key to the whole conspiracy, had disappeared.

Years of work undone in a matter of days. And all because of three people: the American journalist Stone Wallace, that stubborn professor Huw Griffith and his daughter.

Diarmuid's bile was especially reserved, however, for Huw.

He abruptly stopped playing, hitting some discordant notes as he stood up and went to the window. He leaned his short solid form on the window sill to take in the mountain view, aware that in recent months he'd developed a bit of a paunch that he attributed to too many delightful Guinness ales. His immaculately creased fawn slacks and yellow Ralph Lauren sweater would have marked him anywhere as a well-to-do entrepreneur. Only his fathomless grey eyes hinted at a cold, calculating soul devoid of feelings and emotions. With one exception.

His gaze drifted from the scenery to the terrace where Declan sat huddled in blankets in his wheelchair. Seeing Declan brought his anger to a boil once again, tightening his fists until the knuckles whitened. He'd sent Declan to Brittany as a special envoy from his own Tuatha de Danann Druids in Ireland. His eyes began to tear as he thought again of the pain and suffering Declan had endured since he'd been shot during the French raid.

Callaghan blamed Huw Griffiths for Declan's current paraplegic state with a singular hatred. Griffiths knew where King Arthur's sword Excalibur was hidden and knew it was crucial to the Druid's plans but his stubbornness and refusal to tell what he knew meant forces were sent in to get him. In Callaghan's mind it was simple: had Griffiths cooperated the raid would have been unnecessary and Declan would not now be in a wheelchair wracked by constant pain.

Oh yes, Callaghan hated Huw Griffiths. Now, finally, he could do something about it.

Declan's recent return home from rehabilitation hospitals was welcome, even though it stoked his anger again, seeing the terrible impact of his brother's injuries.

He waved to Declan who smiled in return and powered his electric chair across the slate patio to the main doors. Callaghan eased over to the door to greet his brother.

"Diarmuid. You're back." Declan's raspy voice reminded Callaghan again that his brother's wounds had not only shattered his spine but damaged his lungs as well.

"I just got in little brother"

"Just because you're two minutes older than me does not make you the big brother, or me the little one, Diarmuid!" The teasing, hotly disputed when they were young, was now a small sign of affection. They might have been twins and share the same fiery red hair but their personalities were totally different. Where Diarmuid was headstrong and demanding, Declan was thoughtful and patient. Where Diarmuid was outgoing, Declan was more reserved. Where Diarmuid was cold and hard, Declan was caring and soft. They'd always been the perfect complement to each other.

Callaghan wheeled his brother to the living room couch and sat down beside him. Declan's recovery had been of prime importance these last few months. In that time, Callaghan had never discussed the Druids, the horrible debacle in France, or the failure of their glorious plans.

Now that Declan was finally home, he could broach the subject. Declan's eyes shrewdly noted that his brother was bursting with news.

Although Diarmuid had refused to talk about it, Declan's assistants and friends were not as reluctant. Even so, all Declan knew was that there'd been a sudden call for a Gorsedd, or council by who, nobody knew since until now, only the Dragon Master had that authority and she apparently was missing and presumed dead. It intrigued him that the Gorsedd was held at the ruins of Castell y Draig, Dragon Castle, on the island of Anglesey off the North

Wales coast. The castle's history and location on the holy island known to the ancients as Yns Mons, created a special aura around the gathering.

"You are hiding something from me, brother," Declan wheezed out painfully. "You are dying to tell." He looked expectantly at his twin.

"I can't hide anything from you for long, can I little brother? Very well. You are now looking at the new Dragon Master, so you'd better behave and obey all orders from now on."

Callaghan grinned at the look of astonishment on Declan's face.

"It was unanimous. All the other Druid leaders begged me to accept the leadership. So I did." In Callaghan's mind, the slight twisting of facts would make it easier for Declan to accept.

"You have the ability and drive to lead well brother, but where will you lead them?" Declan's green flecked eyes held Diarmuid's as if trying to penetrate Diarmuid's mind.

"Rhiannon tried to get us all together and destroy modern society in order to take us back to the old ways and the old gods." Declan took another shallow breath before continuing. He could only handle short bursts of speech now. His eyes flickered constantly trying to signal his brother on how strongly he felt about the issue. "We all know how that turned out, Diarmuid." He took another breath. "It didn't work. We must persuade the people, not force them. You can do that. You have the charisma." Another breath. "That's why they asked you."

Callaghan shook his head vigorously, his voice dropped to a cold clipped tone.

"I was chosen because it's too late for persuasion, Declan. They have taken out most of our leadership, either through death or imprisonment. The gods must be appeased. Our time is now and it must be seized. The gods will not hand it to us on a platter." He knelt beside the wheelchair and placed both Declan's hands in his and softened his tone.

"You've suffered far more than I, for the cause Declan. I can't even begin to understand the pain and anguish you feel right now. I have asked mother goddess Danu for her guidance. I promise you this, I will lead well. I will be the Dragon Master who restores us to our rightful place. People will see—they already do see—the corruption and emptiness of our current society. I promise you Declan, I will get revenge for the agony you have suffered."

Tears welled up in Declan's eyes; his head waved side to side.

"No Diarmuid, enough. No more killing. No more suffering I beg you." He struggled for breath again. "The gods will bless us if we are at harmony with nature and the gods, not through terror."

Callaghan's voice hardened. "You are getting weak from your wounds, little brother. Those were the days before the Christians destroyed our faith and robbed us of our gods. By Danu, we must eliminate all vestiges of them from the face of the earth. Then we eliminate the Jews and the Muslims. Only then, can we return to the true calling of our ancestors."

The two brothers argued heatedly until, exhausted, Declan suddenly spun his chair and began powering himself to the door. He stopped and turned slightly, now barely able to rise above a whisper. "You've changed Diarmuid. And not for the better," he drew a breath. "The Mother Goddess Tara commends us to peace not war. She would not have us kill for the sake of killing." The whisper became even more pronounced. "Revenge is not the way." He disappeared down the hall into his special rooms. A door slammed to emphasize his upset.

Callaghan glared at Declan as he left. The injuries had obviously impacted his brother's mind, he told himself. But don't worry little brother, he thought grimly, old Diarmuid will not forget. Nor will he forgive. Huw Griffiths will pay but it will not be a swift repayment. No, it will be a slow, lingering punishment. First he will lose his friends and his reputation, then his family then, and only then, his life.

He walked over to the sideboard and poured some mineral water. The minute he was affirmed Dragon Master he swore off alcohol in order to keep his mind clear and functioning. Might as well begin now, he shrugged, downing it in one swig. He wiped his hand across his face and pulled out his mobile phone. In moments he was connected to his assistant.

"Michael, are our people still with Griffiths in Istanbul?" The day after he was named Dragon Master he'd sent his own Tuatha warriors to track and observe the professor, gathering detailed files on his movements, contacts and behavioral patterns.

"Keep Griffiths under close surveillance, but nothing else until they get orders from me personally. Find Griffiths' daughter and put her under the same strict observation." He paused a moment, drumming his fingers against the sideboard before he asked his assistant to contact Liam Fitzpatrick's people in America.

"I want that reporter taken care of. Permanently. Liam's people bungled the attempt at Arlington Cemetery and I want no repeats. I don't care how they do it, but it must be done as soon as possible. And, Michael, I want a photo of his body or what's left of it. I'll take special pleasure sending that to Professor Griffiths as a warning that his time is coming." He paused, smiling coldly in anticipation. "Have Quinn report to me immediately. No matter where he is or what he's up to."

He put the mobile away and strolled back to the piano. As he settled in to play, he smiled and fantasized the many ways he would destroy his enemies.

### Eminonu District, Istanbul

Huw sat at his desk staring out onto the Golden Horn. Beyond the Galata Tower and just to its right he could see part of the first Bosporus Bridge through the lifting clouds and stretching over to the Asian side of the city.

Everywhere he looked, there was busyness; buses roaring in and out of the terminus at the docks, trams and vehicles of all descriptions trundling across Galata Bridge and a myriad of ferries and tour boats scuttling across the water in a chaotic sea dance. In the near distance he could see a large cruise ship docking and beyond it a massive loaded container ship ponderously plowed its way up the Bosporus towards the Black Sea. Although he could not see them from his vantage point, he knew that hundreds of freighters of all sizes and descriptions lay anchored at the entrance to the Bosporus, waiting for their permission to proceed northward. For some the wait would be days.

The frenetic activity reflected Huw's mind set. While Enver's warning came as a shock if he was completely honest, it was not a surprise. Stands to reason they wouldn't just let it go, he reasoned, if whoever was trailing him were in fact Druids. His mind raced to other possibilities. British intelligence making sure he didn't chat about last fall's events? That doesn't hold together logically, he scolded himself. They wouldn't waste manpower and resources on such a nebulous concern. And he had no other enemies that he knew of, at least not enough to follow him in such an exotic locale. No. Logic said it was the Druids. But why? Excalibur was gone, their plot destroyed. If it was revenge wouldn't they have moved against him already?

The questions and reasoning flitted back and forth across his mind. As he sat, one thought jumped out. If they were watching him, they'd be watching

Mandy and Bradstone as well. He still could not call his journalist friend by his shortened familiar name, no matter how much he pleaded. Bradstone he was and Bradstone he would always be.

Only one way to find out if they are being followed, he told himself, reaching for the desk phone. As he picked it up, he stopped, Enver's warnings ringing in his mind.

Quickly he scanned his office, considering his desk and bookshelves to see if they'd been disturbed. Thankfully, he'd kept a copy of the parchment translation in his satchel. He pulled it out, scanned it into his laptop, inserted a flash drive unit, copied it and then deleted the scan off the computer. Satisfied, he put the tiny drive into his pocket, shredded the hard copy of the translation and walked out of the tiny office, carefully locking the door behind him.

Assuming his 'minders', as he now thought of them, were waiting for him on the plaza between his office and the Spice Market, Huw headed the opposite direction, away from the elevator. The hallway led away from the elevator and around a corner to a restaurant that boasted of its harbor views and where he often ate lunches and dinners. Huw slipped in, nodded to the waiter. "Hasan, I want to play a joke on my friend Enver, you know, the university professor. Can you show me how to go out your back door?"

Hassan laughed merrily, delighted to be part of the prank. He signaled Huw to follow, leading him through the kitchen to the service elevator. "I will say nothing to Professor," he said in his cursory tourist English, then winked as Huw disappeared.

In minutes, Huw was pushing his way through the crowds on the back streets past stalls selling fish, produce, ceramics and fabrics. Strong smells of spices and cooked foods permeated the air. Thankfully, the rain had ended and the sun was breaking through the low grey clouds. He wove his way through the teeming throngs past the back entrance to the Spice Market and onto Semin Sah Penlevi Caddesi. Halfway along the street he slipped into an electronics store and bought a cheap mobile phone and long distance card. While waiting to complete the transaction he wandered casually to the store's front window peering up and down to see if he could spot anyone following him. Ruefully, he realized he'd be easy to follow with his limp and silvery-white hair standing out in a crowd of jet black-headed Turks and all the while he hadn't a clue as to who was following him or especially what they looked like.

The street was jammed with tourists and locals which Huw thought served to both shield him from any potential trackers but also kept them invisible as well. After taking a few side streets and narrow passageways he was back on Hudavendigar Caddesi. The wooded enclave that was Gulhane Park and, above it, Topkapi Palace lay directly in front of him. As he approached the corner he noticed a café with outdoor seating. He hurried over, picked a table hidden from the street, and ordered tea and baklava.

Checking carefully that there was no one around him within listening distance, he used his new mobile to place two long distance calls.

# Chapter Three

**Hereford, England**

Dr. Myfanwy Griffiths strolled down the stairs towards her tiny office at the University of The Marches. Her scrunched and pony-tailed burnished mahogany hair bounced as she walked, her bright hazel eyes and ever present grin capturing the attention of passing students who smiled back at the popular new faculty member. Behind the smile though, was both exhaustion and tension. A two hour lecture to first year students always tired her out, but the worry of her father's hurried phone warning added to her stress.

He hadn't said much, just warned her that since he was being watched and followed she'd better take precautions as well. "Give Crown Security a call. They should provide some help," he told her, noting that so far, whoever was involved was only watching from a distance and making no overt threats. Ten minutes after the call, she was in the lecture hall and now, two hours later she was due to meet with three students for a tutoring session.

"Dr. Griffiths, step into my office a moment, would you?"

She looked up to see her department chair, Dr. Archibald Cranshaw, beckoning her to his open office door. Settling herself into one of his comfortable armchairs, she waited while Cranshaw arranged papers on his desk.

"I'm really delighted you are part of our faculty, Mandy. We're so glad you were able to step in so quickly and easily. I know it was a push for you to start in January, but we're awfully pleased that you did." He smiled easily at her. "And the feedback from students and other faculty is very glowing." Mandy smiled her acceptance of the praise, wondering if he'd brought her in just to say that.

"I fear we may have put too much pressure on you at the start. You came highly recommended as a researcher as well as lecturer, and I want to make sure you have the freedom to do both."

He picked up a file folder and handed it to her. "This is the information on Nigel Pitt. He's a doctoral candidate with a graduate degree in history and is highly enthusiastic. I thought he would make a good assistant for you and that you, in turn, would act as a kind of mentor to him. He can ease your load on both the teaching and research ends."

Surprised, Mandy stammered "Thank you Dr. Cranshaw, but I really don't need an assistant. I don't mind the teaching at all and I prefer to work on my own in terms of research. That's the way I've always worked. I really don't need an assistant. Thank you for your consideration, but I work best alone. I like it that way."

Cranshaw tut-tutted her objections. "Nonsense. Nigel won't interfere at all. He's just there to help. Now, no more about it. Read his file. You'll see what a good idea it is."

"But I have to go to Oxford tomorrow for that seminar. I haven't time for reading files on a person I don't need," she pleaded.

Cranshaw waved her objection away and before she could utter another objection he gently but firmly guided her out of his office and deposited her in the hallway. The irrepressible grin was gone and, file in hand, she stormed into her office, briefly stopping to apologize to her waiting students and cancel their tutorial that day.

Behind her closed door she moved books off her desk and angrily slapped the file down. Without touching it, she grabbed an apple out of her desk drawer, picked up her notes for the next day's seminar and stormed out. "Bloody hell!" she muttered banging the door behind her and locking it. "I don't need another problem on my plate today."

## Shenandoah, Virginia

Grim-faced, Chad and Stone jumped out of the shot-up van at the entrance to the agency's safe house deep in the Shenandoah. Guards toting automatics and submachine guns escorted them inside while others disposed of the vehicle. Stone barely had time to admire the classic Colonial white house before he was rushed up the stairs past the impressive pillars and onto a wooden verandah. The mahogany colored front doors opened and the pair stepped quickly into an ornately decorated two-story front hall. Chad led Stone to the right into a book-lined library where Stone dropped onto a comfortably deep ivory sofa while Chad reached the desk.

Without waiting, Chad grabbed a secure landline and was immediately connected to Tyler back in Chantilly. They spoke briefly then Chad hung up.

"Only one agent dead. The rest were protected by the special reinforced glass installed on all our buildings and offices. The glass held long enough for the rest of them to escape down into the tunnel." He hesitated, then added "but it's still a bloody shambles. They've got somebody on the inside who alerted them that we had you safe and that we were exiting through the secure passageway."

"Why now?" Stone and Chad blurted the same thought at the same time. Chad gestured Stone to continue.

"What's happened that has suddenly caused them to start killing again?" Stone mused almost to himself. "There's been nothing in the news indicating that they are suddenly ramping up." He glanced at Chad. "What about Murphy? Is he still in custody?"

Chad nodded. "Tyler checked that first thing when Leon was bringing you in. Murphy is in New Mexico and has had no contact with anyone other than our own agents"

"Yeah, but as you said, you have a leak. One of your agents must be a Murphy plant."

Chad nodded. But before he could pursue the thought further, the landline rang. After a few minutes, Chad looked at Stone. "We pulled a message off your phone. It was from Huw. You'll want to hear this."

Frowning, Stone put the receiver to his ears and listened intently then put it down.

"Well?"

"The Druids must be active again. Huw's in Istanbul and being followed. But so far they've not acted against him. He's warning Mandy as well. But so far I'm the only one who's been attacked. Who else would target the three of us?"

For twenty minutes Stone and Chad discussed various possibilities and scenarios. They scanned internet news sites, frustrated that nothing caught their attention. As they tossed theories around they were interrupted by the growing thwack-thwack of a helicopter. Taking no chances it might be an aerial attack, Chad jumped up and seized an automatic while other agents took up defensive stands around the property. One of them herded Stone out of the house and to a grass and leaf covered bunker a hundred yards away. They watched the unmarked white and red machine head directly at the house then slow and descend onto the manicured lawn. The passenger door opened and Calvin Tyler hopped out, ducking to avoid the whirling blades while running towards the house. Before he even cleared the blades the chopper lifted off hurriedly, swinging back to the east.

By the time Stone and his bodyguard made it back into the house, Chad and Tyler were inside the library. No one said a word as Stone entered but Tyler quietly signaled the guards to leave. As the door closed, a tired, pale-faced Tyler plopped heavily into an armchair while Chad and Stone chose their own seats.

"There's no way around it. We have a serious breach in our security and I won't rest until I discover who it is. In the meantime," he stared directly at Stone, "you are the flavor of the month. You attract bullets and bombs like wasps at a picnic. We've got to remove you from the scene so I can spend my time and effort finding the traitor.

Briefly, he outlined his plan. "I don't want to know where you go or what you are doing. You are the only ones who will know. I want you totally out of contact and somewhere safe until we've cleaned this mess up once and for all."

Tyler slammed his fist against the arm of his chair three times to emphasize his frustration, anger and fear. Chad saw for the first time a man unlike the normally confident and in-control Chief. Now, Tyler was a vulnerable and stressed security chief seeing his organization unravel with disastrous consequences before his very eyes.

As the afternoon wore on Chad and Tyler argued about how to keep the two exiles safe while still maintaining contact. Finally, they agreed on a system of messaging using SID's safe addresses and always creating blind email addresses for themselves.

"Remember," Tyler said, "only use an address once and only in extreme necessity. As soon as you've used it, delete it and create a new one each time. Send to my secure personal web address. And always from a different computer that's untraceable." He looked up at them, a brief smile flashing across his face, "You realize that other than you, the only ones who have access to that address are the President and the Secretary of Defense, so don't abuse it."

After questioning Stone and determining the journalist still had a series of credit cards under various nom-de-plumes he used as a travel writer. Tyler asked for the names Stone used and undertook to put healthy payments in each account. "Buy whatever you both need, but do not return to your home or office. You need to get lost...well and truly lost. Any engagements you have Stone, I'll cancel them for you. Contact nobody yourself."

Suddenly, Tyler jumped up and began pacing across the room and back again, sometimes punching his fist into a hand while other times pausing to slam his hand on the desk to emphasize a point. By the time Tyler finished an even more intensive debrief on the day's events, Stone was exhausted. He suggested to Chad that an early night was probably in order only to be stopped abruptly as Tyler suddenly spun around and shouted at them.

"No. I will be staying here but I want both of you away from here before nightfall. There are vehicles in the north outbuilding. Take one and get out of here. As soon as possible, ditch it and find another mode of transportation. Just get the hell away from here and from Virginia."

Both Chad and Stone were stunned by Tyler's vehemence. Wordlessly, they left the room and headed for the outbuilding. Neither spoke until they were in a non-descript Toyota, heading down a country road towards Sperryville.

His eyes fixed firmly on the road ahead, a subdued Chad muttered "so where to?"

**Eminonu District, Istanbul**

His phone calls to Mandy and Stone concluded, Huw retraced his steps back to the restaurant. Fortunately some deliveries were being made so, smiling and with a nod of his head, he entered the service elevators, rising to the kitchens. Stepping out he noticed Hassan and flashed a huge smile with a comment that 'we surprised him' and headed back into his office. So far as he could tell, nobody had followed him. Whoever was watching him likely did not know he'd slipped away. So now he had to keep up the charade.

He picked up several unimportant files, stuffed them in his case and left the office. As he walked slowly across the plaza in front of the Spice Market he stopped at a hot chestnut vendor and purchased a bag. As he did he glanced casually around to see if he could identify any of his watchers. In the mass crush of people dashing to and fro from the market to the bus station and the ferry docks on the Golden Horn it was an impossible task. He slowly limped his way past the New Mosque up Cami Meydani Sok and onto the bustling Hamidye Caddesi once again. This time, at the corner of Ankara Caddesi he slipped into a baklava shop and ordered chai tea and baklava. He chose a window seat, unobtrusively scanning the people on the street outside.

Half an hour later he was frustrated at not identifying his minders. Not your game Huw, lad. You're a historian not a spy, he grumped. Just as he was about to give up he fixed his eyes again on a short thin bald headed man who'd been leaning on a black metal sidewalk bollard for some time. He was well dressed in a suit and tie but somehow looked out of place and uncomfortable as he stood sideways ostensibly taking in the view of Sirkeci railway station but angled so he could keep an eye on the bakery. Huw settled in to watch and ordered another chai.

Fifteen more minutes passed. Huw tried to be inconspicuous as he sipped the tea and took small bites of the honey coated delicacies he so loved. He glanced out occasionally, sweeping his gaze over the bald man who remained rooted to the corner. Fortunately, Huw thought, the Turks often lingered in restaurants making it a long social occasion. If this was America the waiter would have already dropped the bill on the table and would be tapping toes impatiently waiting for Huw to leave so he could fill the table with more customers.

Huw sighed and took another sip. Suddenly, the man stiffened. Casually, while Huw's lips nursed the chai cup, he peeked out and saw a red headed and bearded figure stroll up and speak to the bald one briefly. The bald one quickly tipped his head to the left indicating the shop then hurriedly sauntered off. The bearded man nonchalantly pulled a pocket camera out and began taking shots of the railway station, the view down to the harbor and the street in front of him including the baklava shop and the man sitting in the window seat. Rather than move on, he stayed in place taking occasional shots up and down the street.

Slowly Huw put his cup down. "Right boyos, I've got you now."

Two minutes later Huw left and crossed to the mid-street tram station, fed coins into the machine for his jeton and took the first tram headed towards Sultanahmet District. He stood in the aisle clinging to a strap as the tram squealed around the corner and was pleased to see that the resplendent bearded man had boarded the car behind. Huw smiled grimly to himself, happy that he'd been able to identify two of his minders but mystified as to what he should do next.

By the time the tram climbed the hill past the bulk of the mighty Hagia Sofia and closed on Sultanahmet Park he was no wiser. He hopped off at the next stop and slowly made his way down the remains of the Byzantine Hippodrome, skirting the walls of the famed Blue Mosque and into the rabbit warren of streets that made up Sultanahmet District. He turned the corner and after a few yards entered his chic boutique hotel.

Inside the relative safety of his room, Huw looked out his window. He could not see the crowded streets below, only the balconies of other flats and hotel rooms. Beyond them he had a wonderful view of the Sea of Marmara and its mass of anchored, waiting freighters. It was a sight that fascinated the nautical side of him. He stared out wishing he had a camera to take a picture. Suddenly, he snapped his fingers.

They took a photo of me surreptitiously, he thought, so why can't I turn the tables and get shots of them and email those shots to someone who might be able to identify the minders?

Rubbing his hands with glee, he stepped over to the room's phone and called Enver. Painfully aware that the phone might be tapped he asked Enver if he could borrow a digital camera from the university so he could take photos of the ruined church site. By the time evening fell, one of Enver's students had dropped off the camera for Huw to get used to it.

With his plan half formed, Huw turned in for the night.

# Chapter Four

**Preseli Mountains, Wales**

Callaghan shivered as a cool wind off the sea picked up. Even though he was protected from the worst of the breeze by the great rock formation, wispy tendrils still wound around and through the cracks and splits in the rock, determined to find his tired body.

Wales is a land of myth and magic, castles and mountains, music and poetry. It's a place where mists cling to green mountainsides and dip into steep terrace-house lined valleys. It's a Principality proud of its unique Celtic past and against all reason insisting that the many huge stone castles built by the English were in fact a purposely designed plan by the Welsh to keep the English out! The overwhelming color of Wales is green—green mountains, green meadows, green valleys, green forests—dotted by blobs of white sheep that seem to outnumber the population. All of this was lost on Diarmuid Callaghan, a proud Irishman in his own right and gratified by his Celtic Druid heritage that stretched back through the mists of time. All he knew or cared about is that Wales had long been a stronghold of the Druid faith. And it was there—Irish or not—that he was drawn.

He'd waited more than four hours already, drawn to the place by a curt enigmatic summons. The unsigned note simply said *"Friday afternoon. Carn Menyn"*. No one at the house saw who delivered it, yet it lay prominently on the floor inside the front door simply addressed "Dragon Master". But in his gut he knew who summoned him.

It had been easy enough to get to the Pembrokeshire hills. From Dublin to Fishguard by ferry then a short drive into the Pembrokeshire countryside before he parked and hiked up into the hills. He cursed himself for being out of shape as he stumbled up the worn rocky path towards the ancient stone circle at Carn Bica and beyond that across the boulder strewn landscape to the massive outcrop of Carn Menyn.

Since arriving just after noon, he'd sat against one of the substantial long thin boulders that dotted the outcrop. Nothing moved in the landscape. Obviously, he thought as he gazed around, this was not the high tourist season. A pint of Guinness would go well right now, he told himself, even if I have sworn off the drink. Overhead, birds wheeled and danced and sang but he paid little heed. Shadows crept across the stone monoliths and scattered boulders as the sun dipped lower into the sky behind some high clouds.

"You are here."

Callaghan jumped, startled by the deep voice behind him. He turned and saw the old man standing precariously on one of the boulders. Without waiting for a reply, the man nimbly jumped down from one rock to another until he was level with Callaghan.

"As you commanded." Callaghan stifled the excitement and surprise welling up within him, commanding his mind and body to remain as cool and calm as the figure before him.

"You are watching the professor, are you not? I believe he is in Istanbul." The flat cold voice was absorbed by the equally cold rocks.

Callaghan nodded, unsurprised by the man's knowledge. "I am also watching his daughter in Hereford and will eliminate the reporter in the United States." No expression crossed the man's face but his eyes bored into Callaghan's soul.

"You want revenge. For your brother. But personal desires are unimportant. Our mission is to bring people back to the old faith. They are too willful to do it by themselves. They must be brought—by force if necessary—to our gods. But personal revenge cannot interfere." The harshness of his voice belied the thin-lipped smile that flashed briefly across his dark visage.

"Follow Griffiths by all means. But do not harm him. Others will have that pleasure. Nor can you harm the girl at this point. The American however, is yours!"

He pointed to a flattened rock and gestured to Callaghan to be seated. As Callaghan obeyed, he swept his arms in an arc around the prehistoric quarry. "These boulders were used by our ancestors in building our great temple that is known today as Stonehenge," he said. "We moved them by muscle and magic across the land and water to that sacred place." Waving his hands over the surreal landscape, he began to pace up and down.

"There is much that our ancestors knew and did that goes back in time. Long after the temple was built, the Romans came and began to destroy our people and our religion. Then later they brought with them the cursed religion of the Nazarene." The venom in his words oozed out of his mouth as he plied Callaghan with a lengthy history of the ancient religion's struggle against what he called "the one god" religions.

"There is a particular document that we know existed until medieval times. We traced it to a particular church and a particular priest in Istanbul; a ruined church that Griffiths is now involved with. We'd planned to insert our own expert into the archaeological team but the university moved first and invited Griffiths. So we watch instead. It is possible that he may discover this scroll. If he does, it is ours. Until then, he must be allowed to continue his research undisturbed. So must his daughter. Oh, you can harass her and worry her, if it gives you pleasure, but she must not be harmed. Once it is over and once we have our hands on what is ours, we will deal with them both."

"What is this precious document that keeps them alive?"

"You question my decision?" the man's voice boomed at Callaghan. "You saw what happened on Yns Mons. Do not make the same mistake."

"I don't question your decisions. I merely seek to understand what we are seeking—what is ours—so that I can better guide our efforts."

The man's eyes bored into Callaghan once again. Then the brief smile returned. "When the time is right, I will perhaps tell you. For now, all you need to know is that Griffiths and the woman are to be closely watched and not hurt." The old man began walking towards the stone barrier.

"We have people other than yours in Istanbul. Rest assured we will know if and when he discovers what we want." As he reached one of the boulders, he pointed past Callaghan. "It is getting late. You need to leave. Obey my instructions."

Callaghan turned to look in the direction he was pointing.

When he turned back to speak to the man, he was gone.

Knowing better than to search, Callaghan began hiking back to his car, his mind reeling with a thousand questions that demanded answers Callaghan knew would not be forthcoming. Yet, if he could, he would discover those secrets with or without the old man's help.

## Niagara Falls

Stone and Chad leaned against the metal tube railings, staring across the mist shrouded Horseshoe Falls at the myriad of sparkling high rise hotels and casinos that dotted the landscape of the Canadian city of Niagara Falls, Ontario. The nearest tourists to them were several yards away and engrossed in the activities of the wave-bobbing tourist boat 'Maid of the Mist' as it neared the base of the Falls.

Chad had bowed to Stone's persuasiveness and agreed to head north, away from Virginia. They ditched the Toyota in Winchester and rented a car. The next morning they were looking at the rumbling, foaming spectacle called Niagara.

"OK, we're here, but we still need to get across that border," Chad spoke quietly. "I can't use my credentials to get us across. The Canadian border guards require documentation like passports—which, by the way, we haven't got. And, in any case, I don't want any record of us crossing any borders. You never know whose hands that information might drop into. The Chief said we were to keep out of sight, out of mind."

"I suggested we come this way because it's a fair distance from Virginia and in a totally unexpected direction. I hope." Stone shifted his position to face Chad. "I can get us across the border quietly; quietly, but illegally. You know that. I did it last year with Mandy," Stone smiled at his glum friend.

Chad snorted, "Yeah, but that was upstate New York by the St. Lawrence River and with a guy that owed you a favor. This area is a lot more crowded and better protected by both countries."

"True. And for that we need passports. That's why I had you stop at that hotel outside Lewisburg last night. I called Colin Maddox in Britain to see if he could help."

"Holy crap! You dragging them in again? Wasn't once enough for you?" Chad sputtered in surprise and annoyance.

"Look, we agreed on the drive up here that it had to be the Druids. Who else could it be? And who knows more about their operations than Colin and the Crown Security Bureau? I spoke to him while you were asleep, persuading him to prepare British passports for us."

Before he could continue, Chad spluttered objections then looked carefully around to see if his raised voice had attracted attention. Satisfied it had not, he hissed at Stone, "that's a crazy idea Stone."

"Exactly. So crazy, let's hope the Druids don't catch on to it. You know pal, you've been a cop and government agent too long. You're too rules and order oriented. You need to think outside the box like me and break the rules once in a while." Stone laughed, delighted he'd thrown his uptight friend for a loop. "Anyway, the Brits owe me big time. The Queen said so herself. So the head of her security branch is not going to refuse. Two British passports are on the way even as we speak. One of Sir Giles' agents will deliver them either today or tomorrow. That's why we're doing the tourist thing until they arrive."

Chad grunted as Stone outlined the plan he and Colin had agreed to. He listened carefully staring out at the churning white waters. "So we just wait here, wandering up and down this path beside the Falls until four o'clock. If nothing happens, we come back at ten tomorrow morning for another two hours and if nothing happens, back at two, and we keep doing that routine until contact is made. Sounds iffy, to me. We don't even know who's making the contact. What if there's a leak in Sir Giles Broadbent's mighty Crown Security Bureau, huh? What then. We get killed, that's what!" He slammed his fist against the railing.

Chad's vehemence startled Stone. In all the years he'd known him, Chad had been the cool, calm, calculating one; the man in control, always planning ahead. Now Stone saw a shaken, insecure Chad. The attack at Chantilly had stunned and upset him deeply. His world had been rocked. The idea of a traitor amongst his closest colleagues must be eating away at his insides, Stone thought.

Although pleased with himself for taking the initiative, Stone dropped the subject realizing Chad had to process the events of the past two days. Stone was amazed at how calm he now was. He'd been shot at, almost blown up and his entire world had suddenly closed to him and made him a refugee. Yet he had put together a plan, no matter how flimsy, and not Chad. Nevertheless, he worried, what if Chad was right.

It had seemed so simple. Stone eagerly pitched his idea to his British friend, filling him in on the attack and Huw's enigmatic phone call. But in the cold light of day he began to doubt himself again. He chastised himself for forging ahead without fully thinking it through or even, as Huw would have certainly recommended, praying about it. His mind flitted back and forth from doubt to confidence and back to doubt again. Wrapped in their own thoughts, the two men stared silently unseeing at the vast wall of water plunging into the gorge.

Well, Stone finally shrugged inwardly, the die is cast. He looked at his watch. "It's four o'clock. Let's grab a bite to eat and look for something to lighten our mood. We have to be back at ten tomorrow."

**Crown Security Bureau, London**

"Bloody hell!"

Sir Giles Broadbent slammed his phone down and ran his fingers through his tuft of snowy white hair. Ever since he'd heard from Tyler, about the attacks in Arlington and Chantilly, he'd had his agents frantically investigating the vestiges of the Druid movement in the United Kingdom. If they were active again, he wanted to know it.

So far they had drawn a blank.

"Freddy! Here. Now." Sir Giles pushed papers aside as his assistant and confidante hurried in. "Any contact in Niagara yet?"

"No, Sir Giles. Not officially. We're keeping them under careful watch first to be sure they are not being followed or targeted." He pushed a piece of paper towards his Guvnor. "Here are the names we're giving them. I also prepared a second set of identities and passports just in case the first ones are breached. Those are the names underneath."

Sir Giles grunted. "Nothing. No hints of Druid activity. No whispers. No movement at all. Don't like it Freddy. Don't like it at all." The Guvnor's habit of speaking in clipped partial sentences underlined his frenetically active mind. Only the essentials mattered, the rest superfluous. Freddy, used to his trimmed speech patterns merely nodded. "Got to be something. Somebody knows." Sir Giles plunged into a cone of silent thought.

Freddy stood patiently in front of the desk then broke the silence. "I sent John Fowler to Wales to look into the remnants of the Druid movement there, but so far he's come up with nothing. The French arm was totally destroyed in the raid last year and our American friends are investigating their end. All we know is that there was a secret meeting on Anglesey several months ago, but it was over before we could get people on it. We can't find out who was there or why. To this point Sir Giles, we're stumped."

Another grunt and the Guvnor looked up. "Tyler says Griffiths and his daughter are also being watched. Check it out." He paused, deep in thought again. He snapped his fingers. "Irish connection! Wasn't there an Irish contingent in that Druid mob? Check that too."

"Certainly, Sir Giles, but our understanding is that they were merely a cultural cover providing music and the Celtic experience for visitors to their compound. Not even Charlie, as close as she was to the Dragon Master, could identify any threats or muscle emanating from the Irish connection."

"They're Irish Freddy. Have to be wisps of the IRA in there somewhere."

At Sir Giles' casual wave of dismissal, Freddy disappeared into his own office. He opened a file on his laptop, searching through his extensive list of contacts. In short order he'd contacted an old acquaintance in the Secret Intelligence Service and arranged a meeting with a contact in MI6 near the service's offices in Vauxhall on the banks of the Thames.

It was a long shot, Freddy determined, but there were few other options turning up.

# Chapter Five

**Dublin, Ireland**

It was a quiet pub, hidden up a narrow alley off Pearse Street. Although just across from Trinity College, it was not a student haunt, which suited Callaghan fine. He casually strolled to the back of the pub and saw his quarry half-hidden in shadow, sitting with his back to the wall as always, scrunched into a corner seat.

"Not drinking anything today Diarmuid. There's different!"

"It's been a long time, Cathal. A long time. I've sworn off the drink, I have."

Cathal raised his thin pale face and glared at Callaghan for what seemed an eternity then looked down at his glass. "Quinn said you wanted to see me. Why? As you said Diarmuid, it's been a long time." As he spoke he stirred the drink with his finger then sucked the finger, smiling in appreciation. "Ah. Nectar of the gods, this is."

Callaghan settled into the booth beside him. "Still in the old game Cathal or have you retired?"

"Ah, now Diarmuid my old friend, that would be telling!" He fixed his glare steadily on Callaghan, oblivious now to the drink in front of him. "Oh, by the way, I was sorry to hear about the injuries Declan suffered. Sure now, and wasn't it in France and did I not hear Diarmuid my boy, that you somehow got religion?"

"Always liked to show off your intelligence sources, didn't you Cathal," Callaghan said with a thin cold smile. "You want people on their toes by letting them know you've done your research, right? Cathal tipped his head in acceptance of the back handed compliment.

"Intelligence is essential, my friend," he said quietly.

"Well, it's a little off this time," Callaghan retorted. "I didn't 'get' religion, I have always had it. I worship the old gods of Ireland and the ways of our ancestors."

Again, Cathal tipped his head in acknowledgement. "Whatever works for you. It is of no interest." He placed his hands on the table in front of them. "But you still haven't told me why you wanted to see me."

"I have a job that requires a man with fine skills. One who can use a knife as well as the best Harley Street surgeons. And were you not known as the best in the IRA in that department during The Troubles? Or were the stories exaggerated?"

"The Troubles are over, have you not heard Diarmuid? We are at peace now. What happened in the past is in a past I choose not to revisit. Especially with those who were not inclined to help." Cathal glared at Callaghan, a scar now faintly visible against the two day stubble on Cathal's chin.

Callaghan calmly placed his hands on the table as well. "As you say Cathal, the past is one we need not visit. The question however, remains. Are you retired or do you know of someone who could help me with this job."

"Sure now. We can talk."

An hour later, Callaghan left the pub smiling but with his pocket lighter by several thousand Euros left in Cathal's grasp back in the bar.

His plan was slowly dropping into place.

### Niagara Falls

Stone and Chad leaned against the railings once again looking at the fury of the Falls. Both wore sunglasses to block the bright sun. Niagara looked particularly spectacular against the cloudless deep blue sky. But the two were oblivious to the scenery, each wondering when the contact would be made.

They'd already spent a restless and somewhat boring evening and night in the American town on the east side of the Niagara River. Across the way was the Canadian city with its spectacular and brightly lit hotels, restaurants and casinos. Even Chad agreed that the American side tried but couldn't compete with its Canadian twin and was nothing more than Niagara's ugly sister.

Morning found them again walking the trail. Every once in a while, Chad raised his camera to take a photograph and surreptitiously survey the many tourists enjoying the view.

"Don't think anyone's coming. Let's grab lunch." Stone muttered as he started walking back towards the city's restaurant area. Chad suddenly gripped his arm, pulling him slightly off balance.

"No way! Look what the wind blew in!"

A grinning Colin Maddox approached. "What kind of mess have you got this time, Stone?" Shaking hands and slapping their backs, Maddox steered them to his car.

"I had no idea you were coming, Colin." Stone settled into the passenger side while Chad took the rear seat. "Have you got passports for us?"

"I've got two sets for you. More importantly, Sir Giles has asked me to stick with you for a while until either your side," Maddox nodded to Chad, "or we get a break."

Twenty minutes later, Stone had turned in his rental car. Armed with passports and British credit cards in their false names, they crossed the border quickly and easily. Before long they were humming along in Maddox's car around Lake Ontario toward the urban megalopolis that was Toronto. Standing erect above the shiny glass and steel skyscrapers that marked the city was the soaring needle of the CN Tower, until recently the tallest tower in the world. Sun glinted off its famed observation tower and restaurant that grew in size and height the closer they got to it. As they skirted the city, Stone explained to him that the city was bigger than Chicago, San Francisco and most other American cities. In fact, Stone declared, it was the fourth largest in North America after Mexico City, New York and Los Angeles. I can believe it, Chad muttered to himself as they sped along the sixteen lane expressway north of the city.

### Hereford, England

Mandy ushered her last student of the day out of her office and fluttered around her tiny office, moving books, stacking files and generally fussing and tidying. Intrigued by his photo and impressive credentials, she'd finally agreed to see her potential new assistant. Illogically, she'd felt the sudden need to impress him rather than the other way around.

Fussing done, she sat at her tiny desk and opened his file, waiting for his knock. Although not always punctual herself, she admired the trait in others and, exactly on time, a sharp rap on the door announced his presence.

As soon as she said "come" a slim, muscular man stepped in. She was impressed as soon as the door opened. The file photograph did not do him justice. His reddish blonde hair was neatly cut yet lingered over his blue shirt collar. A brown tweed sport coat topped the light green open necked shirt. His precisely pleated beige pants finished his interview ensemble. It was casual and understated academic looking while not being overly old fashioned or equally over-the-top-cool. Involuntarily she glanced down. No boat shoes. She mentally shook her head. He didn't look like the man on the train. Paranoia, girl. That's what you've got, she mentally rebuked herself.

An hour later and after intense questioning, Mandy leaned back. She'd stated her qualms frankly about taking on an aide but warmed to the idea slowly as they discussed their approach to both research and teaching. Quickly she found a great commonality in their philosophies towards the past.

"Nigel, I see that some of your personal details are missing from your CV. For example, it doesn't indicate where you were born."

"Ah," Nigel furrowed his brows. "I didn't think to put that in as necessary. But it was a small place in Yorkshire, called Ravenscar."

"Funny. I thought I detected a hint of Irish brogue a couple of times."

Nigel laughed. "Wouldn't be surprised. My mother was from County Antrim in the north. I picked up some of her inflections, I'm sure." His ready grin eased her mind.

"You are older than the normal applicant for a role such as this."

A quick grin creased his face. "Yes, well after my seven years in the army I wanted out and knew that I had to start at the bottom." The grin changed to a frown. "Not that I think working with you is the bottom, mind," he sputtered.

Mandy laughed and walked around the desk hand stretched toward him. "I want to take some more time before I give you my final decision, but I appreciate your enthusiasm and the expertise you would no doubt bring to the university. Thank you." She ushered him politely out of the office.

Back at her desk she shuffled through his CV and her notes. She picked up her phone and dialed the mobile number Huw had given her. She needed his advice about whether to hire him or not and, especially given Huw's extensive contacts in the British university system, if he'd ever heard of him.

## Wicklow Mountains, Ireland

Callaghan chewed his eggs and sausage and sipped his tea, quietly looking at his brother. The morning sun was already breaking through heavy clouds over the Celtic Sea and warming the sitting room. Last night he'd returned from three weeks way only to have another flaming row with Declan, this time over his decision to move his headquarters as Dragon Master to Wales.

Callaghan's reasoning was simple: Wales was where Rhiannon died, where Damien Wyndham had disappeared, and where that cursed professor and his daughter lurked. Finally there was a remote possibility that this was where Excalibur might yet be found. He had his own doubts, but the possibility was enough that the other Druid leaders unquestioningly endorsed his plan.

Declan's objections to the move were equally simple: Keep Diarmuid away from the influence and power of the other Druid lords and hopefully prompt a less violent and vicious way forward for the Druids. There'd been a profound change in Diarmuid since he was raised to Dragon Master. He was now colder, crueler words and actions, and more obsessed with power.

But Declan's bottom line was simple. He loved his twin deeply and, however, reluctantly, was prepared to appease him. "When and where do you want to move, Diarmuid?"

Surprised after all their arguing, Callaghan smiled gratefully at his brother. He put down his cup and pushed his breakfast plate away. "We'll make the move next week little brother. I've got a delightful and totally suitable secure location in the Neath valley in the mountains overlooking Resolven."

He leaned forward enthusiastically, emphasizing his points with forceful gestures. "It's ideally placed, close to the motorway so we can get anywhere fast. Plus it's close to where our own investigation says clues to Excalibur may be hidden." He paused for a moment and added vehemently, "and it is within easy reach of Hereford where Myfanwy Griffiths is."

Declan sighed. The craving for revenge against Huw Griffiths and his daughter was all consuming for Diarmuid. It troubled Declan deeply. This too had been part of their quarrels, with Declan pleading for a conciliatory approach and built upon the harmony and peace he believed Druidism was initially based upon.

He was shocked by Diarmuid's harsh snarl.

"We're in a holy war Declan, and in a holy war there is no middle ground! It is one way—our way—only. Christians and any others who stand in our way must be wiped out. There is no middle ground. No compromise. No concessions. No negotiations."

Declan moved his wheelchair closer but before he could speak, Diarmuid gently gripped his shoulder. "I've already arranged medical care for you and the house is now retrofitted for your chair. It's a wonderful place Declan. High on the mountains overlooking the green Welsh valleys with views in every direction. Not as nice as here in Ireland of course, but close. You'll have all the care you need and I've arranged for a driver and vehicle to take you around and get you out of the house."

Declan nodded, resigned to the decision and aware that he had little choice. He tried to coax a smile on his face. Callaghan, engrossed in his plans, did not notice the hesitant smile that appeared more a grimace. He walked away to stare out the window again.

Silent in his thoughts, Declan wheeled his chair around and silently left the room.

# Chapter Six

### Istanbul, Turkey

Huw huffed and puffed in the hot sun, puttering around the dig, trowel in hand, scraping centuries of dirt away layer by layer. It had taken four days but finally permission to extend the dig time arrived and Huw grabbed every moment available.

He knew his minders were watching him constantly but since they'd not made any overt moves towards him they had drifted to the background of his consciousness. Nevertheless, he'd surreptitiously taken his minders' photos while photographing the dig site. In the next day or so, he'd have to find a way of sending the shots to Crown Security but now it was essential that he concentrate on unearthing the altar.

"Doctor Huw. Over here." One of Enver's Turkish students waved at him and pointed at a corner of flat marble slab he'd just exposed.

"Right, boyo. We may have something by here." Huw eased himself down. Kneeling and troweling were difficult, but he forced himself down into position where he could help dig away at the slab. As it was slowly uncovered Huw grew more excited. "This might be it, Enver. This just might be the altar."

An hour later they'd revealed a white marble block approximately five feet long and three feet wide. It rested on a number of smaller grey stone squares. Enver studied it while Huw knelt beside him. "This might indeed be the base of the altar, my friend," he said smiling and nodding.

"Can we lift it up?" Perhaps along this longer side down by here. It looks easier to get at than that corner over by there," Huw pointed.

Enver gestured to the three students beside him and gave them some orders. Quickly they scraped enough dirt away to insert a small crowbar that they used as a lever. Gently and slowly they then lifted it until the one side was eight inches in the air.

Huw leaned in as soon as he could and began scraping dirt away with his trowel He concentrated on the left corner, slowly moving dirt out deeper and deeper. After ten minutes he shook his head, disappointed. "Not this one. The parchment said they lifted a corner and placed it under the altar. Let's try the next one."

An hour later, they'd excavated two more of the corners with equally frustratingly results. Unperturbed, Huw shuffled over to the fourth corner and began scraping again. A few minutes later he felt his trowel scrape against something harder than the dirt. Excited, he quickly scraped away until a small bronze box began to appear. Enver dropped beside him, troweling rapidly but carefully alongside until finally they gently lifted the box out of its hiding place.

"Brilliant!" Huw shouted in his excitement.

As the students lowered the marble slab, Huw and Enver studied the box to determine how they could open it. Out of the corner of his eye, Huw noticed that one of his minders across the busy Istanbul street was taking telephoto shots as they unearthed the box. Trying to suppress his excitement and the desire to open the box immediately, he turned to Enver.

"Tell you what, boyo. Let's get this back to the lab and look at it by there. If I'm right, we can shut this dig down and turn it back to the authorities after everything is recorded."

Enver quickly agreed and placed the artifact into a clear plastic exhibit bag. He spoke rapidly to his students who immediately began replacing the marble slab and cleaning the area around it. He grabbed Huw by the arm and together the two strode off to Enver's car. Ignoring their dirty outfits they jumped in with the precious object sitting gently in Huw's lap.

As they pulled away, Huw noticed his minders hopping into a yellow taxi, gesticulating at the driver to follow Enver's car.

### Georgian Bay, Ontario, Canada

Chad Lawson sat on a chaise longue on the dock thrusting out into the sparkling blue waters of Georgian Bay. He knew the huge bay was considered by many the sixth Great Lake in the middle of North America. But he was pleasantly surprised at its peaceful beauty. The entire area sparkled with the blues of the water, the greens of the pine, maple and oak forested shores and the sandy browns and grays of the rugged granite rocky outcrops and the yellow-white strips of small beaches. From the dock he could see at least twenty of the thirty thousand islands that dotted the area and stretched northward for nearly sixty miles.

Against the blue horizon interspersed with the green dots and blobs of islands, he saw motorboats and sailing boats enjoying the calm waters and sunny morning. He could hear the throbbing drone of the motorboats and the raucous roar of jet skis. Nearer to the cottage he could see three jet skiers larking about, crisscrossing each other and passing between some of the islands. The day had started out warm and was now, just at lunchtime, beginning to get quite hot. Funny, he thought to himself, I'd always had the idea that Canada was always cold and snowy. This is actually quite pleasant. He turned as he heard footsteps behind him.

"Anything from Tyler?"

"Nothing." Stone dropped into a chair beside him. In deference to his host country he was wearing a bright blue Toronto Blue Jays T shirt and ball cap. "I've got to tell you, I'm getting really irritated. We've been here two weeks and no progress at all."

Despite the warmth, gloom descended upon the pair. The forced exile was wearing upon them both. While grateful that the Canadian Intelligence Service had loaned their secure safe house to Crown Security, they were frustrated. Boredom was taking its toll on both, particularly after Maddox's return to London two days ago. Now, only a couple of friendly but stand-offish Canadians and one British agent stayed with them.

Stone's boredom was enhanced by the fact that he was cut off from his beloved classical music. He had no access to his personal collection at home, he'd left his iPhone with Tyler when they fled Virginia and so far he'd been unable to even find a radio station that played classical. The island location of their refuge precluded even getting FM signals from the Canadian Broadcasting Corporation's station that did broadcast classics. All he could do is summon them up from his vast memory and replay them in his mind.

"This is a lovely spot," Stone nodded at the cottage. "I love the huge rustic log walls. It adds a real wilderness feel to the place." He glanced out into the lake again. "Those jet skiers look like they're having fun." He pointed at the three who were looping around a small rocky island less than a mile from the cottage. Chad sat up straight and stared at them.

"They're a lot closer than they were. They seem to be heading in this direction." He stood and walked to the end of the dock. The jet skiers looped the island once again and angled themselves towards a point of land just to the right of the safe house property.

"Don't know why, but I've got a bad feeling about this." Chad turned and ran up the rock steps to the cottage with Stone behind him. They crossed the front deck and through the glass doors into the rustic interior. Chad shouted for assistance as he reached into a cupboard drawer and pulled out an automatic. There was no response.

"Chad. Those skiers are now headed directly for the dock."

"Check out the kitchen and see where our guys are. I'll keep an eye on the skiers."

Stone raced into the kitchen and jammed to a stop. Through the window he saw Ed Wilson, the lone British agent, racing towards the cottage. All of a sudden the front of his body exploded in a spray of red and he spun and sprawled against the car.

"Oh God." Stone ran to the kitchen's outside screen door and pushed it open. Beyond Wilson's body in the driveway he saw one of the Canadian agents also sprawled in death on the pathway.

"Chad, we've got two dead agents." Before he could say more, a bullet whined by his head. He ducked and scrambled back into the main room as a fusillade of bullets smashed into the window above him. Thankfully, the thick logs absorbed most of the shots. From the front room he heard Chad fire off some shots at the approaching skiers. Stone pulled the wooden table over to the outside door, flipping it and jamming it against the door to prevent entry. It wasn't much, but it might slow up any attack on the rear of the place, he thought.

He ran into the living room and saw Chad firing at the jet skis as they neared the dock. Suddenly there was a massive boom and flames shot into the air as the lead ski blew up, throwing its rider high into the air before he splashed down unmoving into the shallow waters of the bay. His companions veered off, circled around and began another round. This time they approached from different directions hoping to throw off what they believed to be one shooter.

"Lucky shot!" Chad muttered, then shouted at Stone "There's another gun in that drawer."

"I've never used a gun in my life," Stone spluttered.

"Can't think of a better time to learn," Chad responded, reloading and firing again. "Just take your time and try to keep their heads down.

Stone picked up the weapon and ran back into the kitchen, positioning himself by the door and firing as he saw a figure dart between two trees. Stone's shot did the trick, whether it was close or not, as the man dove and rolled behind a granite boulder. In the living room, another of Chad's shots seemed to hit a skier as he suddenly veered off course. The second Jet Ski roared up behind him, shielding him with a rooster tail wake and moving back into the bay.

Taking advantage of the pause in action, Chad raced into the kitchen and fired through the smashed window.

"At least they know we're armed and that the element of surprise is gone."

"Yeah, but I'm betting there's more of them than there are of us. Two on the water and one, maybe two or more in the woods behind, plus they can get back up quickly," Chad responded, firing off another few shots before reloading. "We'd better come up with an idea fast. As it is we're trapped."

### Hereford, England

For the past few weeks Mandy had enjoyed herself. All reluctance about taking Nigel on as an assistant had vanished. He'd proven capable and knowledgeable as she'd expected but also exhibited a great sense of humor coupled with a vast well of trivia knowledge that kept conversations lively, captured the interest of students and generally added a spark to Mandy's day.

The path between the University's library and administration building led down beside a small stream and across a delightfully verdant meadow. It was the long way around, but it was in her mind a much more pleasant walk to her flat than following the main road. The University's location on the Welsh border not far from Hereford was ideal for her because it was on the route to one of her favorite spots in the world, Hay-on-Wye, universally known as the town of bookshops. She loved visiting the tiny village as often as she could, reveling in poking around the hundreds of bookshops that smothered the community.

This was the part of the day she really enjoyed; late afternoon alone, wandering across a meadow feeling the slight breeze in her hair and listening to the birds chirping and singing, while she thought.

Following the enigmatic call from her father a couple of weeks ago, now she worried about his latest news that gunmen had attacked Stone in America. Her feelings about the American confused her. On the one hand she cared deeply for him, perhaps even loved him. But on the other, she wasn't willing to give up her academic career in Britain. Nor it seemed was Stone keen to abandon or drastically change his own career. It was, in many ways, a stalemate.

Her thoughts drifted and swayed like the breeze, gently moving from one topic to another: Stone, her Da, student papers needing attention, Nigel, a potential dig in Cornwall, the Druids…her mind floated on.

Mandy made her way across the stream and up a small knoll to a copse of trees. Her path continued along the edge of the trees, to a gravel path that led past a hedgerow. Absorbed in her thoughts she did not see the man stepping out of the copse until it was too late.

Suddenly he grabbed her arm and dragged her towards the trees. A flash of sun sparked off the open blade in his left hand. Acting instinctively, she swung her purse laden with papers and a large, heavy book. It clipped her attacker on the side of his head. As he stumbled she pulled free and ran back to the path, screaming for help. Swearing, he lurched after her, swinging his blade at her and missing by inches. Terrified, she staggered onto the path only to fall face first onto the gravel, undone by a stray rock. A sharp pain shot through her ankle as she sprawled on the ground.

"Bitch." It was the only word uttered as he stood over her, lowering the knife towards her face.

"Let her go!" A man's voice yelled as he ran towards the scene. Mandy's attacker whipped around and, swearing, suddenly kicked her in the face before he turned and ran into the woods, his pursuer close behind.

Weeping with pain and shock she watched them disappear. She tried to pull herself up as she heard more commotion among the trees. Painfully she staggered to her feet and saw her rescuer reappear, running towards her.

"Nigel!"

"Sorry, Dr. Griffiths, I wasn't able to catch up with him. Are you all right? Sit on this rock here and let me look at you,"

"How did you get here?" Mandy limped over to the rock and plumped down.

"I left the college just after you and I noticed this character hanging around and then follow you. I didn't want to alarm you, so I just tailed him.

He took the shorter route into the woods so I thought I would just stick close to the end of the path out of sight. If he was up to no good, I would be available. If not, I wouldn't have to worry you."

"Well thank God you were here. Help me up."

He expertly tested her ankle. "You've twisted it, but I don't think it's broken. Your face took a beating though, what with scraping it on the gravel and that vicious kick. Wouldn't be surprised if you wind up with a black eye to go along with those cuts and scrapes."

Leaning heavily on his arm they slowly made their way down the path. As they did, she tried to puzzle the attack out. Was it a random attack by a pervert or something more sinister?

"We have to call the police."

There was silence before he replied. "I don't think that will be necessary Dr. Griffiths. He just looked like a tramp and was probably trying to steal your purse. He's probably long gone now."

"Steal my purse? With a wicked looking knife like that?"

"Probably to cut the straps. Look, tell you what. Let's get you home and seen to. I'll report it to the police and, if they need any further information, they can follow up with you. And I'll let university security know so they can make sure he doesn't hang around the school either."

Still in shock and somewhat mollified, she allowed herself to be helped towards her flat. Her landlady, flustering and excited, helped Nigel lead her up the stairs with constant promises to look after her. As Nigel wrapped her ankle in a bandage, the landlady did what all landladies do and promptly brewed a pot of tea. He left with Mandy's profuse thanks ringing in his ears, assuring her he would follow up on the incident.

### Istanbul, Turkey

Huw sat at a desk in the university lab. Gently he handled the document he and Enver had carefully extracted from the bronze box. Remarkably, it still retained its suppleness and the ink used had only faded slightly.

As Huw gazed at the parchment on the desk in front of him, Enver peered over his shoulder. "Can you translate it? Was it worth the extra time and trouble?"

Huw remained silent, conflicted on what to tell his friend and colleague. He could indeed read it and what little he'd already scanned, told him he was holding a powerful yet maleficent item with profound implications if it was true. He thought again before answering

"Enver, I will need to study this carefully before I can really tell you what it says." Not exactly the truth Huw boyo, but neither is it a lie, Huw told himself. "Can you leave it with me for a while? But certainly, you can tell the city that we are finished with the dig and they can now close the site and let the transit engineers take over."

Enver, anxious to move on, nodded smiling. "That is good news, my friend. By all means take the time you need." He hustled off, whistling.

Huw exhaled slowly. His white gloved hands touched the parchment again, bothered by the story Brother Manfred told. If true, in the wrong hands this would be more catastrophically mind-blowing than if those immoral Druids had got their hands on Excalibur.

# Chapter Seven

**Georgian Bay, Ontario, Canada**

"How many out back?" Chad hunkered down behind a massive pine dining room table that he'd flipped on its side to give him some protection. He could see two jet skiers bobbing up and down on the waves conferring and preparing for their next run towards the cottage, out of his range.

Chad could see the wreckage of the first Jet Ski but no body and, if he'd wounded the second skier at all, it was but a glancing shot. Certainly he didn't look the worse for wear as they focused on the cottage gesturing strategy to each other.

He heard two more shots from inside the kitchen before Stone answered. "Can't tell. Two, maybe three."

"Stand in the kitchen doorway so you can see out both front and back."

Without waiting for a reply, Chad crouched low and scrambled to the staircase and the bedrooms above. Inside both his and Stone's rooms he grabbed the small carryalls that contained all their possessions and ran back down. "Anything yet?" he looked at Stone who shook his head.

"We've got one chance. There's a boat in the boathouse down by the dock. We know there's only two left out front." Briefly, he outlined his skimpy plan. A rarely used door on the side of the cottage out of their attackers view led into the pine and bracken filled forest.

"Almost immediately we'll be in trees and bushes. With any luck the guys out back won't see us leave and we'll make our way down to the boathouse, fire up the boat and be out on the water before our skiers know it. You drive. I'll ride shotgun. Literally."

"Nice plan except for one thing. Suppose they know about that side door and have it covered?"

Chad shrugged and tossed a bag at Stone. "If they do, keep running, split up and head into the woods. With any luck we'll meet up at that café in town." He ran for the door, opened it slowly, peeked out and then slipped into the bushes with Stone a half a step behind. Together they crept quietly through the woods, keeping bushes and trees between them and their attackers.

Suddenly a fusillade of shots pounded against the back of the house. Chad grinned. "They don't know we've gone."

At the boathouse they silently opened the door and looked in. The small speedboat bobbed as waves rolled in and the main lakeside door was open. Relieved that their waterborne attackers couldn't see inside, they moved swiftly, releasing the mooring lines before jumping in.

"Ready?" At Chad's quick nod, Stone fired the engine and the boat spat into the small cove. Their sudden appearance caught the skiers by surprise just as they were beginning their run in toward the dock. The nearest skier wobbled as the boat shot towards them. Stone aimed directly at him while Chad fired three quick shots at him before turning his attention to the second. Unbidden, Wagner's 'Ride of the Valkyries' popped into Stone's mind as they bounced over the choppy waters.

Both attackers veered away from the boat hurtling towards them. As they did, the nearest took a wake wave poorly and in seemingly slow motion the skier tumbled head first over the handlebars and smacked into the water. Stone swerved quickly to avoid colliding with the upturned craft but felt a slight bump as he hit the driver.

"One down, one to go" Chad said grimly, firing again at the remaining skier who this time returned fire. They ducked as bullets whined over their heads. Hearing more shots from the shore, Chad hastily turned his head and saw the land attackers run onto the dock.

Stone directed the boat towards two islands directly ahead of him while Chad kept a steady fire at the skier. As they roared out of range, the shooters on shore stopped. Now it was the boat and skier in a deadly ballet on water. They spun around each other, each firing in turn. The windscreen in front of Stone exploded in shards, causing him to lurch and twist off course. At the same time, the wake hit the ski jet and threw the shooter's aim off.

"Aim toward the gap between the islands then at the last minute spin away," Chad shouted in his ear. "See if we can throw our friend off once and for all."

Thrusting the throttle as far forward as possible, Stone kept the boat aimed at the rocky shores. God help us if there are hidden underwater rocks there, he thought as the islands raced towards them at warp speed. At the last second he twisted the wheel violently, turning one hundred and eighty degrees and almost swamping their craft. Without a drop in speed he aimed at the skier. Unconsciously, Stone's jaw clamped tight as he closed the hundred or so yards between them. Never did like the game of chicken he muttered to himself.

At the last second the killer's nerve failed and he swerved violently to the left. It was too late, as the boat smashed a glancing blow, throwing the man into the water. By the time Stone had slowed and circled back, the man's body was beginning to sink. As it did they got the evidence they needed to confirm their suspicions. The last sight they had of the attacker before he dipped beneath the water was his bare right forearm.

Inscribed on it was a black dragon tattoo.

### Istanbul, Turkey

Huw sat on the small sofa in his room studying the papers laid out on a small wooden coffee table in front of him. He ran his hand through his lush grey hair.

Manfred's confession was frightening, startling, and fascinating in turn. Huw had worked hard all day, translating painstakingly to ensure accuracy. His efforts were made easier since Father Manfred had been a literate man with a good grasp of both Latin and Greek. Unusually, the text sometimes slipped from Latin to Greek and back to Latin again. It was almost, Huw thought, as if he was rushed to complete his statement and, if a Latin word or phrase did not fully convey his meaning, he used Greek instead.

He picked up the first page once again.

~~~

I PRAY THAT MY BROTHER BALDRIC WILL DESTROY THE SCROLL I SENT HIM.

DEAR GOD FORGIVE ME FOR MY GREED AND FOR SENDING HIM THE SCROLL INSTEAD OF DESTROYING IT MYSELF. WHEN THE TRAVELERS sold it to me I thought little about it. But for some reason the night after they left I lay troubled, unable to sleep. I tossed and turned until finally I got up, lit the oil lamp by my pallet and made my way to the store room. I picked up the scroll. I paid less than one solidi for it, thinking it but a trivial item. I opened it carefully and began to read. It was difficult to make out some of the script but even though it was a form of Latin from the days of Caesar, I could understand it.

I trembled as I read.

It was the confession of Marcus Lucinius Janus, a centurion who reported that he was the one who crucified our Lord Jesus. He was tormented by his deed and from his words claimed he was possessed by the Evil One himself, who promised great wealth and power for those who bowed down and worshiped him. Church legend claims the centurion's name was Longinus. I realized that this Lucinius might indeed be the one we now call Longinus. But his story was vastly different. If this scroll is real, the legends are all wrong.

The horror came when I realized that Lucinius claimed he was the one who thrust a great spear into our Lord's side as he hung dying on the cross and that same spear was cursed and empowered by Satan. Through it, the Evil One and his hordes would control the world. Lucinius then wrote of all that would befall those who failed to bow before Satan. The lance would be Satan's weapon to destroy the Holy Mother Church and all who followed Christ. Through Lucinius' words, the Evil One himself raged and cursed, swearing great wealth, eternal life and power beyond belief for the one who would find the spear and wield it for him. Finally, he promised the one who delivered the spear would co-rule earth and all its peoples along with Satan himself.

## The Lucifer Scroll

I stopped reading at this time, weeping with shock, confusion and fear. I replaced the scroll in its small cloth sack and crept back to my bed. But sleep evaded me still.

Was this the spear used against our Lord? If so, what of the one the church already venerates, Heilige Lanze, the Holy Lance? Mother Church claims it is blessed by God himself and has remarkable healing powers. Legend also says it will bless and give remarkable powers to whoever owns it. Who is right? Mother Church or the scroll I had before me? For if Lucinius was right, this lance cursed by Satan, was still hidden and the church now celebrates a fake and powerless fraud.

All night I tossed and turned the question of Lucinius' truthfulness over and over in my mind. In the morning I went about my duties as normally as I could, hearing confessions and leading in prayers and worship. But the black cloud would not leave. My mind drifted during confession. I sped through the liturgy, anxious to get it finished. I did not understand my own reactions. At the end of the day, I retired to the tiny garden outside my living space and unrolled the scroll once again. I thought that if I read it in daylight my fears would disappear.

They did not.

If anything, and I blame my own cowardice here, my fears grew worse as I read the final words of Lucinius. It was in a different ink and not as neatly written. He said he had written the first part of Lucifer's message and handed it to his Optio with the promise that he would finally be allowed to die.

In his last hours he rewrote Lucifer's warnings from memory. His last words said he had hidden the lance days before he deserted the Legion and that he alone knew where. Now, at the end, he revealed its location, though it meant little to me for I know nothing of the Holy Land. Besides the Holy Land is in the hands of those same blaspheming Mohammedans who had the audacity to move up an army and threaten our great city.

As I read the scroll again, it became clear to me. The Centurion's final words were not in a different ink and were not poorly written. They were written in his own blood and with his last measure of strength.

For days afterward, I wondered what I should do about the scroll. Destroy it? If I did, I would only be out one solidi and my brother, should he find out, would be furious with me. Baldric is an unpredictable man, for all that he is my brother, but perhaps that is what he needs to be as a seller of relics.

I could also just send it to him. Should it be my concern that a weapon of such potential destruction to the church was possibly still hidden? After all, lots of abbots and nobles believed they already had the great lance as a great holy relic in their churches or palaces. One more or less would make no difference, would it? And besides, who could know if theirs or the one mentioned by Lucinius was the real lance.

If I ignored my worries and sent it to Baldric, would God absolve me of sin knowing that I had the opportunity to destroy the scroll and keep the spear's existence forever out of man's knowledge or temptation?

My greedy side even juggled the idea of selling the scroll and its secret in our ever corrupt city for a vast sum of money. I could then share with Baldric and thus mollify him.

For the next two days and nights I struggled with this decision. As I pondered, I slowly became convinced that the scroll was genuine. Lucinius was real. The lance was real. The Satanic threat was horrifyingly real, far beyond anything I could imagine. I read the scroll many times—particularly

Lucinius' last words where he described the spear's hiding place—and every time I did so, I changed my mind.

I prayed harder during those days than I think I ever had before. My mind had no rest despite the prayers. I felt that God abandoned me to my decision alone. He would let me decide. And bear the consequences of my choice.

Finally, on the day we heard that the Sultan's armies were in Galata on the other shore of the Golden Horn and preparing their attack, I made my decision. I hurriedly packaged the scroll together with some other relics before I could change my mind once again, and took them myself to the Emperor Theodosius' harbor. I paid the necessary bribes to the port authorities and the ship owner and stood on the wharf as the ship was rowed out of the harbor. I watched as its sail was raised and kept watching until I could see it no longer amongst all the other ships coming and going.

I walked slowly up the hill toward the church feeling that at last I could rest and that the weight of the scroll was no longer mine.

I was wrong.

Heaviness came upon me and would not go away no matter how much I prayed and pleaded. Visions of Christ Jesus hanging on that cross and being struck in the side by the spear haunted my days and nights. I saw the spear plunging into the heart of the great cathedral St. Sophia and rivers of blood pouring out of it. I saw the spear slicing through great lines of pilgrims, stabbing and slashing men, women and children. I saw martyrs before the throne of God, blood still pouring from their wounds and the spear floating above their heads.

God forgive me. What had I done?

I should have destroyed the scroll and suffered the consequences of my brother's anger. I had the opportunity to seal

THE FATE OF THE SPEAR BY KEEPING ITS HIDING PLACE FOREVER SECRET. BUT MY SPINELESSNESS MEANT THAT THE SCROLL STILL EXISTED. ANYONE COULD FIND IT AND DISCOVER ITS UNIMAGINED SECRET.

PRAY GOD THAT THE ONE WHO NEXT READS THE SCROLL WILL HAVE THE COURAGE TO DO WHAT I DID NOT AND DESTROY IT.

PRAY GOD TOO THAT IT WOULD NOT FALL INTO THE HANDS OF THOSE WHO ARE ENEMIES OF THE CHURCH. FOR IN THAT SCROLL LIE THE SEEDS OF ITS DESTRUCTION AND POTENTIAL VICTORY FOR THE EVIL ONE.

AS THE MOHAMMEDAN SIEGE CONTINUED FEAR, DEATH, AND HUNGER STALKED THE CITY. I DITHERED FOR DAYS THEN MADE MY DECISION. FIRST, I WOULD WRITE THIS CONFESSION AND LEAVE IT FOR THOSE BETTER AND MORE WORTHY THAN I TO JUDGE. SECOND, THOUGH I COULD NOT GO MYSELF, I WOULD SEND A TRUSTED HELPER TO CARRY MY PLEA TO BALDRIC TO DESTROY THE SCROLL. PERHAPS GOD WOULD MOVE IN BALDRIC'S STONE COLD HEART AND HE WOULD YIELD TO MY PLEAS. I SET MYSELF A TASK OF SAYING ONE MASS EACH MORNING AND TWO PATER NOSTERS EACH MORNING AND EVENING BEGGING GOD TO GUIDE BALDRIC TO DESTROY THE SCROLL.

THUS, I HAVE SET MY HAND TO THIS TASK.

MAY GOD BRING FAVOR UPON THIS DECISION. AND MAY HE FORGIVE ME AND DEAL WITH ME ACCORDING TO HIS GOOD AND GLORIOUS WILL.

AMEN.

BY MY OWN HAND, MANFRED VON PINZGAU, PRIEST AT ST. THEODOR MARTYR

~~~

After Manfred's letter closed, another document followed. As Huw read it, he realized it was Manfred's incomplete translation of the centurion

Lucinius's document. He handled the photocopy gently as if he had Manfred's original still in his hands.

Exhilaration mingled with anxiety as he read. By the time he finished his third reading of the material he still had no clarity of thought, no wisdom, torn as he was by conflicting considerations. One thing was obvious. Manfred had not recorded the location of the lance in his confession or translation. That secret remained locked in the scroll alone.

Having translated the document as a guest historian of the university and city of Istanbul, Huw knew he had a responsibility to share the findings with Enver. But he wavered, fearing the news would launch a frenzy of debate amongst academics, searching by historians and archaeologists and posturing by politicians.

And there was the very real fear that, if Manfred's translation was accurate and the scroll still existed, it would be an icon used against the church if it fell into the wrong hands. Worse, he shuddered inwardly, the scroll might lead to the discovery of the spear itself. Or at the very least set in motion yet another plague of religious conflicts.

Across the pantheon of history, Huw was fully aware of the sometimes conflicting rumors and legends of the lance that speared Jesus' side. Emperors, Popes, despots and church leaders throughout the centuries coveted what became known as The Holy Lance, die Heilige Lanze, or The Spear of Destiny. During the Nazi era, Adolf Hitler and Heinrich Himmler in particular believed the spear embodied occult powers that could be harnessed in order to win the war and ensure the survival of the thousand year Reich.

No matter what he finally decided, it would be fraught with problems, Huw mused. He picked up the phone, forgetting Enver's caution to him, and dialed Mandy in England. He would give a copy of his translation of Manfred's letter to Enver.

The translation of the scroll, however, he would hold back until he saw what way Enver and the Turks would go with the information.

# Chapter Eight

**Vale of Neath, Wales**

"He has served his purpose. You know what to do next." Callaghan thumbed his mobile off and slipped it into his jacket pocket. He smiled. Quinn had done an excellent job, finding that self-righteous buffoon to threaten Huw's daughter. It was one more step on his campaign to slowly increase the pressure and tension on the Griffiths duo.

He sat at the piano once again, playing his favorite jazz piece, smiling and fantasizing the professor's slow demise. The strident double ring of his mobile shattered the bliss he was feeling. He reached for it and answered. Without another word he listened intently, thanked the caller then, face flushed red with anger, flung the mobile across the room, shattering a vase on the way.

"Problems, brother?" Declan had glided smoothly and silently into the living room.

Callaghan whirled, startled, then shrugged. "Bad news from one of my teams, that's all." He looked down at the piano keys once again and tried to pick up where he left off. "Are you settling in all right?"

Declan hated the new house in Wales. Oh, it was luxurious enough and certainly had a fine view of the lush green Welsh valleys and mountains, especially on a day as clear and sunny as today. But it wasn't home. It wasn't Ireland. He knew better though than to pull that scab off and start another fight with Diarmuid. "Fine. Nice."

Insensitive to the message behind those two simple words, Callaghan plunged on. "Good. Now anything you want Declan, you just ask. Your nurse Williams is there to provide whatever you need. Just ask. I'm not going to be around much over the next few weeks, but he'll take care of you. If there's any problem, just call me and I'll sort it out. OK?"

Declan nodded and wheeled into the glass conservatory. He needed to think and here was one spot he could bask in the sun and warmth of the day and think. There was little else for him to do these days. He drank in the vista of thickly wooded Resolven Mountain. A quarter turn of his chair to the right showed him the busy A465 roadway stretching through Neath Vale and towards the market town of Neath and, beyond that, the Bristol Channel.

He sighed deeply. There was a harshness and remoteness to Diarmuid he had not seen before. The fun-loving, caring brother was gone, replaced by a brittle, cold man whose obsession for revenge and brutality was now constantly on display. Declan could see it in his eyes and hear it in his voice.

The Dragon Master had been overtaken by his dragon.

In the main living room, Callaghan strode swiftly across, kicking ceramic shards out of the way and picked up his phone. With a glance at Declan, he turned and headed to the side door seeking the privacy of the outdoor for his next call. There were no pleasantries when his call was answered.

"Where are they now? What happened?" He listened intently while the attack on the Canadian safe house was detailed then exploded in a visceral, profane discussion of his team's incompetence. "Find them. Find them now. And this time finish the job properly," he barked before disconnecting.

He stared malevolently up the Neath Valley tracing its route north and east in his mind until he zoomed in again on the university and Mandy Griffiths. He thought for a moment then dialed again.

### Midland, Ontario, Canada

"We've got to split up. Together, we're attracting Druids like flies to a rotting corpse. Apart, we divide them."

Stone sipped a coffee, hands still trembling after the narrowness and bloodiness of their escape. Across from him Chad constantly flicked his eyes from one customer to another in the coffee shop, glancing occasionally outside at the drive through entrance.

"Apart we also give them a better chance to pick us off." Stone countered. "And I would have preferred a cheerier analogy! Anyway, what good would splitting up do?"

Chad said nothing for a while, letting the idea sink in to Stone's mind. Since the morning's attack he'd begun to shake off his melancholy and reassert himself. Action, however hazardous, was infinitely preferable to lazing around waiting for someone else to solve the problem. In the attack's aftermath they'd raced across the lake and down an inlet to Midland rather than head to the closest dock at nearby Honey Harbour.

"It's more than logical they might have a backup there," Chad reasoned as he argued for the longer trip. "That's what I would do and it's probably where they rented their units. But they can't cover every little town and dock in this area." Rather than debate the idea while they roamed aimlessly around the lake, Stone agreed, anxious to get away to a modicum of safety. Forty minutes later found them nestled in a quiet corner of an outlet of the ubiquitous Canadian coffee franchise, Tim Horton's.

"This is totally ridiculous," Stone murmured into his cup. "We're being chased around, shot at, had some very lucky escapes and generally bounced from pillar to post. Other than we've confirmed that it's Druids after us, we've got nothing. They're always one step ahead of us." He slammed the cup onto the table, "where's the leak Chad? Why can't your outfit find the leak?"

Chad shrugged his shoulders in agreement, unable to answer because he too had the same thoughts tumbling around in his mind. ""Tyler didn't know where we were. My guess is there's breach in Canadian or British security this time. God, what a mess!"

He swirled the coffee around his cup for a moment while he gathered his thoughts.

"We know who's after us, but I doubt its Liam Murphy's crowd. We really do have them under tight surveillance. Their leaders can't even pee without us knowing about it. If these attacks are from the States, it has to be some minor leaders trying to capitalize on the situation. A possibility yes, but unlikely."

He took another sip and shook his head before he lowered his cup "I need to back to the States and start working on those leaks. You? You need to decide for yourself which way you want to go, but I suggest it might be back to the UK and dig from that end with Colin's help. You've got better connections there and that, after all, is where the root of the problem is."

They argued quietly for another ten minutes before Stone reluctantly agreed. "Besides Stone, you know how to use a gun now," Chad smiled at his friend.

"Yeah, but they're illegal in Canada and Britain."

Together they worked out a plan. With hard driving for the next eighteen or more hours, they would cross the wilderness that is northern

Ontario and into the province of Manitoba. In Winnipeg they would split. Still using their fake identities Chad would fly from Winnipeg to Phoenix, Arizona while Stone would make his way either by car or air to Calgary and get a direct flight to Britain.

"Don't call Colin until you get there and I won't inform Tyler until I'm tucked up safe in a hidey hold in New Mexico."

Stone nodded then paused. "One problem. We have no transportation. Our car is still back at the safe house."

The sudden burst of laughter from Chad soon had Stone chuckling. Around them, other customers smiled and then turned back to their own conversations. A quick conversation with one of the patrons established the location of a car rental agency. In short order the pair had cabbed over, rented a car and aimed north up the expressway into the rugged green countryside of lakes, rivers and trees that marked the famed Canadian Shield.

### Istanbul, Turkey.

Enver laid the paper down on his desk and removed his glasses. He pushed his chair back and folded his hands over his portly stomach. Across the desk from him, Huw waited patiently looking around the tiny room. He realized that Enver needed to absorb the immensity of the translated find before him. This museum office was jammed with the bric-a-brac of academia and Huw was sure Enver's university office was no tidier.

Finally Enver looked up. "My dear Huw, this is astounding. Who knew such a thing was hidden so well in such an unimportant church?"

"You realize its significance then?"

"Certainly it is an interesting piece of writing, Huw, but I would hardly call it significant."

Amazed, Huw frowned at him. "But surely if this account is true, then there's the original scroll somewhere in Europe and the possibility of a major archaeological find somewhere in Israel waiting to be found."

Enver shrugged. "It is an interesting addition to the record of machinations and intrigue of the city of Constantinople, of course, but let's be honest, we have no proof that this Manfred was ever a trustworthy or honest correspondent. In fact he condemns himself by openly admitting to the seedy business of relic hunting. Second, our interest is solely in what happened in and around this city, so possible scrolls somewhere in Europe fail to interest me. Third, this must be what, the fiftieth or one hundredth 'sacred lance' we've heard about. You of all people know how many fakes there are in churches and museums across Europe. Lastly, I doubt very much the Israelis would welcome a Muslim Turkish team digging around on their home soil. They wouldn't welcome a lead from us even if we had one to give them."

For the next five minutes while Huw seethed internally, Enver picked Huw's translation apart, praising Huw for his meticulous translation and careful study of the document but dismissing it as a minor piece of historical insignificance.

"No Huw, it's an interesting side story in the history of our city. Nothing more. Nothing less." He stood, reached his arms out to Huw and embraced him in a bear hug. "I am truly grateful that you pushed us to find this unique scrap of our city's history, believe me. And I am grateful for all that you have done to help me solve and close the mystery of St. Theodor Martyr. Please, be the university's guest for another week. Enjoy the hotel and the hospitality of our city."

Slowly he began to usher Huw out of his office. In desperation, Huw pleaded with him to take more than a cursory look at the document and try to determine its veracity. Finally, as they reached the door, Enver grudgingly agreed to let two of his graduate students explore the mystery further "but only for the remaining time you are in Istanbul, my friend. They will call you if they need further information, But after that…" he shrugged "I want their minds engaged on other projects."

As soon as Huw left, Enver crossed to his desk and telephoned the chief of antiquities at the Archaeological Museum. In moments a scanned version was emailed to the chief and Enver moved on to more pressing files on his desk, Manfred's letter already forgotten.

### Hereford, England

Mandy's brows furrowed in worry as she put her mobile down.

"Anything wrong?" Concerned, Nigel crossed the inner courtyard and caught up with her. "You look worried. Students complaining about the workload again?" He grinned at her trying to lighten her mood.

She flashed a quick smile. "Thanks Nigel. No, it's okay. I just got a call from my Da in Istanbul. He's worried that the authorities are not taking a document he found seriously enough. I promised I'd look it over for him if he emailed it, but I think sometimes he goes on too much about things. He just needs to slow down and take it easy."

With assurance that he was always willing to help, Nigel carried on toward the library, a thoughtful look on his face. He suddenly turned and ran back to her. "Sorry, I meant to tell you this but I got distracted when you talked about your father. The police called me this morning. They found a body this morning in the woods about fifteen miles north of here. It matches the description of the man who tried to mug you the other day."

"What happened?"

"Didn't say really. Just that they think it was murder. I offered to help identify the body but they told me it wasn't necessary."

Shocked, Mandy dropped onto a bench beside the path. "Murdered?"

"Mm. Probably fell out with gang members and paid the price." He reached over and gently put his hand on her sleeveless arm. "It's okay Mandy. The man is gone and out of your life. No need to worry about him again."

Mandy looked up at him and placed her own hand on his. "Oh Nigel. You always seem to show up at the right time with just the right words. You not only ease my work burden but you seem to ease my soul as well. You're becoming a real protector and friend."

They sat wordless for a few more moments then, with a "duty calls", Mandy eased herself up and with a cheery wave continued down the path. Nigel remained on the bench staring after her, the thoughtful look still on his face.

**Vale of Neath**

Patience was never a virtue embraced by Callaghan. He paced the floor, looking out the large picture windows, waiting for Quinn. When his trusted lieutenant finally showed up, Callaghan dragged him by the arm into the living room and thrust him into a large leather armchair.

"What took you so long?" Without waiting for an answer, Callaghan plunged into the reason for his demand that Quinn make the sudden and immediate trip from Ireland to Wales for a face-to-face meeting.

"That Istanbul university security guard we've been slathering with Euros has finally paid off." Callaghan said excitedly. "This is what Griffiths was working on over there." He handed Quinn several sheets of paper. "The idiot professor in charge thinks this is nothing and just left Griffiths' translation on top of his desk. Our guard grabbed it and gave it to our man. He sent it to me."

Callaghan thought for a moment. "Arrange for that guard to get a five thousand Euro bonus. And then make sure he is the tragic victim of an unfortunate robbery attempt."

Quinn, a short, stocky, balding man nodded in agreement as he continued to read the material. "What else do you want me to do? Does this clear the way to take care of Griffiths and his daughter?"

"No." Callaghan sighed and dropped into a chair facing Quinn. "Much as I would like to say yes, unfortunately this puts a different perspective on things. Knowing Griffiths as we do, he will now want to pursue this information. He will want to find the scroll. And then he will use the scroll to find the spear. So we watch him even more carefully while he does. And when he finds it, we pounce. Leave him alone for now." He paused and thought a moment longer. "And that regrettably precludes moving against the girl as well. But tighten the watch on her as well."

As Quinn listened, Callaghan outlined a strengthened surveillance regime for Huw and Mandy. "I want to know what he finds an instant after he finds it. Follow him wherever he goes. To Israel, back to Britain, to Europe, wherever!"

Quinn glanced up at his leader, "You are sure this is genuine? You believe such a scroll exists and that it is as the old priest describes?"

"You question the Dragon Master" Callaghan barked at his underling.

"Never, Dragon Master," Quinn hastily assured him, "but can we be sure that the guard copied the real thing?"

"I feel it in my bones, Quinn. A wave of power swept over me when I read this. It is real and so are the scroll and the spear. As is the promise of power and domination contained in the spear. We must get our hands on it." He stood up and began to pace again, gesturing as he spoke. "But we will know the document's reliability for sure when we see what Griffiths does. If he does nothing and just returns to Britain, we'll know it's of no interest to him and that the thing is fake. But," he jabbed a finger at Quinn, "if he begins a search we'll know he believes. And if he believes…" Callaghan smiled and shrugged.

"Don't forget, the spear is real. For centuries our people have known of its existence and its power. We fed information to Hitler and the Nazis in the hopes that they would find it for us. But their own greed and stupidity led them to a fake. That and the pressures of war ended the real search for the spear. We've search for it since the day the Nazarene was executed. Oh yes, Quinn. It is real and it exists, waiting for us to find it and use its promised power."

He sat down in the chair once again, fingers steepled against his face as he contemplated his next step.

"The old Dragon Master was too passive, too unwilling to confront the forces against us. She tried to do everything behind the scenes. We need to let the world know that the Dragon has not lost its roar! It needs to understand that we will destroy those who stand against us or who have emasculated us in the past."

Quickly he outlined his plan. Quinn sucked in his breath at the scope and audacity, hastily jotting notes and trying to keep up as his leader spewed out his bloody ideas.

"There can be no mistakes this time, Quinn. Choose your people carefully. I want no cowards on this. No qualms. Not from you. Not from anyone. The Dragon Master has commanded." He leaned forward, chin thrust out to emphasize the seriousness of his words. "As I told my brother, this is a holy war and in a holy war there are those who are willing to die for the cause. Find me someone who is willing, Quinn, and turn him loose."

"The smaller attacks can begin whenever they are ready, but I want the major one ready in place by Alban Hefin, the summer solstice. Our targets will be there the Sunday after so make it happen then so we can truly celebrate. See to it."

With that, Quinn was dismissed. Callaghan read and re-read the old priest's confession. It still bothered him that the American had somehow escaped his deadly clutches three times and had now disappeared again. Luck and some followers in the Canadian security service pinpointed him in Ontario only to have those idiots screw up the attack and allow the target to live and disappear yet again. But Wallace's luck wouldn't last forever. Sooner or later, he would drop delightfully and bloodily into Callaghan's waiting arms.

Hands outstretched he raised his head and pleaded with the gods to grant him favor; leading him to Wallace and allowing him to be the one who discovered and used the spear of destiny as commanded by Lucifer himself.

# Chapter Nine

### Istanbul

Huw trundled his way up Alemdar Caddesi puffing slightly as he passed the pathway leading to the archaeological museum and the Haghia Sofia and slowly entered Sultanahmet Square. He strode through the crowded park that linked the main square, Topkapi Palace the Haghia Sofia and the famed Blue Mosque. They did not attract his attention. Nor did the sparkling, dancing fountains or the cool painstakingly laid out greenery of the park.

Once in the old site of the Hippodrome he paused by the Egyptian obelisk, ostensibly to examine it. As he did, he quickly glanced around, scanning the crowds coming toward him and was relieved to see his minder in the distance slowing and meandering as he passed the Kaiser Wilhelm fountain. He smiled to himself, pleased that he'd accurately identified his watchers but puzzled by their relative passivity towards him.

Huw was also concerned by Enver's casual dismissal of his finds. For the past three days he'd played the part of tourist as Enver had suggested, visiting many of the city's fabulous historic sites, hoping against hope that Enver would contact him and agree to investigate Father Manfred's confession in more detail or at the very least concede that the university would take it seriously. Now, after three days of silence, Huw was determined to act on his own if Enver wouldn't.

In the coolness and security of his hotel room, he called Mandy on his mobile to tell her he was coming home and on a hunt that would require her research skills. Satisfied, he then used the mobile to contact the Crown Security Bureau and emailed the photos he'd taken of his minders. Maybe they would be able to identify them or maybe they wouldn't, but at least he'd passed it along to them. He had a gut feeling that the passivity was just a waiting game. With the Bureau involved he might be able to get some help if things hit the fan again.

His last calls were to Enver, thanking him for the opportunity to work on the St. Theodor Martyr dig, and to British Airways, securing a flight to Heathrow the next afternoon.

### Manchester, England

Stone entered Piccadilly Gardens watching for the car he'd been told would pick him up. From the moment he'd landed at Manchester International after the long flight from Calgary his nerves had been on edge.

He'd agreed to Chad's wild idea but now that he was back in Britain, he was not so sure.

Was he putting his head into the Druid's maws by hanging out in their backyard? Even going through passport control had been traumatic. Stone glanced suspiciously at the agent, wondering if he was on the Druids' payroll and he kept a sharp eye on other airport or airline workers as they passed by. His jangled nerves saw enemies everywhere.

Stone forced himself to keep cool as he went through the immigration and customs rituals hoping the British passport and the unshaven look he'd cultivated the past two days would let him slip in undetected. Adding to what he hoped was a deception, he'd donned his Blue Jays cap with its peak pulled down and shading the top part of his face

From Manchester airport it was a quick walk over to the attached railway station and just over an hour later he was at Manchester Piccadilly, the city's major rail terminus. Another quick walk and he'd checked into the Hilton. In his room he called the special number Colin Maddox had given him back in Canada.

Three long tedious hours later, as he sat in the hotel's lounge a man approached him. The man briefly leaned down and spoke quietly to Stone. Ten minutes later Stone was crossing through Piccadilly Gardens. He spied the car described and slipped into it, relieved to see a solemn Maddox waiting in the rear seat.

Grimly, the British agent signaled the driver to move away. He turned to the American. "You'll be checked out and your luggage brought to you. Now, give me details."

As he filled Colin in on the events of the past week, Stone noticed the driver smoothly weaved through traffic and was soon on the M6 headed north. Interesting, he thought, we're not heading south towards London. "Where are we going?"

"The Lake District," Colin answered curtly and quietly, eyes constantly scanning their surroundings as they sped up the motorway.

Stone grunted. "Hope it's safer than the last place."

"Look we lost an agent there as well, Stone. Thank God you and Chad got out okay, but we suffered too," Colin barked.

Feeling a little ashamed Stone blurted a quick apology which was accepted by a nod.

"As I said, thank God you made it. Where's Chad? I expected to be picking you both up."

"We split up. He's gone somewhere—he wouldn't say where—to snoop. We agreed that I'd come here and get you involved again."

They both fell silent as they sped northward. In less than ninety minutes they swung onto the A591 and travelled smoothly along through Windermere, skirting the eastern shores of a calm sun-lit Lake Windermere. Beyond the lake he could just see the rising mass of what was called the Old Man of Coniston. Stone remembered the area from his several visits as a travel writer. He enjoyed the peaceful tranquility of the rugged hills, called fells locally, and the sparkling waters that dotted the area. It was one of his favorite regions of Britain so, since Colin was uncharacteristically quiet, he settled back to enjoy the drive as they continued north through Ambleside, past Wordsworth's cottage in Grasmere, rolling swiftly north.

Clouds were descending over the higher peaks as they swung onto a narrow roadway around the thick green forested western side of Buttermere one of the smaller lakes. Above them and across the waters loomed Buttermere Fell and High Snockrigg which were already disappearing into the grey mists of the fast-falling clouds. A quick left turn took them through some gates and up a winding driveway to a brooding stone mansion, two of its walls covered with ivy, and the whole house guarded on three sides by tall stately conifers. Behind them, now hidden by the clouds, Stone knew was the looming mass of Scafell Pike, the highest peak in England at well over three thousand feet. A lush green carpet of a lawn swept down the hillside to disappear into more woods. Beyond that, Stone realized, lay the calm waters of Buttermere.

Inside the house, Stone looked around the cavernous wood paneled entry hall, impressed by the display of armor and weaponry that decorated the walls and directed attention to the massive central stone staircase that led to the upper reaches and a wooden balcony that overlooked the hall itself. The black and white tiled floor lent an echo-like quality to every sound, including their footsteps. A massive circular glass tabletop on four stone claw feet stood in the centre of the hall, holding only a large blue and white porcelain urn. Its display of spring flowers and greenery gave the only real color to the hall.

He heard a slight cough and saw Colin gesturing to him as a tall, thin silver-haired woman dressed in a knee-length tweed skirt and beige woolen sweater approached.

"Welcome to Greyfell Abbey, Mr. Wallace." The woman smiled warmly and extended her hand. Her long fingers encircled Stone's hand and shook it with a surprisingly strong grasp. "I'm Nees, one of your hosts while you're here. My husband will join us shortly. He's been out seeking information."

Surprised at her warm though brisk manner, Stone smiled back. "Thank you, Ma'am. If you don't mind my saying, you have a fascinating name and this is an interesting place."

Nees laughed delightedly as she linked her arm in Stone's and led him into a warm well-lit sitting room filled with comfortable looking furniture and a vast array of fascinating paintings, figurines, photos and other bric-a-brac. "My full name is the Honorable Lavinia Denise Rose Longthwait. So you see why I find most of those names pretentious and prefer the shortened form of Nees even better than Denise!" She turned to Colin as they sat, "and will you be staying with us Mr. Maddox?" At his nod of assent she called a servant into the room, requested refreshments, and then settled back onto the sofa.

"So Mr. Stone. Our old friend Giles Broadbent tells me that you have stirred up the Druid's nest yet again." Before he could respond she waved her hand dismissingly, "oh it's all right to talk about it. Giles told us about Excalibur and the way you found it and then let it disappear in that Welsh earthquake." She smiled even more broadly at him. "But it was awfully naughty of you to not give it to poor Giles. He so wanted it for the Crown Jewels."

Her tinkling laugh took the sting out of her words and caused Stone to chortle out loud for the first time in days. Even Colin grinned, remembering the tense discussions about Excalibur and the aftermath of Stone's decision.

Soon tea, milk, sugar, scones, jam and a massive plateful of triangular sandwiches were laid out on the coffee table before them. Nees offered tea and milk to both her guests and continued, "Let's just enjoy these before Edward gets here. We can talk business then. Or perhaps you'd prefer to wait until morning, Mr. Wallace since I'm sure you're tired after your long journey from Canada."

Stone smiled. "Thanks Nees. Perhaps when your husband comes we can have a brief chat. I'm tired and confused so I may not make much sense myself and probably won't take in half of what I'm told. But I do want to know what this place is and how you know so much about me and my past. Oh, and by the way, please call me Stone. Everyone else does."

Nees smiled again and put her cup down gently on the saucer.

"Patience, Stone. Patience. For now, just enjoy these tidbits." With that she picked up a sandwich. It was obvious that nothing more would be forthcoming.

Stone resigned himself to wait while he devoured the delicacies before him.

### Silver City, New Mexico

The heat had finally let up as Chad gained elevation driving towards the Gila mountain range. Silver City, his destination, was only fifteen minutes away now and would be a thankful end to his long journey from Ontario. For nearly two of the past three days he and Stone had driven hard through Northern Ontario. Then he'd had a restless overnight in Winnipeg, Manitoba before they split and he caught his flight to Phoenix. Now, finally, his exhausting trip was almost over.

A quick stop in Lourdsburg for gas and food gave him a chance to finally call Silver City and get an okay for the first part of his plan. The long drive was enough to convince him that there were only two seasons in Arizona and New Mexico: hot and hotter. Thank God for air conditioning, he mused.

Mile after mile of dusty yellow-brown desert scrubland had revised his opinion of northern Ontario slightly. He'd thought that was bad enough, with its endless wilderness of rocks, trees, lakes and rivers interspersed occasionally by small dilapidated towns. Now, with nearly four hours of Arizona and New Mexico under his belt he that realized the unrelenting sun-smeared earth of browns and tans pock-marked only by polka-dots of the green brush and stunted trees of the southwest desert was marginally more boring than Ontario. Not much comfort, when you think about it, he muttered to himself.

Chad continued northeast on State Route 90 and wound his way through the historic mining town before branching off on a little used road that was more rutted dirt track than paved highway. In the distance he could see the dark blue and grays of the mountain peaks, their sharp tips ripping into the sky like dinosaur teeth. The directions to the ranch were easy to follow and he soon rounded a small hill and dropped into a small, somewhat greener, valley. To his left were outbuildings and behind them he briefly glimpsed what looked like a straight paved road. Before he could take it in, the track led him away and around another scrub hill with a magnificent view of grey-blue mountains in the background. The setting sun over his right shoulder was beginning to paint their tips lush red and orange to match the fiery sky.

A sprawling adobe bungalow lay tucked in a small side canyon. There was no sign of life. Cautiously, aware that he was unarmed, Chad stepped out of his rented SUV. "Hello the house" he called, standing behind the vehicle's open door, its engine still running. In the silence, he scanned the surrounding area, paying particular attention to a large clump of bushes halfway up the slope. He squinted at the undergrowth but could see nothing. Carefully he reached into the vehicle and turned the engine off, cocking his head to listen for any sounds out of the ordinary, but keeping his hands firmly on the car door ready to react instantly. He stared at the house, squinting into the shadows around the door and still saw nothing.

Chad took another quick look around before heading for the house itself. Before he'd taken five steps a voice barked at him to stay where he was. He spun around to see a mustachioed man carrying a powerful-looking assault rifle crawling out of a well camouflaged ditch behind him.

"Wiz! You scared the crap out of me." Together they slapped each other's backs and shook hands vigorously. Oscar Zanelli, a solid Directorate agent in his day, had taken the rookie Chad under his wings, teaching him the tricks of the trade and, instilling a sense of integrity into him while they both made their way through the muck and mire of an often dirty business. Because Wiz had always signed letters and reports with his initials, O.Z., he soon became known as "Oz". Later, because of his increasing success on various cases and problems, he became "The Wizard of Oz" and finally the shortened nickname "Wiz". Chad absorbed Wiz's resolve to do the job with honor and he'd missed the man's fierce determination to see a job through to the end. Seeing him reminded Chad again that he'd made a lousy effort to keep in touch since Wiz's premature retirement.

Beneath his Stetson hat and silvered sun glasses, Wiz grinned through his bushy sandy grey moustache as he dusted himself off after crawling out of his trench. He led Chad into the cool interior of the bungalow.

Inside the cool main room Chad took in the thick adobe walls and the thick ceiling beams. He enjoyed the rustic look but was surprised at the lush furnishings in such a simple building.

Noticing his guest studying the interior, Wiz quietly remarked. "Just 'cause I live in the desert doesn't mean I've got to live like a nomad." He swept his hand possessively around the room. "Best of everything here. And the most modern and up to date,"

"How many acres?"

"Fifty. And before you ask, yes it's secure. It might not be fenced, but I have surveillance cameras everywhere. Saw you on the highway long before you hit the track into the house. Gives me plenty of time to take precautions before guests—expected or unexpected—arrive on the doorstep." He waved Chad to a comfortable black leather armchair. Beside it was a heavy carved wood end table. On the table was a bowl full of ice and a frosty-looking bottle of Chad's favorite beer.

"Let's cut the crap and get to the point junior. You need a safe place to hide out for a while." Wiz said without waiting for Chad to speak and began to tick items off on his fingers. "First, you haven't tried to see me or contact me in any way since I left the office three years ago. Second, you suddenly call this afternoon out of the blue and tell me you're just outside Silver City and wonder if you could stay with me for a couple of days. You're in trouble son, and you need a hideout. Well, you're in luck. Even Billy the Kid and Butch Cassidy hid out in these mountains, so I guess we'll find a spot for you."

He was pleased to see Chad's jaw drop. "You forget I still have friends inside. I hear you were the target of an attack and then disappeared. You need a safety net and I'm it. Correct?" Wiz's smile was not forced but Chad could see questions in his piercing blue eyes.

"Absolutely correct," Chad acknowledged as his host directed him to a comfortable arm chair, "And yes, I've been derelict in contacting you, Wiz.

But things have caught up with me—especially over past year; I need a place to stay while I do a little investigating on my own. Tyler doesn't know where I am and doesn't want to know.

"I also need weapons, transportation and communications equipment like a laptop and cell phone. I want to hide the SUV here and find some other method of moving around."

Wiz leaned the rifle against the wall beside the door and pointed to a stuffed black leather couch.

"Sit down. I have a feeling this may take a while

### Crown Security Bureau, London

Freddy stepped into Sir Giles' office aware of the frowning scowl on his guvnor's face.

"Better have something good. God knows we need it."

"I don't know whether it's good or bad, Sir Giles, but it is a step forward."

He put a file on the desk and watched as Sir Giles read it and then picked up the attached photo.

"Recognize him." He stared thoughtfully at the photo for a few more minutes then snapped his fingers. "Knew it. Cathal O'Leary. IRA knife man," Sir Giles said tapping the photo with his finger. "Almost had him back in Antrim but he got away. Knifed two of my best informants. Slit their throats stem to stern."

Freddy pointed to the file. "Those are the police details. Cathal O'Leary's body was found about five miles outside the little village of Credenhill up near Hereford. A long way from his usual haunts in Dublin." He paused before completing his sentence. "Credenhill is only a few miles from the University of the Marches where Mandy Griffiths is teaching."

Sir Giles merely grunted. Freddy continued. "I also got some information from an old friend of mine in MI6. I kept it discreet and personal. Nothing went through official channels. He's been a deep mole in Eire until fairly recently." Freddy put a sheet of paper and some more photos on top of the file. "It's a list of Irish Druids. Apparently the Irish police have been looking into them surreptitiously for some years. You'll note that one of the prominent names on that list is Diarmuid Callaghan. My contact suggested I take a deeper look at him." Freddy paused dramatically, then added, "He's been to Wales six times in the past three months. Once to Holyhead on

Anglesey and the rest to Fishguard in the south." Freddy saved his best for last. "Not only that, but he has supposedly moved to Wales in the past two weeks, giving an address in Swansea. That's proved negative, but I've got eyes on the ground looking for him. His picture has been distributed to all our people plus the South Wales Constabulary."

Freddy pointed to several other photographs. "More importantly, his twin brother Declan was in Paimpont, France last fall attending a so-called conference at the Druid compound. He was badly wounded in the fire fight."

Sir Giles whistled. "Good work, my boy. Good work indeed. Now we've got something to get on with those. Check out this Declan's medical records. See what we can dig up."

In short order Freddy was told to ensure that Colin Maddox received copies of the information especially now he'd been dispatched to Greyfell Abbey. "No idea why the American agent wasn't there. Incommunicado with him and Tyler." Sir Giles also ordered Freddy to step up surveillance on both Mandy and Huw Griffiths.

"Find out if Griffiths is still in Istanbul and when, if, he comes home. There's a connection with all three again. Feel it in my bones,"

Ten minutes later, Freddy was again at Sir Giles' door this time excitedly waving another file at his guvnor. "Just got this from Huw Griffiths," he said as he handed over the photos Huw had forwarded. "The photos came in about an hour ago but we just identified the men in these pictures. Huw says they've been following him all over Istanbul. Both are members of the Irish Druid sect called the Tuatha run by guess who? Diarmuid Callaghan! Oh, and the professor says he's coming home tomorrow and would someone from our crowd meet him at Heathrow?"

The old man behind the desk leaned back in his comfortable chair, a quiet smile appearing on his face. "On the hunt now, Freddy. The game, as Sherlock Holmes would say, is afoot!"

# Chapter Ten

### Greyfell Abbey, Lake District

Stone briefly met Nees's husband, more properly called Lord Greyfell, later that evening. Greyfell explained that the house was actually a center for studying what he called "the ancient and mysterious powers." The manor house stood on the grounds of an old Cistercian abbey, one of many seized by Henry VIII during the Dissolution of the abbeys and turned over to court favorites.

"We've been flying under the radar for many years now. Nees was embroiled in a Wiccan coven when she was a young girl. I was able to liberate her from their clutches, but it caused the two of us to take a deeper interest in Wicca and its various offshoots. As time went on and I inherited this house, we made a conscious decision to make it a study center for the occult."

Greyfell was an imposing man of contrasts. His bright blue eyes were cloaked beneath large black glasses that made him look serious and scholarly but when removed they sparkled with a constant hint of humor and mischief. His massive shoulders shook when he laughed, yet his handshake was firm but gentle. He wore an impeccably laundered and pressed light blue golf shirt matched with an incongruously grubby pair of jeans. He was, Stone, decided, a man of many parts and many permutations.

After his brief explanation, Greyfell smiled apologetically at Stone. "I am so sorry, Stone. I don't mean to bend your ear on all this. You're exhausted after all your experiences and travels. Why don't we call it a night? Lots of time tomorrow to get you up to speed. And, besides, Colin and I have to update each other."

The night had passed peacefully. Crawling into the huge four-poster bed he wrapped a gigantic warm duvet around him like a soft security blanket. After tossing and turning briefly, wishing he could fall asleep to his beloved Pachelbel's *"Canon"*, Stone's last conscious thought was 'I feel safe here. For the first time in weeks, I feel safe."

After ten hours of blissful, deep slumber he'd forced himself to get up, shower, dress and make his way downstairs for breakfast. He felt human again as he jogged down the stairs in his casual beige slacks and deep red golf shirt.

He sat down at a large glass table on a patio outside the main living room. French doors opened up onto the green vista of the Greyfell Abbey's lawn and beyond, Stone saw flashes of sun glistening on the waves of nearby Buttermere. Even this early in the morning, the sun warmed the stone veranda. His host, Lord Greyfell, sat across from him wearing a tan sweater over a white dress shirt unbuttoned at the neck.

Over an enormous platter of eggs, sausage, beans, tomatoes, and bacon accompanied by gallons of hot steaming coffee, Greyfell explained his interest in the ties between Wicca, the occult and, over the past five years, the Druids.

"I'm talking about the real Druids here Stone, not the play-acting, costume-wearing, poetry-weaving pseudo-Druids who partake in cultural festivals and the Welsh eisteddfods. No, our Druids reach back through the dark clouds of history, past the Bronze Age and who knows how much farther back. They worship what they call the old gods, but who today would be identified as demonic or satanic beings. That's who you are up against Mr. Wallace. These Druids are very real and very terrifying, make no mistake. And they do not forget. Or forgive."

Greyfell squeezed more ketchup onto his plate and peered at Stone over his glasses. "Do you believe in God, Mr. Wallace? Because if you don't, I fear for your safety, your sanity and your life in this battle. Make no mistake. These are not just simple hardcore terrorists intent on temporal power. This is a struggle well beyond anything you have ever imagined.

"Still, we are not dismayed and we are not downcast, right old chap?" Greyfell's grin as he forked another mouthful of sausage and egg, again underlined the contrasts in the man.

"Look, Lord Greyfell…" Stone began.

"Call me Eddie, please Stone."

"Okay, Eddie, how much do you know about these Druids. Do you know why they are attacking again? Can you explain why I am here other than this being a hideout? Because I assume from what you've told me, there's a lot more behind this and you have pertinent information to share. Correct?"

Before answering, Greyfell turned and shouted into the house. "Come on out and join us, Nees my dear. We need to give Mr. Wallace a real briefing." He swung to face Stone again. "To answer your question, I told you that they do not forget or forgive. In their eyes, you and your companions stole Excalibur. You sabotaged their plans to dominate western society and destroy Christianity. You must, therefore, be eliminated. It's as simple as that in their eyes."

Nees and Colin Maddox stepped out onto the patio. Sweeping his arm to encompass both of them, Greyfell continued, "and it is our job, Stone, to see that they fail and that you and your companions not only survive, but triumph."

Before he could continue, Nees interrupted, announcing that Maddox had to leave for London immediately, before she sat and poured orange juice into a glass.

'"I got these from Sir Giles," Maddox said, placing copies of Huw's photos on the table in front of both Greyfell and Stone. "We ID'd them just now. They are members of the Irish Druids. Meanwhile, I'm heading to Heathrow to pick up Huw and bring him back here. Apparently, he has some other interesting news for us as well." He turned to Greyfell. "You'll tell him about Callaghan?"

As Colin left, Nees silently helped herself to coffee. Greyfell replaced his glasses and resumed his grave demeanor. His warm pale blue eyes gripped Stone in a penetrating stare.

"I was most serious when I asked you if you believed in God."

Seeing the conflict and puzzled look on Stone's face, Greyfell silently spread strawberry jam on his toast and raised it to his mouth. "I don't require an answer, Stone. Ever. It's not a subject you need to share with me at all. But you do need to think about it. And you do need to know the answer for yourself. Because these people believe in powerful ancient gods that have a malevolent and evil presence in this world.

"The occult, the supernatural or call it whatever you want, is all too chillingly real no matter how much modern culture and science likes to pooh-pooh it or turn it into fantasies suitable for films or Telly."

He slathered more jam on the toast and chewed, watching Stone carefully. So far, the American had remained silent, processing Greyfell's warning as his mind spun rapidly grappling with the implications of Greyfell's question.

"My last word on this subject. If you are not prepared to deal with this magnitude of war—for war it is—then I strongly urge you to return home to America, ask your contacts there to create a new identify for you and then totally drop out of sight, never to be seen or heard of again. And then hope and pray that the Druids never find you. As I said earlier, they will hunt you down relentlessly, because they never forget and will never forgive!"

## Hereford, England

Mandy was confused. Her relationship with Nigel was evolving—a little too fast she sometimes thought—though she admitted to herself that she enjoyed it. The attention she received from him was like a breath of fresh air, taking her out of her precious books and helping her see a different side of life. She had to be careful, she scolded herself. There were professional ethics involved; she was the superior and technically the employer, while he was the employee.

But he was also fun to be around. He had a charm and wit that lifted her out of her gloom some days. He'd rescued her in the woods that day and handled it all with the police, shielding her from questions and ensuring her wellbeing. They'd had deep discussions about their philosophical approaches to history and research and shared favorite books and authors with each other.

A couple of times they'd also grabbed a pub lunch between classes. Last night, she finally broke down and agreed to go out with him. They enjoyed a fine dinner at The Pinnacle, one of Hereford's finest restaurants located just outside Hereford's city center. Over sizzlingly delicious beef filets and red wine they'd slowly strayed from shop talk to more personal things. She'd learned about his eclectic work life from working as a waiter in a pub through to his army life before setting his sights on a university teaching and research career. He'd even persuaded her to use the diminutive of his name when they were alone. "All my good friends call me Nige, and I would be so pleased if you would do so as well." He smiled shyly at her through the dimmed atmospheric lights.

She, in turn, replayed her own eclectic life, studying, reading and doing her own research while also helping her father with his research. She almost slipped up, beginning to talk about the search for Excalibur and her run-in with the Druids but caught herself. She'd been sworn to silence and, if there was anything she prided herself on, it was her faithfulness to duty. And the Official Secrets Act *was* her duty. Quickly she changed the subject to her plans for her upcoming research trip to Cornwall.

In the fading twilight, the pleasant evening was topped off by a stroll along a quiet path on the banks of the Wye River.

Now she was in a dilemma. What should she do about this burgeoning relationship? What about her on again-off again bond with Stone? And now, she'd just heard from her father. He was suddenly returning from Istanbul and bubbling over with excitement about something—something he wouldn't talk about over the phone. Just a simple "call you when I can when I get back, *cariad*."

She jumped at the rap on her office door then relaxed as Nigel's beaming smile peaked around the corner. "Any chance we could do lunch again? It's a lovely day and I found a wonderful little pub just up towards Hay-on-Wye. You have no classes this afternoon and no tutorials, so maybe we could then continue on and indulge in some browsing in the bookshops."

"Sounds like fun Nige but I'm afraid I can't. Lots of other work to do and I just heard from my father. He's coming home from Istanbul with some new discovery, so I need to stick around here and wait for his call."

Nigel eased himself into the chair across from her desk. "Well, you've got a mobile haven't you. He could call you on that."

She shook her head, amused at his persistence but realizing above all she needed to speak to Huw in private. "Thanks anyway Nige but I really think it's better if I stay here. Mind you, if you do go up to Hay, I wonder if you could look out for one of these." She handed him a scribbled note naming four books she wanted to get her hands on.

"Mandy, I really need to talk to you. I would have preferred to do it over lunch." He gulped, "but now is as good a time as any." He slowly exhaled. "The fact of the matter is, I've decided to resign."

"What? Why?"

He waved his hand desperately at her, trying to stem her questions. "Let me explain. You've become very special to me. I've enjoyed working with you, talking to you and just generally enjoying your presence in my life, especially after that lovely time last night. I realize that this places you in a very awkward situation as my supervisor, so rather than do that I will leave." He searched her face for a response." Even if you only see me as a friend, I can't pretend. It is not professional or ethical for me to try and pursue a relationship with you when you are my boss."

Tears began to well up in her eyes. "Nigel, you are wonderful and becoming very special to me as well. It does create problems at the university, but maybe we can get around them somehow." She struggled to understand her feelings, confused and upset and yet strangely warmed by his declarations. "What will you do, if you leave here?"

He shrugged. "I have a little money left over from my army days plus what I earned here. I'll be all right. Especially if I can see you and not have to hide my feelings."

They spent another ten minutes talking, whispering, smiling before he reluctantly got up and started out the door. "I mean it, you know. I want you as more than my boss. I'm going to the Dean's office right now and hand in my letter."

As he left, Mandy collapsed into her chair, tears streaming down her face. Why, oh God, why, did life have to be so complicated? What did she truly feel about Nigel and what did she feel about Stone? More than anything she needed to talk to her father.

**Silver City, New Mexico**

Chad and Wiz drove past the unmarked dirt road that led towards the government's special cases penal center, euphemistically called The Spa. They did not slow down and Chad only gave it a peripheral glance knowing that well-hidden surveillance cameras monitored every vehicle passing by.

"It's about five miles away, tucked into a small canyon over that way," Wiz said quietly, gesturing slightly towards the west. He chuckled. "Tyler certainly had a sense of humor planting Murphy in this place."

Chad laughed as well. "Yeah, there's a certain irony in isolating Murphy near a town called Truth of Consequences, isn't there?"

In the three days they'd been together Chad and Wiz had examined the issue from all sides. Was there a leak in the security at The Spa? Was it possible that there was an unknown way into the place? Finally, Chad said he needed to 'eyeball' the location and the ever surprising Wiz obliged.

Two hours later they were in Wiz's blue and white Cessna 182 taking off along the "straight paved road" Chad had seen behind Wiz's ranch when he first arrived. To Chad's unspoken question, Wiz muttered quietly "just another of the many tricks our masters taught me. Then I got me a plane of my very own when I moved here."

Just over two hours later, after circling well south of Silver City and following a circuitous route past Deming and Las Cruces, they'd landed at Truth or Consequences, a non-descript town named after a defunct television game show. Wiz borrowed their pickup truck from an old friend who'd merely met them and turned over the keys. They followed the interstate north from the municipal airport. Some fifteen miles north of the airport, Chad estimated, they'd turned off onto state route 107 and were soon deep into barren desert scrubland dotted with rundown shanty-type homes. Mountain ranges hovered in the background wherever they looked as they followed the highway, meandering north and west until they passed the turn-off to the secure house.

"There's no cover is there?" Chad asked. "No place we can pull over and do a recon."

"Nope. And there's no settlement anywhere near here. There is absolutely nothing here. The Spa is truly remote, which is why Tyler arranged for Murphy to be incarcerated here." He pulled off to the side, executed a three point turn and headed back down the highway. Chad fixed his eyes straight ahead as they passed the dirt road once again. If any cameras were fixed on the truck cab they would see two mirror sunglassed men shaded by dark Stetson hats and focused on the road ahead.

Wiz drove back toward Truth or Consequences. He called his friend and made arrangements to meet at a bar where they could have a cold drink or two before they were driven back to the airport. "We'll fly out towards The Spa. I know it's a no-fly zone but we might spot something from eight thousand feet that we didn't see from the ground." Chad grunted agreement, his eyes scanning the singularly bland and unimpressive townscape.

Five minutes later as they made their way to the business core of the town, Chad stiffened in his seat. "Wiz, turn around and go into that gas station." Eyebrow raised but without comment, Wiz swung the vehicle around as requested. "Park so that I can see the entrance of that burger joint."

"What are you looking at?"

"Wait a couple of minutes and see."

Ten minutes passed then five more. Wiz began to get restive. The heat was beginning to filter through the windows in spite of the air conditioning in the truck. Chad suddenly grabbed his arm. "There. Coming out now. Who is that?"

Wiz pulled his sunglasses down to take a serious look. "Isn't that Helena Martinez from Tyler's personal staff?"

"Yeah. Wonder what she's doing here."

"Probably checking out security at The Spa."

"Doubt it. She's not a field agent. This wouldn't be her specialty."

"Why don't you check with Tyler?"

The pair watched as Martinez chatted with her driver as they got into a white Buick SUV then drive off down the highway. Wiz wheeled out of the gas station.

"Keep back. I don't want to be spotted," Chad said anxiously.

"Don't try to teach your father to suck eggs, sunshine. Remember. I taught you!" responded Wiz gruffly. Allowing several cars to get between them, Wiz dropped back but kept the SUV in sight. "I wish I had a camera so we could ID that driver," Chad muttered. They watched as it turned right onto a residential street. Wiz gunned his truck and sped to the next corner, spinning right onto the parallel street and driving as quickly as possible. Five blocks later he turned right again so that he wound up on the SUV's street. He stopped at the corner but neither of them could see it.

"He must have pulled off somewhere," Wiz muttered, turning and driving slowly down the street. "Keep your eyes peeled right and I'll keep looking left. See if you can spot him."

Three blocks later Chad saw the car pulled up tight against a non-descript bungalow painted a light brick red. They drove by cautiously but saw nobody. "Back to the plane. We'll skip the drinks and add this house to our aerial tour."

As he finished the call to his friend and arranged to pick him up he turned to Chad. "You do whatever you need to do to get confirmation that Martinez is either here on duty or whatever."

### Istanbul

The three men stood among the crowds in the departure area, trying to look as unobtrusive as possible. Ironically, their relative inactivity in the bustling chaos that was Ataturk Airport's international departure area, made them stand out even more.

They watched Huw Griffiths wrestle his bags onto the check-in counter then grab his carry-on bag and wander over to a newsstand. For more than an hour they waited, taking up new positions sporadically until finally they saw their quarry headed towards the security checks and then onwards to his departure gate. As Huw disappeared past security, the taller red head and bearded one pulled out his cell phone and made a quick call, listened carefully, acknowledged briefly. He turned to his companions and spoke to the shorter one who was wearing a cheaply made version of the Donald Trump toupee.

"You wait here until his flight has left, then join me back at the hotel. The Dragon Master has changed the plan slightly. We've got to get the security guard's help one more time at the university before we dispose of him. He's got to obtain an ancient document for us." He spun on his heels and left immediately.

Neither of them noticed four other watchers strategically placed around the airport concourse. As one discreetly followed the bearded man, the second flashed a pass and went through security, strolling in the same direction Huw had disappeared. The third and fourth remained, carefully but furtively watching their other target, switching locations and viewing points frequently and generally showing a surveillance professionalism their targets did not have.

# Chapter Eleven

### CSB offices, London

The attacks began without warning.

At Winchester Cathedral in the ancient royal city, congregants were stunned at their Sunday morning service when five visitors coolly standing at the back of the church suddenly whipped out machine pistols and began running down the centre aisle, firing indiscriminately and tossing small grenades.

In the panic, people screamed and dove for cover where there was none. The gunmen calmly kept on firing, stopping every once in a while to ensure that a victim was dead. Blood began to flow amongst the upturned wooden folding chairs. One man stood and threw a chair at the nearest attacker in a vain attempt to fight back. His chest exploded in blood and tissue as bullets from three of the attackers hit him. A four year old girl cried as her mother collapsed in a pool of blood before her. While choristers tried to duck behind the more substantial thickly carved wooden protection of their choir desks and chairs, a grenade blasted the choir master into the air, landing him in a bloody heap at the foot of the stone elevated pulpit.

As fast as it began, it ended. The unscathed gunmen disappeared into a smaller side chapel and out a smaller side door a short way down the hall. The last gunman stopped at the door, turned and shouted "Ta muid anseo." He too then disappeared.

Within the hour reports from other parts of England and Wales described similar atrocities at churches—Catholic, Church of England, Baptist and evangelical—in a variety of similar locations. Each targeted church was either a well-known vibrant local church or a local historic tourist draw.

Freddy sat on the sofa opposite Sir Giles' desk. Both of them had bowed heads as Freddy reported quietly. "In all a total of fourteen churches were attacked though most were not as bloody as Winchester."

"How many?"

Without looking at the sheet in front of him, Freddy replied softly, "In total, Twenty six dead, four critical and eighteen more with wounds of varying severity." As he spoke the television in the office blared away, with a series of microphones in front of the Prime Minister on the steps of 10 Downing Street. Flanked by the Lord Chancellor, the Home Secretary and the Secretary of State for Defense, police and other officials, he confirmed that no group had yet taken credit for the well-coordinated assaults. Furthermore, the Prime Minister was saying, there were very few clues for authorities to go on although, he promised, the perpetrators would be hunted down without mercy.

Sir Giles snorted. "Damn fool to go on the air with so little information."

"The nation needed to hear from him as quickly as possible. The people need to know that someone is in charge and fighting back," Freddy explained patiently. "Remember when the World Trade Centre was attacked? President Bush virtually disappeared for several days without a word to the country. It destabilized an already jittery nation,"

Sir Giles snorted again and turned the set off. "Closed circuit tape from Winchester. Do we have it yet?"

Freddy pulled a flash drive out of his jacket pocket. "I had it rushed over to us from our friends at MI5." He slipped the drive into his laptop, set it on the desk and they both began to watch the murderous attack unfold. Five times the camera view switched enabling them to see most aspects of the violent assault. They watched each segment repeatedly, carefully and quietly watching for the slightest clue. Suddenly, Sir Giles shouted.

"Stop. Right there. Repeat that. Slow it right down."

Freddy obediently replayed the segment. "Look! Right there." Sir Giles pointed at the last gunman just before he disappeared. "He's saying something."

Freddy agreed but pointed out the obvious, there was no sound so they could never know what he was saying or to whom.

Sir Giles shook his head impatiently. "Not shouting orders to the others Freddy. He's addressing the crowd. Doubt they heard in the chaos though." He smiled as he studied the video once again. "Get a lip reader in. Enhance this section of the tape. I want to know what this cretin is saying."

## Vale of Neath

Quinn arrived on schedule. In short order, Callaghan outlined his plan to his stone-faced subordinate then summoned Declan.

"I have to leave for a time. Quinn here will be responsible for the house and anything associated with it. If you need anything, ask Quinn and he will make it happen." Callaghan glared at Quinn to emphasize his point. "I will be on Dragon Master work and incommunicado. If anyone comes looking for me—authorities, anyone—you do not know where I am, where I've gone or when or if I will return. Got it?"

Without waiting for an answer, he grabbed Quinn by the arm and drew him out onto the patio for a private conversation.

Declan looked sadly at his brother as he left the room, then wheeled his chair around and returned to the glass conservatory that he'd made into his personal domain. There was nothing he could say to Diarmuid anymore.

## Silver City, New Mexico

Chad relaxed on the couch in the coolness of the late evening. Ceiling fans droned slowly over his head, wafting a cool breeze onto his otherwise sweating body. He waited impatiently for a response to his query to Tyler about Helena Martinez. He'd been circumspect about it, asking Tyler only if Martinez was available or around. He gave no hint that he had seen her in Truth or Consequences thus giving away his location.

The flight over the house had shown nothing. The SUV was gone by the time they'd been able to get into the air over the town. Even then, Wiz was careful not to directly overfly the house. A similar flight took them out towards The Spa but it too proved fruitless. Chad was able to follow the line of the dirt road with his eyes but lost it as it disappeared into the canyons that lead into the mountains. Wiz shook his head when asked to fly closer, citing the no-fly restrictions over that part of the desert. "Can't even approach it from above the mountains. They'd track us and identify us immediately and bang goes your anonymity sunshine," was his only comment during that part of the flight.

Chad's laptop dinged, informing him an email had arrived. He called it up and frowned.

"Well?" Wiz wandered into the room with some ice cold drinks.

"Apparently she's on vacation in Europe for two weeks."

Wiz dropped into the huge leather armchair and pushed a drink across the coffee table. "You think that's your leak? She's the one who ratted on you and Stone and took out the Chantilly operation?"

"Need more proof than this. But it sure looks suspicious."

The two batted the issue around most of the evening. Wiz played devil's advocate at times, swatting down Chad's suspicions. At other times, Chad found himself arguing the opposite side while Wiz played district attorney.

In the background Chad could hear the stirrings and sounds of night creatures as silence fell upon the ranch house itself. He got up and opened the door, standing in the doorway and drinking in the rich experience of a New Mexico night. Above him a myriad of stars shone brightly, unencumbered by harsh man-made city lights. The Milky Way gleamed in the cloudless night, the nearly full moon creating vivid shadows of the house on the ground.

"We've got to go back to Truth or Consequences."

"And do what," Wiz drawled as he ambled over to the door.

"Take her."

### Greyfell Abbey, Lake District

Stone was tired after an exhausting morning listening to Nees and Eddie walk him through the links between the occult and authentic Druidism. From Wicca to necromancy to witchcraft to Satan worship, they covered it all. He appreciated that they'd tried to keep it simple as possible, not knowing what, or if, he believed in anything. Stone grudgingly acknowledged to himself that not even he really knew what he believed other than he was still trying to work things out in his own mind. Huw's many admonishments to pray seemed good ideas at the time, but his desire to do so certainly waxed and waned depending upon his moods and situations. Fervent prayer, scattered and ineloquent was top of mind when he was being shot at. But for simple decisions—even the one to come to Britain again—well, they were less of a payer priority.

Through the morning they'd carefully laid out their hypothesis and thread by thread, rope by rope tied together the supernatural world and the Druidism Stone had encountered. Eloquently and effectively they led him through a dissertation on the supernatural in general, and then specifically tied it to the history of Celtic Druids leading up to the modern violent version.

"Look at it this way," Eddie said, pacing up and down the patio in front of the massive French windows, "Christianity, Judaism and Islam are what you would call 'revealed religions'. That is, their belief systems are based on revealed teachings in the Bible, the Torah or the Koran."

Believers in the occult, on the other hand, delve into a hidden belief system whether they worship Satan, are animists or Shamans or our Druid opponents. Their teachings are based upon oral tradition where mysteries are verbally passed down generation to generation. Secret incantations, shadowy powers and covert connections are their basis of power."

Nees took up the teaching. "Most people today consider themselves sophisticated and above such nonsense. Science trumps all belief systems, whether revealed or hidden in the darkness. But they are wrong: Terribly, terrifyingly and completely wrong." She paused for a moment and caught Stone's eyes, holding them in a firm embrace and whispered, "Eddie and I have seen the power of the supernatural at first hand and I was almost lost. Thank God Eddie was there to save me." She shuddered.

"Look around you. Look at the evil lurking in society today. Do you seriously think that terrorism is simply and only about power grabs? Money? Ego? Look behind those basic motivations and peel away the sociological justifications and you will find evil. Pure unadulterated evil.

"Why else would innocent bystanders be executed, beheaded, blown to bits, raped or mutilated. These atrocities are guided by a blood lust that permeates these actions and goes well beyond the desire for power or money. It is seeping throughout society even or, more accurately, especially, in our sophisticated educated western world. Child sex abuse—even in the church, for God's sake—child sex slavery, mass murders and shootings, I could go on. Do you seriously think these are just about simple base motivations? Underlying all of them is a base evil—sometimes known and sought by its practitioners, sometimes unconsciously embedded in the individual—but evil nonetheless."

Nees stopped speaking. The entire morning, Stone's comfort level dropped like a stone. He'd considered himself a well-educated and inquisitive journalist. But now he was in waters so deep he thought he'd never see the surface again.

"This may seem overwhelming to you, Stone, perhaps even bordering on the bizarre. You've been patient and basically silent while we talked." Eddie leaned forward. "But this is real. And you need to understand what you're up against."

Their discussion was interrupted by a ringing bell. "Lunch." Nees jumped up and swept her arm into Stone's, guiding him through the French doors and into the well laid out dining room.

"Cheer up, old man. Its heavy duty but I assure you there's good at the end of this. You know what they say: the best idea the Devil ever had was to convince people that he didn't exist!"

There was the abrupt change of direction once again. Stone turned a pained face towards his hosts. He liked them. He felt they were sincere and they certainly were treating him well. But this shower, no, make that a massive bath of information, was overwhelming.

He couldn't wait for Huw to arrive. Maybe his mentor could help him sort out the muddle in his head.

### Anglesey, North Wales

A cold mist-filled wind whistled in off the Irish Sea. From the heights of Castell y Draig you could sometimes see the Isle of Man and Ireland on a clear day. Today was not such a day. Heavy scudding clouds, showers, and now the wind buffeted the crumbling stone walls of the ruined castle.

In the old keep, Diarmuid Callaghan knelt by a small fire, oblivious to the weather. As always, a musty putrid odor hugged the ground in the interior of the ruins despite the fact that winds often howled through the ruins that were always open to the skies. Above him the jet black ravens that infested the carcass of the old castle cawed and circled, screeching their anger at the human intrusion of their territory. The flickering flames were reflected in his fixed unseeing eyes. His trance held him even as his lips moved in an unspoken incantation.

> GODS OF THE SKIES, GODS OF THE EARTH
>
> GODS OF FIRE AND FLAME; ENTER WITH POWER
>
> TO YOUR RULE GIVE BIRTH
>
> GODS OF THE WOODLANDS, GODS OF THE CREATURES

UNDER THE LANDS AND OVER THE SEAS
LET BLOOD FLOW AND ENTRAILS FLOOD
THE GODDESS WE WORSHIP, LET HER POWER INCREASE
HOOF AND HORN, HOOF AND HORN
ALL THAT DIES SHALL BE REBORN
CORN AND GRAIN, CORN AND GRAIN
ALL THAT FALLS WILL RISE AGAIN.

As he chanted quietly he called upon the gods of the underworld to grant him victory and, more importantly, to deliver his new and deepest desire, the scroll and the lance. From what he'd read, he knew the actual scroll would lead him to the all-powerful spear. With it, he would be able to serve the gods of the underworld as no other had. And with its power he could take revenge on all his enemies. But he knew that the gods had to approve his desires and guide him.

Sparks flew from the fire. They lifted up into the midday sky that was already darkening with dense rain-bearing clouds. He shifted his position to sit on a flat stone and pulled his windbreaker around him a little tighter. He waited. For what, he didn't know. But if his pleas to the gods had any impact he knew he had to wait.

The past three days he'd moved around to different homes in Ireland and North Wales. His supporters and devotees gladly opened their homes to him. Now, on the ancient holy island of the Druids he'd accepted the keys to a well-appointed home on the north shore. The modern house stood high enough on a hill to allow stunning views of Wylfa Head and Cemlyn Bay. As a bonus it was only three miles across admittedly narrow lanes to the ruins of Castell y Draig. If he was going to go into hiding, then he damn well was going to hide in luxury he told himself. Except for this self-imposed sojourn to the castle.

As he waited, he heard the winds howl around the walls. The sparks flew higher and the flames flickered menacingly as he put more wood on the blaze. He tilted his head to one side as the howling wind became a moan. He shifted his seat once again and looked into the depths of the old keep. Where before light had crinkled through the holes and cracks of the wall, now a light-absorbing blackness waved and bobbed in the shadows. The moaning noise began to take on a hissing sound, warbling and rising as he began to approach the wall.

His head tilted to one side Callaghan sought to determine if the shadow was caused by natural phenomena or was, in fact, the answer to his summons. He got colder as he advanced towards it. But the sounds became slightly more comprehensible. He suddenly stopped as his whole body was suddenly hit by a freezing cold beyond anything he'd experience before. The iciness penetrated his clothes through his body and to the very depths of his organs. He could not move his legs one step closer to the shadow. His head, however, remained warm. Squinting, he focused on the darkness, training his ears to hear the sound the shadow was making.

"Spear. You want me to get the spear," he whispered to the shadow. Above him, the skies darkened, thunder rolled and lightning crackled. As he watched, the impenetrable darkness flowed and shifted, streaming around itself and spiraling upward, getting thinner and thinner as well as higher and higher. Finally, it was a long, snake-like apparition before it suddenly dissipated. As soon as it was gone, his body warmed.

He smiled to himself. The gods had answered him. The spear of the scroll was now more important than personal revenge on Huw Griffiths, though he promised himself that if there was any way he could kill both birds with one stone, he would do so. And enjoy it.

# Chapter Twelve

### Greyfell Abbey, Lake District

"Austria?! Have you lost your mind totally?"

Huw smiled benignly, amused that he'd thrown the cat amongst the pigeons as he watched Stone's and Colin's reactions. Out of the corner of his eye he also noticed Nees and Eddie glance at each other then back at him. But nothing on their faces betrayed their feelings.

"Calm yourself Bradstone. You too Mr. Maddox. Indeed and to goodness, I am in my right mind. I have thought about nothing else for the past two days. I know what I am doing." He turned to Eddie. "Lord Greyfell, if you have any maps of central Europe—particularly Germany and Austria—I would be most grateful."

"I do indeed Professor, and please call me Eddie."

Before Huw could open his mouth Stone blurted "won't do you any good, Eddie. I don't think he believes in nicknames or short forms. He still refuses to call me Stone after all these years." A soft smile creased Huw's face and he nodded acknowledgement to Stone.

Eddie, respecting Huw's wishes, disappeared into the library. Nees shuffled out of her seat, told the men she had work to do and disappeared into another portion of the house.

Colin, Stone and Huw sat alone in the sitting room. Finally Greyfell returned with a map and spread it out on the table.

"I made a phenomenal discovery in Istanbul that I must follow up on, look you. And it hints at a place called Finsternisdorf in Germania, which in the mid 1400's was part of the Holy Roman Empire. I have been looking for this place and, sure enough, there's still a place called Finsternisdorf but it's not in Germany, it's in Austria in the Tyrolean Alps between Salzburg and Innsbruck".

Excitedly, Huw walked them through his search and rationale before settling on his plan to search in Austria. As he spoke he plunked his finger onto the village called Finsternisdorf.

"How do you know this place is the same one mentioned in your parchment, Huw?" Stone asked. "It's been six hundred years or more. Place names change, towns and villages disappear or get swallowed up by larger towns and cities. It's a very slim link between finding a name in an old parchment and a similar name on a modern map."

"Bradstone, my boy, you are of course correct. That is why I need Mandy to work her magic and look up whatever historic documents she can find from the mid 1400's to today. And I need her to try and find a knight named Baldric who ruled from a castle there and who, it seems, was a trader in relics and icons." He looked up from the map as his finger still tapped the spot, "But the best way to find out is to go there and see for myself. I have found out one thing though, and that is that Finsternisdorf did have a castle, Schloss Finsternis. That's where I would begin my hunt. But first, Bradstone and Colin, I think you need to read this." He reached into an old scratched, beaten and weather-worn leather satchel and pulled some papers and handed them across.

Colin picked his up. "Before I read it Huw, would you telephone Mandy and tell her that our men will pick her up at the university this afternoon and bring her up to Greyfell. There are things that all three of you need to know and I would rather just tell it once."

He looked at Stone. "You've been kept out of the loop in terms of news too, and you'll have noticed there's no radio or television here at the big house. Nor will you find any newspapers. We've done that deliberately to keep your mind focused on what Eddie and Nees have to teach you. But if you will just wait till Mandy gets here before we read, I have some news that I think might impact both of you. So let's take a break before we do anything else and just enjoy this relaxing place."

He handed Huw his mobile. "I think my news may also change your mind about Austria."

### Hereford, England

"You don't have to go with them. Tell me where your father is and I will take you." Nigel slowed his pace to match Mandy's. "You don't even know who these people are. They could be anyone from anywhere with all kinds of ulterior motives. Besides, you know me," he ended lamely.

"I really appreciate the offer, Nige. Really I do. But I do know these men and I do know where they're from. I will be fine."

"Who are they then? Why won't you tell me?"

Mandy shook her head. "Nige, much as I might want to tell you, at this point I can't." She slipped her arm into his. "Look, walk me down to the administration building. I'm meeting them there and you can see for yourself that all is well." Her ready grin was hard to ignore. "Besides, you still haven't gone to Hay-on-Wye and got those books for me yet."

As she spoke, they rounded the corner of the central university complex. An undistinguished blue sedan waited in front of the main doors. Mandy's grin became broader as she recognized the man waiting. "Freddy!" She began to pull Nigel faster in her haste to meet her friend but she was pulled up short.

Baffled, she looked at Nigel. He had lost his warm smile. "Look. It's probably best if we part here and then you can go on with your friend. The bus stop is just over there and I can get the next bus to Hay." He reached down and gave her a quick kiss on top of her pony-tailed head then walked quickly away. Mandy stared after him a while, puzzled by his inexplicably sudden attitude change. Slowly and thoughtfully, she turned and walked towards Freddy. When she reached him, she shook his hand, flashed her brilliant smile and jumped in to the back seat he indicated. He got in beside her and signaled to the driver.

As they pulled out onto the main road Freddy asked about her companion. "Oh, that was my teaching assistant Nigel. I think he's a little put out because he wanted to take me to Da himself. Plus I wouldn't tell him who you were." She grinned at him again. "I couldn't exactly tell him I was bound to silence under The Official Secrets Act, could I?"

Freddy chuckled. "No. That in itself would have been a breach of the Act. By the way, I stopped at your flat as you asked and picked up your suitcase. Your landlady is a tough one. She wouldn't let me anywhere near your door. I had to show her my Queen's Warrant."

He grinned at the memory of how the woman's eyes widened in surprise and curiosity. "I had to swear her to secrecy and let her know I was working for you. You'll have her eating out of your hands when you come home."

The car headed down the A438, picking up speed after it wound through the heart of Hereford. "Where are we going?" Mandy asked.

"First to Worcester then over to the M5 and north from there," Freddy said enigmatically. "We'll stop for a quick bite to eat in Worcester then relax for a few hours."

"Scotland?"

"Let's just say further north than Birmingham and not as far as Glasgow." With that, he stopped talking and, taking the hint, Mandy reached into her purse and drew out an ever-present book. She decided that at least she was going to make the most of the next few hours reading.

In the courtyard of the university complex, Nigel had watched them drive away, a scowl on his face. He turned his face as the car neared him and he did not acknowledge Mandy's wave. As the vehicle rounded the corner out of the university and onto the main road, he followed it with his eyes.

Once it was out of sight he reached into his pocket and pulled out his mobile, punched some numbers with his left thumb as he walked, and began speaking.

### Istanbul

Dr. Enver Turel, the renowned and always under control director of archaeology, paced frantically back and forth beside his desk. Beside him, museum security guards and several policemen were examining his desk and safe. While one carefully brushed the safe's lock, another in surgical gloves was sifting through papers on Enver's desk.

"And you say you found the safe door open when you first arrived." A stockily built man with a shaved but tanned bullet head and enormous black bushy moustache leaned against the filing cabinets in the corner. His thick neck was almost bursting the top button of his rumpled white shirt. Only a slightly grubby obviously well used red tie loosely held the shirt together. For the past hour Enver had repeated the story at least three times. First to the security guard who came running at his shouts, then the first policemen on the scene, then his own Dean. Now that the stocky man who identified himself as Detective Beyanzid Kizil of the National Police was in the office, Enver had to go through the story again.

As he did, the detective lit up yet another cigarette, sucked in heavily and slowly exhaled the smoke through his nose. "And you say the only thing missing is an old manuscript?"

"Yes. It was in a small bronze box and that's gone too."

The detective took another drag. "Was it valuable, this manuscript?"

Enver shook his head. "Not really. Just one interesting story dug up from the ruins of an old Christian church excavated as part of the Marmara subway project. My British colleague and I found it a few days ago."

"Why would they take that, whoever it is?"

Enver stopped his pacing to run his hands through his hair. "I really don't know. It has no real value that I can tell, just a report of the final few days of the Byzantine Empire before Sultan Mehmet captured the city."

Another drag on the cigarette and Kizil straightened up and walked over to the safe. He knelt down and studied it carefully. "It hasn't been broken in any way," he said, pointing to the handle.

"Of course not," Enver snorted. "It was always left open. I told you. Nothing of value was ever kept in there."

"Then why put the box and the document into the safe?"

"To keep it out of the way and not get it all mixed up with the rest of this stuff," Enver waved his hand at the myriad of items dotting every available space in his office. Bits and pieces of broken pottery shared shelves with books and figurines interspersed with fragments of old timber. "Look. I just wanted to report the theft and get your men looking for it. It might not have much intrinsic value but it is a rarity. The illegal antiquities trade would snap something like this right up and it would be lost to the city and the nation forever."

Kizil nodded thoughtfully. "Any chance your British friend could have taken it?"

Enver tossed his head back and laughed. "Huw? Ridiculous. He would never do anything against the law. Besides, he left Istanbul yesterday afternoon and it was here last night. I saw it myself."

Kizil stood and was about to speak when another policeman opened the office door and beckoned him out. Kizil followed the officer, closing the door carefully behind him. Ten minutes later he stalked back into the room again, a frown pulling his moustache down even lower than it normally sat.

"You say these items were not valuable?"

"Correct."

"Then can you explain to me please, why the night security guard who serviced this office and this floor and who was on duty last night, has just been found on the grounds of the Hagia Sophia just now? The man's throat was sliced from end to end and he was found in a large puddle of blood beside one of the ancient stoneworks outside the main entrance." He plopped himself into Enver's desk chair and drummed his fingers on the desk. "Something so lacking in value, yet worth taking a man's life? The man whose job it was to ensure the safety of these offices."

He looked up at Enver and stopped drumming. "Why do you think that might be Dr. Turel?"

### Truth or Consequences, New Mexico

Picking up Helene Martinez actually proved much easier than either Chad or Wiz had expected—or planned. They'd conceived and disposed of a number of scenarios, including breaking into the house and seizing her, abducting her on the street at night, pulling her car over and taking her, along with a myriad of others. Most of them were rejected, even laughed at, as soon as one or the other threw it out. At one point, tired after hours of thinking, they even tried to outdo each other with the most outrageous and unlikely ideas just to get a laugh and relieve the tension.

"Any one of these ideas would get us arrested and in jail before we could even blink," Chad groused after they agreed to get serious again. "If she goes anywhere near The Spa and we try to seize her there, we'll probably be on surveillance cameras and they'd alert half the state's police forces before we got more than five miles."

'Wiz thought for a moment. "She knows you and she knows you've been ordered into hiding. She won't expect you to be in this town any more than you expected to see her. So let's use that to our advantage."

"What do you mean?"

"Well first thing is that beard you've grown. That and your sunglasses might just throw her off long enough." Wiz then began to walk Chad through his plan. He conceded that it was still paper thin, but gave them a better chance than anything they'd yet produced.

"We've been watching her for two days. You're right. She's not a field agent because she never varies her daily routine. Out at 11:45 each day, into the local burger joint with her order and then back to the house. Other than

Martinez and whoever is in that house and drives her, there seems to be nobody else. That's our best opportunity to seize her."

The pickup had gone according to plan. As soon as she arrived at the restaurant the next day, Chad and Wiz had driven up beside her. While Chad got out and followed her inside, Wiz strolled around and approached her driver feigning a problem trying to light his cigarette. When the driver opened his window in response to Wiz's knock on the glass, he fired a miniature tranquilizer dart into the man's neck. "Take a nap for the next half hour," Wiz muttered as he strolled casually back to his truck.

Inside, Chad held back while she placed her order. He made sure he was not in her line of sight while she paid and quietly approached her when she stopped to get condiments for her take out order. As soon as he stood behind her, shielding her back from the view of the few uninterested staff and customers, he poked her back with his Glock 22 pistol.

"Helena. What an interesting surprise," he said quietly. "Just act normal please. I would really hate to use this. It would make such a mess. Just casually stroll right outside and into my car."

"Lawson!" she hissed. "What the hell are you doing here and what the hell are you playing at."

"Shut up and do as you're told."

As they passed her vehicle she gasped as she saw the driver slumped over. "You killed my brother?" she hissed.

"Tranquilized. He'll be asleep for another fifteen minutes or so, then wake up with a massive headache. Now move!"

Ten minutes later they were in the car heading to the airport. Fifteen minutes after that they were airborne but not before Wiz tranquilized her as well. "Don't want her seeing where we're going and certainly don't want her to kick up a fuss while we're in the air. I have a distinct desire to avoid crashing." Nevertheless Chad cuffed her using plastic hand restraints conveniently provided by Wiz from his magic box of tricks, as he called it.

Back at Wiz's ranch they carried her inert body into one of the side buildings Wiz had prepared. They laid her on an old blanket covered army cot and waited for the tranquilizer to wear off. The only light in the building was an old sixty watt standing lamp in one corner. The sole window was sealed with black plastic covering. When the drug finally wore off, Chad was the only one visible in the otherwise empty room. He was casually seated backwards on a hard plastic folding chair, leaning over its back while still wearing his Stetson.

"Welcome back to the real world Helena," he motioned to her to sit up on the cot. As she struggled to do so with her hands manacled before her, she glared at him and began cursing in both English and Spanish.

"Language, language, Helena. Please keep it clean. Are you enjoying your European vacation?"

"You bastard," she spit out. "They were supposed to get you as well as that reporter."

Chad smiled. "Well at least we don't have to dance around the room doing the 'I-don't-know-what-you're-talking about' polka," he said amiably. "How long have you been a Druid?"

She laughed and spit at him. "I'm not. But they pay a hell of a lot more than your precious Tyler." She struggled again to shift her position. "You think you're going to get away with this? They have people all over. They were in place before Murphy pulled out of the election and are still there. He'll be back. And bigger and more powerful than ever before."

"Why did you do it Helena? Was it just the money? I hope they gave you lots, because your family will need it. You're going to be away for a long time." Chad leaned forward. "Maybe Tyler will take pity on you and arrange for you to be at The Spa with your buddy Murphy. And you'll be close enough that your family can visit." He paused dramatically. "Oh, wait. Guests at The Spa don't get visitors do they, because nobody knows exactly where they are or where The Spa is."

Her response was a hate-filled glare as she clamped her mouth shut then turned away from him.

The interrogation went on for three more hours. While the woman did not deny involvement in the Druid attacks on the Chantilly headquarters or the attempt on Stone's life, Chad could get very little more out of her. She would say nothing about her Druid contacts or how she connected with Murphy. She refused to tell him how much money she'd received for her betrayal. Apart from her first stunned outburst, she dropped into a monosyllabic response to every question, devoid of any feelings. Whenever she looked at him, daggers flew out of her blazing eyes but for all the emotion they contained, her voice stayed flat and cold.

Chad was into another round of repeated questions when the door opened and natural light seeped in to the room. Wiz walked quietly in.

"Zarelli. I should have figured."

"Nice to see you too, Ms. Martinez," Wiz countered amiably. "I'll sit and wait with her for a while. We'll be having visitors shortly." He placed a plastic bottle of cold water and a sandwich on a cot beside her. "Sorry I can't release your hands, but you should be able to figure out how to eat and drink with those cuffs on."

"You recorded all this, no doubt." Martinez' flat voice could not disguise the hatred she seethed at both men.

Wiz was about to answer when they heard a helicopter arrive. "Go meet him, Chad. I'll stay with our charming guest."

Outside, dusk was beginning to fall. The peaks were getting fired up and glowing red and orange once again. As the helicopter landed, Chad recognized the bulky rumpled figure who jumped out. He was followed immediately by four more armed men. As they ran towards Chad the chopper lifted off again and he heard Tyler's unmistakable booming voice fired out an order to the men behind him. "Set up a perimeter."

He ran towards Chad, shouting at him that he'd disobeyed orders to go into hiding and stay out of the investigation while gleefully acknowledging the good work Chad and Wiz had done. As he did, a second helicopter began its approach onto Wiz's landing strip.

Inside the building he looked down at Martinez, palpable anger reddening his face. "I'll see you in hell," he fumed at her. She said nothing and merely spat in his direction.

"We're going to take her out of here and interrogate her some more." He turned to Martinez. "And you can be sure that we will not be as gentle in our questioning as Mr. Lawson was." Two men from the second chopper arrived in the room, lifted her up as if she weighed no more than a feather and moved her out towards the waiting aircraft.

Tyler flopped down on the vacant chair, wiping his red face with a crumpled white handkerchief. Wiz stepped over and handed him some discs. "Other than her first outburst, there's nothing, Chief. But she does admit working with the Druids and being part of the attack on both the offices and the reporter."

Tyler mopped his face again. "Damn heat. Don't you have any air conditioning in this place Wiz?"

"Wasn't expecting guests. Had to jury rig this old barn into an interrogation centre overnight, Chief."

Tyler looked at Chad. "Don't want to know how or why you got here, Chad. I do know you were in Canada and got involved in a shootout on some lake up there. Took a lot of talking and explaining to clear that with our Canadian cousins, I can tell you."

"Now what have you got so far and where do we go from here?"

# Chapter Thirteen

### Greyfell Abbey, Lake District

The afternoon sunshine had suddenly turned grey and gloomy. Within minutes, Scafell Pike to the south disappeared and Skidaw peak to the northeast also disappeared. The rain began drumming down heavier and heavier as Huw stood in the open French doorway gazing out pensively at the view, waiting impatiently for his daughter to arrive.

"Brwr hen wragged a ffyn" he muttered to himself.

"What was that, Huw?" Stone walked up behind him, a cup of coffee in hand. Colin Maddox still sat comfortably on the sofa checking his mobile.

"Welsh, my dear Bradstone. It means literally that it's raining old wives and walking sticks." He turned away and shut the doors, "So you think this Diarmuid Callaghan is behind all of these attacks."

Colin stretched. "We have information that he was named Dragon Master to replace Rhiannon. Apparently, according to Lord Greyfell's sources, there was a Gorsedd—that's something like a conference of Druid leaders—earlier this year on Anglesey in North Wales. It seems they have an old ruined castle on the island that is somewhat sacred to them. They had their meeting there."

Lord Greyfell entered the room followed by Nees bearing refreshments. As they set them down on the table, Greyfell added "the place is called Castell y Draig in Welsh; what we would call Dragon Castle. We've tried to find out what's up there, but it is very well protected; Electric fences all around the property at the bottom of the hill and probably security cameras as well. The castle itself sits up on the promontory looking out over the Irish Sea towards the Isle of Man. There's a farmhouse nearby that they use. The farmer and his wife have some pretty ferocious dogs that are allowed free range within the property."

He offered the plate of sandwiches around while Nees picked up the narrative. Stone had noticed that the two of them were always in perfect synch, able to spell each other off in their discourses without ever missing a beat, losing the train of thought or contradicting each other.

"There was a young man savaged by the dogs just about a year ago. He was found bloodied and barely alive on the other side of the fence. Passersby on the road found him and called an ambulance. We understand the police were called and investigated but the farmer paid the fines, allowed one of the dogs to be put down and paid for the young man's medical expenses. From what we can discern however, they merely replaced the dog with another equally savage animal."

Lord Greyfell chimed in. "We tried to trace the money in that case. Where did the farmer get the money to pay the fines and expenses, we wondered? Certainly if you look at the farm operation up there it does not seem a very prosperous place. But we got nowhere. The money trail was too well hidden."

The chatter about Callaghan continued with Lord Greyfell, Nees and Colin providing what details they could about Callaghan and the Tuatha De Danann Druids in Ireland. Stone still stood sipping his coffee and punctuating the discussion with questions. Huw, he noted surprisingly, was fairly silent, offering only the occasional comment. Normally, Huw—ever the professor—would have been pontificating on points, adding bits of information, asking probing questions and generally participating in the discussion with relish.

"Are you okay, Huw?"

"Fine, my boy, fine. Just trying to absorb all this and fit it in to my discovery in Istanbul." He turned to Colin. "Do you think your boys might be able to persuade the higher-ups to authorize regular satellite passes over that castle and give you any information they might glean." His eyes twinkled, "and I know you are all listening in on mobiles and sifting through that. Any chance we could tap in to that as well?"

Colin smiled. "Way ahead of you Huw. Sir Giles enquired through some back channels a couple of days ago. Unfortunately, we have very little to go on other than suspicions. We're not going to get that kind of assistance without more solid evidence to back up our fears."

"Surely if they had any part in those church atrocities it would be enough,"

"Can't prove anything yet. The police investigation is still ongoing, Huw. Unless we get something solid, we can't shift the police into looking at a Druid connection."

Lord Greyfell snorted. "Of course they're involved. That's probably what their bloody Gorsedd was about—planning the massacre."

"Now, now, Eddie. That's your abhorrence of the Druids coming through. We have no way of knowing they really did plan it." Nees offered another sandwich to Huw and he eagerly took it, "long time since I had good old British sandwiches, Nees. *Diolch yn fawre*. Thank you. Love the smoked salmon." He took a second before she moved away.

Stone snapped his finger. "Colin, is there any way we could figure out if there's another meeting coming soon? Maybe we could launch a drone and take aerial shots instead of wasting time with satellites."

Colin looked up eagerly from his comfortable position on the sofa, "Hadn't thought of that. I could pass it by the Guvnor and see what he thinks." His smile lessened somewhat as he added "mind you, I don't know how or if we could find out when such a meeting was scheduled." He reminded Stone and Huw that the Crown Security Bureau, while an essential part of the government's intelligence and counter-intelligence establishment, was relatively small in terms of manpower, resources and budget. "Really, this whole Druid thing is beyond our mandate. It's only because of the attempt on Her Majesty last autumn that we're allowed to investigate this far. Sir Giles has made sure that the Queen's express desire we remain involved got passed along to the proper channels." He took a bite of the small lemon tart offered by Nees. "The thing is," he added, "much of the time all the Guvnor does is fight turf wars with the Metropolitan Police, MI5, MI6 and other intelligence bodies you don't even know about."

The discussion continued until they heard a car crunching on the yellow gravel driveway outside. "They're here," a relived Huw said quietly. "And after we've listened to your information, Colin, perhaps you'll listen to mine and you'll see why I still need to pursue my discoveries in Europe."

Huw pointed his finger at both Stone and Colin. "You'll see. I think my discovery and this increased Druid activity are connected.

"Austria, gentlemen, is the key!"

## Istanbul, Turkey

Detective Kizil sat in a borrowed office in the Tourist Police headquarters at number 6 Yerebatan Caddesi, just across the street from the entrance to the Basilica Cisterns and around the corner from Sultanahmet Square and the Haghia Sofia. It reeked of strong stale Turkish cigarettes and the desk was cluttered with files and papers, most of them bearing at least one coffee stain or cup ring. There seemed little order to the pile so Kizil grabbed most of them and pushed them into a small hump to his left. He loosened his already loose tie, took out a pen and began laboriously going over his notes.

He ignored the nervous man sitting across from him while he read. As he read, he surreptitiously kept an eye on the man in front of him. He was not convinced that a well-known archaeologist like Dr. Turel could be so innocent, so naïve, as to leave valuable documents and artifacts lying around his office.

He lit another cigarette, took a long drag and slowly let the smoke seep out of his nostrils. "You see, Dr. Turel," he boomed, finally acknowledging the man across the desk, "I have a real problem understanding this. You say this box and its contents were of no value. Yet you especially asked for this British professor to help you with the excavation. Further, you were willing to wait weeks for him while he recovered from some injury. Then you and he convinced the authorities to continue the dig long after it was supposed to end. And finally, in the last few days you get your hands on this remarkable little bronze box that you all worked so hard to find. And then you just… dismiss it? It is of no value and you send your British friend home?" He tapped his pen rapidly against the desk. And dropped his voice "You see why I find this a little unsettling. A little strange."

Enver Turel rubbed his hand around the neck of his shirt, biting at his lips. Never in his life had he been faced with such a frightening problem. He'd never had difficulties with police of any kind. Yet now he was under suspicion of something, though he didn't quite know what. But this was still Constantinople in everything but name, he reminded himself, where intrigue and plotting reigned supreme and where people disappeared at the mere hint of suspicion.

He shuddered and licked his lips, squinting his eyes to force his mind to think. Finally, he threw up his hands.

"I don't know what to think. I asked for Professor Griffiths because he is one of the best in the world at understanding ancient documents. I was willing to wait on the project at St. Theodor Martyr because I had numerous other projects on the go at the same time." He pulled a handkerchief out of his suit pocket and wiped sweat from his face. "When we found the document, as I said, it was an interesting and unusual piece of history but nothing outstanding or valuable." He shrugged his shoulders in defeat. "Other than that...."

The policeman studied him intensely, letting the silence build and letting the man suffer a little longer. "Were you aware that there were men watching all of your work, watching you and your professor friend?"

Startled, Enver thought for a moment then smiled slightly. "I saw some men watching Huw and I did warn him to be careful." He spread his hands in a gesture of 'what can you do,'"but nothing really came of it. I have no idea who they were, nor did he. But they didn't threaten us in any way. Nor did they interfere. They just watched him, not me, from a distance."

Just before the policeman began to ask another question, Enver suddenly leaned forward. "I did ask one of my students to find out what they wanted. But it was obvious that they were not Turkish."

"Did you know that they followed your friend right to Ataturk and made sure he got on his flight?" Kizil's eyebrows rose while he studied Enver's reaction. Before he could respond, Kizil changed direction.

"What was in this ancient document that was so interesting? Do you have a copy so that I might read it for myself?"

Enver winced. "I had copies made but now they're lost too. I kept one on my desk but it disappeared a couple of days ago. I'd sent one to the city's chief archaeologist as well, but when mine went missing, I asked him to send it back. He did, and I put it in the safe with the others. Now it's gone too."

"Curious, wouldn't you say, Dr. Turel? Or even suspicious?"

The questioning went on for another half hour. By then, Kizil wondered if Turel wasn't indeed as naive and innocent as he seemed when it came to the workings of the modern world. He's trapped in the old world of his own making, Kizil decided. For the life of him he could not see what part, if any, the professor had played in the disappearance of the box and its mysterious documents and even less, the murder of the guard, yet he was sure that there was a connection between Turel, the British scholar and the men following them. And, his gut told him, it was all connected to the box.

Finally, after another hour of questioning he left the archaeologist alone for a further fifteen minutes. From a darkened room next door, Kizil watched Turel closely through a one-way glass window. Turel never moved from his chair nor did he look at the darkened mirror that hid the window. He merely sat and fidgeted, wiping sweat off his face regularly and sipping from the glass of water Kizil had provided.

If he was guilty of anything, then he had nerves of steel and was a good actor, Kizil decided. With no hard evidence and no other options left to him, the policeman re-entered the office and let Turel leave with cautions about calling immediately if he found anything or thought of something he'd forgotten no matter how trivial. He was also warned not to leave Istanbul in the near future.

Kizil watched the archaeologist leave the building and cross the street, weaving his way between trams, trucks and cars. As planned one of his own men quickly followed behind him. *You may indeed be uninvolved in this, Kizil mused, but I'm going to be absolutely sure of it before I let you go totally.*

He returned to the borrowed office and called in his assistant. "Call that British security office. They wanted us to help them by keeping tabs on their Dr. Griffiths and the ones who were watching him. Now it's their turn to help us with a theft and a murder."

He stubbed out his smoke and immediately lit another, stretching back and demanding a pot of chai as quickly as possible. *Nothing like a good smoke and a good tea to settle you down,* he thought.

### Silver City, New Mexico

"To think I had that viper in my own office, privy to everything." Calvin Tyler paced back and forth across the living room while Chad and Wiz relaxed in comfortable chairs. "How could one group of extremists develop so many powerful friends and key positions?" He shook his head in disbelief. "And I thought we had the best of the best working for us."

"Hey Chief, you can't outbid these guys. If they want to buy someone they can do it. You don't have the budget. They seem to have an uncanny knack for identifying the weakest link." Wiz sipped his cold beer. "Bet you'll find Martinez had a real need for money once you do the background checks."

"Or the bitch was just plain greedy," Chad spat, his lips curling in disgust. Even now, Chad could barely restrain his anger at the traitor they'd uncovered. He'd steeled himself to be calm and professional during the takedown and throughout the initial interrogation. Now that she was out of his hands, he allowed his feelings to bubble over and together he and Tyler let their rage pour out.

Wiz let them vent for a few more minutes then brought them back to earth with one quick question. "What next?"

Tyler sunk onto the long leather couch exhausted by his long day, the tiring flight from Washington and the visceral emotions of meeting his betrayer. He slowed his breathing and accepted a drink from Wiz.

"So where's Stone? And how did you wind up here? And what happened in Canada?" The questions tumbled out one on top of the other and it was clear to Chad that none of them was going to get much sleep until they'd done a full and proper briefing.

Halfway through, one of the SID agents stepped into the house to report the perimeter was quiet and that Martinez herself had been helicoptered to Holloman Air Base outside Alamogordo where she'd been quickly transferred to a waiting private jet and whisked to a supposedly derelict airfield in North Dakota. "We've got a place up there where we can question her," Tyler explained. "As far as anyone is concerned, all we know is that she's in Europe somewhere on vacation, if anyone asks."

He dismissed the agent with orders to step up observation on the house in Truth or Consequences.

He turned to the others. "Everyone on duty at The Spa will be rotated out and a new, screened team will take over. And every one of them will be vetted again to see if there are any more traitors. Chad, you and I are going to pay a special visit to our friend Liam Murphy tomorrow. Wiz, you'll be our driver but I want you to wander around the facility and double check security, personnel, facilities, resources, everything. We'll take an IT guy with us. He can do a scan of all the computer equipment and communications devices in there. If it looks suspicious, seize it." Now that his wrath had dropped down a degree or two, he was back to being all business-like.

Wiz cleared his throat. "Uh, Chief, you seem to forget something. I'm retired and happily living on a ranch in New Mexico. Remember?"

"You're back on duty now, Agent Zarelli, as of three days ago. At your old pay grade. All your expenses up to now will be covered. Including housing and feeding this sad specimen," he said, pointing at Chad. "When all this is over, we'll consider your resignation again."

"Well since you put it that way, Chief. Say, would the expenses run to an upgrade on my Cessna?" Tyler merely glared in response. Wiz shrugged and muttered "can't blame a guy for trying."

Tyler began pacing again. "No more screwing around and being nice guys with either Murphy or the current Spa team. Each one of them will be isolated and scrutinized to the nth degree. I want to know what time they pee, how many warts they have on their asses and who and what contacts they have outside the facility. Nothing is to be glossed over. And none of them will be allowed to return to duty until they've been cleared, re-cleared and cleared again.

"And the two other 'guests' at The Spa will be removed. From now on, Murphy must be in isolation."

### Crown Security Offices, London

"What joy?" Sir Giles looked expectantly at the young woman who entered his office. Her golden brown finely coiffed hair complemented her deep blue skirt and white blouse. "I see you're an Oxford grad, Susan."

The woman snapped her head up, startled at Sir Giles' pronouncement. "How did you know?"

"Skirt. Oxford Blue. Correct."

"Why yes."

"What College? Let me guess. Either Trinity or Jesus."

"Jesus College, Sir Giles. That's pretty amazing, how you did that from one blue skirt."

He nodded his head modestly. "Yes, amazing." He paused dramatically. "Particularly after you've also read an individual's resume."

She had the grace to blush while he laughed quietly at her embarrassment.

"Sorry, m'dear. Couldn't resist. Now, seriously, what joy?"

She smiled faintly then turned all business. "We have examined the tape from a number of angles. Plus, we were able to engage a lip reader. We got a rough read although he claimed it was very difficult due to the graininess of the video plus the smoke and dust that permeated the scene. Once he gave us the words, we discreetly asked the investigating officers to question survivors. Some of them agreed they heard one gunman shouting but couldn't agree what he said. One survivor said it was most definitely not English."

"Mm. What did our expert say?"

"He agreed it was not English. So he did it phonetically. As you know, Sir Giles, Jesus College is known as 'The Welsh College' at Oxford, largely because of the high concentration of Welsh students and the Celtic studies department. I took the liberty of taking the phonetic script he gave us and putting it together."

She slipped a piece of paper onto his desk. He took the paper but kept his eyes on her. Then closed them tightly as he said "tell me what it says."

"As near as I can get, the gunman was saying *ta muid anseo*. Or, The Master has spoken"

Sir Giles sighed. "Thank you." He opened his eyes and added, "Get hold of Freddy."

She nodded and disappeared into the outer office, closing the door behind her.

In his massive desk chair, Sir Giles rested his elbows on the desk, templed his fingers over his brow and with eyes closed, muttered. "Knew it. Damned Druids!"

# Chapter Fourteen

### Greyfell Abbey, Lake District

When Freddy escorted Mandy into the main sitting room there were happy exclamations from both Stone and Colin while Huw rushed over and embraced her. Mandy's infectious grin added a sparkle of light and happiness to what had been a somber mood.

Huw wrapped his arm lovingly around her shoulder and introduced her to Lord Greyfell and Nees. "My brilliant daughter and historian Myfanwy." As they shook hands Mandy laughed and invited them to "call me Mandy. Everyone does. Personally, I am not enamored of the name Myfanwy," she joked, smiling fondly at her father as she said it, "but I get its Welsh significance and I am Welsh after all."

Nees beamed back at her. "My dear, Myfanwy is nothing compared to mine. It's…"

"Not now Nees dear," Greyfell interrupted and smiled at both "We haven't enough time left in the day!" While the rest of the group laughed, Nees leaned over and whispered to Mandy that she'd explain later.

Stone moved towards Mandy but before he could move more than three steps she rushed over to him and embraced him. Tears flooded her eyes as she murmured "I am so glad you are here and safe, Stone. Thank God he has kept you in his care." She hugged him tight, glad to see him and trying to convince herself that she loved him in spite of their two continent lives. Stone held her tight, then both abruptly noticed the silence in the room and felt everyone's eyes upon them.

Huw coughed and then addressed the group in a general way. "Well somebody—I presume the Crown Security Bureau—has brought us all together for a reason. So let's get right down to it." The scholar in him could not resist the opportunity to lead. "Why don't you tell us what you've got gentlemen, and then I'll share my news. Lord Greyfell, perhaps you and Nees could listen in and help us fit things together with everything you know about the Druids."

Mandy broke away from Stone and awkwardly stepped away from him and across the room, her mind even more confused about her feelings. Puzzled, Stone watched her but finally turned away as Colin began speaking.

As quickly as they could the two British agents brought the team up to date. With the mention of Callaghan's name, Greyfell and Nees exchanged glances and nodded. Freddy caused the most shock as he outlined the past Sunday's attacks on churches across Britain. At the mention of the Winchester attack leader's final words a rumble of anger and disgust swept the room. When Freddy and Colin finished, a hush fell over the assemblage.

Finally Huw stood, his arm still comfortably around Mandy's shoulders. "Now that you're here *cariad*, I can share the news about Istanbul.

"Given what we've just been told, I think this will also be of interest to all of you," he said, "and will explain why I need to pursue further investigation in Austria."

Huw moved to the centre of the room facing the group. Stone was amused to see Huw transform from friend and doting father to the lecturing professor, hands on hips and reading glasses sliding slowly down his nose then unconsciously poked to the top again only to begin the process all over. Huw paced before them, telling his story and asking probing questions as he proceeded.

"As Colin has informed us, the men who were following me and watching me were in fact Druids. Now why would they be interested in my Turkish dig, I asked myself. Certainly if it was just revenge, they would have attacked in some way or form. No, as soon as they realized I really was on an archaeological dig and that it was not a cover of some kind, they disappeared."

"Sorry Huw, but you're wrong," Freddy interrupted. "They kept following you right up to the moment you stepped on the plane to return home."

Huw was stunned. "Are you sure?" He dropped into the deep accent of the valleys and pronounced it 'ar 'ew shuah' before he added the equally colloquial Welsh expression of surprise. "Duw, Duw."

"Once we identified them Sir Giles pulled in a favor and asked the Turkish police to follow your followers. I just got a text," he held up his cellphone, "and the Turks confirmed that three men followed you to Ataturk

Airport and waited until you got on the flight before leaving. They're still trying to find them in Istanbul to see if they caught a later flight back home."

Flustered, Huw murmured "Duw, Duw. So it was me they were after." He shot a glance at Freddy, "Why did they not try to kill me then?"

"Don't know. But we do know now that the night you left, the museum was robbed and the security guard was killed." He paused a moment. "They took the bronze box you found as well as the transcript."

Huw flopped into a chair, his head in his hands. Nobody moved or spoke as they watched him grapple with the latest news. Mandy crossed over to him and gave him a hug which Huw shrugged off.

"Thank you *cariad*, I'm OK. It just means that it is even more vital that we go to Austria." He dug into his leather satchel and pulled out papers, distributing them to the assembled group.

"This is my translation. Read it and you will see why the Druids are so interested in this and why they will stop at nothing to get their hands on this icon." He stopped and let them read.

As they each finished, Huw fixed them with his stare and continued. "I believe that the scroll must have made it to Manfred's brother. I have done a lot of online research the last few days and have possibly identified Baldric's castle near Salzburg. Nothing is heard of this scroll since it left Constantinople. It's possible of course that it never arrived in Finsternisdorf. If it did, either it has been destroyed—and with the war that is a distinct possibility—or it is still somewhere around the ruins of the Schloss. If it had been found it would have been mentioned somewhere in documents but, as I said, we have nothing. The scroll contains the secret of the hiding place of the real spear that sliced into Jesus' side on the cross. I believe that the scroll and the lance are real and the lance...if it is real, must still be waiting to be found somewhere in the Holy Land."

His declaration sparked a vigorous debate in the room. Mandy broke in at several points, questioning his reasoning and arguing the veracity of Manfred's confession.

"Da, you rushed this whole translation from your own knowledge of Latin and Greek. Before you can draw any valid conclusions, it has to be thoroughly and carefully examined and translated." She blushed, realizing that she had inadvertently called her own father's scholarly credibility into question. "Of course, you've seen the source material and we haven't," she added lamely to soften the criticism.

"Hold on Huw," Stone protested. "There are all kinds of holy lances, spears of destiny and what have you. I've seen one in the Hofburg Palace Museum in Vienna myself and there's another one supposedly at the Vatican though they keep it out of the public eye. Both claim to be the genuine spear that pierced Jesus's side. The choices are simple: one of them is real, which means it's already been found; or the lance really is something out of Christian fervor and legend and nothing more."

"Possibly, my boy, possibly. Or, both of them are fakes and the real thing is still in existence out there? Suppose it is still hidden right where our centurion friend Maximus Lucinius Janus put it?" The professor surfaced in him once again and he began pacing the room, enthralling his listeners with his logical approach to the problem.

"If either of the Vatican or Hofburg Palace lances are in fact the real thing, then this scroll is ridiculous. If the lance gives unearthly power to its holder, then it certainly has not worked so far has it, no matter which you prefer to believe is real?" He was warming up to his subject now, bursting with the information he'd researched the final few days in Istanbul. Thank God, he ruefully admitted, for the internet and its abundance of information. All you had to do was sift through the rubbish to find the truth.

"We know that Hitler and the Nazis were convinced of the power of what they called *Die Heilige Lanze*, or Holy Lance. Hitler was obsessed with it as was Heinrich Himmler. Both, but especially Himmler, were deep into the occult. Huge resources both before and during the war were diverted and millions of Deutsch Marks were poured into the search for it and similar icons."

Mandy, still working Huw's latest pronouncements through her tidy academic mind, blurted out. "Church legend says that the Centurion who was in charge of the crucifixion was a man named Longinus who later was converted, martyred and became a saint.'

"Ah, *cariad*. And is it not possible that 'Longinus' is merely a corruption of the name Lucinius; a much more common Roman name than Longinus."

She nodded, "Maybe. But it's all speculation so far."

Delighted with her contribution Huw beamed, "of course it is. Everything is speculation. That's why we need to do research. Austria's where we follow up on one trail while I need you back at your uni doing the hard basic research you're so good at.'

"All of this, I agree, is based upon the accuracy of the original document. Was there a scroll? Did Manfred buy it and then send it on to his brother? That, *cariad*, is one of the things I need you to investigate. I have done meagre research so far that shows there was a Baldric at Finsternisdorf in the appropriate time period. I need you to dig and confirm that information."

He turned to his rapt audience once again.

"Hitler believed the holder of the lance would have total authority and dominance over the world. The whole Aryan master race concept revolved around the history of the lance as much as anything. In the Holy Roman Empire Charlemagne owned it as did Emperor Otto I—and both were supreme and powerful rulers. Therefore Hitler wanted the lance and Himmler was determined to get it for him. Did he get it? Rumors abound that the Hofburg Lance is a counterfeit forged in the midst of the war by Himmler and his SS. If so, where is the real Lance—if Hitler ever had it?"

Stone shifted uncomfortably in his seat. "There are stories that the Lance and other valuable treasures and icons stolen by the Nazis were smuggled out of Germany in U Boats during the last days of the war. Depending upon who you talk to they are either at the bottom of the ocean—one such U Boat is supposedly off the Florida coast and another off North Carolina. Still others suggest that the U Boats made it to places like South America and even Antarctica where the Nazis allegedly had a secret base under the ice."

He looked around and shrugged as the others stared at him. "I did a series of stories about the Nazi looting of art and historic items a few years ago."

Huw nodded his head like a professor proud of a particularly good student. He swept his eyes across every person sitting in the room, jabbing his fingers to make his points.

"Ladies and Gentlemen, if the lance still exists at all, the Druids want it just as desperately as Hitler did and they are willing to kill for it. For them, it will bring back the power of the underworld and their pagan gods. They won't need to assassinate the Queen or our political leaders. The lance will give them all the murderous power they want or need. And it will be worldwide power, not just in Europe or America."

Silence enveloped the room. Each looked at the other, grappling with the information they'd just been given and baffled about their possible response.

"No, we will not fight these Druids here in Britain, or in America. In fact, I fear that the battle will not be fought in this world at all. Rather it will be fought in the realm of the spiritual and the demonic." He stopped dramatically to let his words sink in.

"That's why I must go to Austria, Mandy. To examine the source documents. It must be done carefully and completely. But our battle starts in Austria. We must get to the scroll, if it exists, before our enemies do. Our survival is at stake."

Lord Greyfell stood up and stretched. "I think we all need a bit of a break. Certainly I do. What say we lighten the mood somewhat and have some refreshments while we each consider what we've just heard and read. I have some thoughts already, but I need to think them through even more clearly before I speak." He signaled to Nees who stepped out to oversee her husband's suggestion. As she did, a general hubbub of noise swept over the room as if the dam of silence was broken.

"Walk with me." Colin spoke quietly to Stone and led him outside. The skies were leaden, the rain had settled into a fine drizzle, and the chill wind was cutting, but Colin strode unrelentingly through it all, straight up the vast green lawn behind the house, climbing steadily into a wall of trees. Stone struggled to keep up as he closed his jacket and pulled the hood over his head. Not a word passed between them until they were deep into the woods.

Finally Colin stopped and leaned against the trunk of a fallen tree. Apart from the steady dripping of rainwater on the leaves and the whistle of the cold wind, the woods were silent.

"We need to stop Huw from following this insane quest of his," Colin said bluntly, fixing Stone with a grim look. "These Druids have intensified their murderous actions. We need to protect both Huw and Mandy and the best place is here at Greyfell. I can't go to Austria and I'm not sure the guvnor has the resources or manpower to provide an escort for him."

"Is here any safer than that place in Canada?" Stone couldn't resist. Colin glared as Stone waved an apologetic hand. "My point is, neither you nor Chad Lawson's outfit can guarantee anyone's safety. Look what I went through at their headquarters, not to mention Georgian Bay. Perhaps if Huw was digging around in Austria he might actually be safer than here in the UK."

"Help would be closer at hand here."

"Maybe. But there are no guarantees anywhere. Look, Huw is a very strong, very determined man. Once he gets his teeth into something he will see it through to the end." Stone shook his head. "I really don't know how to dissuade him from going to Austria even if I wanted to. And I'm not sure I want to."

They argued back and forth for several minutes, neither convincing the other totally, yet each acknowledged strength in the other's point of view. Finally Colin stood up, brushed bits of leaves and dirt off his trousers and sighed. "Leave it with me for a bit. Let me think."

The pair headed back down towards the house squelching through the trimmed wet grass.

As they neared the flagstone patio, Colin snapped his fingers. "Stone," he said quietly, "why don't you go with Huw and help him. If you're convinced it's just as safe there as here, maybe it would be safer for you and Mandy as well."

Stone didn't answer as they stepped through the French doors and into the sitting room.

### Anglesey, North Wales

Callaghan smiled as he put down his mobile phone. The news was very good, he thought as a satisfied smile creased across his face. There had been so little to smile about these last weeks; he knew that Declan was unhappy and yet he could not convince his twin that the path he'd chosen was the right one that would bring the Druids back to power once again.

But now, within days, he would hold in his hands the bronze box that damnable professor had found. Paradoxically, he considered, that damnable professor had now enabled him to find the spear and unlock the powers of the underworld.

He stepped out of the house and walked down the lane towards the castle. There were very few hills in Anglesey, unlike the mountainous rest of North Wales, but already as the lane twisted north, he could see the hill and the ruins of Castell y Draig. Resolutely, he crossed over the road and climbed the fence, walking steadily towards the ruins. He stayed away from contact with the farmer and he had no fear of the dogs, viscous though they were. They cowed before him anytime he came near, aware deep in their animal brains that there was a power within him.

He didn't fully realize what or how much power he'd obtained; he only knew it grew stronger as he got closer to the castle. He also knew that the old man would be there. Callaghan never contacted him. He had no way of doing so—no phone number, no address, no information at all. Yet Callaghan knew that the old man would meet him.

Each time he entered the ruins Callaghan cast his eyes about, looking for a secret entrance to a cave or something beneath the ruins. He convinced himself that the old man lived somewhere in the castle vicinity, probably the old dungeons, and that the old man saw him coming each time. And each time, as Callaghan wondered about the old man, an icy cold shiver swept through his body no matter how warm the day. It started in his extremities then flowed into his core. One time he even felt himself leave his body and stare down at himself. Another time he felt himself travel inside his body and watch his heart beat slower and slower until it almost stopped. Each experience left him shaking and sweating yet at the same time exhilarated at these new powers taking hold of him.

He sat on the Dragon Master's stone and waited. Above him the ravens, as always, swooped and cawed letting the world know of an intrusion on their solitude.

"You have news". The closeness and coldness of the voice startled him momentarily. He spun around and faced the old man. His usual garb of black slacks and shirt and jacket was now covered by a long black overcoat despite the warm sunshine. One of the jet black ravens circled over the old man's head then landed gently on his shoulder, never moving his body but with his eyes fixed firmly, unblinkingly on Callaghan. Despite himself, Callaghan shivered under the bird's gaze that seemed to reach deep inside him. It's just a dumb bird he mentally scolded himself, then raised his eyes to meet the old man's scrutiny.

"Yes. We have our hands on the original manuscript. I suspect the professor will begin a search for the scroll as will we. But I have him and his daughter under tight surveillance. I anticipate that either we will find it first or he will lead us to it and from it to the lance. Either way it will mean our success and their deaths."

"Good. We have been searching for the lance for a long time." The two spoke quietly for a time, with Callaghan mostly listening.

In the raucous noise of the ravens, neither heard a slight buzz high above them and didn't notice the flitting shadow.

# Chapter Fifteen

### The Spa, New Mexico

Chad looked around the sparsely furnished room. His boss stood beside him. A smallish window dominated a short wall leading to a corridor and the room's front entrance. Below the window was a small kitchenette-type table and two chairs. As he examined the window, Chad realized that it was sealed shut and probably had bombproof glass as well, he thought. Directly across was a brown tweed sofa and one matching tweed armchair. Above it was a non-descript reproduction print showing a ubiquitous Southwest scene of a sunset and desert mesas. A three shelf book case packed with books was the only indicator of personality in the room. Two more bland beige chairs flanked the bookcase with a small side table between them. Along the opposite wall two doorways opened up, one into a small bathroom and one into an equally small bedroom.

Liam Murphy walked out of the bedroom briefly acknowledging his two visitors before plunking himself down into the sofa. Although locked away at The Spa for more than six months, he retained his haughty patrician demeanor. At just over six feet tall he still looked like the presidential candidate who came within a whisker of winning the top job last November. Black well-trimmed eyebrows and a sharp hooked nose dominated his face partly hiding the setback dark brown eyes. But the staff at The Spa obviously kept his famous tossed and wavy jet black hair closely cropped. It was the one major difference between the current Murphy and the myriad of smiling campaign photographs the nation had become enamored of last year. His crisp blue golf shirt and beige slacks were set off incongruously by a pair of battered blue plastic sandals.

He signaled the two to sit and smiled coolly at them. "Well, I am honored. The great Calvin Tyler, my chief torturer himself." He locked eyes with

Tyler, each refusing to back down on the staring contest until Murphy finally asked "and who's your companion, Mr. Tyler. No, wait, don't tell me. I believe I have the inestimable honor of meeting the famed Chad Lawson himself."

"Obviously you are well informed Murphy," Tyler challenged, letting Murphy's smooth entrance get under his skin. The man's arrogance and condescension was trying to reverse their current position of prisoner and jailer and it rankled Tyler. "But let me tell you all this changes as of today. New staff all carefully scrutinized. No more perks," he waved towards the books, "and no more games."

Unruffled, Murphy yawned and glanced at his Rolex as if to put Tyler on notice that he had only a short time before Murphy would end the session. Even Chad was both annoyed and impressed by the performance.

Tyler huffed. "You and your crowd are a major threat to the safety of this nation. But, as our other enemies over the years have found out, we will not be beaten. You are our guest here for now because you're charged with subverting the course of democracy both by trying to steal the election and then plotting to put our nation under the domination of a foreign power. Well Murphy, your Druids failed in Britain and France. Their nations were not overthrown. We discovered theirs and your criminal plots. You failed, Murphy. Completely, spectacularly and miserably." In spite of himself, Tyler could not help sounding pompous.

Murphy glared daggers at Tyler as he continued. "Enough of your followers have come forward and confessed. But then, you know all this, don't you. You know that we have congressmen and key bureaucrats at the federal and even some state levels who've confessed and are even now serving time."

The malevolent stare continued but still Murphy said nothing. "Your moneyman Damien Wyndham is dead. Your Dragon Master, Rhiannon, is dead. Your French storm trooper Tonnerre is dead. There's nobody left Murphy. Nobody at all. There's nothing left for you."

Tyler reached his hand out to Chad who gave him a thin file folder. "All you have to do is sign this document, Murphy." He extended the file to Murphy who ignored it. "Sign it and you can leave here," Tyler added, though he carefully kept a future destination out of the conversation.

A hard thin smile creased across Murphy's face. "And I am supposed to fold in the face of your bluster, am I? I'm to flit away like some scolded child to contemplate my sins?" He leaned forward and began jabbing his finger at both agents.

"You have no evidence against me. If you did, I would already be under indictment and we'd be heading to some sort of trial. That is if you really believe in the rule of laws. No Tyler, you've shelved me for a while, but I will be free before long…and without signing your confession or whatever it is you have. Very powerful friends are already working to expose my illegal and unwarranted seizure and incarceration without right of legal counsel or defense."

He sat back. "No, Tyler, it is you who have acted against the Constitution. It is you and your kind who have undermined the process of democracy. You are the one who perverted the course of the last election and prevented my election as President." He smiled smugly. "Give it a few more weeks or months and our roles will be reversed. You will be sitting in this godforsaken hell hole and I will be in charge." He paused a moment. "I wonder how considerate a jailer I will be?"

"You disgust me Murphy." Tyler snarled at the unruffled Murphy. "You think it nothing to kill and destroy just so you can get power."

Angrily, Murphy leaped up. "Wrong, Tyler. It is not about power, it is about correcting a floundering, failing situation. Our current system with its basically paralyzed government is the problem. There's a void of leadership. The volume of rhetoric in Congress is matched only by its unbelievable failure to do anything, pass any legislation, or in any way provide leadership. And why?"

He stood face to face with Tyler. "Because this nation has been suckered into believing that it is a Christian nation where faith is the core. But faith in what, Tyler? Praying to the Christian God or to his symbol, the Nazarene?" He sneered in Tyler's face. "Of all the useless exercises! Prayer to your God is pointless, needless, useless, arrogant, lazy and above all narcissistic.

"All you have to do in this country, whether you're an athlete, celebrity or politician is throw out the word Jesus and the people are like sheep, blithely accepting whatever trash surrounds it without any critical analysis or any real concept of what their own religion teaches. So you have so-called Christian leaders committing all kinds of crimes—including murder, theft and corruption—in the name of their faith. And you condemn the Druids? Look to your own house gentlemen. Your religious ghetto is the blind leading the blind. The Druids will clean house, eliminate the poison. If there are some unfortunate deaths, well, so be it. They are what your beloved military leaders would call collateral damage."

The two glared at each other for a minute, neither willing to back down. Finally, Tyler snapped icily, "I don't need to get into a religious debate with a traitor." He spun on his heels and waved Chad out. "Let's leave this turd to wallow in his own filth."

At the door he turned. "By the way Murphy. Your nest of vipers in my office has been cleaned out. Ms. Martinez is no longer your pipeline to information. And, as you can see, Mr. Lawson survived your assassination attempts. As did our good friend Mr. Wallace who, even now is alive and well and working towards your destruction."

After they left Murphy stood for a while then slammed his fist into the wall. Why oh why did the gods not answer his hourly pleas for release and revenge? Why did they dither? For all his bluster with the two intelligence agents he knew how close his organization was to collapse in the United States. Obviously the situation was just as dire in the true Celtic lands in Europe as well. He closed his eyes and raised his head and arms to the sky, calling on Arawn, god of death and revenge, to satisfy his lust for Tyler's demise.

### Istanbul, Turkey

Kizil threw the report across his desk in disgust and lit another of his incessant cigarettes. Drumming the fingers of one hand on the desk, he grabbed the phone with the other and barked a command to the unlucky receptionist who answered. Five minutes later there was a knock on his office door and a slim sweater-and-blue-jeaned man slipped in and stood to attention in front of the desk.

"You lost them? You followed them from the airport and then what? Just lost them?" Kizil oozed sarcasm as he scowled at the man in front of him.

"I followed the first man from Ataturk all the way to Sultanahmet. Fortunately he took the Metro to Zeytinburnu and changed to the tram. He got off at Sultanahmet then walked up Divanyolu. I trailed him pretty carefully at a distance until we got to Beyazit and I realized that he was heading into the Grand Bazaar. I closed up with him but lost him as a huge crowd of tourists got between us. I tried to force my way through them, but by the time I did he was gone. The others also followed their targets and, as I said in my report, they followed different routes to Sultanahmet, but they too disappeared in the Bazaar."

"Idiot! You had no backup? Even the most elementary course in trailing a suspect would insist on having additional manpower on hand for just such a situation as this." Kizil cursed and sucked his cigarette and sucked again, smoke pouring out his nostrils and mouth.

"I thought we were just tracking them to see where they went after they left the British man. We had no information that they were wanted for anything. If we had…." He was interrupted as the detective slammed his fist on the desk. Papers and pencils flew off onto the floor as the empty chai glass and spoon rattled on the glass saucer. Kizil launched into an extended tirade against the quaking policeman, pulling in his vast array of Turkish, Kurdish, Russian and Greek curses and questioning his subordinate's intelligence, breeding and parenthood.

Finally, he pointed at the door, shooing his subordinate out. "Get out. And when you're out of this office you'd better contact those other two imbeciles you were with and pray to Allah the merciful that you find your targets. Check every hotel, every taxi, every tourist spot, every shuttle van and anyone else your lame little brains can dig up. Find them. There can't be too many red headed and bearded tourists around who don't speak Turkish. Concentrate on the old city. I doubt they even crossed the Horn and went over to the new city or Taksim Square, let alone go to the Asian side. Find them dammit. I have a strong suspicion that they're involved in the theft and murder at the museum. It's been four days and this is the only potential lead we had and you let it slip away. You lost them four days ago and I only find out about it now, in this worthless report. Idiots! I am surrounded by idiots!"

As the object of his wrath disappeared hastily through the door, Kizil stubbed out his smoke and lit another. This is going to be a long day, he thought, picking up the reports and murder file again.

### Greyfell Abbey

"*Cariad*, you seem troubled. Are you really that set against my going to Austria?" Huw Griffiths held a comforting arm around Mandy's shoulders. They stood on the stone patio overlooking Buttermere Water. Fresh breezes wafted through the air but the leaden clouds were already drowning out the sun and the twilight was rapidly disappearing into blackness.

"Da, it's not just that"

"What is it then? Trouble at the Uni?"

"You could say that." She sighed. "It's my assistant—the one Dr. Cranshaw suggested I hire." She turned to face her father and looked into his caring eyes. "I wasn't going to take him on, but Nigel and I seemed so compatible in terms of our approach to history, research and everything. Our philosophy matched and, well," she hesitated, "it's become somewhat more than that lately. I have grown very fond of him and, well…"

"What about Bradstone?" Huw's voice was gentle in the rustling breezes.

"That's just it, Da. When I saw Stone today I was just overwhelmed. Partly because I was so relieved to see him safe and well but also because I realized how very much I am taken with him, perhaps even love him. But then I think about Nigel and how much I appreciate him. I'm very fond of him too." She began to weep softly, "Oh Da, it's just such a mess in my mind." She sniffed, "and then I think about those horrid Druids killing so many people and trying to kill you and Stone."

Silent, she reached into her purse and pulled out some papers. "Here's his resume, Da. And his photo. Read it and you'll see why he and I connect so completely.

Huw scanned the papers then held her tight and let her cry, realizing she had to break the dam of emotions pent up inside. But he also realized how totally unprepared he was to deal with issues of the heart. His own happy marriage had ended fifteen years ago when a drunk driver claimed his beloved Mari's life. Since then he'd thrown himself into his work while still trying to raise a daughter—not the easiest task either he confessed to himself. His own life situation made it easier for him to understand and care about the terrible isolation Bradstone had built into his life. His fondness for the journalist and his appreciation for Bradstone's efforts to save his life last fall may be coloring his reaction to Mandy's state, he suddenly realized. Ah for the simplicity of dealing with an ancient manuscript he thought.

"This may sound trite and I don't mean it to be," he said as Mandy began to wipe her eyes with a tissue, "but have you prayed about it?"

"Oh Da. People are being killed for their faith and there is greed, corruption and death at all levels of society in all countries. God doesn't worry about minuscule things like this."

Huw paused. "That's your emotions talking, *cariad*. You know he does care, but sometimes we just have to trust and wait."

"Yes, Da, patience. Like you always exhibit patience," Mandy laughed in spite of herself. The deep relationship between the father and daughter was enough to bring a spark of agreement on the topic. She sighed again and hugged him back.

Huw hugged her again. "You know me too well, *cariad*. Tell you what. I believe God really does care and he will show you unmistakably what you are to do. I'll pray for you. Now, dry your eyes and let's get back inside. We still have those blasted Druids to deal with!"

Inside, warm cozy lights lit the sitting room and a warm fire crackled in the stone fireplace that dominated one side of the room. A servant was cleaning up the refreshments while Colin and Stone huddled in a corner near the fire deep in quiet conversation. As Nees sipped her tea, Lord Greyfell entered with some material from his next door library. "It's not much to go on, I know, but there are some old documents that tell an interesting though vague story," he said loudly enough to catch everyone's attention.

"All of you know that the 'history' of the Druids and the ancient Celts of Great Britain was largely an oral tradition. How accurate those oral histories are remains a matter of speculation. However, they are stories that seeped through the passage of time, larded no doubt with lots of imagination and hidden agendas. Beowulf is a good example of the oral tradition translated into written form. Anyway, I have this volume that has gathered dust for many years. It's a record of oral stories and traditions of the British Isles and written in the mid-1600s."

He laid the large leather bound book on the coffee table and, slipping on some white cloth gloves, opened it gently. His rapt audience gathered around, curious to see what he had.

"As I said, it's not much and it may not be applicable in this situation, but there is a recording here that in what were called 'ye olden days', some travelers 'from the 'wildes and mountains of Wales travelled to Rome and the many lands of our worlde'. You'll see here," he pointed with a gloved finger, "that they were seeking a shaft of great power."

He left the book open so that they could all study it. "As I said, it's not much and we are doing a huge leap of conjecture to link this with our lance. They might just indeed have been relic hunters. But it was the expression 'from the wildes and mountains of Wales' that intrigued me when I first read it some years ago. Who would be traveling from Wales overseas in that day? Monks or priests seeking holy icons for a church in Wales?"

Before he could go further, Huw interrupted. "Druids. If it was priests or monks there would be other records, written records in the church. You said this was a record of oral histories, did you not, Lord Greyfell? And who specialized in oral histories and traditions? You reached the same conclusion, correct?"

Chuckling, Greyfell nodded his head. "Right you are Huw. When I read it back then it sparked my curiosity. I purchased the book and a number of others from the estate of a deceased lawyer back in 2005. I bought them because the man was a life-long druid. I doubt his fellow Druids really understood the mine of information he had in his library. If they had, I wouldn't have stood a ghost's chance of getting it. As it is, I have some very interesting and informative materials in my library."

A buzz of comments flew back and forth, particularly from Huw and Mandy.

"As I said, it's not a lot to go on and I am making a great leap. But it was listening to your story and reading your translations that clicked in my mind, and I remembered this book. I'm not a true scholar like you, Huw, but I think there's enough meat on this sparse bone that we cannot ignore it."

Beaming with excitement, Huw rubbed his hands together. "If this holds together, then it suggests a great and long lasting interest on the part of the Druids, does it not?" he appealed to the group. "It should underline the need to go to Austria and track the scroll down, to at least see if it exists."

While the buzz died down and each began to think through the consequences of the information they'd just received, Freddy stood up.

"Much as I would love to stay and wrestle this decision through with you, and I really am intrigued by all this, I have to return to London. For one thing I have other work to do and for another, the guvnor needs to be brought up to speed. Colin, you change your plans and stay here with Lord Greyfell and dig into this a bit more. Make this your head office for a while.' He turned to Huw and Mandy. "Whatever you decide to do, keep Colin here fully informed, will you?" As he left the room he shook hands with them all, leaving Stone to the last. As he shook Stone's hand he leaned forward and whispered quietly, "Mr. Wallace, I understand Colin has made some suggestions to you. Just to let you know, I concur." With that, he grabbed his coat and scarf and left the room.

Stone caught Colin's eye and murmured "you really do know how to put the cat among the pigeons, don't you?"

# Chapter Sixteen

### Bavaria

For the first time in it seemed months, Stone was relaxed and mellowed out. He adjusted the earpiece on his newly purchased iPod and let the smooth tones of Beethoven's stirring seventh symphony wash over him. Across the narrow aisle Huw was, as usual, nose buried in a couple of books and several piles of papers all laid out on the seat directly across from him.

Once they'd decided to go to Austria, Mandy took a lot of persuading to not join them but instead return to her university and work on the project. Finally, she agreed and left Greyfell Abbey earlier in the morning anxious and eager, now that she had been convinced, to get started.

Stone and Huw meanwhile agreed to Colin's plan to get them to Austria. A quick drive through the Lake District soon brought them to Carlisle where they worked their way around the north end of the city and onto the A689 to Carlisle airport. Colin drove past the retired RAF Vulcan bomber on display, straight up to the self-contained stairs leading into a Learjet 45 business jet.

"We've arranged for this rather than commercial to get you to Austria We're taking no chances, so you'll be landing at a small government field in Bavaria, just north of the Austrian border. A field agent will meet you there and take you the rest of the way."

As Stone settled into his grey leather seat he admired the polished rosewood paneling and took full advantage of the meal and drinks the steward placed in front of him shortly after takeoff even though they'd had a quick light breakfast before leaving. Huw, as usual, could not be bothered to eat while he was buried in his studies.

Just over an hour later Stone looked out of the jet's window. They were passing swiftly to the south of Munich or, as the Germans preferred,

Munchen, and beginning a slow descent. As they came out of the puffy marshmallow clouds he could see the red tiled roofs that stretched wherever the eye could see. In the distance he could see Munich's skyline pockmarked by the spires of its many churches as well as a few skyscrapers and the famous Olympic Tower, symbol of the city's marred 1972 Olympic Games.

As the jet lost altitude Huw began gathering his pile and stuffing them into his satchel. Stone was part way through one of the Bach Brandenburg concertos as he looked out and saw the shimmering waters of Chiemsee, often known as the Bavarian Sea. The flight plan took them just south of the lake and he could see the green treed island of Herreninsel and King Ludwig II's unfinished replica of the Palace of Versailles. Ludwig's castle building mania in the late 1870's had bankrupted Bavaria and ended in the loss of his crown. But it also provided the German state with some of its finest tourist attractions including Schloss Herreninsel, the lofty grandeur of Neuschwanstein, Linderhoff and others.

The landing warning came almost immediately as the island swept by and the plane banked to the right, now descending sharply, dropping onto the Bavarian plains in the shadow of the mighty Alps. In minutes they were taxiing to a small building after landing on a small, obviously military, airfield. As they rolled to a stop Stone could see several helicopters and two small jets, all of them prominently identified as Luftwaffe with the iconic silver and black iron cross prominent on their fuselage.

As soon as the plane stopped, the crew opened the door and extended the self-contained stairs. A bored looking uniformed man beckoned to them and pointed towards a blue Mercedes Benz station wagon that was bustling around the corner of the building. They threw their bags into the trunk and hopped inside, startled to see the big beaming smile of a cheery looking woman behind the wheel.

"Hi. I'm Brenda McClelland, Sir Giles asked me to meet you and take care of you while you're here." Without waiting, she slipped the car into gear and they pulled past their jet which was already beginning its taxi to return home.

"We're just south of Traunstein near the town of Seigsdorf," their driver said merrily, "I've got you booked into a small Gasthof, or hotel, near Zell am See. I was told you want to explore around Finsternisdorf. Zell is the nearest town and would make a good jumping off spot."

Stone, sitting in the passenger seat, looked at her quizzically. "If you don't mind my saying so, you don't sound British but you say you work for Sir Giles."

"Oh sorry," she said, passing an ID wallet across to him. "I should have given this to you right away. Show my bona fides so to speak. And you're right. I'm not British even though I do work for Crown Security. I'm Canadian and very familiar with this part of central Europe. I did a lot of work here over the years. So whenever Sir Giles needs an unobtrusive non-Brit agent—I do look unobtrusive don't I?—they call upon me."

The trip through the Alps followed ancient passes that had been trading routes since ancient times. Huw sat engrossed in the passing scenery and eagerly anticipating the beginning of their hunt. "Definitely bigger than Snowdon" he muttered to himself as he compared Wales' highest mountain to the jagged snow-covered peaks that swallowed the road as it zigged and zagged its way through the narrow valleys. From the snow caps the mountains seemed cloaked in fine dark forest green blankets that dropped down from the white until, at the very bottom, they opened into the velvet emerald green dresses that were the lower meadows and pastures. Above them like dots of bright yellow-green against the green-blue of the forests, they could see high Alpine meadows glistening in the sun. They passed village after village and farm after farm, each looking like the other with their stereotypical wooden chalet houses with gingerbread paneling, steep roofs with boulders on them, and overflowing flowerboxes exploding in color.

As they drove, Stone gleaned more information about their driver and her eclectic career with the Canadian Security Service CSIS and, more lately, the Crown Security Bureau. "I just wanted a smaller, less bureaucratic and political outfit to work for," she confided. "I did some work for Sir Giles when the Queen was in Ontario and Quebec and the rest, as they say, is history."

She noted Stone's wary look the moment she mentioned CSIS. "Don't let that chaotic disaster in Georgian Bay color your views about CSIS," she said quietly, "a few rotten apples betrayed a good service and a bunch of good people. We lost agents there too." Stone said nothing. "If Sir Giles didn't think I could do the job or was one of those treacherous Druids, I wouldn't be here, believe me. I'd be locked up in the Tower of London or some such place. As the saying goes, Sir Giles don't suffer no fools gladly." She smiled again, and then concentrated on the road ahead.

Outside Zell am See she turned off the main 311 highway and followed the signs to a place called Schmitten. As they left the built up area the road twisted and turned as it climbed up the steep mountain side. Finally she turned in at the Gasthof Kremml, stopped the car and nimbly jumped out directing them to the front door where a young blonde woman stood waiting. She was dressed in the Austrian dirndl with white blouse and black bodice and skirt. A small blond child—Stone could not tell if it was a boy or girl—huddled hidden behind her skirt, clutching a stuffed bear.

"Gruss Gott," Brenda smiled at the woman. She introduced her as the host and innkeeper as well as wife of the farmer who owned the little hotel. "She speaks a little English," Brenda told Stone as they entered and were shown to their rooms. "We're the only ones here. I've booked all five rooms, even though we only need three. Don't want any strangers around the hotel while we're here, do we?"

Stone admired her brusque no-nonsense style as she dealt with the woman. Huw stood uncharacteristically quiet as he contemplated the hotel and its surroundings.

"Tidy. Very tidy. Just what we needed. They'll never find us here," he smiled at Stone.

**Truth or Consequences, New Mexico**

"Get down!"

Chad and Tyler heard the shout from Wiz and reacted instinctively as they left the main complex at The Spa. As they splattered themselves against the dusty rock strewn dirt, bullets hammered into the walls and doors behind them.

Chad pulled his gun and rolled sideways. Tyler did not move. Wiz opened up with his own weapon, allowing Chad to sprint to the relative cover of their car. Other guns opened up, some towards the unseen shooter and others at the car and building. From his spot behind an adobe wall, Wiz yelled at Chad to "get Tyler" and then put up a fusillade of shots in the direction of their assailant.

Without wasting a second, Chad raced to the unconscious Tyler's side and saw he'd been wounded in the first barrage of shots. He grabbed Tyler under the right arm and dragged him unceremoniously across the rugged ground to the cover of the vehicle.

The blazing sun did not help Chad as he popped his head from behind the car to search for the shooter. The sun, lower on the afternoon horizon, blinded him.

"At your one o'clock behind the brush on those red rocks above the entrance gate" Wiz shouted, realizing instinctively what Chad's problem was." Chad ripped off more shots at the brush then ducked down to see to Tyler. Blood was seeping from Tyler's left shoulder. More blood was evident on his right pant leg. His quick examination did not uncover any major wounds that he could see. His cursory first aid training assured him that for now, Tyler was not critical. It freed him to concentrate on the shooter.

Two Spa guards suddenly burst through the facility's main door, racing for positions behind other adobe walls. Ensconced in relative safety they too opened up on the main shooter.

From his vantage point Chad realized their attacker's firing speed and accuracy was dropping although one or two shots came uncomfortably close. As one of the front tires suddenly exploded he prayed that none of the shots would hit the nearly full fuel tank.

Wiz was directing fire from his own position and shouting commands to the other guards who'd raced into the fight. From behind a boulder on a small hill overlooking the entrance road, a man suddenly stood up with a shoulder-mounted apparatus. There was as sudden whoosh just as the man spun and jumped in a death dance.

"RPG" yelled Wiz and dropped to the ground as the wall behind him suddenly disintegrated in an explosion. Dust and debris littered the area, but the guards and Chad kept firing. Apart from the crashing of wood and rubble as it fell back to earth, there was silence; no more shots from their assailant.

As the dust settled The Spa security team skillfully raced from cover to cover, approaching the rocky outcrop. Finally one reached the rock itself and stood straight, signaling to the others. A second guard reached the body of the man who fired the rocket grenade. Satisfied that the attack was over, Chad stood and called for medical aid for Tyler. Out of the corner of his eye, he saw a dust-covered Wiz emerge from behind a pile of rubble, brushing himself off and limping slightly.

"I heard one shot and saw one of our guys go down, then you came out the entrance so I yelled. How's Tyler?"

"A couple of wounds in the shoulder and leg but he must have hit his head on one of the rocks as he fell. He's out cold," Chad said as Tyler's body was hustled inside. In the distance he could already hear sirens of the approaching police and ambulances. He knew that the general alert had gone out and that backup troops from Holloman Air Force Base would be on the ground with them in minutes.

Wiz brushed off Chad's concerns about his own injuries with a brisk "took a hit from a hunk of wood on the back of my leg. Be fine in a minute or two once I work the kinks out." He nodded at the various Spa personnel heading towards Chad. "I guess you're in charge for the moment sunshine, well until Tyler recovers anyway."

In rapid succession Chad was assured that Tyler's wounds were not critical though he was still unconscious, that Murphy was secured in his room with guards already in place at the door and the outside window. "He was pretty shook up, even though he figured it was his people doing the shooting," the Superintendent of The Spa, a rugged ex-West Pointer and Ranger, reported. "There were two shooters. We're trying to ID them now. The bodies are over there" he said, pointing at one of the outbuildings. Chad accepted the statement and asked him to report to Chantilly.

Half an hour later he and Wiz sat at the administrator's desk. Chad was on a secure line briefing the second-in-command at the Virginia base. "Yeah, looks like Tyler'll be OK. We're going to medevac him from Hollman in an hour." Chad nodded a couple of times, made some notes then hung up.

"They've left me in charge down here, Wiz. So, since Tyler put you back on the payroll, you are now my 2IC. Let's see what we've got." Quickly they reviewed the known facts. Already, one of the shooters had been identified as the man who'd driven Martinez to the burger joint and been tranquilized by Wiz.

"She said he was her brother when we hustled her out of the place," Wiz said, "so it could just have been a revenge thing." He bent over and rubbed his sore leg again. "But who was the other one with the RPG? Stands to reason they were both connected to these Druids of yours and that they had help from the inside. This place was sealed up tighter than a drum and yet they were able to drift in, find potential firing spots all without detection or alarms going off."

Chad grunted, looking at the pile of papers on the desk. He rummaged through them and found what he wanted. "Here's a roster of who was on duty yesterday and today. Have them checked out thoroughly. One of more of them might be the insiders we're trying to get."

The throbbing rumble of approaching helicopters interrupted them. "The replacements Tyler ordered yesterday," Wiz commented, looking out the window as first one then a second chopper disgorged personnel. "We'll send Tyler back to Hollman on one of them."

As they considered the Spa roster, a slightly built man with balding hair, a bad comb over and large coke bottle glasses, stuck his head inside the open door. "I've got some stuff here that might interest you, Chad." He hesitated a moment, then walked forward and placed a laptop on the desk. "We found this buried under clothes and shoes in Murphy's room. He had another laptop that he used most of the time, but that was out in the open. This was secreted and I wondered why."

Chad knew that once Nelson McAdam, the SID's top IT wizard got going, nothing could stop him, so he settled down for a long involved explanation of whatever it was McAdam had unearthed. Ten minutes later he was rewarded. "So you see, all the heavy-duty encryption on this device is what delayed me. That and sorting out the encryption on Murphy's hidden iPhone."

Chad jerked at that. "He had a hidden phone?"

"Correctamundo. But I pulled all the numbers and decrypted the text messages as well and they corroborate some of the material we got off the laptop."

McAdam laid some papers, still warm from the printer, on the desk and waited smugly for Chad to read them.

"So Murphy has been in touch by phone and email with this Diarmuid Callaghan in Ireland. The two are working together."

"Correct again. And you will notice that this Callaghan is now what they call the Dragon Master."

"We've got to get this to the UK as soon as possible," Chad said, mostly to Wiz who'd been eagerly reading the material as well.

"Wait a second though, Chad. You haven't read the juicy stuff yet. They're planning some kind of major attack again. Look here," McAdam said, poking a paragraph on the third page.

"They did that already. Attacks on those churches all over Britain." Wiz growled.

"No. They were only the prelude. See here," McAdam began running his finger along some lines. "The opening salvo will be nothing compared to what we intend to do the Sunday after Alban Hefin. I looked that up. It's the summer solstice which is a big Druid holy day. I'm trying to see if there's anything else of interest in here."

Chad let out a long sustained whistle. "Best get that to Sir Giles as well." He let McAdam continue to work on the computer realizing the man was already engrossed again in his beloved tech toys and oblivious to the furor and discussion around him.

He slumped back into his chair, calling for the Superintendent to come to the office. Seconds later the man strode through the door and stood waiting for Chad's instructions even though it was his own office.

"Thanks for letting me use your desk and chair Colonel Bryson." Chad smiled at him and indicated to him to sit in the chair Wiz vacated. "It's been a tough day."

"Tough?" the man growled. "Disastrous as hell I would say. First I get told there's a leak in my team and they're all to be replaced. I didn't believe it. Then this attack. Had to be an inside job, so I checked our manpower. The guy firing the RPG was one of ours but he was supposed to be on leave. And our main guy at the entrance gate is missing." He shook his head in disgust, barely able to keep his voice in check overwhelmed as he was by the treasonous acts of his own people plus the shock of the attack and its aftermath. "The Chief will have my resignation immediately."

"You'll have to report that to the Chief himself, but he's en route to Virginia. As it is, we have new people on site to help re-establish and secure this place. So right now, we need you to stick in place and help clean out the snakes. Wiz here will stay and help you. You need to get the new people in place. We'll be out of your office in a minute."

That said, the Colonel stood, looked as if he wanted to salute, then just nodded and spun on his heels walking briskly but still ramrod straight out of the office.

"I think he's a good guy," Wiz looked at Chad. "He's been shaken by this stuff but it will make him tougher than ever, which is just what we need. I'll stick around too. Maybe check into a hotel around town for a week or so. What are your plans now?"

"Depends on Tyler. How he is and what he wants. I'll stick around here till that's decided, but in the meantime I need a secure line to call Britain."

A cough brought them back into the reality of the room and they realized McAdam was still in place, still peering at his papers and playing with the laptop. "If you don't mind, I'd like see if there are any other encrypted devices Murphy or others may have hidden." He continued pounding at the keys, shaking his head and pounding new keys. He paused a moment and looked up at Chad, a quizzical look on his face.

"Say, a little while ago I heard some banging crashing and then one almighty bang. What was all that about. And where's the Chief?"

# Chapter Seventeen

## Hereford

The first thing Mandy did on her return to the University was raid the library for documents, books and other materials related to both medieval relic hunting and the Holy Lance. With them in hand she cleared the desk in her office of other materials and asked the custodian to bring in an extra table that she squeezed between the file cabinet and the door. Her second act was to call Dr. Cranshaw and request time off from some of her tutorial duties. She ran into a bit of an argument with him as he reminded her of Nigel's resignation, but his need for her presence on the faculty overcame his objections and he reluctantly agreed, particularly as it was near term end. Only then did she do the third thing on her list—call Nigel.

She'd thought about it all through the long car ride down from the Lake District. Although she would be circumspect about the whys and wherefores of the research, she felt that Nigel could indeed do some of the leg work for her, if he was willing. She was still unsure about her personal feelings towards him, but told herself if they were professional about it all, it just might work.

It was a difficult conversation at first. Nigel, satisfied that she was safe and back in her office, kept asking in various ways where she had been and who she'd been with. "Jealous?" she finally burst out. "You've no reason to be. We have no claims on each other and, actually, I spend most of my time with my father." Carefully wording her request so that she did not breach the security parameters Freddy insisted on, she let Nigel know that she needed his help on a private research project. He finally agreed to meet with her to discuss it, but insisted it be over a quiet dinner in Hereford, an idea she quickly settled on.

Two hours later, with the succulent and aromatic prime roast beef, roasted potatoes and vegetables washed down with a glass of Italian Prosecco wine, Mandy raised the project with Nigel. As they talked, the waiter cleared the table and lit the lone candle. The discussion continued through the desert and tea.

"And this search for Baldric in Germania. You want me to find out if he ever existed and as full a biography as possible. Why is he so important? How did you latch onto this person?"

"Let's just say he's a person of interest and part of a larger research project my father is involved in as a result of his Istanbul dig."

"He must have found something incredibly interesting there then. What was it?"

"It's not really important at this point, Nige, we just need to confirm who he was and as much as we can about his life. He is reported to have been a relic hunter or seller, particularly to the Holy Roman Empire and the churches of medieval Europe. He was also reported to have lived near Salzburg"

"You're not giving me a lot to go on, are you?"

"No, because I'm not really sure about all of it myself. I wonder sometimes if this man ever really was. It's daft, I know, but I want to help my father and it is very important to him so it's important to me. I just thought you might be willing to help me."

He said nothing, sipping his tea and holding the cup in both hands. She waited. Finally he put the cup down and leaned towards her, forearms resting on the deep maroon tablecloth. "For you!" He leaned back and smiled, his white teeth glinting in the flickering candle. "Where do you want me to begin?"

Relief swept through Mandy as she mentally reviewed the many steps she'd methodically thought out. "I've already cleared out the University's meagre selection of medieval material. I plan on heading down to Oxford in the next day or so to check out the Bodleian Library. The Ashmolean will be of no use. If you could go online and also check out the Austrian embassy in London to see if they have any archival material, that would help."

"All right. I could also contact the German Federal Archives in Koblenz and the Austrian archives in Vienna." Now that he'd committed himself, his enthusiasm began to take hold. "If necessary, I could even go to Vienna. I need a bit of a holiday anyway. Their archives have material going back to the

800's, so if this fella was around they'll probably have him." He leaned back and looked Mandy in the eye, his bright smile never leaving his face.

"Right then. That's sorted. Now let's talk about us!"

**Zell am See, Austria**

The drive through Zell am See to Finsternisdorf was a relaxed, enjoyable one. Rested after their night in the Gasthof, Stone and Huw spent breakfast making plans for the day. Huw, predictably, grumped about the typical Austrian breakfast of bread, rolls, muesli, cold meats and cheeses. "Why can't they eat decent breakfasts like we do," he complained in the car later. "Eggs, sausage, bacon, tomatoes, beans, mushrooms and maybe even some blood pudding or, better yet, some cockles and laverbread."

"Laverbread," Stone snorted. "That stuff is disgusting. Seaweed that looks like some black gelatinous grunge that was scraped off the rocks after an oil spill."

"You have no taste, Bradstone my boy. No taste at all. Laverbread, properly fried in bacon grease and served with cockles and toast is pure manna from heaven."

The argument continued unabated as Brenda sat quietly in the driver's seat letting them hash out their culinary preferences. She interrupted at one point to tell them they were entering the tunnel that the Austrians had bored through the mountain to take traffic around the town and cut out the worst of the in-town traffic chaos. "This way, we do eighty klicks all the way through, with no traffic lights, no delivery trucks obstructing the streets and no slow moving pedestrians."

On the south side of town she deftly spun onto the 311 highway and headed east. As they approached the town of Krossenbach she pointed up towards an old castle peeking out amongst the trees and sitting high above the town itself. "That's Schloss Fischhorn. It was a satellite concentration camp for Dachau and a place where the Nazis stored some of the art treasures and historic artifacts they looted. It's also where the Americans captured Herman Goering in 1945."

"Nazi treasures, you say," Huw leaned forward from the back seat.

"Yes. Apparently when the Americans entered they found it crammed with treasures plundered from Poland and The Netherlands. Crates of old masters, books from pillaged libraries, furniture and even, they say, Chopin's piano stolen from the National Museum in Warsaw."

"Maybe after we've looked around Finsternisdorf, we could take a look around there."

Brenda shook her head. "Sorry, professor. It's privately owned now and under reconstruction. Nobody is allowed in."

Past the town of Bruck und der Grossglocknerstrasse the highway ran parallel to the Salzach River and the main railway line between Zell am See and Salzburg. At the first bridge, they crossed over the Salzach and began a slow, steady climb up a switchback road until they were several hundred feet above the river. They pulled into a small parking area.

"Sorry gentlemen, but we walk from here." All three got out of the car, Huw had his ever present satchel while Stone took the digital SLR camera he'd bought in Carlisle in a hurried stop on the way to the airport. Brenda reached into the glove compartment and took out a hefty looking pistol. Noticing their glances she just shrugged. "Never hurts to be prepared."

A fresh breeze swept across the mountain as they gingerly followed a rocky path, working their way between the trees and occasionally getting a breathtaking view of the wider part of the valley with its meadows and farms. They could see well down the valley with the Salzach winding its way through every craggier and higher snow-capped peaks towards Salzburg. The sun, the warmth, the greenery that surrounded them, the birds chirping and singing, all made it seem more like a picnic hike in the late spring than a serious historical research effort. In the distance they could hear the rhythmic clanging of a myriad of different noted cow bells and the pungent smell of fertilized fields wafted even this far up the hillside. Below them they could hear the steady roar of traffic on the highway interspersed at times with the faint rustling waters of the river.

Finally, they broke through the woods into a large clearing dominated by the ruins of an old castle. "This gentlemen, is all that is left of the old Schloss Finsternis," Brenda announced.

One wall was little more than rubble. Stone could see where many of the castle's massive building stones had rumbled down the hillside, carving their way through the trees down towards the river in the many storms that often laced the Alps. They clambered over the remains of the wall and entered a quiet rock and rubble strewn area that must once have been the castle

*The Lucifer Scroll*

courtyard. Seen from the inside, the castle looked formidable but small as Austrian Schlosses went.

"So this is where our Baldric lived,"

"We're not even sure he even existed, Huw. Don't get ahead of yourself." The skeptical journalist in Stone raised its head yet again.

"Don't be daft, boyo. Of course he existed. Here in this castle. I can feel it in my bones. Manfred's letter is truth. I believe it. The scroll must have come here. But where did it go afterwards. Or is it still here?" Huw's uncharacteristic punchy sentences betrayed how excited he was.

"We have to think like medieval knights and barons, Bradstone. Where would you keep valued treasures and belongings if you lived in a sturdy castle like this?"

"Down in the dungeon area, I suppose. But too, he could have sold it on to someone else, some bishop or church perhaps."

"Possible, but we agreed did we not, that if he had sold it on somewhere, there would be a record of it. Such a scroll in possession of some bishop or cardinal would have been a key to a new crusade to the holy land and perhaps even the papacy for the man who found the real holy lance. It would have been something to shout from the rooftops. Instead there is nothing but silence from this point on. And I believe this silence is shouting at us that the scroll was here!"

"That's assuming it even reached Baldric in the first place, Huw. We have no information about the scroll from the moment it left Manfred's hands. Suppose it never even made it out of Constantinople, or was stolen by pirates on the way to Venice. Or perhaps some brigands stole it on the trip overland."

Huw sighed. "Are you always so negative, Bradstone, my boy? When did you become such a pessimist?"

"Realist, Huw. Realist."

Huw made a face and continued wandering around the courtyard. "The layout of many of these castles was similar." He pointed to the ruins of part of the living quarters, rising three floors above them. "I agree Baldric would have kept his treasures in the strongest, most secure part of his castle; perhaps the dungeons or perhaps just some cellars below the main housing section. You take this side, I'll take the other."

"And just what are we looking for?"

"A depression in the floor, the remains of steps going down, anything that might indicate a cellar or dungeon entrance."

Stone shook his head in disbelief. "You really don't think we're going to magically find some opening, trot on down the steps and there lo and behold behind a hidden door, we find the scroll?"

"Of course not, boyo. Don't be daft. And don't be obtuse. I just want to satisfy myself that there was such a potential hiding spot. After that…" his shrugged and his voice trailed off as he peered close at the ground and began walking slowly around his section of the castle.

Bemused, Stone too began staring at the ground as he slowly made his way over the rubble and detritus of a ruined castle. Out of the corner of his eye he could see Brenda, stationed carefully by a shoulder high section of wall, keeping an eye on the path they'd taken.

For thirty minutes, as the sun grew hotter, they carefully and slowly trudged the grounds. The musical cowbells tolled in the distance and Stone noticed Huw suddenly drop to the ground and pull a trowel out of his ever-present leather bag. "Come help me move this rock" he called over his shoulder.

As they struggled with the waist high stone, Huw told Stone to push against it while he troweled under it. Five sweaty minutes later he'd unearthed it enough that Stone's final heave pushed the stone over onto its side.

"The entrance?" Stone asked hopefully.

"No, I don't think so, but I thought I saw a glint of something over by there," Huw said, pointing at a corner of the rock. He got back down on his hands and knees and carefully scraped away the grass and moss with his trowel, stopping every once in a while to examine the dirt underneath. "Ah ha!" he shouted and a few seconds later sat back on his heels, his dirty fingers rubbing something in his hand then he wiped it with a handkerchief.

Stone leaned forward. "What do you think? Significant?"

He offered the item to Stone. It was a small gold or bronze item. As he examined it closer, he noticed two crooked diagonal lines and a small bump. He shook his head at Huw. "Nope, no idea what it is."

"Ah, the blessed innocence of the post-war generations; that my boy is a bronze insignia of an officer of the SS, the Schutzstaffel, the Nazi's bully boys, thugs and murderers."

Huw stood gingerly, still favoring his leg. He looked around the castle pensively and saw Brenda still observing the path. He turned and looked at Stone examining the artifact. "You know what this suggests, don't you?"

"That the Nazis were here sometime during the war and obviously had an interest in this castle."

"Right you are then. And why would they have an interest in this place? Could it be that somehow they got wind of the scroll and knew that this was Baldric's castle and that it might be hidden here still?"

"Hold on a second there Huw. I give you that as a possibility. But consider this. That Schloss we passed this morning on our way was also a Nazi treasure place as well as a concentration camp satellite. What's to say Schloss Finsternis wasn't a camp too? Or a rest place for SS officers? Most of the castles in this area were used by the Nazis in one way or another. After all its only eighty kilometers or so to Berchtesgarten where Hitler hung out."

"True. But the Nazis were also very methodical and meticulous. Why would they set up a sub-camp here when there's one just down the road at Fischhorn? And why would they set a rest place here where there's nothing except a narrowing valley and lots of farming? Remember, we have no records of Finsternis being used for anything during the war.

"And, let's not forget the Nazis had a pathological obsession with the occult and the mystical trappings of power. Hitler and Himmler desperately wanted *Die Heilige Lanze* and they searched painstakingly through records and histories not only of Germany but of Austria after the *Anschluss* and all the other occupied countries. Isn't it possible that they found some reference to the scroll and Baldric that led them here?"

"I don't mean to interrupt you gentlemen," Brenda spoke quickly and quietly as she hastened up to them, "but this conversation might be better done in a more secluded place. Like over here." She pushed and dragged the surprised men over the walls and up the slope until they were behind a thick bush. "I think we might be about to have company," she whispered, leading them along a path where they were hidden by the dense bushes and trees. At a small rocky ledge, she signaled them to remain quiet and lie down. Pistol pulled, she slithered and edged her way forward and signaled Stone to creep up beside her.

"I noticed that we were being followed on the way here, but I thought I lost them on the highway. Anyway, I noticed that the birds had suddenly gone silent. Then I heard some branches breaking and decided to bring you up here."

Stone stared at her. "How did you know this even existed?"

"The day before you arrived I scouted out this place. Always have a plan B is my motto. Now, quiet!"

She watched the Schloss ruins intently then stiffened. Stone looked down and saw two hulking men arrive at the edge of the woods. They froze in place and then, not hearing anything, crept forward slowly. As they reached the ruined walls and peeked over, they realized their quarry was gone. Carefully and methodically they entered the ruins and searched.

Brenda hand signaled Stone to take photos.

When it was evident that their quarry had gone, the men walked carefully over to the tree line and peered along another path leading sideways across the slope and heading towards a farm further along.

As soon as they disappeared along the path, Brenda whispered to Stone and Huw to move quickly and quietly. Ten minutes later they were in the parking area. As the two of them got in their rental, Brenda ran silently up the road and found a Mercedes tucked in behind a rock spill at the side of the road. She pulled a knife out of her casual jacket and quickly slashed all four tires then ran back as quietly as possible, jumped in the driver's seat and took off as quickly as she could.

"Did you listen to them?" she asked. "They were speaking German. Either they are hired goons working for the Druids or they're another group all together. Have you upset anyone besides the Druids, professor?"

The entire drive back to Zell the three of them batted theories back and forth. "Is it possible," Stone finally asked, "that we somehow stumbled upon somebody trying to protect some secret of the Nazis. I mean they certainly didn't look friendly and they were definitely armed, but we've had no attacks on us and I doubt the Druids know where we are yet."

To throw any possible trackers off their scent, Brenda avoided the highway tunnel, choosing instead to wander through the crowded streets of Zell. With Huw in the back seat monitoring all traffic behind them and Stone looking both ahead and behind, Brenda was free to maneuver the narrow streets past quaint souvenir shops and open air cafes. Though he was carefully scanning the roads ahead and behind for potential trouble, Stone's travel writer persona couldn't help but admire the multi-colored pastel houses and shops they passed, varying from pink to green to yellows and adorned with elaborate painted decorations.

Near the Zell railway station overlooking the lake, Brenda pulled in and parked beside the green Eurocar office. "This vehicle's been compromised. Time to get a new one," she said in explanation as she ushered them out. Half an hour later they were on the road again in a white Volkswagen Passat.

In the Gasthof's small lounge that evening they dissected the day's events, after carefully checking that their hosts were nowhere around and that nobody was lurking outside the door and windows. Although they had little to go on, the final consensus was to err on the safe side and assume that their trackers, whether they were working with the Druids or not, had no good will towards them. Further, they agree to split some online research. Huw would continue to search for information on the scroll and Baldric and would touch base with Mandy. Brenda would check with her contacts to see if there were any neo-Nazi groups operating in Austria. Stone was to investigate Hitler's obsession with the Lance and other sacred treasures as well as to check out the history of both Schloss Fischhorn and Schloss Finsternis.

Throughout the entire discussion Huw had been meticulously cleaning their day's find. "You see, I told you. An SS insignia." He held it up for them to see the infamous Death's Head and double lightning bolt symbols of the deadly organization, shiny and glinting in the light. "They were at Finsternis. We need to find out why."

"One thing's for sure," Stone remarked as they split up and headed to their respective rooms. "Colin thought we'd be safer in Austria but it seems we've landed in the middle of a wasp nest."

# Chapter Eighteen

### Greyfell Abbey

"Lord Greyfell. What is Alban Hefin?" Colin Maddox walked into the sitting room where Greyfell and Nees were enjoying a quiet cup of tea, sitting comfortably in their matching beige leather recliners.

"That's the summer solstice and one of the big three 'spirit nights' along with Beltain and Samhein. Why?"

Colin handed him his mobile phone and pointed to the message it contained. "It's from Stone's friend Chad Lawson, the SID agent. Callaghan and Liam Murphy were in contact about some big event they're planning after Alban Hefin." He waited while Greyfell read the brief message.

"I also got these from the Guvnor." He handed Greyfell a photo. "We took the suggestion and put a drone up over Castell y Draig. It was a test really. Had no idea someone would actually be there, let alone get a picture of them."

Greyfell studied the picture. "The one in the jacket is Callaghan for sure. Do we have any better shots of the second man, the one in the black coat?" Colin handed over some more photos that Greyfell looked at. He paused at one and then asked Nees to hand him a magnifying glass. As she did, he said "Not totally sure about this. If we can get some enhanced views of this picture, especially of the face, I might be surer, but if he is what I think he is, then we have real problems."

"Like what."

Greyfell studied the picture some more with the magnifying glass, then put them on the coffee table. He paused before he beckoned Colin to sit on the couch across from him.

"We are dealing with some very deep and very dark issues here Mr. Maddox. Issues and situations I'm not sure you really want to believe or explore."

"Try me. And please, all my friends call me Colin."

"Very well Colin, if I am correct, and enhanced views may help me in this, I believe that we are looking at a photograph of something that is known as a *Sidhe*, not a man, with Callaghan." He pronounced it '*seethe*'. "Look, are you sure you want to hear this?"

Colin nodded.

"The Sidhe are a race of beings that belong to what the Druids call the Otherworld. They are considered by the Druids to be a different race of beings and in the Tuatha de Danann book, the Book of Leinster, they were described as 'gods and not gods'.

"The closest modern man can come is to believe they are some kind of faerie folk. In the old Irish talks they were descendants of the gods and who have had much contact with mortals over the centuries. There are many documented testimonies in Irish or Celtic libraries attesting to this.

"They are believed to have the ability to move quickly through the air and be in different places within seconds. The Druids also believe that the Sidhe are capable of changing shape at will."

"You're kidding right? You're pulling my leg."

"Not so, Colin. I wish I was. Unfortunately Nees and I made studies that show, unbelievable though it may seem, there may indeed be some truth to these folk tales. There is something above and beyond our mortal ken, both good and evil. The Druids and their ilk have chosen evil as a means to gain controlling power over mankind. I happen to believe that Christianity, especially as practiced by those who are true followers of Jesus Christ, is the very antithesis of that; a power for the good of mankind."

Colin shook his head in dismay. "That's telling me you also believe in ghosts and Father Christmas."

"Well, if you are a Druid, you most certainly do believe in ghosts. This Alban Hefin is like Samhein and Beltain. They are times when the veil between our world and the Otherworld is thinnest and faeries and ghosts are abroad and easily visible to those who believe. You see, Colin, it really does not matter what you believe or what I believe. What matters is that they believe and therefore we must act as if everything was in fact true. Only then can you counter it."

Greyfell thought for a moment and then looked piercingly at Colin. "A moment ago you wondered if I was joking about the *Sidhe*. Let me tell you this. Both Nees and I have had situations in our lives where we have encountered events and individuals that cannot be explained in human terms; people who suddenly appear and disappear, cold chills in the presence of someone yet on a very warm and humid night, and unexplainable accidents when such individuals are in close proximity. I could go on. My point is this; for all our scientific knowledge and all the rational thinking and education we've been subjected to, there is a very real and very strong aspect of life that we as a society have ignored or choose to not acknowledge. Call it the supernatural, call it otherworldly, call it what you will. But it exists. Whether you or I or anyone else chooses not to believe is frankly irrelevant. It does exist."

He looked sternly at Colin. "I told Stone this and I will tell you. We are engaged in a battle that by far surmounts anything you or the Crown Security Bureau or MI5 or MI6 or any other agency we have has ever come up against. This is an unparalleled war that will be fought as much in the area of the supernatural as it will in the here and now. We are up against a terrifying power that is going to take what all of us can give and then some. I asked Stone and I will ask you, though I require no answer; do you believe in God? Because I believe we are up against enemies who not only believe in their gods but who draw upon their power in chilling ways. You need to seriously consider this."

Silence permeated the room. In the background, Colin could hear the antique dining room grandfather clock ticking slowly and resolutely away. He shifted uncomfortably from one foot to another. Greyfell waved him to the armchair across from him.

"I think we're going to need some more tea and biscuits, Nees dear. We have a lot to share with Colin."

## Zell am See

Sunlight flooded the kitchen and dining area of the Gasthof and Stone and Brenda cheerfully dove into the generous breakfast spread before them. Even Huw, still grumbling that it was not a proper breakfast, helped himself. The three chatted about the weather and the various sights around Zell am See, deliberately avoiding the topic they were all anxious to tackle; Finsternis, the SS pin and their findings during the night's research. Those discussions they'd mutually agreed last night would only be held somewhere safe.

Once in the car, they drove into the heart of the town and parked. Following Brenda's instructions to "keep close" they walked down the pedestrianized streets crowded with tourists and across the main square until they came to the railway tracks. They waited while the crossing gates flashed and lowered as the morning train to the ski resort towns of Kitzbuhel and Innsbruck slowed for the station stop at Zell. As the last coach rumbled by and the gate began to rise, they crossed the tracks and walked down the slight slope towards the lake. A palatial white hotel loomed above them, but they turned right and walked along the pathway that paralleled the lake.

"We'll take the Rundfahrt and find a quiet spot on deck, away from people," Brenda said, pointing at the tourist boat that did a round the lake ferry service. Once aboard they grabbed three seats close to the stern on the boat's upper deck and shared their findings. It wasn't much, they agreed.

Brenda led, speaking softly and reading from her rough notes. "There are some neo-Nazi groups in Austria but they're not as well defined or organized or even financed as their counterparts in Germany. Most of them are splinters of, or supporters of, the right-wing parties such as Austria Freedom Party or Alliance for the Future. There was one particularly brutal group, Burschenschaffen and its leader Gottfried Kussel, but they lost some of their steam when Kussel was jailed for eight years. One of my contacts suggested that there might be a small group semi active in this region and they operate out of a place called *Die Bruderhaus*, 'The Brothers House' up the Pinzgau valley towards Mittersill. But other than that, there's very little."

Behind them the town of Zell disappeared as the boat silently pushed its way down towards the south end of the lake. Above the snowcapped peaks the sun fought a running battle with white puffy clouds leaving the peaks glistening then shadowed, then glistening again. The peaceful scenery and lake were a contrast to the churning in the minds and stomachs of all three as they talked.

Huw spoke up next. "I've got nothing. I couldn't even reach Mandy by phone," he said glumly. "Baldric is as mysterious as ever."

"I'm not sure exactly how this relates to our situation," Stone said, "but I found out quite a lot. You were right Huw. Himmler and Hitler were deep into the occult. That movie *Raiders of the Lost Ark* had more than a touch of truth in it. Hitler wanted the Ark of the Covenant and sent teams out as early as 1936 in Ethiopia to check out the claims of the Coptic Church that it had the Ark. They scoured the entire Middle East for it and also searched amongst the records of the Cathars and the Templar Knights to find traces. And it was not just the Ark. Hitler was determined to track down the Holy Grail as well."

He was getting so excited discussing his findings that his voice was beginning to rise and carry. "Sush, my boy. Quietly." Huw admonished, and then let Stone continue. The reporter acknowledged his words with a quick nod and dropped his volume.

"The thing is, Hitler wanted all these holy relics because he thought they would give him power beyond anything any other human leader had achieved. But the key for him, was the Holy Lance. Apparently he visited Vienna and the Kunsthistorisches Museum at the Hofburg Palace when he was still in his early twenties and had some kind of mystical experience when he saw the Lance. As late as the 60's a British newspaper, the *Sunday Dispatch*, published excerpts from the memoirs of an Austrian historian, Dr. Walter Johannes Stein. Stein said the Fuhrer had a deep fanatical desire to own the Lance and believed he could harness its power. Stein added that throughout the war, the Lance was Hitler's secret talisman."

Stone leaned back and looked quickly around. So far as he could determine, most of the passengers were either closer to the bow or leaning over the rails enjoying the passing scenery. He motioned to the others to be quiet as the boat pulled into its first stop at Erlberg on the western side of the lake. After just a few passengers got off and a few others got on, the boat pulled away and began moving up the lake towards its second stop at Thumersbach. With one more look around, he began speaking again.

"Hitler and Himmler drew in two other important players in this search, an SS Colonel named Conrad Buch and another named Hans Ostermann. Buch was the overall commander of a special force assigned to make sure the Lance and some of the other relics of the Holy Roman Empire were removed from the Hofburg and repatriated to Germany on the day of Anschluss. They wound up in Nuremburg in a purpose build museum in the city Hitler had decided would be the mystical and religious centre of his Reich the way Rome was to Catholicism. Ostermann was to do the dirty work and actually find the other relics including the real Lance. It gets a bit murky from here, but the rumor is that as the war was coming to its end, Hitler realized that the Hofburg Lance was counterfeit. Himmler arranged for an elaborate and well-made fake of the Lance to be left in Nuremburg while he took the original one to his own castle in Wewelsburg. Ostermann and his team were pulled off every other project and told to find the real spear. When the Americans captured Nuremburg and later sent the Holy Roman Empire collection back to Vienna, it's believed that they returned Himmler's fakes. The real relics were then either hidden or smuggled out of Germany by U-boats as I mentioned the other night."

"But all of that is supposing that the Hofburg Lance was real," Huw noted. "My contention is the Hofburg Lance, whether Himmler later faked it or not, was itself a fraud. I have heard or seen nothing yet that would persuade me that the Lance has in fact ever been found. Rather, it is still somewhere in the Holy Land as our centurion has written, and the scroll is somewhere around here still. Either in Baldric's castle at Finsternis or possibly at Fischorn."

He looked up at Stone. "You said Hitler had an SS Colonel searching for the Lance, did you not, Bradstone? If so, suppose the Nazis had some indication that the scroll existed and was here and that Colonel Ostermann was sent to investigate. That might explain our little souvenir from yesterday."

"I hate to be a downer Huw, but even if Baldric existed and was at Finsternis, how would the Nazis have known about the scroll to search there."

There was silence, then Huw very quietly nodded and said, "you have a valid point there Bradstone. We must find what the connection was. Did Hitler somehow find out that the scroll existed and would lead him to the Lance."

By now the boat had left Thumersbach and was pulling into its final stop at the north end of the lake, Wiesenlehen. They sat back to enjoy the return trip south to Zell and enjoy the slowly passing countryside with the green mountains and white peaks and dotted with the ever present chalets and onion-domed churches.

"One thing's for sure," Huw said as he stood and stretched his legs. "We may have more questions than answers right now, but I believe deep in my heart and soul that things will begin to come clear for us. We'll track that scroll down yet. And then we'll know,"

### Crown Security Offices, London

Freddy knocked briefly then walked into Sir Giles' office. "Here's the latest from our American friends. Lawson says they questioned Murphy intently about Callaghan's plans for Alban Hefin. They couldn't get anything out of him. Murphy's associates in custody were also questioned but while they knew what Alban Hefin was, they had no knowledge about any attack. Lawson says he's convinced they were sincere and that only Murphy knew something was planned. He's not even convinced that Callaghan told Murphy any details which may explain why Lawson says Murphy was so smug about his silence on the matter."

"Mm. Know where Callaghan is yet?"

"Yes sir. We have finally traced him to a house in the Vale of Neath near Swansea. So far as we know though, only his brother and a companion and some medical people are actually there. There's been no sighting of Callaghan himself for more than a week."

"Hm. Bugger's gone to ground."

Sir Giles shifted in his seat and handed a note to Freddy. "Friend of mine in MI6. Went to the same college. Served in same regiment. Has a new toy and wants to try out its capabilities." His eyes twinkled as he looked at Freddy. "New drone. Much better than that one we sent over the Anglesey castle. Might want to contact him. Try it out over Callaghan's houses? Particularly that one he rented near Neath."

Freddy smiled and took the paper. "I'll call him immediately."

## Hereford

Mandy couldn't help shake the feeling that she'd said too much last night. Their long dinner discussion had warmed up when Nigel agreed to do some research for her. As much as she resisted providing too much information, she had to acknowledge that to do his research properly, he needed a bit more information. Bit by bit, it had come out; Baldric had a scroll sent to him by his brother, a priest in Constantinople at the time it fell to the Ottomans.

He hadn't blinked an eye as she told him that. "Well that gives me some dates to work on anyway. I have to find out if and where he was around 1453 to say, 1456."

She had resisted mentioning the spear, but did acknowledge that Baldric was a relic hunter and that the scroll apparently contained information about a sacred relic. "Mind you, we're not sure the scroll even existed or, if it did, that it ever got to Baldric in the first place. This might all be a wild goose chase," she remembered telling him.

As the evening wore on, she'd grown more comfortable talking to him while trying to answer his probing questions cautiously. His sharp questioning mind was what had attracted her in the first place, so the discomfort of giving vague answers troubled her. Walking the tightrope between needing his expertise and remembering she was bound by the Official Secrets Act was wearing on her. Finally, she admitted to herself that she slipped up a bit by revealing Huw's whereabouts though it really seemed to create no reaction in Nigel at all. He'd merely nodded and continued asking questions.

"I have a friend who's an expert in the Holy Roman Empire's obsession with holy relics. Maybe he's heard of this Baldric, or at least might give me some clues as to where to look. He's at The British Museum in London. Why don't I pop down there tomorrow and see if he can help. It would be good to spend time with him and I think this is something more easily explained in person than over the phone or email."

The rest of the evening had gone well. She'd enjoyed his company, laughed at his many stories and was sorry when they arrived back at her flat. "Don't you worry Mandy. If Baldric exists, I will find him and you can ease your father's burden somewhat."

He'd smiled, then leaned forward and gently wrapped his arms around her, kissing her firmly before releasing her and waving goodbye.

Now she pushed papers around her table, replaying the evening again and again in her mind. Her reveries were broken by the ringtone of her mobile. She checked the display and smiled. "Hello Da, how are you and have you found the scroll yet?"

She listened carefully, making notes as she did. "So you also want me to check out these two SS colonels and see where they were in 1944 and 1945." She made further notes as he filled her in. "And you're sure those men were not Druids? You're sure they spoke German? Oh Da. What have you gotten yourself into this time? Murderous Druids are surely enough but now you've got others after you as well!"

He tried to calm her down and assure her that while the men might have acted suspiciously, so far they'd posed no threat. Indeed, he told her, they were actually enjoying a round-the-lake cruise in Zell and, he argued, they wouldn't be doing that if there was any danger.

Somewhat mollified she told him she'd found nothing yet but was still looking. Guiltily, she refrained from mentioning Nigel's participation in the hunt. "Look Da, I know you say everything is okay, but I'm at least going to call Freddy at Crown Security and see if he can dig up something on this SS colonel and also if he has any clues as to who those men would be."

"Any message you want me to give Bradstone while I've got you on the line?"

Huw's question came at her like a bolt. Mandy waited for several seconds before responding. "No Da. Just say hello from me and thank him for sticking with you."

She said goodbye and disconnected. She flopped into her chair and slammed the phone down on the desk staring at the wall, her mind a riot of confusion and guilt as she considered not only her personal relationships but worried she'd already told Nigel too much.

Her emotions overwhelmed her and tears began to trickle then flow, down her cheeks, "Lord God, what a mess I've got myself into," she sobbed to herself, happy at least that she was alone and would not be interrupted. "Help me, please? Father show me the right way, the right decisions. Guard me from those who would harm me, but mostly, guard me from myself."

The tears continued unabated.

# Chapter Nineteen

**Anglesey, Wales**

Callaghan's phone conversations were always kept deliberately short in case government agencies might be monitoring him. Indeed, his paranoia was such that he was already on his third disposable mobile phone this month.

After receiving assurances and information from his callers, Callaghan contacted Quinn. He listened while Quinn provided a brief update on his brother then simply told Quinn "the material is arriving soon. Take care of it. Get it to your team. And remember, no failures this time. And get the Istanbul team home. They are needed here."

He tried another text message to Liam Murphy again with no response. Callaghan was convinced that Murphy's ability to communicate was shut down. He wasn't overly upset because he'd only been giving the American a vague heads up anyway; but the silence was disconcerting nevertheless. He was also frustrated because it had taken a lot of quiet and unobtrusive work to find him and communicate with him, especially since as it turned out he was locked away in a remote facility in the American desert; work that was now wasted. He frowned aware that he'd likely have to begin the work all over again.

He flopped onto the couch and picked up the package from Istanbul yet again. He still hoped to find a hidden clue that would expose the location of the spear. Whoever this Baldric was, he'd been the man who'd received the scroll from Istanbul. That, at least, seemed to be what Huw Griffiths believed and that was good enough for Callaghan. Something inside told him that Manfred's letter was genuine. Therefore all other claimants as the Spear of Destiny were counterfeits.

Callaghan picked up additional research his own people had found. One report particularly intrigued him. His Druid predecessors had carefully noted that their hard work to help Hitler find the spear and other icons he so blatantly salivated after.

He re-read one report to the Dragon Master of 1940. A Druid leader was inserted into the SS in 1939 rising quickly to become one of Himmler's trusted aides in the *Einsatzgruppen* or 'death squads'. As *Obergruppenfuhrer* he'd led several *Sonderkommando* groups on the search for holy relics. Based at Himmler's "Castle of the Teutonic Knights" at Wewelsburg, the headquarters of the Nazi occult movement, Obergruppenfuhrer Hans Ostermann was the primary information channel between the Druids and the Nazis.

Ostermann carefully recorded the many expeditions and searches and kept his Druid masters fully informed. Ostermann, better known to the Druids as Michael O'Flaherty, was the son of a fisherman from Galway to which he later returned. Seeing the Third Reich collapse around him he escaped along with some gold and art treasures on a U-Boat three days before the war in Europe ended. Two days after the Nazi surrender, just after midnight, O'Flaherty was rowed ashore from the U-Boat to resume his Irish identity.

Key portions of O'Flaherty's reports showed that both Hitler and Himmler slowly became convinced that the Hofburg Lance was not real, especially as the war turned steadily against them.

"There were blazing rows between Himmler and Hitler," O'Flaherty recorded, "with Hitler, spittle running down the sides of his mouth, screaming that Himmler had betrayed him; that the lance they now had in Nuremburg was a fake and that Himmler was keeping the real lance hidden. Himmler, equally furious declared his innocence arguing that earlier generations had perpetrated the fraud. Himmler assured the Fuhrer that the real Lance would be found and that he would order me, his picked man, to lead a Sonderkommando unit in Austria to find it based on information our intelligence people had found."

Callaghan ruefully noted that whatever the lead was, O'Flaherty had not written it down. As he had done with the Istanbul material, he scoured O'Flaherty's notes for the smallest clue but found nothing. Nor could he question the man himself. O'Flaherty was killed in a firefight between the IRA and British troops on the Eire-Ulster border in 1972. Although the old man was 74 at the time, he was still a vigorous, demanding, and totally ruthless fighter.

As Callaghan contemplated the piles of papers, his mobile rang. He listened, smiled, and said "stay with it. Find out as much as you can, stay close, and keep me informed. I'll arrange for cover there." He disconnected and began to whistle. It was times like this that he regretted not having a piano so he could enjoy some mellow jazz. He settled for a CD and poured himself a pint of Guinness, the first he'd had since he'd sworn off alcohol. But this day, he told himself, things are coming together and it's only right to celebrate. Even if it was by himself.

He called Quinn and ordered him to dispatch a team immediately.

**Istanbul**

Detective Kizil was pleased with his men, though he did not let them know it. After days of slogging investigation they had tracked the missing British men to a small hotel several blocks from the Blue Mosque.

"Bring them in," he ordered then countermanded it a few minutes later. It would be good, he decided, to do a bit of field work himself. He'd been in the office too long recently. He told his subordinates to keep the men under surveillance and that he himself would arrest them.

His unmarked car threaded its way slowly through the mass of cars, trucks, tourist buses and crowds. The radio crackled suddenly, warning that the men had spotted the uniformed police coming towards them as they exited the hotel. An overeager uniformed officer had shouted to them to surrender and they'd jumped into a taxi and fled.

Frustrated, Kizil listened as the taxi's number was broadcast, and then grew increasingly frustrated as his men chased the taxi on foot, watching it twisting and turning in the heavy traffic, scattering pedestrians on the narrow sidewalks and narrowly missing a parked bus. Police cars began to converge and it became clear that the taxi was trying to make its way to Kennedy Caddesi, the broad highway that skirted the old city and the Sea of Marmara leading to Ataturk airport.

Kizil suddenly pulled his car around in a screaming turn that scattered pedestrians and left a cacophony of blaring horns behind him. He raced down the street determined to head the taxi off, all the while shouting instructions over the radio. He jerked the car right and left, swerving around cars, buses and trucks, making hard turns onto different but equally narrow and crowded roads.

Horn blasting he swung onto Kennedy Caddesi as his men reported the taxi was racing down Akbiyik Caddesi. With any luck, he thought, I can block them before they reach Kennedy. He gunned his vehicle, pressing the accelerator as hard as he could until he thought he'd push it through the floor. Swerving and weaving in and out of the heavy mid-day traffic, he kept his right hand on the steering wheel while his left, clutching his police badge, waved out the window trying to justify his worse than normal driving. The hands switched every few seconds as he changed gears then switched back to his left hand waving out the window. He yelled and screamed at the traffic in front of him, dropping his volume every couple of seconds to radio instructions.

Traffic in the old cramped part of the city helped him. As much as the taxi and the trailing police cars tried, they found it a slower but harrowing drive. At one point, his men radioed, a curbside fruit and vegetable stand was completely demolished by the taxi which somehow kept moving. The police car screeched to a halt as debris fell around, then picked up speed again, squashing and crushing the remnants.

"They're closing in on Kennedy. Coming down Aksafal" Kizil heard. "So am I," he muttered, willing his vehicle to greater speed. He was thinking of slowing just a tad in order to make the turn onto Aksafal when he saw the taxi hurtling towards him. He plunged the car ahead, clipping the cab on the driver's side just behind the passenger door, spinning the cab into a hurtling, whirling time bomb that bounced over the cement boulevard that separated the busy highway's lanes. Kizil wrenched the wheel and sprung his car over the same barricade.

In the background he could hear the wild mee-maw's of police and emergency vehicles. Both vehicles spun to stops in front of the elegant-looking Catladikapi restaurant that overlooked the Marmara.

Kizil eased himself out of his wrecked car, pulled his gun out of his underarm holster and walked slowly forward, left hand raised and still holding his credentials. The driver was slumped over the wheel, blood spurting from his head. The front passenger had smashed his head against the side window, his head at an awkward angle and a wicked looking knife in his hand. A quick glance into the rear showed one of the two men beginning to move while the other moaned.

Kizil felt rather than heard his men rush to the wreck and pull the doors open. Seconds later ambulance attendants arrived and began the process of treatment and extrication. He replaced his gun then collapsed against the cab's front undamaged fender. He looked up to see one of his team and a medic moving in on him. He waved the medic away and glared at the cop. "Find the sakal, the idiot, who shouted and tipped them off and have him report to me." He nodded towards the restaurant "and get me a chai!"

Fifteen minutes later, after finally allowing a medic to look at him and tend to a head wound he'd never felt or noticed, Kizil sat on the steps leading up to the restaurant. He and another officer were going through the luggage retrieved from the cab's trunk. Kizil was peering hard at the laptop. He played around with the keyboard, opening documents and reading them, whistling and then smiling to himself.

"Not much really, just the bags with some clothes, books and papers and that laptop," his partner remarked. "All three of the passengers had strange black tattoos on their arms. Something like a lizard or large dinosaur."

"The driver?"

"No tattoos or any distinguishing marks. He died on impact, but the doctor says he has a knife wound on his right side. Serious, but not enough to kill him. The crash did that."

The cop raised his head slightly to look at Kizil who ignored the comment, grunted and merely lifted his mobile to his ear, thumbing a number as he did. He got up and walked out of hearing. Two minutes later he walked back to the policeman.

"Collect this stuff up and deliver it to my office. And make sure that their hotel room is thoroughly searched. Anything interesting there, send it to my office"

"The front passenger is dead, boss; the two rear passengers in serious condition."

"Stay with them. I want them isolated and guarded at all times. Nobody but the doctors and nurses get near them, and I want anyone treating them to have full security clearances. No clearance, no entry okay?"

The officer nodded and handed over a plastic bag. "Three passports plus their wallets."

"These men were Irish. More importantly, they were on a surveillance mission in Istanbul," he pointed to the laptop, "and were the ones who stole those artifacts at the museum as well as killing the security guard."

He stood up, stretched and then winced in pain, raising his hand to the bandage over his left eye. "This is much deeper than we thought. Not just a simple robbery and murder." He stared at the laptop again, "these guys are into some serious stuff that goes beyond our borders. I can't believe they were so careless as to not put security on their emails and documents." He shook his head in bewilderment and winced again. "I need to meet with those British agents as soon as possible."

Kizil looked at the plastic bag then folded it into his jacket pocket. "Get me a ride back to my office, will you. I have one hell of a headache."

**Zell am See, Austria**

A long coffee break at an outside café after the boat ride saw both Huw and Stone argue quietly between themselves while their Crown Service minder, her back carefully positioned against the wall, carefully kept watch while listening to their discussion.

"Look here Bradstone. We need to return to Finsternis. We found one artifact there with just a desultory poke around. With a more concentrated search of the tower ruins who knows what we might find?"

"One SS pin does not a Nazi treasure hunt make, Huw," Stone shook his head. "It is too slim a straw to build up any kind of argument."

Huw interrupted. "Because we only made a quick search boyo! If we find nothing after a longer more planned examination then I agree, we move on."

"You're forgetting our visitors Huw. We don't know who they were or why they were tracking us, but I doubt very much it was for our health and benefit." He turned to their companion. "What do you think Brenda? Would it be wise to return to Finsternis?"

"My mandate is to keep you safe. Beyond that, I'm ordered to provide whatever help I can plus provide you with the best advice." She shook her head. "I have my concerns about those men too, but I have no information about them yet. I emailed those photos you took, Stone, and so far nobody in London has been able to identify them, nor has Vienna or Berlin. So who they were or are remains a mystery." She looked them both in the eye. "At this point unfortunately, I have no reason to either agree to a return or discourage it."

The argument continued for another half hour broken intermittently when waiters approached. Finally Stone threw his hands in the air in exasperation. "You are the most doggedly stubborn man I have ever met Dr. Huw Griffiths! You get the bone in your teeth and you will not let go. You simply will not listen to reason."

"Answer me this, then Bradstone. Give me one sound, logical and proven reason why we should not return to Finsternis? We both have reams of conjecture supporting our positions; I grant you that I certainly do. But can you provide one solid verified argument against?" He reached over and held Stone's arm. "We have to do something. Sitting in this café is not helping, nor is going around and around the same arguments. We have to act. And act now." He leaned back and fixed Stones eyes with a professorial gaze. "Look you, if we don't return to the castle then what do you suggest? That we go back to Britain, tail between our legs? That we back off entirely and let the scroll and eventually the lance drop into the Druids' hands while we enjoy a Tyrolean holiday?"

Forty minutes later with Stone still in a slight funk, they pulled into the parking area at Finsternis. As arranged, they stayed in the car while Brenda surveyed the path ahead then, at her signal they exited and followed along to the ruins. Inside the old Schloss grounds, Huw headed straight to the spot he'd found the pin. Brenda took up her looking post while Stone joined Huw.

For over an hour, they sweated in the warm late spring sunshine, pulling at stones and dislodging them then poking around in the uncovered ground. If anything the surrounding countryside seemed greener, the skies bluer and the air clearer this time around; even the jangle of cow bells sounded louder.

Exhausted after moving one particularly stubborn piece of rubble, Stone leaned heavily against one of the half destroyed interior walls. Without warning it gave way. As he tumbled over the wall his flailing feet dislodged another weakened portion of the wall that crashed to the ground. As he lurched to his feet and began to dust himself off he looked down at his feet and called for Huw, beckoning Brenda to stay where she was.

They both stared down at one of the dislodged stones. Gleefully, Huw rubbed his hands over it. "It's a carved letter 'B' you found boyo," he exulted. On his hands and knees he carefully pulled it away from the rubble. "It was sitting up there," he pointed, "above eye level yet in plain sight." Stone helped him up and stared at it. "You know what this means don't you? The B stands for Baldric. It must. This is the place. He existed."

Pleased as he was about his clumsy success, Stone was still hesitant to go along with the excited Welshman. He bent over to look at the discovery.

"Very good gentlemen. Whatever you have found now belongs to us!"

Huw and Stone both spun around to find two armed men, guns raised, looking at them. Behind them, Stone could see Brenda's slumped body and another armed man behind her.

"If you've killed her...."Stone sprang towards them only to feel rather than hear the bullet whistle by his head.

"Stay where you are!" The taller man with sparse white buzz cut hair, gestured with his gun. "She is not dead, just incapacitated. Now both of you very slowly put your arms to your sides and move away from those stones."

Huw and Stone obeyed, with Huw's demands to know who they were cut off by a curt command to be silent. As they stood to the side, the second man swiftly searched each of them.

"Nothing, *Herr Sturmbannfuhrer*"

He gestured to the unconscious woman. "Pick her up and follow." Without another word he slipped in behind them, weapon held as still as the mountains. Whoever he was, Stone thought, he's a pro with steel nerves.

Together he and Huw cradled Brenda's arms over their shoulders and slowly picked their way through the rubble and grassy interior of the Schloss and down the path to the parking area.

High above them a watching figure put her binoculars away and slipped down a rough path silently, keeping the small party in constant view.

From a bushy wooded knoll she watched the armed men force their captives into a green van. As they did she whipped out her binoculars again, paused then put them down and grabbed a mobile from her pocket and began thumbing frantically. When she finished she put the phone away and waited while the van disappeared down the road. She sat behind the bushes, waiting until she was satisfied she wasn't observed then began walking down towards the river

# Chapter Twenty

### Hereford

Mandy's quick visit to Oxford's Bodleian Library had been a massive waste of time and effort though, as she admitted to herself, it always was a long shot. She'd pored over all kinds of information and old manuscripts about medieval relic hunters and sellers, but nowhere did she find a reference to one named Baldric in the Holy Roman Empire or anywhere else for that matter. Nor did she find records relating to any claimants to the title Spear of Destiny or Holy Lance other than those they already knew about in the Vatican and Vienna.

The message light was flashing on her office phone when she opened the door. She had, she confessed to herself, mixed emotions when she listened; pleased that it was Nigel but disappointed and worried that it wasn't her father. She'd not heard from him for more than three days now and was beginning to feel tendrils of fear seeping into her mind.

Nigel's message was more encouraging. His visit to London proved fruitful. Although he'd not identified the man Baldric, his friend at the British Museum had located references to three relic sellers from Germania who'd been active in the mid-1400's. No names, but some leads. Plus, he reported excitedly, "the Austrian embassy here has arranged a special pass into the Hofburg museum to speak to the curator about their Holy Lance plus they're arranging a private meeting for me with some of the archivists at the State Archives. I am leaving for Vienna first thing tomorrow then I'm going to Koblenz and examine the German archives." There was a slight pause and then he added "just a heads up. I used my university credentials even though I'm no longer on the faculty. Hope you'll back me up if someone should come calling."

She placed the phone back in its cradle and moved over to the table piled high with the papers, articles and assorted books she'd requested from the university's library. An hour later she was still plodding through the dry material trying to winnow out a modicum of information. Mandy acknowledged that her understanding of the medieval veneration and trade of religious icons from bones to severed fingers to hair to stones from the Holy Land had grown exponentially in the time she'd been researching Baldric. But, she sighed, she was no closer to finding useful information for her father than she had the minute he'd enlisted her aid. And it bugged her. Until now she'd taken a professional pride in being an excellent researcher who always comes through; now she was staring failure in the face and letting her Da down as well.

Frustrated she flung the paper she was reading, across the table. She contemplated phoning her father or Stone but remembered Freddy's admonition to not initiate contact, especially from her university phone. Let him call you if he needs to, Freddy had said and, so far, she'd obeyed.

She snapped her fingers. Freddy. Minutes later she was speaking with the man himself, sharing her concerns at not hearing from either of the two men or of progress from her end either. She listened as his calming, soothing voice allayed her fears slightly. With mutual assurances that they would inform each other the minute they heard something, she rang off.

Truth be known, she scolded herself, it's not just Da you're worried about. It's that stubborn reporter. Unbidden, the tears sprang up again.

### Crown Security Offices, London

Freddy knocked, then slipped into the Guvnor's office. "Two things sir. First, these printouts of the video shot by that new drone. Second, I just heard from Mandy Griffiths. She hasn't heard from either Huw or Stone for several days and seems quite worried about it. I just checked and we've not heard from them either, nor our agent."

Sir Giles nodded and held out his hand for the printouts. "Brenda's good. Worrying if she's not reported. Check if the Austrian police have anything."

He studied the drone shots closely, lifting a magnifying glass from his desk drawer to peer at one in particular. He tapped the sheet with his glass. "Something familiar about that chap. Can't place him. But I will."

Freddy could not conceal his grin, pleased that he was one step ahead of his guvnor. "Facial features, Sir Giles. Take a close look at the nose and eyebrows." He waited while Sir Giles did so then began to speak. "Anson Quinn. The son of…" before he could finish Sir Giles blurted out "Mick O'Flaherty!"

Sir Giles and Freddy shared smiles. "Knew there was an IRA connection. O'Flaherty was killed on the Ulster border. Took out a police station but got caught up with our Paratroopers as they were trying to cross the border." Sir Giles looked pensive. "Information on Quinn?"

"He's stayed under our radar for sure. I checked with our people in Wales and it seems like he's some kind of major domo and babysitter for Declan Callaghan, the one who was paralyzed in Brittany. He's got no form on our side of the Irish Sea and he's been squeaky clean in Eire according to my contact."

"Keep that drone over the house regularly. Callaghan has to come back at some point." He peered questioningly at Freddy. "Sure they won't notice it flying over their heads?"

Freddy laughed. "This is a super drone. It flies at over 40,000 feet and has a special battery pack that will keep it up for hours at a time. All we have to do is program it. They can't see it or hear it, but the imagery is unbelievable even from that distance. You can see how sharp the images are. We can pick out the wart on Quinn's face. Look here, Sir Giles and you can actually read the headlines on the newspaper Declan is reading."

Sir Giles uttered a pleased grunt. "Nevertheless. Find out more about Quinn. Family. Contacts. Friends. Enemies. Get it all. Want to see shots from the drone every time they're downloaded."

Freddy jotted a couple of notes then, using his pen as a pointer, drew the guvnor's attention to some long crates just behind Quinn. "We don't know what they are," he said, "but they were delivered just before Declan came outside." He drew out some more photos and slowly flipped through them as Sir Giles studied them intently.

"Find out what's in those crates. And also check out what's happening in Austria."

With that dismissal Freddy left the office and a pensive Sir Giles sat staring out his office window, rocking in his creaky desk chair.

## Die Bruderhaus, outside Zell am See, Austria

The room was totally dark. All Stone could remember was being bundled into the room blindfolded and then feeling a sharp prick against his skin. Everything then went blank. He blinked several times and slowly began to recall where he was. His hands and arms were free so he quickly checked himself over. He heard a moan and hissed into the dark. "Huw. Brenda."

An answering voice told him to "be quiet will you, I'm listening." Stone was relieved to hear Brenda's quiet voice. "Huw's in there being interrogated. This is called *Die Bruderhaus* apparently and it's the headquarters for what they call The Brotherhood."

"Who are they? What do they want?"

"Near as I can tell they're a bunch of old Nazis and want to know why you and Huw are poking around the castle. They already knew who I am and who I work for but they're really curious about you."

She stopped suddenly and whispered "they're coming. Make like you're still out."

Seconds later a flood of light entered the room as the door opened. Stone, his head still in shadow, saw through his partially closed eyes that Huw was upright and indignant as he was pushed into the room. "I'll pray for you *mein herr* and for your men that you would find peace in the present rather than trying to revive the past." A barrage of German swearing followed as two men shoved Huw roughly into a chair. They then briskly strode over, looped their arms under Stone's and dragged him out into the main room.

The light blinded him at first but as his eyes adjusted he saw a room dominated by the tall bullet-headed man with the sparse white buzz cut. He stood by a wooden table which held what looked like their passports. The two men led Stone to a lone couch in front of the table and dropped him unceremoniously onto it. Three other armed men stood along the perimeter of the room, two by the door leading into the dark room, the other by what he assumed was the main door leading to other parts of the house.

"Why are you here, Herr Wallace? What is it you seek at the Schloss?" the man's strong guttural German accent made it sound like a cold bark. "And don't pretend you're not awake. The drug does not last that long."

Stone looked up, shaking his head, "don't know what you're talking about."

"Don't waste time. You and your friends have been searching Schloss Finsternis. One of your friends is an agent with a British security agency. I have been gentle so far with your companions, but my patience is wearing thin. I ask again, Herr Wallace. What are you looking for?"

"I am a journalist. I write travel pieces and I'm doing research for a piece." The man stepped forward quickly and with a sharp, fierce backhand, slugged Stone so that he slumped into the couch. "Do not play games. What were you looking for?"

Stone shook his head again. "I was looking for information on old castles in the Tyrol for a piece I am writing. My friends came along to keep me company." Again, the man stepped forward and punched Stone. Then nodded to his two henchmen who proceeded to pull Stone off the couch onto the floor, beating and kicking him as they did.

Two minutes later, a groggy Stone, one eye partially closed and with blood streaming from his nose and cuts on his forehead, struggled to focus with his one good eye. The two men hauled him off the floor and threw him into the couch again.

"You are a stubborn man, Herr Wallace. I despise stubborn men." He turned suddenly to his underlings. "Bring the others out here. We'll let him watch while we interrogate the woman."

Together they dragged Brenda and Huw into the room. Horror rippled across their faces as they saw Stone.

Suddenly Brenda saw masked faces at the window against the dark night and yelled "Huw, Stone. Down!" As she did the three men spun around startled by her shout and then by the sudden sound of breaking glass and the sudden spit of silenced weapons. First one man spun around then the second. The three armed men began firing back at the window while their leader dropped to his knees and drew his own gun, pulled the table down, sheltering behind it and firing back at the window.

In the confusion, Stone rolled off the couch and over towards Huw and Brenda. With a massive bang a smoke grenade exploded and began to fill the room with insidious, noxious smoke. The main door burst open and two more armed Austrians burst into the room, one dropping almost immediately as shots ripped into his side.

Chaos in the room was now compounded as angry shouts and orders from both inside the house and outside mixed with the sound of weapons being discharged. More smoke and tear gas canisters were fired into the room.

Brenda and Huw began crawling and pulling Stone into their former prison room despite their coughing and choking on the toxic smoke. Bullets slammed into the walls above their heads. Inside the room, Brenda slammed the door shut, jumped up and began pulling Huw and Stone towards the back corner of the room. "There's a door here too, she said," pulling on it, grateful that it opened easily. It led to a narrow hallway. Above them and to the side they could hear more people running and firing. Smoke began seeping into the hallway and amidst all the cacophony of noise there was now the still quiet but unmistakable crackling of flames coming from the main room.

"Come on, we haven't got much time." Huw grabbed the door handle on a room just down the hall and away from the chaos. He stood silent for a second, eyes closed, then with a deep breath suddenly opened the door. The room was empty, so Brenda shut the door quietly behind her while Huw helped Stone stagger over to a window. "No choice," Huw said as he picked up a chair and smashed it through the window. Without a second thought he jumped out, half pulling Stone behind him while Brenda pushed. Together they fell into the bushes beside the house.

The firing seemed to be on one side of the house only. The three ran as quickly as possible up a sloping small lawn and into the tree line just beyond. In the background they heard more shouting and firing as figures suddenly sprinted around the corner, still firing at the house through open windows. They could see a glow in one of the rooms as the fire began to take hold. Suddenly one of the figures tossed something into the window they'd just escaped from while another fired an automatic weapon indiscriminately into the room. With a sudden *whump* flames flared up and the room began to burn.

Crouched behind the bushes they were startled to suddenly hear one of the figures bark out in an unmistakable female voice "Withdraw. That will finish all of them. The Nazis as well as Wallace and Griffiths. Ta muid anseo. The master has spoken."

The figures began running down the slope towards the front of the building.

"Come on, we've got to get away from here. Now." Brenda pushed and pulled the two men until they began moving. "Stay in the shadows of the trees and let the darkness hide you." In the background they could hear the sirens and mee-maws of emergency vehicles racing to the scene from the nearby town of Mittersill.

Making their way as quickly as they could, they found themselves on the edge of the main road. Motioning Huw and Stone to stay put, Brenda crept along the empty road towards the house. They could hear the emergency vehicles getting closer and by now it was clear that the back of the main house was engulfed in flames.

Stone sat on the edge of the road, hidden slightly by a small hedge. Huw handed him a handkerchief to help him wipe away the drying blood. They suddenly crouched, pushing themselves against the grass verge as a vehicle with no lights unexpectedly raced towards them and slowed down as it neared their position. Someone was leaning out of the driver's window. "Huw, Stone. Quick." They scrambled across the road, relieved to find Brenda at the wheel. Before they were fully inside she gunned the old Volkswagen van and raced off towards Zell am See.

"Fools left the keys in. It was hidden about one hundred feet from the entrance to the house. Don't know whether it belongs to the Nazis or the others, but it belongs to us now." The steely determination in her voice sparked a quick discussion.

"It was Druids. You heard what that woman shouted. She thought she'd killed us as well as those neo-Nazi thugs." Huw helped Stone sit up. "Are you okay boyo?"

"Yeah. I'm all right. A bum eye and my whole body aches and I can just feel it popping black and blue bruises as we speak." Stone coughed and winced with the pain. "But how did they know we were there? Nobody knew we were in Austria, yet they pegged us immediately and knew we were in that house. Did those Austrians tip them off?"

"Doubt it. Don't forget, they were firing to kill everyone in that house. It was an attack against them as much as us." Brenda spun the wheel of the van as they dodged around a large truck and plunged into the tunnel that bypassed Zell.

"Hey, watch it. Don't attract attention. We don't want to be pulled over by the police." Brenda silently nodded in acceptance of Stone's rebuke and eased her foot off the gas pedal.

An hour later they were well on their way to Munich after a quick stop at the Gasthof Kremml to gather their belongings. On their way, after much argument, it was agreed that Brenda would drop them outside the main train station in Munich. There they would split. Brenda would ditch the old van and make contact with London while Stone and Huw took the train to Koblenz where they hoped to search the German archives.

"It's obvious they tracked us to Austria," Stone argued, "and they know that there's three of us. Those Druid forces escaped before the fire department could arrive. Who knows how many were in the building and survived, but it will soon become obvious to them that we survived. So they'll be on the lookout for us. If we get to Koblenz and the archives by tomorrow, they won't be expecting it. They'll be watching train stations and airports in Austria, not Munich.

"Problem." Brenda spoke up. "None of us have passports. We'll have to get some before we move on."

For the first time that evening Stone smiled and reached into his jacket pocket. "Surprise!" He pulled out three passports. "Bullet head tipped the table over as a shield and these fell at my feet. I grabbed them."

As they laughed, Stone, slowly recovering from his beating, peered into the rearview mirror and winced. "Unfortunately now I look nothing like my mug shots." He leaned back against the seat. "I just don't understand how the Druids knew where we were. It's like they have a homing device on us or something."

With that thought tumbling around in his mind, he allowed silence to descend as Huw tried to catch a bit of sleep. It doesn't matter, he thought, because in two hours we'll be in Munich and six hours after that, Koblenz.

# Chapter Twenty-One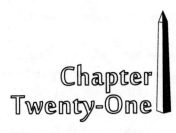

### County Meath, Ireland

The sun was setting in the west as Callaghan finally arrived at the small out-of-the-way farm cottage in the heart of County Meath. It was good to be home in Ireland again he thought, as he settled himself into a black leather armchair. He heard his driver bustling away in the kitchen, preparing a quick meal.

The sudden decision to shift headquarters back to Ireland was partly strategic—keep the authorities guessing if they're looking for me, he thought—and partly longing to return home. It was easy enough to arrange a small sailing vessel to meet him at the small jetty in Cemaes on Anglesey and spirit him across the waters to Balbriggan. Untypically, the Irish Sea had been calm the entire voyage with good southeast winds pushing them to Ireland. From Balbriggan it was a short drive around Navan to his destination, another place of refuge offered by his loyal Tuatha de Danann Druids.

His ebullient mood over being back in his homeland was muted. A curt phone call as they left Balbriggan put him in a rage. Despite his reluctant order to keep Huw Griffiths alive, the team Quinn sent to Austria had tracked him and his companions to a house where they were apparently prisoners. Taking no chances the team attacked swiftly and brutally, determined to wipe out the pair and as well as their kidnappers. Callaghan was mollified somewhat that Griffiths survived but infuriated at the undisciplined way his team acted. More importantly they now had no idea where the two men had gone; they'd disappeared into the Alps. He was about to order the team leader's immediate execution when Quinn told him the woman lost both her husband and brother in the French debacle. Remembering his raw emotions and desire for revenge over Declan's situation, he relented and ordered her home; she would, however, be punished severely and before all her peers in the Tuatha.

With the meal in front of him Callaghan dismissed the man who'd brought it with thanks. As he chewed his sandwich he thought long and hard about the next move. The Alban Hefin plan was proceeding. Quinn had chosen a man. The equipment had been delivered. Callaghan deliberately stayed away from the sophisticated weaponry favored by Damien Wyndham. That elaborate plan had failed miserably, Callaghan remembered, and cost Wyndham his life. No, he told himself, simpler is better. Alban Hefin was proceeding well with the next phase tomorrow; all leading to the main event when people would be forced to pay attention.

But the Lance. The Lance. It gnawed away at his mind, rolling over and over as he tried to sleep. Many nights he simply sat up and visualized the Lance. He could see it beckoning to him in his mind's eye, ripe and ready for the one who could truly control it and wipe all memory of the new religions from existence.

His hands and head began to sweat as they always did when he thought about the Lance. He jumped up and began pacing the room. He had to get the scroll. It was the key to finding the Lance. Unfortunately, right now the professor seemed to be the best lead to the scroll. Losing him could mean losing the scroll. Callaghan cried out to his gods, pleading with them for wisdom. In his mind he could see the Lance again, black against a blue sky. He tried to grasp it but it danced away from him, always seeming to be just beyond his reach.

A sudden banging on the door snapped him out of his trance. Quickly he pulled a revolver out of his jacket and approached the door cautiously. Leaning with his back against the wall, he gently reached forward and flipped the door latch. As the door swung slowly open Callaghan dropped to one knee, revolver in firing position.

A cold wind swept through the door. Silently the black-cloaked old man swept in. "You left. Why?" A cold fear gripped Callaghan. "I warned you that I expect absolute obedience. I was not informed."

The icy black eyes bored into Callaghan as he slowly rose and lowered the gun. "It is part of my plan, Master. To keep moving from place to place frequently. It will keep the authorities guessing."

"You fear them after your attacks on their churches? Or do you want them unaware of what you are planning until after Alban Hefin?"

Callaghan choked. "You know about this? How? Only a few of my closest…" The old man's hand rose and stopped his sputtering. "I know everything. Yet you keep things hidden from me." His voice suddenly changed from a frosty cold tone to a gentler, oily one. "Tell me Dragon Master, what will you do with the Lance when you have it?"

Callaghan paused before answering, trying to fathom the mind of the strange malevolent man in front of him. He knew, and had seen, the old man had power to take life by simply lifting a finger. He sweated more as he realized he needed to be wiser than ever as he answered.

"I will bring it to you Master, of course."

"But it holds great power for the one who possesses it does it not Dragon Master? You could rule the world, could you not?" The old man had not blinked, but kept Callaghan fixed in his gaze.

"The Lance is indeed powerful Master. But I have sworn to offer it to the old gods and their service."

He tried to hold the old man's gaze in the silence that followed until it was broken by the soft buzzing of Callaghan's mobile phone. He jerked his eyes away and grabbed the phone. The quick report confirmed that no bodies fitting the description of the professor or reporter were found in the gutted remains of the wooden chalet his team had destroyed. He listened then barked "Whatever you need to do, find them. They can't have gone far." He dropped the phone onto the chair and turned again to face the Master.

The room was empty. The wooden cottage door flapped open but the old man was gone. Callaghan stepped outside squinting to see in the deepening gloom. There were no cars on the isolated track leading to the house or on the road that he could see. No lights. No noise, just the wind picking up and rustling the leaves in the few trees that surrounded the old farmstead.

Despite the thick woolen jacket and sweater he still wore from the boat trip, he shivered. And it was a shiver that reached into the depths of his bowels.

It was two days before he got the phone call pinpointing Wallace and Griffiths again.

### Crown Security Offices, London

It was surprisingly warm and sunny in London, especially since the BBC weather report predicted rain and cool winds for the capital. Sir Giles stared out his office window at the narrow street road into the mews and, beyond, the barely glimpsed roof of his primary concern Buckingham Palace.

Ever since the foiled attack on Her Majesty, the Druids had occupied a lot of his attention at the Queen's specific request. Still there were other threats against the Royal Family that had to be investigated and thwarted. Normally he avoided the city on weekends, especially Sundays. But things were stuck and he hoped the office on a quiet Sunday might shake some cobwebs loose in his mind. Hands on hips, he sighed. His mind chewed the facts over and over again. His staff was working hard, going around and around, sniffing at the edges, but so far getting nowhere. Sooner or later surely they had to catch a break, he reasoned. But where? And when? And would it be too late?

As he turned away from his window, the effervescent Freddy bounced into his office, "Just heard from Brenda. She's back in Vienna and the men are in Koblenz apparently." Sir Giles simply stared, so Freddy continued. "They were captured by some neo-Nazis while poking around an Austrian castle ruin."

"Nazis?"

"Yes sir, but here's the thing. They were being interrogated in an old house near Zell am See when the house was attacked." Freddy paused, watching Sir Giles bushy eyebrows raise. "The attackers were Druids apparently determined to kill everyone in the house. Brenda said she and the men were able to jump out a back window and hide in the woods when the firing started. They heard a woman shouting the Druid slogan as fire began to take hold of the building."

"What happened?"

"They escaped as the Druids evacuated the area and just before the fire brigade arrived." Freddy checked the paper he was holding. "Earliest Austrian reports are that when the firemen extinguished the blaze they found five bodies burned beyond recognition. Apparently there were four others severely injured but able to escape the building. They're under police guard but apparently uncommunicative."

"My God. Gets murkier and murkier." Sir Giles plopped into his chair and looked up at Freddy. "What else?"

"Huw and Stone split with Brenda. Sent her back to Vienna while they headed for Koblenz and the German State Archives."

"Bloody hell." Sir Giles slammed his fist onto the desk. "Getting nowhere on this, Freddy. Why?"

"Well Guvnor, things are slowly getting put together. We now know Huw was probably right in his assumptions. Whatever is in that scroll I told you about, the Druids want it badly. We know Callaghan has gone to ground." He pulled out another piece of paper from the file he was carrying. "We got a break yesterday. This is an audio transcript of a conversation between Quinn and Callaghan. That drone can also listen in on mobiles." He pointed to a highlighted section. "Callaghan is apparently planning something major on the Sunday after Alban Hefin, the summer solstice. That's tomorrow. So we're looking at something major on the Sunday after, which is June 28. Next Sunday."

"Any clue what they're planning?"

"Not at this point, no sir."

"Get on it. Best brains in the outfit. Find out what's happening Sunday. Anything else?"

"We've investigated Anson Quinn and know he had a wife who died ten years ago and a son who went to University College Dublin. At this point, all Quinn seems to be doing is looking after the injured brother in Wales. We're read a label on those boxes but so far have not been able to track it to find out what was inside. Lastly, Guvnor, a Turkish police detective sent us this. Its material he found in the laptop of some men who were trailing Huw in Istanbul. Seems they stole the originals of the material he found and killed a security guard. It all confirms what we know or suspected."

Sir Giles grunted agreement.

Just then, there was an urgent knock on the door. A slim man slipped in apologizing and said simply "There's a situation sir."

"Report." Sir Giles growled.

Three more churches were attacked this morning. One in Scotland, one in Norfolk and one in Cornwall. So far, about ten dead, dozens more wounded."

Sir Giles swore vehemently.

"The Home Office would like to see you this afternoon sir. They want your input on these church attacks."

Acknowledging the request, the CSB head glared at Freddy. "Find them. Freddy. Find every one of them and destroy that nest of vipers. Especially Callaghan. Why can't we find him?"

"Bit of luck there too, sir. We were able to back track on a mobile call to the house in Neath. We've traced it to the Irish coast north of Dublin. My guess is Callaghan is returning to Ireland because we'd followed leads that placed him in North Wales and were getting close."

"Probably dumped the phone anyway," Sir Giles said gloomily. "Be careful. Don't want to step on Irish toes. But find him, Freddy. Find him. And stop whatever it is from happening on Sunday."

## Koblenz, Germany

The Bundesarchiv proved a gold mine of information about the Holy Roman Empire from the time of Charlemagne to the moment Napoleon dissolved it in 1806. But the German national archives fell exceedingly short on relic hunters and collectors. Especially anyone named Baldric in the Tyrolean Alps. For two days, from opening to closing, Huw and Stone pored over documents, letters and reports.

"Have to say the Germans live up to their reputation as meticulous," Stone said at one point as they took a break. He stretched and noticed a distracted Huw glancing over another part of the busy room. Men and women delving into various research projects dotted the room.

"Bradstone, my boy, take a picture of me in the archives will you? In fact, take a few—wide angle if possible and get as much of the room if you can," he said and placed himself at the other end of the table, smiling. Surprised, Stone nodded and pulled out his camera.

"You never want your picture taken, Huw. You're the most camera-shy person I know."

"Shut up and shoot," Huw hissed.

Stone shrugged, grateful his cell phone also had a camera on board. When he was done, nothing more was said about photos as Huw dove back into the boxes of files. At the end of the second day, he admitted defeat and said as much to one of the archive's curators. As they talked, he became intrigued with Huw's laundered version of their Austrian sojourn.

The curator listened and thought carefully, determined to help the renowned British professor. "If what you seek was indeed at a Schloss in that area, then it is possible that it was plundered by the Nazis. You say you found some Nazi artifacts there?" He and Huw continued to discuss the issue in low voices. Finally the curator took out a pen and paper and wrote a name and address down, handing the paper to Huw. "*Herr Professor*, this man might be able to help you. Klaus Dengler is a very private man but he specializes in tracking art and antiques stolen by the Nazis. He lives in Metternich, just west of Koblenz. You may use my name and tell him I suggested you call. He might be able to assist."

In their rented car, Huw used Stone's cell phone to contact Dengler and arrange a meeting later that evening. "A quick supper now is what we want, boyo," Huw said.

"Fine with me, Huw. Say, what was that nonsense with the photos back in the archives?"

Huw's demeanor changed. "At the back of the room I saw a man. I recognized his face but can't for the life of me place him. Somehow it bothered me. He was just staring at us but made no attempt to wave or acknowledge us."

Stone shrugged. "Probably met him at some conference somewhere or perhaps a profoundly unmemorable student."

At the restaurant as they were waiting for the food, Huw asked to see the shots Stone had taken. Finally, he found the face he wanted and asked Stone to zoom in and crop it. Still puzzled, he stared at the face for a while then asked Stone to email it to Crown Security. "Just in case, my boy. I'd rather be safe than dead."

At Dengler's house they were greeted by a stern looking older housekeeper who kept a stone face and spoke little as she led them into the front room. There they met a frail-looking, small, wrinkled old man bent at the waist, his lightly striped navy suit all rumpled and stained. A pair of wire glasses perched on his bulbous nose. A few strands of white hair framed his red and freckled bald head.

Their initial impressions were soon squashed. Dengler was in fact a lively, intelligent and energetic old man, hauling boxes of papers around with the ease of a twenty-year old. And, they soon found, he was indeed an expert on Nazi treasure troves.

More importantly, from Huw's perspective, Dengler was deeply interested in the Nazi fascination with the occult particularly, as it turned out, the Lance. "Of course the one in Vienna is a fake. There's no provenance whatsoever for it except the word of Heinrich Himmler and he was not the most reliable of individuals," Dengler chuckled.

Their evening was enjoyable as well as instructive. They pored over more documents and reports, mostly German, about the incredibly organized and systematic looting of Europe's treasures in the occupied nations or owned by Jewish families.

After hearing Huw's sanitized version of their search, Dengler finally pulled a box towards Huw. "These are American army reports about items seized and removed from Schloss Fischorn and Schloss Finsternis as well as some other locations in and around Zell am See. Fischorn is where they captured Goering. See if there's anything in there."

This time it was Huw who turned up the critical item. He read a piece of paper, whistled, and re-read it, shaking his head and muttering "Duw Duw" as he did.

"What?" Stone leaned towards him. "You've got something?"

Huw pushed the paper towards him. Stone scanned it rapidly. It was a military report of a search of Finsternis. There were clear references to a "collection of Count Baldric" sent to the American Sector's headquarters in Salzburg. Stone whistled too when he read the inventory of items sent to Salzburg. "A silver tube".

Before Stone could utter a word, he noticed a frowning shake of the head from Huw. He resisted the questions, comments and excitement bubbling up inside of him and forced himself to remain silent.

Huw casually turned to Dengler. "Tell me, Herr Dengler, do you have any more information about shipments of items sent from Zell to Salzburg?"

"Ach, my friend, you have found something that helps your search perhaps." Dengler's eyes twinkled with happiness that he'd pleased his esteemed visitors.

No flies on Dengler, Stone thought, as the man scurried off to find more files. Huw and Stone remained silent, barely able to contain their excitement. When Dengler returned he handed them a brown folder marked US Zone Command, Salzburg. As they flipped through the pages, Huw's shook his head with disappointment. Most of the items listed in the inventory were included in a series shipment back to the United States by the 202nd Engineering and Transport Company. There was no mention of a silver tube.

More files and folders proved unhelpful until finally, with thanks and a last glass of red wine, Huw and Stone thanked their host profusely. He smiled and handed them a piece of paper. "It is what you want, yes? A copy of the inventory?"

Back at their hotel Huw and Stone eagerly surveyed the inventory and report once again. "It's got to be the scroll, Bradstone. No other explanation. It says Count Baldric's collection, so it must have been in the castle as part of the décor for nearly five hundred years. The American army took it—probably their Monuments and Fine Arts section—and sent it to their command headquarters."

"And they in turn sent it all back to the States," Stone added glumly. "Where it might be in the Smithsonian archives or even an old warehouse somewhere just languishing." He thought for a moment. "Let me see if I can reach Chad. He may be able to track something down from his end.

The next morning, during a hearty British breakfast in a sparsely filled Irish pub near their hotel, Stone reported he'd finally made phone contact with Chad after more than an hour of frustration. They agreed another visit to Dengler's house was in order. As the final slices of toast were sliding down, Stone suddenly jerked up as he heard Klaus Dengler's name on the pub's TV.

He watched in horror as a reporter stood outside Dengler's house. Stone's less than fluent German was good enough to understand that Dengler and his housekeeper had been brutally murdered in the night. Breathlessly the reporter noted that police were actively seeking two persons of interest seen entering the house the previous evening. Questioned by the eager reporter, a police spokesman said a passerby saw an older white haired man and a tall younger man exiting the house close to midnight. Police were seeking the pair for questioning. He also confirmed police were also following up leads that Dengler's interest in Nazi treasures might be a motive since so many boxes and files on the subject were found littered around the room where Dengler's body was found.

Stone grabbed Huw firmly by the arm, threw some Euros on the table to pay for the meal, and hustled the professor outside as quickly but unobtrusively as he could. They hurried across the pedestrianized plaza while Stone explained. Huw's face turned white. "We must go to the police immediately. Tell them what we know."

"We can't Huw. We're the last ones to see Dengler alive other than the killer. They won't believe us. We're travelling on false passports and we're up to our necks in that business in Austria which they're sure to find out about. No, we've got to get away."

"We'll tell them to call Sir Giles at Crown Security. That will clear us."

"Sorry Huw. I'm as law abiding as the next man, but it doesn't work that way. We'll be taken in and interrogated. All Sir Giles can do is ensure that we get proper representation at the consular level. At least he will for you. I'm American, so he won't even be able to provide that for me."

He hustled Huw into the front seat and pulled out into the flow of traffic. "Even if we are eventually cleared, it will mean weeks, maybe even months where we are locked up in a German prison with no bail. Weeks or months when the Druids are free to wreak their havoc; weeks or months when they're free to search for the scroll. You can bet if they're so close behind us they know where we were last night, they'll also find out what we found out. If they didn't already steal that list from Dengler's house."

He grimly drove as quickly as he could out of the city until he hit the autobahn. "Where are you going," Huw asked quietly.

"Don't know really. We've got to get back to the UK as quickly as possible but I don't know how, yet. So I'm heading west towards the Channel."

As he drove at a steady 120 kilometers per hour, he frequently glanced into the rearview to see if any police cars were following them. Who knew, he thought, maybe the passerby also noted the car license. He stared at the road ahead, his mind whirling in confusion, horror and fear.

Stone kept up with traffic, staying primarily in the middle lane as they passed long convoys of trucks heading towards the Channel ports like Ostend, Dunkerque and Antwerp. Even though they'd crossed into Belgium he maintained a wary watch for police.

The shock was only now beginning to settle in. Stone mentally ran through the events of the past few days. The swelling around his eye had gone, replaced by a sickly yellow green bruise. Other assorted bruises across his body still ached. He had no doubt it was the Druids who'd killed Dengler, but he was puzzled as to how quickly they'd found them in Koblenz and how swiftly they'd struck.

As they skirted the southern suburbs of Antwerp, Stone glanced over at Huw who sat slumped quietly in the front seat, eyes closed.

"You okay, Huw?"

"Be quiet boy! I am doing what I have failed miserably to do all along. And what you too should be doing, Bradstone. For we need this now more than we ever have before."

"And what's that?"

"Prayer my boy, prayer. I am praying for wisdom for us both, praying for all those who've been hurt or killed because I insisted on forcing this hunt. I am praying for Mandy and her needs and concerns. I am praying for you as always. But most of all I am praying for myself; for forgiveness." He turned a quizzical eye towards Stone. "You might try the same."

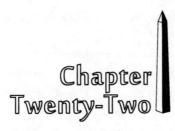

# Chapter Twenty-Two

**Greyfell Abbey**

Colin Maddox had undergone a massive tutorial in Celtic myths and legends the past few days, particularly as they related to the *Sidhe*. He and Lord Greyfell pulled out books and files and sifted through all the material and stories seeking to separate myth from fact.

The skeptical Colin slowly found himself immersed in the topic and faced with the uncomfortable acknowledgement that there was indeed factual evidence indicating strange and unexplained events and situations from unassailable witnesses.

"If this man is indeed one of these beings, what does his relationship with Callaghan mean? And how can he and Callaghan be stopped?"

Before Greyfell could respond, Nees entered the room and handed Colin a phone. He answered, listened and then quietly slumped back in the couch still gripping the phone. "They've attacked again. Three churches spread across Britain." He straightened up and leaned forward, eyes moving from Lord Greyfell to Nees and back again.

"Apparently they're planning something for the Sunday after Alban Hefin. That's next Sunday. We have no idea what but, as Freddy just said, it has to be bigger than the church attacks so far."

Greyfell knotted his brows, deep in thought. "Obviously Callaghan wants to make a huge statement, bigger than he has to this point. He will want it to be spectacular and yet....our reading of Callaghan all along is that he is much more thuggish and direct than Rhiannon or Wyndham ever were. Isn't that right, Nees?

"Yes. Rhiannon was much more subtle. And Wyndham reached well beyond the norm for his impact."

"Nothing subtle about an attack on the Queen and government during the State Opening of Parliament," Colin said.

"No. But think about the methodology involved. What happened last November was a grandstand play by Wyndham with the aim of seizing power. Callaghan doesn't think that big so therefore doesn't need such a sophisticated plan. No, he wants to make a major statement—a bloody one—and shock a lot of people. Other than that…" Greyfell shrugged. He turned to his wife. "Nees, dear, would you fire up the laptops and let's do some poking around."

He quickly assigned Nees to troll Druid websites—which, he told Colin, she'd learned to hack—while he too surveyed Druid sites for information on planned Alban Hefin activities to see if there were any hints or clues he could follow. "Colin, if you wouldn't mind, contact Sir Giles and ask him to send up copies of any photos or information he has. I want to see the hard copy, not just rely on a verbal or email synopsis. We might catch something that others don't."

An hour later they took a break for lunch. Greyfell returned to the subject of Alban Hefin. "Most people today might not know the name of the holiday, but they'll know that Druids and quasi-Druids gather at Stonehenge to see the first light come over the 'hele stone' on that day. You'll see news clips of it on the BBC tomorrow, no doubt, because that's Alban Hefin."

He sipped some tea. "It's supposed to be a celebration of joy and welcoming of summer. But it also has a darker side. Like Samhein it's a time that the fabric between our world and the underworld is thin. It is a time when people pass between the worlds."

As he ate the casual meal and spoke, Greyfell still searched the internet. Frustrated, he leaned back and said, as much to himself as the others in the room, "Maybe we're looking for the wrong information in the wrong place."

Twenty minutes later he slapped his hand to his head. "Yes, of course! That must be it."

Colin and Nees both leaned over to see what he was looking at. It was the Times of London news site. "See here? The Archbishop of Canterbury and the Catholic Archbishop of Westminster are gathering for an outdoor service following their week long joint synod; the first such meeting since the church split in the Tudor era."

"So what?" Colin's blunt response startled Greyfell. He studied the field agent's face but found no belligerence, only a puzzled look.

"We know that Callaghan wants to make a big statement. We believe he prefers blunt, straightforward measures as opposed to sophisticated or subtle means to achieve his goals.

He has mounted attacks against various churches of different denominations the past month, but we know he's planning a 'big' operation. What could be bigger and yet less blunt than an attack against the leaders of the two major churches in Britain in the heart of London?"

"It's a guess. We have no proof; not even a hint that this is what he's organizing."

"Absolutely true. And I am not suggesting for one second that we should stop looking in other directions. But this would seem to fit the bill. The Queen will be out of the country on a State Visit, the House of Commons is taking a break and the Prime Minister is heading for a NATO conference on Wednesday. So there are no 'big' targets. No. If he's going to make a mark, this would seem to fit."

Nees and Colin continued to debate the possibilities with Greyfell until Colin reluctantly agreed to call Sir Giles and float the idea past him. "Even if this is his plan, I don't see how we can fully protect against it. The service is in Hyde Park so stepping up security to the nth degree will be difficult if not impossible. And against what? A lone assassin; a full out frontal attack by armed squads of Druids; A bomb?" The questions were still ringing in his head as he dialed London.

"This is it. I am positive that this is the target," Greyfell muttered softly to his wife. "It fits."

### Crown Security Offices, London

"Huw, Stone, how very good to see you safe and sound!" Sir Giles bounded to his feet and rushed to grasp each of them firmly and welcomingly in his hands, as they were ushered into his office by Freddy. "Fill me in." He waved them to his comfortable leather couch and pulled up a chair in front of them, preferring it to sitting behind the desk. Freddy perched on the corner of the Guvnor's desk, notepad and some files in hand.

"You tell stories better than I do, Bradstone. I don't want to inadvertently turn this into one of my lectures. Besides I'm still shaking a bit."

Stone nodded. He himself was still shaking, unnerved by the suddenness of the murders and their escape from Koblenz. It was still a bit of a dream—make that nightmare—that he could not shake. Nor could he shake the feeling that somehow he and Huw had been responsible for Dengler's murder by leading the Druids to him. Stone had no doubt as to the identity of the killers even if he had no proof. He waited a few moments, collecting his thoughts. How do you recount the past thirty six hours and explain the gut-wrenching, sweat-inducing fear of driving for your life through foreign nations not knowing if the car ahead, behind or beside was an unmarked police vehicle or, worse, killer Druids.

Quietly he began to walk his listeners through the tension-filled day and night. He described their run down the autobahns of Germany and into Belgium, skirting towns and hoping against hope that their license plate had not been reported. Finally, just outside Brussels he'd stopped at the small town of Halle. There they'd parked the rental on a side street, quickly walked to the center of town and hailed a cab. Then a quick trip to Halle's railway station and a train to the heart of Brussels. The short trip was over before they'd barely had time to sit down and breathe.

"Originally, I'd thought about heading for the ferry ports but I realized that would mean hours on the crossing. So I headed to Brussels instead, figuring we could catch the Eurostar to London. I was hoping that the manhunt still centered on the Koblenz area. If so, they wouldn't think of Brussels immediately." From there, he pointed out, it had been fairly easy: no problems with passport control, a quick call from St. Pancras station when they arrived in London and half an hour later they were ushered into the great man's office.

"Good. Wise move. Police likely had no idea you would head for Britain. Tell me more about Austria."

Sir Giles listened patiently while Stone talked, interrupting occasionally to clarify a point. "But if those neo-Nazis took you captive how did the Druids find you? And how did they know you were in Koblenz?"

"Questions we've been asking ourselves constantly," Huw agreed.

"Did you get those photos we sent from the Archives in Koblenz?"

"I still don't know how or why the neo-Nazis got involved in the first place," Stone muttered.

"Ah," Freddy responded. "Brenda did some checking on that. Apparently the Schloss is used as their covert meeting spot. They tracked you on your first visit and then found out you were connected to British intelligence. They thought you were investigating them and were going to scare you off."

Freddy then leaned forward and pulled something from his ever-present folder. "Is this the man you were wondering about?" He showed Huw an enlargement of the face behind Huw in the Koblenz archives. "What made you take this picture?" he asked softly.

Huw studied the print. "Yes that's the one." He paused for a moment. "I don't know why I insisted on the photo really. It's just that I think I have seen that face before but can't recall where or when."

Stone examined the picture. "Can't say I've ever seen him or know who he is. But he must be some kind of chameleon."

"Oh, we know who he is alright." Freddy surprised everyone in the room. He handed a copy of the picture to his guvnor. "His name is Norris Quinn. His father is Anson Quinn, currently serving Diarmuid Callaghan. More importantly, his grandfather Mick O'Flaherty was one of the leading IRA terrorists until he was killed."

"Plot grows murkier and murkier," growled Sir Giles. He stood up and moved to the bookshelf, running his fingers lovingly down the spine of a Winston Churchill book. "What's the connection?"

"More than we might want, Sir Giles." Freddy removed another piece from his folder. "Our friend at MI6 sent this over." He handed copies to everyone. "Quinn the younger was thought to have dropped off the map, but a little more elaborate and deeper digging reveals he's been a bit of a naughty boy. He's been working with the so-called Real IRA, nasty mob who've refused to abide by the peace agreement and has been involved in a number of terrorist acts trying to start The Troubles all over again. Call themselves the 'New" IRA now."

"Nasty inhuman bastards." Sir Giles swore. "Michael McKevitt's their leader. Murderous filth. Involved in extortion, drugs and god knows what other criminal activity to fund their actions."

"Just so. But it seems that Norris Quinn has been a bridge between the Druids and the Real IRA. Some of the people who joined the Breton wing of the Druids were trained by McKevitt's people, including Quinn," Freddy added. "Remember, the French group was rightly considered the thugs of the Druid movement, so it makes sense that the more radical and violent of the Irish Druids were over there."

Sir Giles snorted. "If not deliberately sent by Callaghan. Never did believe he was into all the cultural and nicey-nicey nonsense."

Silence enveloped the room as each studied the photo and information.

"Track this man down Freddy. Imperative. Take him in." Sir Giles turned to Huw and Stone. "Might as well be aware. More churches attacked last week and there's an attack planned for this Sunday as well. Supposed to be something called Alban Heflin. Summer solstice. Big event in their calendar." His shoulders dropped in frustration. "Greyfell believes it will be an attack on the Archbishop of Canterbury at the open air service. Hyde Park. Sunday."

He sat down and faced Stone and Huw again. "Need your help again. Anything you can think of. Any clues you might have. Let us know. Work with Greyfell on it."

Sir Giles thanked them again and gestured to Freddy to escort them out. As they reached the door, Stone suddenly turned.

"One favor, Sir Giles. Could you contact Chad Lawson's group in the States and get him looking for something? It's important and relates to the scroll we're looking for."

At a nod from Sir Giles, Freddy moved them into the other room while Stone explained that Dengler had given them the US Army inventory. "We need to find out if this inventory shows up in army files in Washington and, if possible, how these various items were disposed of. Particularly the silver tube."

"You think that's the scroll, don't you?"

Stone nodded.

"Quid pro quo, Stone. Huw, you get up to Greyfell and do some research. Get Mandy to help you if she will. Stone I need you to stick around London and use your journalistic skills to help us stop Sunday's attack."

"Why not just cancel the service at Hyde Park?"

"Tried that. Sir Giles spent hours with the Archbishop and his people yesterday trying to persuade them. They will not back down from terrorist threats. Direct quote from the man himself. Plus, as he pointed out, we have no proof, just speculation."

"I'll do what I can. But I sure hope Lord Greyfell is wrong about this."

"So do I, Stone. So do I."

### County Meath, Ireland

Callaghan sat back with a relaxed smile on his face. The latest phone call sent shivers of anticipation throughout his body. They were close. He could feel it. The weeks of loneliness and isolation had begun to play on his nerves. Apart from those who cooked and cleaned for him and moved him from place to place when necessary, he interacted with nobody. His rigid self-imposed exile meant he talked to nobody except via the briefest phone conversations. He spoke to no one unless absolutely necessary, and kept his deepest hopes and fears deep within himself. Nobody visited him. Except the old man, of course. He shuddered.

But it didn't matter. Now they were on to something. Now there was a solid lead. The scroll would be his and with it the key to finding the Lance. Spear of Destiny, indeed, he thought as he rolled the name around in his mind. My destiny.

He reached for his mobile and thumbed a number. Within minutes he'd outlined his needs and shared the information he'd received, nodding and responding occasionally as his listener on the other end ran over the plan and requirements.

"Make it clear to him if you can reach him. As the Dragon Master, I am commanding this. Make no mistake. If you can't contact him then I expect you as his second in command to obey. As soon as you have something definitive, let me know. I will come over immediately."

He disconnected and sat back with a satisfied smile. It was the longest call he'd made in almost two months. But, with any luck, it wouldn't matter if they tracked him. He wouldn't be there.

He walked outside in the early morning rain, uncaring about the drizzle that ran down his face and neck, under his shirt. He stood in the small grove of stones he'd constructed and raised his face and arms to the sky, giving thanks to the gods of the underworld for their favor and offering them a blood sacrifice and calling for the destruction of all who opposed him.

### Hereford, England

Nigel's phone call was a surprise. Even more surprising was his suggestion that she join him in London where he had unearthed vital information regarding Baldric and the scroll. He refused to say more on the phone, but the excitement in his voice was palpable. "It's best that you see this information in person. I don't want to scan it and email in. You have to see it for yourself." With assurances that he would meet her at noon tomorrow at Paddington Station, he rang off.

Mandy gathered her files together neatly on the desk. She put a few files and books into her laptop case, remembering suddenly to add the phone charger, and bustled around making sure she had everything. She thought about calling someone and letting them know her plans but paused. The only one who needed to know really, was her father and she didn't know how to contact him. Crown Security and Greyfell Abbey would not be interested and there was time enough to let them in on it if, indeed, Nigel had really found something crucial. Anyway, she reasoned, it was Friday and who cared what she did on her weekends.

She turned the office light off and locked the door. If she hurried she could catch a train to Birmingham and then down to London Euston. There would not be a direct train to Paddington until tomorrow. After a short stop to pack a small suitcase and call a taxi, she was ready. On the way to the station she called her favorite London hotel and reserved a room. She would wait until morning before contacting Nigel and arranging to meet.

Despite her outward business-like actions, Mandy was worried about her Da and Stone. Her meeting with Nigel, she decided, would be strictly business; no long luxurious lunches in the latest out of the way 'cool' restaurant. And, when she was finished looking at whatever Nigel had, she'd go over to the Crown Security offices and see what news they had.

At the ornate red-brick station she purchased her ticket, stopped at the small café and purchased a tea and walked across the bridge to her platform. Satisfied with her plans, she sat on the bench, started in on her tea and instinctively pulled out a book to read as she waited for the train. It was only then she realized that while she had her phone charger, she'd left the phone itself on the kitchen counter. Oh well, she consoled herself, I'll be back tomorrow and I can use the hotel phone to call Nigel tomorrow.

### Vale of Neath, Wales

The pain increased daily. Phantom pain, the doctors had told Diarmuid because his brother's injuries meant that he couldn't really feel pain. Live in my body, Declan silently sneered at them when Diarmuid reported their comments. Then you'll know that it's real pain, not phantom and most certainly not a figment of his imagination. One doctor had prescribed a powerful drug Zemuron, normally used as a neuromuscular blocker in surgery or for those needing mechanical breathing. It totally blocked the pain most days and, in normal people, created a form of temporary muscular paralysis. Their minds were fully operational but their body was incapable of movement and feeling. For Declan it provided a blessed time of relief. The doctor left instructions on how to use it, with warnings about addiction. Declan had laughed at that; the possibility of addiction was the least of his problems.

Today was particularly awful. His legs felt like they were on fire. His back ached to the point that he just wanted to cut his body in half and discard the remainder. And now his lungs were searing in agony as he took even simple breaths, let alone trying to talk to the sullen Quinn who served as his babysitter and guard. He guided his chair down the slight ramp into the kitchen.

"Have you heard from Diarmuid yet? Do you know where he is?"

Quinn looked up from the stove where he was warming some soup. He shook his head then turned again to the saucepan of soup.

Declan took a deep painful breath and rasped. "Quinn. I asked you a question. Have the decency to answer."

A black look came over Quinn as he turned to face his charge. He snarled his response. "If I hear anything I will tell you."

Declan handed him a list. "I need some things. Please get them for me."

Quinn looked it over, raising an eyebrow quizzically. "Dart gun? Target?"

"I'm bored. I thought I would try seeing if I could shoot again, but don't want to use a real gun. Get them for me."

Declan wheeled his electric chair around and purred back up the ramp, through the hall and back into his bedroom which had become a sanctuary of sorts away from the churlish Quinn. Ever since they'd left Wicklow and moved here he'd sensed a blackness about the house. He didn't understand, because the house itself was warm and inviting, located on the side of a lovely forested mountain overlooking a picturesque valley. And the few Welsh people he'd been in contact with were friendly and compassionate. Yet the house oozed malevolence and darkness that he could not fathom. He'd prayed to the gods for understanding, pleading with them to show their power and wisdom. But even as he did, he felt the weight of evil press on his already damaged body. He knew deep in his heart, but could not prove, that Diarmuid was responsible for the attacks on churches across Britain. Tears streaked his face as he thought of the dead and maimed—perhaps some even wounded like him—all because of the blood lust for power.

If his body had the strength and his voice the power, he would speak out against the murderous activities of his fellow Druids. He wanted people to know that Druids worshipped the earth and nature and reveled in poetry, music and oral histories. He hated the violence that was now being associated with the Druids and he was appalled at the darkness that had enveloped his beloved brother.

He wheeled his chair to the open window. A fresh warm breeze wafted into the room. He heard voices outside and struggled to get closer to the window. All he could see was the top half an unmarked white Transit panel van on the driveway. He heard at least two people speaking quietly and they were obviously loading it. Then he heard Quinn's cold Irish brogue warn the driver to be careful with the load because it was packing a powerful message. After an assurance that they indeed knew exactly where and when to deliver the load, Declan heard the van doors slam and saw it drive slowly off.

It was odd, he thought, that the van was taking something bulky and valuable away from the house since most deliveries were materials and supplies coming in. He heard the phone ring and quickly wheeled the chair out into the hall where he could listen.

"Yes Dragon Master, they just left with the material for Norris," Quinn was speaking quietly into the phone. "I'll join him on Saturday and make sure everything's in order. I've got a nurse coming up from Neath to take care of Declan." The conversation continued for several minutes, then Quinn hung up and went towards the kitchen.

Declan, hidden in the hall shadows, sighed. Tears trickled down his cheeks as he turned the chair around and wheeled back into his room. The feeling of estrangement from Diarmuid was strong and he sensed the darkness creeping over his soul. Without Diarmuid, there was little of life left for him, but his beloved brother seemed indeed to have deserted him and become absorbed by the all-consuming desire for power and revenge. He shut the door quietly.

Whatever it was Diarmuid was doing and planning so surreptitiously was wrong. Of that he had no doubt now and he was sickened that his brother so gleefully embraced the black side of the spiritual world.

He sat in his chair motionless. Tears still flowed. He was frustrated and felt powerless. Given his pathetic condition, until now all could he do to save his brother from himself was plead with the gods; gods who did not hear or care.

But he had to stop Diarmuid. He had to. He just didn't know how.

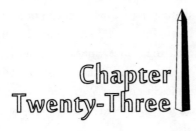

# Chapter Twenty-Three

**Crown Security Offices, London**

Crowds of shoppers and tourists flooded the buses and tube in the capital. The trip from Waterloo towards the Palace was slow. The Jubilee Line from Waterloo to Westminster was not operating for the interminable weekend upgrades and maintenance. The double decker on the 211 route was jammed but Sir Giles found a seat at the back of the rear top deck. Predictably, the bus sailed across Westminster Bridge then crawled in heavy traffic around Parliament Square and down Victoria Street. Normally he didn't come in on Saturday mornings, but this was no normal situation. He'd demanded that all hands appear at the office that day; in fact several had already been there all night, consumed with the mission of preventing an attack.

When the dam began to break, it cracked in several places.

First up was a call from Huw at Greyfell Abbey. He was panicked because he couldn't find Mandy anywhere. Her phone at both the university and her flat went unanswered and colleagues at the university could not recall seeing her past Friday afternoon. Nor was she answering her mobile. The other reason for his alarm was quickly explained to Freddy. "That man who was in Koblenz at the archives. He was at the university teaching with Mandy; working for her." His normal professorial voice was shaky and rose in pitch as he tried to explain. "She'd hired him as an assistant at the university's insistence and brought his resume to show me when I was here at Greyfell. His photo was attached to the resume. It was obvious she was also developing feelings for him. Mandy left the whole file here when she returned to Hereford. She knew him as Nigel Pitt, but it's the same man all right; Norris Quinn."

As he tried to calm Huw down with reassurances that Crown Security would do everything it could, he managed to scribble a note to one of his assistants with Nigel Pitt's name scrawled on it and an order to check UK Border Control for either Nigel Pitt or Norris Quinn travelling between Britain and Koblenz. Once off the phone, and after a quick update with the guvnor, he also spread word through Scotland Yard and MI5 who were running the church attack investigation, that Pitt/Quinn should be brought in for questioning. He asked Huw to scan the resume into an email and fire it to London as soon as possible.

Freddy called Stone on a newly-provided mobile. After teasing him briefly about the number of mobiles he'd gone through in the space of several weeks, he got serious. "We've identified Norris Quinn's alias and I'm afraid it's not good news. He was masquerading as a teaching assistant for Mandy at the University. Worse, none of us can contact Mandy. Can you come here as soon as possible?" He assured Stone there was no need to go to Hereford, that a CSB agent was already en route. Further, police and security agencies were already looking for Quinn and trying to track his movements to and from Germany.

Ten minutes later, as he waited for Stone's arrival and juggled phone calls to and from various contacts and agencies, he got another call, this time from the United States.

"Chad. You have news?"

"Absolutely. Is Huw or Stone available?" Freddy rapidly filled him in on the events of the day and then noticed Stone enter the offices. He waved him over and handed him the phone, letting him know who was calling.

"You've got something on the Schloss inventory?"

"Sure have buddy. According to the records, all that material is right here in the good ol' US of A!"

Stone whistled and signaled for someone to hand him a pen and paper. "Shoot."

"Three crate loads of material, including all the stuff on your inventory, was shipped in January 1946 from Salzburg to Frankfurt and then by air to Camp Ellis in Illinois, near Bernadotte. It was handled by the Army's 728 Quartermaster Salvage Collection Company and kept at Camp Ellis until the Camp was decommissioned in 1949. Interestingly, Camp Ellis was also a POW camp. The whole shipment was apparently under the guard of the 581 Military Police Escort Guard Company, but never opened and never looked at.

"When the Camp was closed as an active base and turned over to the Illinois National Guard, all the crates of that and other shipments were sent to a large government owned warehouse on the banks of the Mississippi in Quincy, Illinois."

"Nobody opened the crates? Nobody inspected the contents?"

"Apparently not. Reports say there was so much stuff coming in from Europe including stolen artworks, libraries, paintings, archive materials and so on, it was overwhelming. The powers that be decided all the material should be distributed around the country for various universities and museums to collate and catalogue. Your shipment was designated for the University of Illinois, but so far as I can tell, the university has never bothered to check it out."

They spoke for several more minutes, with both of them bringing the other up to date on their activities. Finally Stone explained about Mandy's situation. "I've got to go and see what's happening there, Chad, but could you do me a favor and somehow get permission to get into that warehouse and see if those crates are still intact. If they are, can you search for that silver tube it mentions? We think that's what the Druids are after. I'll fill you in on it later, but it's really important."

"Already on it Stone. Tyler is still a little woozy from his injuries and taking time off, but I got him to call the President and get an official order to let me into the warehouse. I should have it soon. If there's tube there I'll find it." After assurances that Stone would call and fill him in that evening British time, they hung up.

Stone looked at Freddy. "You heard?"

Freddy nodded. "I'll call Greyfell. Huw will be pleased and it might help take his mind off Mandy. But in the meantime, we've got to find Quinn and Mandy and also figure out how and who will attack tomorrow."

"And where," Stone added. "There's no hint that it really will be at the open air service. That's just speculation on Lord Greyfell's part."

"Yes. But right now it's all we've got. You know, in a way, Greyfell is right. It does make sense; spectacular enough to make a statement. My money is on a bomb of some kind, after all, that was the IRA's trademark so police and special branch are combing the entire area and will keep doing so until the service is over."

Freddy handed Stone a folder. "These are the transcripts of the latest phone taps made by the drone. I haven't had a chance to go over them yet, but perhaps you could look at them first. See if there's anything useful."

Stone took the transcripts to a free desk and sat down. His mind was whirling at warp speed; worried about Mandy, worried about what tomorrow would bring, worried about the search for the scroll. Everything was crashing in on him at once on top of the stress and trauma he'd experienced the past couple of months.

He looked at the first page and saw only lines of text. He took a deep breath and tried to read it, but his concentration flitted from one thing to another. He took another deep breath and suddenly remembered something Huw had said to him in the car while they were fleeing Koblenz. After admonishing Stone to pray, Huw had added, "and I don't mean meaningless babble to an unknown person. Prayer is a conversation with a real and living person who loves you. God is not Santa Claus, so don't give him your list of wants. Talk to him. Plainly. Simply. Express your fears, your hopes, your issues. Think. Make your prayers solid so that they have power and strength. How would you ask your boss to let you cover your dream assignment, Bradstone? Would you stutter and stammer, repeating your request over and over and sounding like a little child? No. You would do it with strength and confidence, with respect for who your boss is. That's the kind of prayer you need. But always with a spirit of faith and obedience."

As Stone replayed the conversation he remembered trying to do exactly what Huw suggested. He remembered a calm settling over him. It was soon after that he changed his mind and chose Eurostar over the ferry.

He kept his eyes open, staring at the paper in front of him but mentally began to think and pray, silently but with strength. He rejected the childish phrasing he'd heard in too many of the American churches he'd attended since last fall. Instead he concentrated on clear and simple expressions of his thoughts and worries. Not much point telling God about Mandy and the scroll, he thought. He already knows. I need wisdom and strength to continue. For everyone's sake.

His quick prayer over, he returned to the folder and became engrossed in its contents. Dimly he heard a phone ring in the background as he read and re-read one line and then a second line. He signaled to Freddy who came running up.

"We've got to find Quinn. He's the key to this whole thing. Look at this conversation here. Callaghan and Anson Quinn are talking about tomorrow. Quinn confirms that everything is in place and he has sent material to Norris.

My guess it's the equipment for the attack. If we find him we can stop whatever is planned."

Freddy smiled briefly. "We're doing everything we can, but I can pull some people off other assignments and make Quinn the focus. I think you're right. Find him, find the key."

"Here's another thing," Stone said, pointing to a spot on the resume. "He says he was born in Ravenscar, Yorkshire. That's a clue right there that the whole thing was fake. There is no town called Ravenscar."

Freddy looked at him quizzically.

"I did a travel piece on the place a couple of years ago. Ravenscar was a grand visionary seaside resort community planned by a Victorian fraudster who diddled hundreds of people out of their money to finance the development. Trouble is, it sits high on a cliff overlooking the North Sea with no way to get down to the beach. And even if people did, the beach was covered with massive rocks and boulders and no sand. Today it's a forlorn abandoned spot with only a few barren grass and weed overgrown roads going from nowhere to nowhere on top of the cliff. It's isolated with only a few houses. I've been there. Ravenscar never existed."

They were still pouring over other transcripts when Stone heard a woman's voice suddenly shout at the top of her voice, "Yes!"

Both men turned and saw a tall, striking blonde rushing towards them. "Got him sir. Nigel Pitt left London Gatwick on Monday for Vienna on easyJet flight 5351 arriving around noon. He left Vienna on Wednesday morning on Austrian Airlines flight 129 for Frankfurt. Then yesterday he left Frankfurt on Swiss flight 1069 to Zurich and from Zurich to London City airport on Swiss 466. He's in London."

"Yes, but where in London?"

"Security cameras at the airport would show him leaving in either a car or a cab," she answered quickly. "My guess is a cab. If we can track the cab, the driver might be able to tell us where he dropped him. But we've got his photo so why not also check all the major railway stations and airports to see if we've got him on visuals somewhere."

Freddy's brusque "do it" was followed by a request that someone check with Brenda back in Vienna, to see if she could track their man from Monday to Wednesday. Stone considered and remarked that no doubt she'd find Quinn had visited the museum and investigated Die Heilige Lanze.

Stone marveled at the certainty the British had that they could follow Norris from one spot to another across the city thanks to the omnipresent and all-seeing surveillance cameras. They'd tracked the July 7 terrorist bombers that way back in 2005 and the cameras were even more universal and powerful now with over six million cameras in use by both government agencies and private organizations.

As the blonde scurried away, Stone asked if the same level of surveillance was maintained across the country. Assured that there was indeed a high level, especially at event locations or on major transportation routes, Stone casually suggested that they try to track Mandy from Hereford the same way. Freddy grinned and charged off to assign the task.

Stone slumped back in his seat. The worry was still present. The fear and uncertainty gnawed at his gut. He heard Huw's voice in his mind: "prayer, my boy. Prayer." He shook his head in wonder as he thought of Huw's steadfast beliefs even in the face of the unbelievable.

"I don't know how you do it Huw," he muttered to himself. "I am not strong enough and not worthy enough. I wish I was."

### Paddington Station, London

Nigel waved when he saw her. He was standing by a retail and café area euphemistically known as 'The Lawn'. She smiled as he hugged her and gave her a kiss.

"I expected you on the train from Hereford, but you weren't on it."

"I arrived at Euston last night. I went via Birmingham because I wanted to be nice and fresh today for when you show me this wonderful breakthrough, not worn out by train travel." She grinned at him. "So, here I am. Show me."

He smiled back and took her elbow and began leading her down the concourse towards the eastern end of the station. "Ah yes. Well we have to go somewhere first."

Puzzled, she looked at him. "Where Nige? Can't you tell me as we go and then show me?"

"No. I want to see your face when we get there." He shushed further conversation and together they walked the width of the station and took the lifts one floor up and onto the taxi rank. They lined up briefly as luggage-laden passengers struggled and pulled their bags inch by inch to the front of the rank. Once inside the cab, she was bewildered when he ordered the cab to take them to the Grosvenor Hotel.

"Look you, don't be taking me for a fancy lunch before you show me what you found. I couldn't possibly wait that long."

Nigel laughed and promised no lunch, just business. Less than ten minutes later they pulled up at the hotel's entrance. Hopping out, Nigel handed the cabbie a ten pound note and led her inside. They entered the ornate marble-filled and maroon carpeted foyer with its magnificent grand staircase at the end. Without hesitating, he was leading her towards the lift when the concierge stepped forward. "The material for your presentation has arrived sir. I've had it placed in your suite." A quick thank you and another twenty pound note followed.

As they rode up to the top floor, Mandy asked "What presentation Nigel? Who are you making a presentation to and what's it got to do with Baldric and our problem?"

"All will be revealed," was the enigmatic answer as they exited the lift and walked down the classically simple yet lavish hallway. He opened the door into the suite and swept Mandy in. From the suite's white marble foyer she looked into the lushly decorated room with its warm burgundy carpet and highly polished cherry furnishings. Floor to ceiling burgundy drapes and white sheers were tied to each side and she could see the open spaces of Hyde Park across busy Park Lane. An open side door led into a bedroom with its neatly perfectly made bed peeking out. Against one wall were two long boxes and three smaller crates.

She looked questioningly at Nigel who stared back at her. This time there was no warm smile on his face. A hard look came across him as he led her to a chair. Before she could react, he pulled her hand tight against the arm of the chair and pulled a pair of handcuffs out of his pocket and clapped them against the arm. Mandy screamed and began using her other arm to beat him, her legs kicking out at him.

"What'd are you doing Nigel, What's going on?" she shouted.

He deftly avoided her kicks, swept around behind the chair and nimbly caught her other hand, pulled it to the arm and used a second cuff to secure her. She struggled and bounced in the chair and almost tipped it over. Quickly he fished behind the small ornate love seat and pulled out a thick rope. As he tied her feet securely to the chair he glanced up at her.

"You might as well stop, you know. This floor is empty with no other guests. An eccentric artist—me—booked all the other rooms just to be sure. No one will hear all your screaming and banging." Calmly he went into the bathroom and came out with a hypodermic needle. His powerful arm held her right arm tight and he kneeled on her lap to keep her from bouncing the chair while he administered the injection. "This will calm you down, but enable you to hear and understand. You'll also be able to talk. But your arms and legs will be numb and immobile."

Tears coursed down her cheeks. "Who are you, Nigel. You're not the man I thought you were. I thought you loved me. I thought you were helping me."

He sneered. "So foolish. A few sweet words and a few minuscule efforts, and your feminine heart turns to jelly."

He walked over to the large window and picked up a pair of binoculars, focusing them on the frenzied efforts across the road as final preparations continued on the huge outdoor platform they were building for the service of reconciliation the next day.

Ignoring a still struggling Mandy, he grabbed a utility knife from the fireplace mantle, stepped over to the boxes and began ripping them open. Gently, he placed each item on the floor as he removed it from the larger boxes. In short order he'd assembled a large tube like object with an eye piece on top and a metal tripod stand.

Mandy was horrified as she realized what it was and saw the shorter missiles coming out of the smaller crates. She tried to struggle but her arms and feet were numb, unresponsive to her brain's commands.

Nigel coolly strolled over to the small sofa and sat down, casually throwing one knee over the other, waving his hand towards the newly assembled materials. "You've likely gathered what this is dear Mandy. After all, you're a smart woman."

He chuckled. "And of course you realize that my name is not Nigel Pitt. There never was a Nigel Pitt. My name is actually Norris Quinn. I do have a very good education and a deep interest in history. The army bit is true as well. Mind you, it was the New Irish Republican Army not the British Army as you so easily assumed."

"You're a terrorist," Mandy weakly screamed. "A damnable Irish terrorist."

"No so, dear Mandy, not so. The IRA trained me yes, and indeed I did do some months training with some Al Qaeda units in Libya a number of years ago. But my loyalty is, and always has been, to the Tuatha de Danann and the Dragon Master."

Mandy's eyes widened and she whispered "You are a bloody Druid. You've been spying on me and my father. Why? Revenge? Why didn't you just kill me? After all, you had ample opportunity."

"True. That was the Dragon Master's original plan for you and your father. We have long memories and you and your father destroyed our plans and stole Excalibur. But when your father found that little letter in Istanbul it changed everything."

A black scowl came across his once charming, smiling face. "The Dragon Master wants that scroll. With it he will become the finder and owner of the Spear of Destiny. It is ours. We have searched for it for centuries. My grandfather even joined the Nazi SS to search for it during the war. He was close, so close. But Hitler refused to listen to reason and pushed for conquest too far and too fast. The fool really believed the lance in Nuremburg was real. He found out too late that it was fake." He sneered with contempt. "But we knew the real lance existed and that eventually we would find it."

He suddenly smiled at Mandy. "Ironically, your father was the one who discovered the evidence we needed. It brought him and you a stay of execution, one might say, until we could find it. I saw your father in Koblenz you know, at the German archives. He didn't know who I was, of course, but I followed him and his friend Wallace to an old man's house in the city. That pathetic fool collected all kinds of documents and information about the Nazi treasure looting. Fortunately for me, he also had an inventory of treasures taken from Austria. It included a reference to the scroll and we know it was taken to the United States."

He shifted in the sofa. "All that remains now is to find the scroll. And our Washington sources already know where it is. Then we'll find the lance. Our long search will be over, the Spear of Destiny will be ours and with it the power to conquer and control the world."

Shocked and frightened, Mandy could only squeeze her eyes shut as the tears poured out. "What do you want from me?"

"Ah yes. Well, everything is coming together. There is one small matter to be taken care of tomorrow morning. Then, my dear, the Dragon Master has allowed me the pleasure of ending your existence."

A gasp of horror shot from her mouth. Her brain was exploding in protest and struggle to free herself from the grasp of this insane creature, but her body remained motionless.

"So, I'm afraid you'll have to stay here for the night. Don't worry, I'll give regular injections so that you remain calm and motionless. And I'll even make it painless for you at the end because you really are—were—a sweet girl."

A knock on the door startled her. Nigel/Norris laughed at the flash of hope that crossed her face.

"Don't worry. Nobody's coming in. I arranged for my meals to be brought up. The staff has instructions to leave it at the door and knock to simply tell me it's ready. I told them I want nobody to disturb me because I am working on a very important and delicate presentation. The staff here are particularly gracious and accommodating when it comes to odd requests from equally odd guests."

He got up, stretched, and moved slowly towards the door. "I'm sorry, my dear Mandy, but there is no food or drink for you. You couldn't eat it in your state anyway. I hope you don't mind."

He stopped at the door and listened carefully. He turned and looked at her from the foyer.

"Cheer up! By this time tomorrow it will all be over."

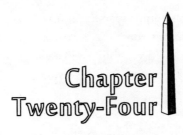

# Chapter Twenty-Four

**Vale of Neath, Wales**

Quinn had left the previous afternoon. A sudden telephone call in the morning and Quinn was quickly packing. "Your brother called. He needs me to join him on a quick trip. I will be back in a day or so," he said coldly. "The arrangements for you are the same."

Now Declan was eating an early Sunday morning breakfast prepared by one of the ladies who helped clean the house during the week. "Eat up, my love. It will be good for you," she smiled at Declan, pouring another cup of tea for him. "Williams the Nurse should be up to the house soon."

She bustled around the kitchen, cleaning up and putting away the dishes as she gabbed away in her soft lilting Welsh voice. "There's lucky you are that your brother is able to provide for you even when he's away on business, isn't it. But I'm sure he'll be back now in a minute."

Declan didn't have the heart to argue with her. No he was not lucky. And it was unlikely he would be back. Diarmuid had abandoned him and most other people emotionally and mentally as well as physically. She could do nothing about it anyway. Nor could the male nurse, William Williams, known in the quaint Welsh way of identifying people and occupations, as Williams the Nurse. That name was the only light moment that cracked an otherwise oppressive gloom enveloping the house.

Quinn's departure had one benefit however. It allowed Declan an opportunity he'd not had before, to roam the single level house without that ugly man glaring at him, questioning him and keeping him away from most of the rooms. Quinn's haste to leave and a traffic delay on the roads outside Neath meant a gap of more than an hour before the nurse arrived. Declan used the time well.

Most of the house was empty, sparsely furnished and decorated. But he'd picked the lock on Quinn's room—a trick one of the Breton Druids taught him last year. He moved carefully and slowly as he examined the room, partly because of his limitations but also trying not to make it obvious he'd been snooping.

When he opened the lower drawer of Quinn's night table he found a cryptic note in Quinn's handwriting. It was partly in Gaelic, partly in English and seemed to be a transcription of Diarmuid's instructions to Quinn. He recognized the names Huw and Mandy Griffiths. He had no clue as to who "Norris" was; nor did he understand the initials AOC or HP or GH. His time in Brittany did clue him in to the meaning of RPG and he certainly understood the term missile. But other than that he was frustrated. There were no guns, no weapons of any kind in the house unless you considered kitchen knives a weapon. The RPG must have been in the boxes he'd seen loaded into that van, he thought. But he did not know where it was heading, so even if he was right, the knowledge did him no good. And nowhere in Quinn's room could he find a phone number or contact information for Diarmuid.

The house was, to all intents and purposes, a sterile environment occupied by a crippled man. His brother had not only well and truly isolated himself but also turned Declan into a pitiable non-entity.

Declan tossed and turned all night. Even if he could decipher the note, what could he do about it? He was trapped. There was no land phone and Quinn had the only mobile. If he did figure out what it all meant, there was no one he could look to for help other than one of his daily visitors. But would they believe him or would they, more probably, consider his injuries were now impacting him mentally.

He watched the cleaning woman leave then wheeled himself onto the back patio. The sophisticated dart gun Quinn had provided for him was the only means Declan had of getting rid of his frustrations. All yesterday he'd fired the gun at the target. Over and over, moving further and further away until he was able to hit the bulls eye nine times out of ten from almost forty yards. It exhausted him and added to his pain, but he relished the emotional release it provided.

He picked up the gun again, aimed and fired, reloading quickly and smoothly. He grinned in spite of himself; four out of five on target in less than thirty seconds. There was no one around to share his victory, but he celebrated inside himself. For the first time since returning to Diarmuid's presence Declan had accomplished something by himself, for himself.

He laid the gun on his lap. The warm sunny morning was beginning to cloud over; a cool breeze was coming off the sea and whisping gently up the valley. Even that short amount of time shooting had drained him physically and caused his damaged lungs to protest with fiery fervor. He shivered and wheeled himself back into the house. For all the momentary joy his dart shooting had provided, the heavy dark weight still sat on his mind. It was exacerbated by Quinn's cryptic note. Deep down, he knew that it was something evil that Diarmuid and Quinn had plotted. But what?

He dropped his head into his hands, weeping softly with frustration and fear.

Diarmuid, my brother, what are you doing, he cried out in his mind. What evil is in your mind?

Before Williams the Nurse left that evening, Declan persuaded him that the pain was getting more and more severe. He asked him for some more Zemuron that he could inject into himself in the middle of the night since that was when the pain hit hardest. He took the three vials Williams reluctantly offered and placed them in his night table drawer.

"You won't be doing anything silly now will you, Declan bach?" The kindly Williams asked.

"Silly? No, I never do anything silly Williams; I never do anything silly."

### Crown Security offices, London

Dusk was falling. For Stone the day was an exercise in frustration. He'd been handed a variety of files and maps but realized it was more a 'make work and keep the poor sod occupied' employment rather than a useful job. Not even the classical radio station he tried to listen to online could help. Finally, he shut the computer down.

Exasperated, he went in search of Freddy and found him hunched over a monitor carefully studying jerky videos he recognized as frames from surveillance cameras. Freddy acknowledged him with a quick nod of the head. "We picked up Quinn outside London City Airport. He got into a cab. Susan here," Freddy pointed to the young woman who'd tracked Quinn's European sojourn, "checked the various cab owners and drivers and finally found the one who picked Quinn up. That cab dropped him at Cannon Street station where he got on the tube. We've traced him on the Circle Line to Earl's Court. He then took the C1 bus and doubled back to Victoria Station. Watch. Quinn is right there sitting at a café on the concourse. Then, as you see, he suddenly jumps up and runs out of the station." He flicked the computer mouse to show a street view. "As you can see he crosses Wilton road and gets into that black van. We got a partial plate number, but it looks like we lost him for a bit."

While Susan contacted the vehicle licensing bureau and Scotland Yard for help seeking the van, Freddy and Stone reviewed the videos again.

"He must be on to the fact that we're trying to find him with all the backtracking and gamesmanship." Stone stared at the screen, willing it to show him answers.

"I don't think so. He'd have no way of knowing we're on to him. I think he's just being super cautious. Not that it helps us either way."

"What about the surveillance videos on Mandy. If we can track her, we might find her. My guess is she's going to meet him somewhere, probably in London. Find her, find him, hopefully."

"The Guvnor is already pulling strings and bullying the provincials to get the videos to us as soon as possible. He's also putting pressure on the railways to get their video to us, but unfortunately it takes time." He paused and looked up at Stone, worry creasing his face.

"And time, I'm afraid is what we don't have a lot of."

**Grosvenor Hotel, London**

Mandy prayed like she had never prayed before. She remembered the times in her teenage years she'd either ignored her 'fuddy-duddy' father or thought him completely bonkers. She'd even been angry with him when he leaned heavily on his faith after her mother died.

But in the dread of the evening and night, secured to a chair and aware of the ominous presence of evil and death in the hotel suite, she now began to understand how insecure life is, how very special and strong her father is and she surprised herself by how deep her own faith really was.

Hope had jumped momentarily in the early evening when her tormentor answered a rapid knocking on the suite door. He opened it immediately and a short heavy woman stepped in. Her heart sank when Nigel told her she was to act as a second guard through the night while he slept. She would also take care of Mandy's "physical needs" as he delicately put it, including bathroom breaks, helping her with an occasional drink of water and ensuring an injection every four hours.

As the night wore on, the woman stretched out on the couch beside her, eyes wide open, while Nigel disappeared into the bedroom. The assembled weapon lay on the floor by the open window. As reality began to set in a sense of resignation swept over her but not hopelessness; it was, she realized, more a sense of internal mental, emotional and spiritual preparation. She was going to die in a few hours. She would never have the chance to tell her father how deeply she loved and appreciated him, even with all his idiosyncrasies.

As dawn broke she realized some feeling was slowly returning to her extremities. The woman had forgotten the 3a.m. injection. The faint hope it raised was dashed by the realization that she could never hope to overwhelm Nigel even if she could loosen the bindings around her.

Mandy also lashed herself for being so completely fooled by Nigel and taken in both professionally and personally. Her deepest regret was that her reaction to Nigel had suppressed her feelings for Stone. Instead of cultivating and enjoying the romance that had developed between them last year, she had trampled on it, ground it into the dust and spit on it. Despite her conflicted feelings when she saw him at Greyfell Abbey, she ruefully acknowledged to herself that she'd remained cool and aloof around him.

Light began to break through the curtains. Nigel bounced out of the bedroom dressed in black pants and turtleneck. He nodded at the woman who, without saying a word, picked up the few items she'd brought with her and left as taciturn as she been throughout her stay.

He ignored Mandy as she slumped in the chair and stood to the side of the large window, binoculars focused on the large temporary stage constructed in the park across from him. Already a team of bustling workers was setting out hundreds of folding chairs while another team decorated the stage area with plants and flowers, draping and carpeting. Even across Park Lane he could hear the muted noise of busyness. He estimated the angle again, then picked up the portable sights and recalibrated. The Dragon Master had secured an excellent device for the day's affair, he admitted; the Serpent launcher was lightweight, powerful, with a range of almost eight hundred yards, and a sighting device that not only corrected for distance but also atmospheric conditions including humidity. Good for rain or shine, he smiled to himself, but from the looks of the weather today it will be shine all the way.

"Only a couple more hours my dear Mandy and it will all be over." He smirked at her disheveled look of anger. "What's the matter love? Cat got your tongue?"

He turned away from her, and began to push a small chest of drawers in front of the window. He carefully placed it a foot back from the windowsill then reached around and opened the window, cranking it as far open as he could. Satisfied, he drew the white sheers across then picked up the tripod, the sighting equipment and then the launcher and began putting them together on top of the chest. He pulled the stubby HEAA rockets beside the chest and placed one beside the assembled weapon. He only needed one, but just in case, he wanted the extras beside him. He pulled a chair up and sat to the side of the launcher, adjusting its height and location on the chest until he was satisfied that he could comfortably sit on the chair out of sight of any alert security people and still fire one, maybe two rounds before he had to leave.

"You won't succeed you know." Mandy spoke quietly but forcefully as she glared at him.

"Of course I will. By the time they figure out what happened, I will be long gone from this place. When they do enter this room, all they'll find is you."

"But you will be found and you will be punished. They know about Callaghan and they're closing in on him. They'll connect my death to the Druids and, believe me, they will not rest until you and the rest are rotting in hell!" Her voice remained soft and devoid of emotion even as she spit out the words.

"Brave words, my dear Mandy. Brave words. That's what I always liked about you. Smart, resourceful and, yes, courageous; I salute you. But this time there is no reprieve, no salvation. And WE will prosper and WE will triumph. The old gods will reward us and reclaim their position."

"God will not allow it," she said simply. "He has the victory. Not your gods. Not your blood dripping Druids."

He stepped over smartly and backhanded her face, drawing blood from her lips and nose.

"Shut up!" he snarled. "Your God is finished. You Christians are done. All you are now is a sideshow in society, ripe for the old gods to destroy. And few people will even notice let alone care. I'm merely helping cleanse society of a sanctimonious plague that has long since lost its power."

Blood trickled from her nose, dripping over her lips and chin onto her white blouse. She looked defiantly at him, bracing herself for another blow. "You can destroy me and others physically. But you will never destroy the living faith we have. It transcends your hatred replacing it with love and compassion."

He lurched toward her and she shut her eyes waiting for the hit. When it didn't come she opened her eyes and saw him, hand raised and hesitating. He turned away instead. "Don't try to rile me, woman. I have other things to think about. If you cannot be silent, I will gag you."

He sat on the chair and checked the weapon sights again. He glared again at her.

"Soon, Mandy. Soon"

### Crown Security offices, London

"We got some tapes from the west," Freddy shouted, beckoning Stone over. It had been a hard night. Stone slept fitfully on a camp cot brought in with several others. From time to time, he sensed movement as tired men and women switched places, getting a few hours rest and then returning to the hunt. He was up four times during the night, sharing from the bottomless urns of coffee and tea, trying to think, re-reading files and sharing wild in-the-middle-of-the-night thoughts with anyone who would listen to him.

Freddy was scrutinizing the tapes as Stone ran over. "She arrived at Hereford station Friday evening and took the 18:10 to Birmingham. We've got her at Birmingham New Street station and she travelled to London Euston on the 21:10 arriving at around 22:45." He switched to another video. "This shows her leaving Euston in a cab. But we need to track the cab and find out where he dropped her."

Stone studied the jerky videos showing a relaxed Mandy walking across Euston's concourse and out to the cab rank. It was a sucker punch to his gut and he realized how much she meant to him and how helpless he felt.

The ever competent Susan slipped a piece of paper to Freddy. "Hmm. The cab took her to the Imperial hotel on Russell Square in Bloomsbury."

"Figures," Stone interrupted. "It's right by the British Museum."

"Yes, well Susan spoke with reception. Mandy checked in alone last night and then checked out just before noon. She took a taxi and the doorman overheard her tell the cabbie to take her to Paddington."

"Is she going to take a train to Cardiff or Swansea?" Stone considered the thought. "If that was her destination, why not travel direct from Hereford without coming all the way to London? Trains from Paddington go to the West Country as well as Wales. Would she have business there, I wonder?"

"What if she was meeting someone, say Norris, there?" Freddy's mind was filtering through all the possibilities.

"Possible. But why?"

Freddy snapped his finger. "Maybe a personal relationship? You do live in America, after all, Stone." Freddy raised his hand to stem the burst of anger from Stone and quickly continued, "Then again he was working with her, helping her research Baldric and the scroll." The two argued while Freddy dragged Stone out of the office and down to the street where he pushed Stone into a car. "We can't wait for them to send tapes. We're going to Paddington and look at them there."

After verifying their identity the station master at Paddington led them to the security control room. In short order, they were carefully scrutinizing the crowded station concourse. It took a number of minutes before Stone asked them to replay one section. "That's her," he said, watching a figure walk onto the concourse from the Praed Street entrance.

They watched as she stopped and surveyed the crowds, then wave. A man rushed up to her. "Norris!" Stone and Freddy blurted at the same time. They followed them on the cameras to the cab rank, watching them speak to each other animatedly.

"Doesn't seem to be a problem. They seem friendly enough. She certainly isn't being coerced to go with him." Freddy stood up. "I've seen enough." Within seconds he was on the phone, ordering his staff to track the cab number he gave them and find out where it had dropped the pair.

Stone peered at his watch. "It's 9:45. What time is the Archbishop's service?"

Freddy shuddered. "Don't remind me. It's set for 11 o'clock. We're running out of time."

# Chapter Twenty-Five

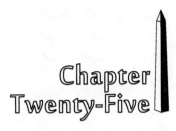

**Quincy, Illinois**

Chad Lawson's black Suburban SUV slowed along South Front Street opposite a non-descript gray warehouse. Ahead of them a diesel shunter was pushing some boxcars along the tracks parallel to the road and into a small siding. The vehicle turned right and bounced across the single track and up to a wire mesh fence topped by barbed wire. They stopped at the gate where a grumpy overweight security guard glared at Chad, annoyed that his early Sunday morning was disturbed by the urgent call to get to the warehouse and let some people in.

Without saying a word Chad handed him his SID credentials then handed over the letter. The guard snatched the letter then did a double take, looking at the letterhead and then at the signature below. Jaw open, he looked up amazed. "Is this legit?"

"It is. The President of the United States has authorized immediate access to this warehouse and demands your immediate cooperation." Chad smiled at him to soften the situation and was slightly amused to see the complete reversal in the guard's demeanor as Chad introduced himself and fellow agents McConnell and Kryer.

He waved them through the gate. Inside the small parking area Chad could see the Mississippi River and beyond, the state of Missouri. They got out of the SUV and walked to the large rolling corrugated door on the side of the building. They waited while the chubby man jogged towards them. Chad hooked a thumb in the direction of a rusty orange weather-worn fork lift beside the door. "You know how to operate this?" At the guard's panting yes, Chad told him to open up the warehouse door and bring the fork lift inside. "I'm sure that what we're seeking is buried high up and at the back of a massive amount of material," he said more to himself than to the two SID agents accompanying him.

Inside the dimly lit building he ruefully acknowledged he'd been right. Stacks of shelving crammed with crates and boxes of various sizes, ran down both sides of a central aisle. Even though it was early morning, the outside temperature was rapidly pushing over seventy degrees Fahrenheit. Inside, despite the seedy look of the outside, it was remarkably cool thanks, said the guard, to an efficient heating/cooling system that kept the building at a steady temperature year round to preserve the accumulated crates and their contents.

"So where do we begin?" The taller agent, McConnell, asked as they stared at the vastness of the task. Chad looked at the chubby guard who merely shrugged. "Don't really know what's in here," he said, still sitting in the fork lift's cab.

"We're looking for US Army crates and boxes dating around 1946."

The guard thought for a moment. "Then it won't be up here. This stuff was just moved in within the last five years," he pointed at the boxes beside them on both sides. "I was here when they brought them in." He settled himself more comfortably into the seat and started the machine. "I think for that far back you'll have to go far back," he said, chuckling at his lame attempt of humor.

With the agents trotting along beside him, the old fork lift trundled down the aisle until it reached the very back of the long warehouse. McConnell ran his hand over his balding head then reached out for the wheeled ladder leaning against one of the shelving units. He climbed it and peered at the labels on the boxes. "University of Illinois. Records from 1955 to 65," he shouted down. They moved the ladder to another unit and he repeated the process. Again he shouted down the results, this time more university materials but dating from the 1950's.

"We're in the right area then," Chad shouted back. "We want US Army crates. They might be marked Camp Ellis, or the 728th Quartermaster Salvage Company or 581 Military Police."

"Nothing like that yet, Chad. You guys move me along on the ladder to another unit." Four times they moved the agent slowly but shakily along. The fourth time he shouted " Now I'm seeing university boxes and crates for 1945 and 1946 Chad, but nothing with US Army stamps or labels."

Chad told him to come down then told the warehouse guard to use the fork lift and move some of containers down. As he did, the balding agent asked for a flashlight. "There are some other boxes buried behind these, but I can't make out their labels."

They waited while the crates were removed, then McConnell scampered agilely up the ladder again. He clung to the top rung, shining his flashlight into the gloom at the back of the shelves. "I think there's something there. I think I see a faded stars and stripes label but can't make out what it says." He scrambled back down and more crates were removed until the subject crate was delicately lifted and moved.

The machine's forks were extended to their highest limit and, for a second, the weight of the crate threatened to tip the unbalanced unit. The guard maneuvered the fork lift slightly, getting a better angle on the crate and lifted again. He reversed and turned so that there was an empty spot on the aisle in front of him and gently lowered the crate. As he removed the fork blades, Chad was already on his knees examining the labels. The guard leaned over in the cab, joining in the eagerness of the search and so focused on the fact that he was obeying the President's command that he left the machine running.

"This must be it!" Chad's voice rose with excitement as he brushed way decades of dust and cobwebs off the label. "Camp Ellis 728 Quartermaster Salvage Company," he shouted. Then he rubbed away the dirt on another label. "Yes! Yes! UFA Salzburg."

"What's that mean? UFA Salzburg," Agent Kryer crouched beside Chad.

"United States Forces in Austria. That was the name given the post-war occupation troops in Austria. Salzburg was the headquarters. According to my sources, the shipment we're looking for was sent to Ellis via Salzburg."

As he told his two companions to take some crowbars and open the crate, he reached into his jacket pocket and pulled out the inventory form sent to him by Crown Security.

Like children at Christmas, they carefully pulled piles of straw out of the crate, sifting then dumping it on the cement floor. As each individual item was uncrated, Chad placed it on either the floor or the boxes beside, checking it first against the list he held.

Small delicately carved marble statues, ornately framed paintings both large and small and obviously antique, and gilt-trimmed leather bound books all took their place one by one.

Finally, Chad reached down and brushed away some straw, pulling out a wool blanket. He knelt and laid it on the cement, cautiously unwrapping it. He knelt for a minute looking at the treasure on the floor in front of him. It was a large round silver engraved tube bearing an ornately engraved "B" surrounded by filigrees and leaves. He estimated it was four inches wide and at least a foot long. It was sealed at both ends with equally ornate silver caps, each also bearing the initial B.

"So, you gonna open it?" The security guard leaned down from the cab of his still throbbing fork lift having watched the drama and excitement unfold beneath him.

"No. This will have to be carefully opened in sterile conditions because if it's what I think it is, it is about two thousand years old."

The guard let out a long whistle which was abruptly interrupted by a cold voice with an Irish brogue. "Quite wise!"

Chad and his companions snapped their heads around but froze when a burst of automatic fire hit the wall behind them. "Move so much as an inch and my men's aim will be much, much better."

A neatly dressed man stepped forward. Behind him, two others kept their weapons steady, aimed at Chad and his group.

"The silver tube, if you please."

"Who are you? What's going on?" Chad growled, though his mind had already answered the question.

"Diarmuid Callaghan at your service, Mr. Lawson. And my friends here are Mr. Quinn and Mr. Nolan. But you may know me better as The Dragon Master. I have gone to considerable effort and expense chasing this little item down, Mr. Lawson and I am surprised that you beat me to it even if only by an hour or two. Nevertheless, it is mine now. Kindly hand it over. But move slowly and carefully. Put it on that crate over there." Callaghan motioned toward the large wooden crate standing waist high that had been deposited on the cement floor by the fork lift just minutes earlier.

"And, just to be certain you won't try any of your American Wild West antics, remove your weapons and place them on the ground. All of you."

Chad slowly reached inside his jacket and put his gun on the ground in front of him. He made no effort to touch the tube. Callaghan gestured quickly and another burst of automatic fire split the air just above his head. The other agents dropped to the ground. The security guard seemed frozen in place in the fork lift's cab.

"For the last time, Mr. Lawson. The tube. Now!"

Slowly Chad rose to his feet, tube in hand, and moved to the designated crate. He placed it gently on top then stepped away. Callaghan gestured with his head. "Quinn. Cover me." As Quinn stepped forward his weapon steadily facing Chad and his agents, Callaghan slipped in behind him. With Quinn in place, Callaghan reached out and lovingly picked up the tube, caressing it and turning it over and over in his hands. His eyes fixed on the tube and he breathed a quiet 'at last' as he stepped back.

"Nolan. With me. My apologies gentlemen, but our business is done. I regret that you won't see the results." He paused and laughed a short sharp bark. "No, in retrospect and all honesty I don't regret it one little bit." He motioned Quinn forward. "Quinn. You know what to do and where to meet me next." With that Callaghan turned and began running back down the main aisle towards the warehouse entrance. Nolan ran behind him, slowing every once in a while to drop black packages.

A cold evil smile came over Quinn's face as he heard Callaghan exit the building. He raised his weapon and began to curl his finger on the trigger. Suddenly the security guard swore and jammed his foot onto the fork lift's accelerator. It lurched forward, startling Quinn who began firing immediately. Instantaneously one of the fork lift prongs caught him in the gut and he doubled over, gun firing wildly into the ground and bullets ricocheting everywhere. One caught the security guard who slumped over the wheel, his weight still holding the accelerator down. As Quinn fell between the prongs, it rolled over his crumbled body.

At the same time, a massive series of explosions hit the warehouse as the small black mines dropped by Nolan detonated and spread flames to the wooden crates and cardboard packages that filled the building.

At the moment Quinn began firing Chad flung himself to the side, rolling and picking up his gun. Out of the corner of his eye he saw McConnell sprawled against one of the crates they'd brought down off the shelving, blood seeping from his body. Without waiting, Chad focused on Quinn's body now being crushed under the weight of the fork lift. He fired three shots into the body and began to run towards the back of the warehouse, desperate to catch Callaghan and retrieve the tube.

The first blasts threw him backwards. As he stumbled to his feet, a wall of flame suddenly shot across the central passage. The flames, sudden and ferocious, caused him to stumble back. More explosions followed driving him further back.

Chad ducked behind the fork lift, and checked the wounded security guard. Although he was bleeding severely, the man was still conscious as Chad pulled him from the machine. He saw Kryer desperately working on McConnell.

"We've got to get out of here. Is there another door?"

The security guard waved feebly to his left. "Security door," he gasped, "behind the second tier of shelves."

Wasting no time, Chad dragged the guard behind the boxes and up to the door, shouting and coughing as he urged Kryer to drag McConnell to the door. The heat was increasing exponentially and the smoke was affecting his breathing.

"It's locked. You got a key?" he turned to the security guard only to see him slumped unconscious on the floor. Chad rifled through the man's pockets as Kryer, hacking and coughing in the thick acrid smoke tried to tie a tourniquet on the downed agent's leg. They could hear mini-explosions and crackling as the artifact crates, dry as bones after years of storage, succumbed to the flames. Finally he found a key ring, frustrated at the more than twenty keys attached.

Desperately Chad tried fitting one after another into the lock. He was disoriented by the smoke, felt the intense heat and was terrified that a flashover might occur at any moment. He was on his tenth key when it smoothly slipped into the lock and turned. He flung the door open, gasping at the fresh air. Chad dragged the others out and away from the burning warehouse aware dimly of the sirens that were disturbing the early Sunday morning slumber of so many Quincy citizens. Together he and Kryer pulled the two badly wounded men across the train tracks. Chad stood and waved at two railroad workers who'd jumped off the shunting diesel at the first explosions, calling for their help.

The metal roof of the warehouse was already buckling as the inferno raged. With the help of the railroad workers he and Kryer worked on the two wounded men as police, fire and ambulance arrived on the scene.

Still hacking and coughing, dirty and singed Chad identified himself to the police as they arrived, tersely asking them to help track down and seize Callaghan. At the same time, paramedics worked on the wounded. He looked at McConell then at Kryer who slowly shook his head. "Not looking good, Chad. The security guard looks like he'll make it though."

"Stick with them," Chad said simply. He looked at his watch. Less than thirty minutes had passed from the time they'd found the crate. Now the warehouse was a blazing furnace with thousands of precious unknown artifacts and documents destroyed, and the one he was charged to find, in the hands of a murderous madman. He slumped against a tree, filthy and disheveled, a borrowed cell phone in hand reporting back to Chantilly.

"I need a ride to the airport top speed," he said to a police officer, again flashing his ID. As they raced through the town, Chad tried calling the airport only to be informed by recording about the airport's hours and the airport's only scheduled air link to St. Louis. Although the airport was in flat farmland and traffic was light, the nearly fifteen mile trip seemed endless.

After a frantic search of the nearly deserted terminal building, Chad finally found someone who acknowledged some authority. A man barely out of his teens called himself the airport's weekend duty manager and reluctantly admitted the existence of such a flight. He'd been unimpressed by Chad's grimy looks and skeptical of his ID and only when forcefully told to cooperate by the accompanying police officer did he open up.

"They were here just over an hour. Parked in the general aviation area over there," he waved weakly in the direction of some hangers.

"I want all the information you have on that aircraft and especially its flight plan."

"Can't give that to you."

"Why not?"

"Don't have it." The man smirked then wiped it off when the Quincy cop glared at him. "We got a notification that there was a minor problem with the plane and they were setting down at Quincy to take a look at it. While they were on the ground, some guys got out and were met by a car. They jumped in and disappeared off towards town. A little later they came back, got in the plane and took off. I assumed they were just continuing their original flight plan."

Chad leaned on the man's desk, thrusting his head, still reeking from the smoke, into the man's face. "You have ten seconds to start cooperating and get that aircraft information to me or you will be arrested as a security threat. It's a federal offense and I can promise you, that means you'll be facing a considerable number of years in federal prison. Now. What aircraft? Where was it going?"

The man blanched and quickly produced what he had. "It was a Challenger 604, with a registration EI-ORT. The pilot reported that he was heading to Europe but said since he'd already filed flight plans he didn't need to do it again with us. There's no air traffic as you can see, so they were up and away in less than five minutes. I had no reason to question it and he was gone out of our airspace, so no big deal."

"EI. That's an Irish registration." Chad pulled his cell phone out and dialed Chantilly, requesting all assistance from the military and FAA in tracking the aircraft. "I want to speak to anyone who had any contact with the people on that plane," Chad demanded as he dropped into a vacant chair. The man nodded and began telephoning but even as he did, Chad closed his eyes and reluctantly admitted to himself that the chances were few that they could identify and find the aircraft let alone try to divert it to an American airport.

The Dragon Master had swooped in and stolen the precious scroll that Stone and Crown Security were so concerned about. It was, as the Brits say, 'a right cock up' he admitted.

# Chapter Twenty-Six

### London

For twenty agonizing minutes Stone and Freddy reviewed the Paddington videos again and again, searching for any additional clues; other people who approached or spoke to either Mandy or Norris, signals from Norris to others, or simply if anyone seemed to be following them. They'd drawn a blank. Resigned, they thanked the railway security officials for their help and headed back to the car. Freddy's hands clenched and unclenched in frustration; Stone slammed a door open and closed as they left the non-public area of the station. Neither spoke.

The car was merging onto Bayswater Lane when Freddy's mobile rang. "Where?" He looked at Stone with a touch of a smile and hope. "Almost there. Meet us at the desk." The car jerked forward with the sudden acceleration as Freddy nimbly flicked the car from one lane to the other, jostling around cabs and red double deck buses. As he drove he told Stone they'd tracked the cab. 'He's at the Grosvenor Hotel just down here on Park Lane. Checked in yesterday and has not checked out yet." He glanced quickly over at Stone as he moved into the right lane for the traffic flow around Marble Arch. "It's across from Hyde Park. Right where the service will be held."

As they spun through the light traffic onto Park Lane he also told Stone that Colin and Huw had driven down from the Lake District through the night. Huw, against his wishes, was at the Bureau's offices with Sir Giles. Colin was on the way to the hotel.

Arriving at the hotel, they saw Colin and three other men running toward them. A quick conversation with the reception desk gave them the information they needed. One man stayed at the desk to ensure that no warning would be given. Freddy, Colin and Stone ran towards the lifts and pushed the button for the floor below Norris' suite. "I'm taking charge of this operation," Colin said bluntly, "I know you rank above me, but I'm the field man Freddy, not you. The police will be right behind us, so will Special Branch and MI5." With Freddy's nod of acquiescence, they left the lift and walked quietly towards the staircase, Colin leading and opening the door quietly. Inside the stairwell Colin and the agent with him drew their weapons and passed a third over to Freddy. "You're not authorized for gun use here," Freddy whispered into Stone's ear as they paused at the top floor. "And stay in the hall until we give an all clear."

Gently and with deliberate slowness Colin opened the heavy metal stairway door, concerned in case it squeaked. The corridor was totally empty and silent. On the rich burgundy carpet, Colin took off his shoes and gestured for the others to do the same then led them soundlessly down the hall to the designated suite door.

### Quincy, Illinois

Chad Lawson paced the hospital corridor impatiently. After weaning out of him what little information the airport manager had, Chad raced back to the local hospital only to find that both McConnell and the security guard were both in surgery. While he'd waited he'd debriefed the Quincy police on the events at the warehouse. The fire was out, he was told, but the building still unsafe for fire crews to enter. To this point they'd not been able to extricate Quinn's body. "You were lucky, very lucky," one cop remarked, folding up his notebook. "That security guy should get a medal." Chad nodded agreement and resumed pacing. He sent Kryer for a break and to get coffee for the pair of them.

As he paced he called Chantilly again. The latest information showed the target jet flew across Illinois crossing Lake Michigan just north of Chicago, and the state of Michigan before entering Canadian territory over Manitoulin Island in northern Ontario. Chad's gut told him Callaghan was on board that jet but with no evidence, it was difficult to persuade authorities to force the plane to land. The thought was redundant any way, since the jet was now well over international territory.

As Kryer arrived back with the coffee, a doctor walked towards then and led them into a small anteroom. "Both of them are still in critical condition," the doctor got right to the point. "But I think they'll survive. Mr. McConnell is still touch and go, quite frankly. He got hit by two bullets, one of which hit an artery in his leg. As a result, he lost a lot of blood. Plus there was some smoke inhalation and burns. The security guard has a wound in the right abdomen that fortunately missed any vital organs. He also has a minor wound on the head. I suspect, from what I've learned of the situation, by a ricocheting bullet. It knocked him unconscious but it didn't enter his brain, so we're grateful for that. He too has smoke damage and burns."

After more questions, Chad thanked the doctor. With the doctor's permission he went into the critical care unit where he met briefly with the security guard's wife and told her of her husband's heroism. "He saved all our lives and I'm sorry, but I didn't even get his name."

"Joe. Joe Schrieber," the small stout woman whispered, worriedly looking at the still white form protruding tubes and wires connected to various beeping and pinging monitors.

"Mrs. Schrieber, he was acting this morning under the direct orders of the President of the United States. And I will make sure he gets a Presidential Citation for bravery." Chad held her left hand gently as she wiped tears from her eyes with the other. After a few more moments, Chad excused himself.

Back in the hall, he motioned to Kryer. "Stay here and keep me posted on both men. I'm going down to police headquarters. I have to let London know what happened. And they're not going to be happy."

**Grosvenor Hotel, London**

Through his binoculars Nigel could see the morning's service underway on the open stage. Bright sunshine and warm sun bathed the entire area.

It was a simple set with a central long table covered in white material acting as an altar and with gold communion chalices and trays at the ready. On each side of the altar stood a large gold cross of equal height; one was a plain cross while the other was a crucifix, representing the two denominations celebrating the joint synod. Large white wicker baskets of white flowers adorned the floor on each side of the altar. In front and off to the side was a simple clear acrylic podium. At the back of the entire assemblage, a large wooden cross had been erected and draped with purple material. The only other accoutrements were large white chairs with plush red seats, one on each side of the altar.

Nigel checked again and smiled to himself as he saw the Archbishop of Canterbury move from the Altar to the podium and begin to pray. According to the published programme, the next item on the agenda would be the moment when the Archbishop and the Cardinal Archbishop of Westminster would come together at the altar and begin the Eucharist liturgy. That was when he would fire.

Through the open window he could hear the combined Westminster Abbey and Cathedral choirs singing a hymn. While other priests bustled around in front of the stage preparing to share the communion with the congregation, the Archbishop of Canterbury moved from the podium towards the altar. At the same time, the Archbishop of Westminster rose and began moving towards him.

Nigel put the binoculars down and raised the weapon to his shoulders, settling the launcher comfortably onto a towel draped over his shoulders and protecting his neck. He'd already loaded one rocket into the weapon and slowly, calmly put the eyepiece up to his eye. With his left hand, he adjusted the calibration slightly. His finger moved to the trigger.

As he pulled his finger back a sudden crash startled him. In that fraction of a second, his shoulder jerked minutely as the missile fired.

"Drop it!" The shout was simultaneous with the crash of the door bursting open. In the flare of the missile's firing, he dropped the launcher and, as he rolled off the chair onto the floor he pulled his pistol out and began firing back into the room.

In the chaos of the backdraft flame and smoke and bullets flying, Colin and Freddy also dropped to the floor, firing back. They could hear their assailant shout and swear in Gaelic then suddenly gasp in mid-word. Colin fired once again at the prone body lying beside the dresser and launcher.

Silence dropped over the room, until they heard a moan coming from their left. Colin jumped up and ran over to Quinn's body, kicking Quinn's pistol out of the way. Freddy rolled to his right then got up and sprinted towards the sofa. He saw Mandy collapsed in a chair that had tipped over backwards, still shackled to the arms and legs of the chair. The moans were coming from her.

Dimly he could hear hundreds of sirens but all he could really hear was his own voice calling for assistance. He reached her and saw blood saturating her blouse. He tried to pull on the cuffs holding her arms and legs but was afraid to pull too hard. He grabbed a pillow from the sofa and tucked it behind her head, talking to her, trying to get her attention.

Stone had raced into the room as soon as the firing stopped and he too dropped beside Mandy. "Mandy love, it's me Stone. Everything's going to be okay. You're safe now."

He kept talking to her while Freddy ran to the bathroom for towels to try and stop the bleeding.

Across the room, Colin and the second Crown agent were checking Quinn's body. The agent swore as he looked out the window and saw the chaos in the park as flames engulfed part of the stage and people were screaming in pain and fear while fire engines and ambulances converged on the scene.

Suddenly the room was alive with police, security people and some paramedics. While one checked over Quinn, two other attendants pushed Freddy and Stone aside while they worked on Mandy. While one ripped her blouse away to check the wound, the other pulled a small circular saw out of his kitbag and began removing the shackles. When he finished he told Stone to help him gently lift her up while Freddy pulled the chair out of the way.

While the medics prepped her for transport to hospital, Stone kept talking to her. "Stay with us Mandy. It's all over. Open your eyes sweetheart; show me that you can hear."

Mandy was in a pain-induced fog. When the bang occurred she lurched backwards with all the strength she could muster from her drug-frozen legs. It wasn't much, but she vaguely felt herself falling backwards when a sharp pain fired up the right side of her body. She could hear shouting and voices but couldn't move her hands or legs. Then she felt hands gently touching her, and her hands and legs getting freed, the chair being pulled from beneath her.

Voices. She heard voices. But not Nigel's. Thank God not Nigel. Was she dead then? Is that it? Where was the bright light? The welcoming face of Jesus?"

Dimly she heard another voice urgently calling to her, asking her to open her eyes. It was familiar. It sounded warm yet imperative. She mentally struggled with the fog in her mind frantically trying to make sense of everything. Then, for a moment, it cleared. Stone. The voice was Stone.

Mandy struggled to obey the voice, trying to get her eyelids to comply with the voice and open. It seemed the fog was not just in her mind. Her eyes cracked open slightly to a heavy misty view of faces hovering over her. She fought to focus dimly and saw Stone's hazy, blurred face close to her. She tried to smile then the strength went out of her. The eyes closed. Everything went blank.

"God almighty. No!"

Stone's painful cry reverberated around the room.

### Crown Security Offices, London

Sir Giles hung up the phone slowly and quietly. He took a deep breath and crossed the office to the door, opened it and looked out at Huw Griffiths patiently waiting while the guvnor's Oxford educated agent Susan poured some more tea for both of them as they discussed various aspects of Oxford versus other—in their minds—lesser universities at home and abroad. Huw's long association with Oxford at Balliol College and Susan's own time at Jesus was a common link and Sir Giles had deliberately got them together to keep Huw's mind occupied while they tried to find and save Mandy.

Sir Giles coughed slightly. "Huw. A word, please." His soft voice and gesture for Huw to enter his office was marked by all in the area. Despite the clamorous ringing of phones a hush descended. Susan shared a worried look with each of her two other colleagues in the office as Huw moved into Sir Giles' domain.

Inside the office, Sir Giles quietly asked Huw to be seated, deciding to be direct with the professor. "I have some news, Huw. We found Mandy and Norris Quinn in a hotel suite overlooking Hyde Park. Quinn was in the process of firing at the two Archbishops when Freddy and Colin broke in on them. Quinn was killed and Mandy was critically wounded. She is being transported to St. Mary's Hospital in Paddington as we speak. Stone is with her and I've arranged for a police car to take you there immediately. That's all I know at present. I'm sorry to be the one to break this to you."

Huw closed his eyes tight and said nothing for a moment. His shoulders drooped. When he opened them, Sir Giles could see them begin to glisten with tears. Huw swallowed twice then asked, "what about the others?"

"There seem to be dead and wounded in Hyde Park. Apparently our people arrived just as Quinn was firing. It may just have thrown his aim off, Colin thinks, but at this point I don't know about the Archbishops or other casualties. None of our own people were hurt." He drummed his fingers on the desktop. "Mandy was tied up in a chair. We think Quinn shot her as he himself was being gunned down. As I said, we'll get you over to St. Mary's as quickly as possible. All I know is that the paramedics would not give Colin or Stone any information but allowed Stone to travel with her."

"Then all we have left is prayer," Huw said quietly. "And if that's all we have, then we have hope."

Sir Giles stood up and escorted him out of the office. As he passed Susan he signaled her to his side. Briefly he filled her in and asked her to accompany Huw to the hospital. When they left, the Guvnor reported the news to the others and ordered them to reach out to their sources and get the latest information on the Hyde Park attack. He retreated into his office and closed the door.

### St. Mary's Hospital, Paddington

The quick trip from the Grosvenor Hotel up Park Lane and then Edgeware Road to the hospital on Praed Street was both quiet and chaotic. As the siren screamed it added to the mee-maws, sirens and cacophony of emergency vehicles rushing to the Hyde Park disaster site. Inside the ambulance there were just the quiet professional actions of the paramedics. The only breaks in the silence were quiet one or two word instructions passed back and forth between the woman medic and her partner and with the ambulance driver.

At the hospital, Mandy was assessed and rushed into surgery before Stone had time to take a deep breath. Freddy was beside him and they walked down a corridor to a small waiting room. Stone instantly had a flashback to the time he waited at George Washington University Hospital back in Washington for another Griffiths to undergo emergency surgery.

He sat silent in the hard plastic chair and looked out of the little anteroom. Down the corridor he could see the controlled chaos of the emergency room as other wounded survivors from the Hyde Park carnage arrived. He began to shake uncontrollably. Until now he'd been stoic and strong; his nerves began to fail him and tears welled up in his eyes. The ever alert Freddy quickly went for some tea, leaving Stone momentarily in the care of a police escort who'd come with them. Stone didn't notice; not even when Freddy pushed a mug into his hands and urged him to drink. Robot-like, Stone raised the cup to his lips and sipped. A single tear flowed down his right cheek. Cradling the hot mug in his hands he looked across at Freddy.

"She'll be all right, won't she Freddy?" he asked plaintively.

"She's in the best accident and emergency hospital in this end of London. The best doctors and surgeons are with her now. If anyone can make it, she will." He did not want to raise false hope in Stone when none of them had information on her condition, but by the same token he knew Stone needed hope and reassurance.

Stone nodded. "I've been praying hard since we were in that blasted hotel room. That's all I can give her now." He looked up at Freddy. "I love her, you know. Just never showed it to her properly. Not willing to act on it. I just thought the words would suffice."

Freddy's mobile rang and he answered it then simply hung up. "Huw is on his way. They're bringing him to the hospital now."

By the time Stone had finished his tea, Huw was rushing up the corridor towards him. "Bradstone, my boy. Anything?"

"Nothing. They took her into surgery right away but so far we've not heard a word."

Freddy stood up. "We'll leave you two alone for a bit while we get some more tea and maybe a sandwich or bun for you." He and Susan headed back down the hallway.

Stone looked up as Huw sat down beside him. "I feel awful, Huw. Helpless. Seeing her there trussed up like a chicken and bleeding and there was nothing I could do." Tears flowed freely.

"I know my boy. I know." Tears flowed down Huw's face as well. "I too feel helpless. Helpless because I did not protect her; helpless because I cannot help her now; and helpless because I dragged her into this whole mess."

The two men hugged each other as they wept then dried their eyes.

"I feel helpless. But I know that God is able," was all Huw said. "She is in his hands now, no matter what." He reached into his pocket and pulled out a well-worn New Testament, opened it and began reading. From time to time he pointed to the portions he was reading and Stone looked over, nodding from time to time and sometimes smiling.

When Freddy and Susan returned with the tea and snacks, nothing had changed. More and more people were entering the small waiting room, brought in as their loved ones were being treated. At Stone's suggestion the four of them went into the hallway giving up their seats to a young woman crying uncontrollably with two children hugging her. Her husband, one of the priests serving communion, was also in critical condition.

"Such evil. Such incomparable incalculable evil. Callaghan and the entire wicked nest must be brought wiped out," Huw muttered. "No faith, no religion can survive that creates such carnage and grief. God will not allow it!"

There was a melodious tone and Freddy answered on the first ring.

"We've got rooms for you at the Marriott near Regents Park when you're ready for a rest. Susan is going to stay with you but Sir Giles wants me back at the office. I will check in with you regularly but you must let me know the moment you have news. We'll have cars available for your use at any time, day or night. Just have Susan call and ask."

"We will be fine here Freddy. Thank you."

As Freddy left, Stone and Huw looked at each other. "We're in for a long wait, I believe. A long, dark wait," Huw said quietly.

"I know Huw. I know."

### Crown Security offices, London

Sir Giles collapsed exhausted on his less than comfortable office couch. His eyes were bloodshot and his body slumped as he sat in his crumpled clothes. Wrinkled they may be, but his old-school values insisted that he retain his jacket and tie professional image. Thank God the office door was closed, he thought. Wouldn't do for the troops to see him weaken whether in looks or attitude. After a brief rest he forced himself up again and pulled an electric shaver out of a drawer, giving himself a quick once over.

A sharp knock on the door and Freddy entered having rushed back to the office, all the while gathering as much information as he could. "More news from the attack. The rocket seems to have missed the entire stage area, Sir Giles. It actually exploded about one hundred feet behind the stage. The blast was big enough to blow both archbishops off the platform with severe shrapnel wounds and burns. Same for the congregation and choir, though they were saved by the fact that the rocket hit behind the platform and it took the brunt of the explosion. Lots of injuries from the debris though."

He looked over his notes again before continuing. "At this point the Archbishop of Canterbury is in critical condition and, frankly, not expected to survive. The Archbishop of Westminster is also critical but they're not making any long term evaluations at this point. Another seven in critical condition. We have three policemen and a Special Branch man killed. They were looking after security and patrolling the area behind the platform. Another dozen or so have critical injuries. In all about seventy-five wounded and four dead plus some not expected to survive."

"Bad business. Bad business all around. What happened at the hotel? What about Quinn?" Freddy briefed the guvnor as quickly but as completely as he could, describing the moment they'd smashed into the room and surprised Quinn just as he was firing the launcher.

"So he's dead. You're sure he shot Mandy as he fell?"

"Yes, Sir Giles. I saw him fire at her before aimed at us. By then it was too late and we we'd already shot him."

Sir Giles grunted and picked up a pencil from his desk. He began to tap it. Used to his ways, Freddy waited quietly. Finally the guvnor looked up at him. "Ta muid anseo. As the Master has spoken." He grunted again. "Words to haunt them Freddy. Bet they never thought it would rebound on them."

One of the other CSB agents then slipped into the doorway. "Phone, Sir Giles. Chad Lawson from the United States."

Sir Giles listened as Chad reported, beckoning Freddy to stay in the office until it was finished. It was a long report, but finally and with thanks, Sir Giles hung up.

"Wasted! All our effort wasted Freddy!" He flung his pencil across the room and a book on the desk soon followed it, crashing into the wall before dropping on the floor.

He looked grimly at Freddy.

"Bastards have the Scroll. Callaghan snatched it right out of Lawson's hands. God I want to get my hands on them. May they burn in hell!"

# Chapter Twenty-Seven

**Crown Security offices, London**

Sir Giles had resigned himself to a night spent in the office again. Latest word from the hospital reported that Mandy had made it through a second operation but was still in a coma. While he understood their initial refusal, he pleaded with both Huw and Stone to consider going to the hotel. After much arguing and persuasion they reluctantly agreed, with Stone taking the first break. Huw would stay at the hospital with Mandy. If all went well, they would switch after a few hours.

The other news from the hospital was not as good. Both Archbishops succumbed to their injuries early Monday morning, as did two of the other casualties brought in. That raised the death toll to seven with more expected. Hospital accident and emergency wards around west London were inundated with victims. The media was in an uproar. Already the Prime Minister had returned to London and visited St. Mary's hospital, speaking with some of the victims and with the families and close associates of both clerics.

In an unprecedented move, the Queen had cancelled the remainder of her State Visit and was returning to London immediately.

All Monday Sir Giles spent working with the Home Secretary and police officials. The Secretary and his officials acknowledged the Crown Security team for their dogged pursuit of the Druids and praised them for killing the assassin and disrupting his aim which, even the head of the Metropolitan Police agreed saved many more lives. Had the missile hit the center of the stage the devastation would have been far greater and the number of deaths much higher. Nevertheless, the Home Secretary turned the investigation over to MI5 and the Met.

Crown Security was shunted aside; no longer needed in the aftermath.

Sir Giles knew better. Callaghan, mastermind of the atrocities, was still loose and the Scroll Huw believed so vital was now in his hands. If Huw was correct, they might be facing atrocities and events that would be far worse. No, although his arguments were tut-tutted by the other agencies, he realized they were concentrating on past events. Sir Giles and his people were gripped by the potential future.

"Bloody turf wars," he grumbled to Freddy as they grabbed a quick sandwich and tea for a late supper. "They want credit of course." He pulled the wrapping off another sandwich and took a huge bite, chewed and swallowed before continuing. "Only fair I suppose. Want to keep us out of media and public scrutiny. Keep us in the shadows. Gives us independence and keeps our accountability to Her Majesty only."

Freddy tossed his sandwich wrapping into a rubbish bin. "Any information on that plane yet, sir?"

From the moment Chad had told him about the Irish registered Challenger, Sir Giles had worked his monumental list of contacts in various government agencies at home and overseas. Over the past few hours a pattern had emerged. Like Chad, he believed the plane contained both Callaghan and the Scroll. It crossed into Canada and tracked across the remote wilderness of both northern Ontario and Quebec. After a brief fuel stop in Goose Bay, Labrador it was now somewhere over the North Atlantic headed where exactly?

"Ireland, most likely." Freddy munched into another sandwich and sipped his tea.

Sir Giles shook his head. "No. One loose element. Wales!" He reminded Freddy that the paralyzed brother was still in the house near Neath. He began listing off the information on his fingers. "One. Our people in Wales have been investigating. Two. The brother has Welsh day help including a male nurse. Three. Quinn senior was in charge but left suddenly. Told the nurse Williams he would return in a few days. Four. Chad reports the man killed in the warehouse was named Quinn." He drummed his fingers against the desktop then drank some tea.

"Somehow. Soon. Callaghan will return to Wales. His brother is still there."

There was a sudden increase of noise in the main offices with lots of voices, some strident. The Guvnor and Freddy stepped out to see what the fuss was about.

"You have the wrong office sir, I'm sorry. This is a genealogy tracing company."

"Bollocks!"

Sir Giles and Freddy emerged to see a strapping man in tweeds and a country cap being gently but forcefully held up by the chunky form of Roger Abbot, one of Crown Security's strongest field agents. Behind them a tall graceful white haired woman stood smiling. Sir Giles and Freddy both burst out laughing.

"It's all right Roger, let him go. He's got the right place." A chuckling Sir Giles thrust his hand out. "So good to see you again Eddie. Lovely to have you with us Lady Greyfell."

Freddy trumped the situation, introducing Roger to Lord Greyfell. The agent blanched at the thought he'd been manhandling a peer of the realm. Lord Greyfell slapped him on the back, "Just doing your job old boy. Good for you." Then he and Nees followed Sir Giles and Freddy into the inner sanctum.

"Genealogy tracing company?" Lord Greyfell's eyebrows rose.

"Useful cover for unwanted visitors," Sir Giles chuckled, ushering them to the couch where he proceeded to bring them up to date on the Hyde Park attack and its aftermath as well as the latest on the Scroll.

"But what brings you here?"

"Couldn't reach Huw and with Colin gone I felt we were missing all the action. So I decided we would bring our news in person."

"Go on."

"As you know Giles, Nees and I have many underground contacts within the Druid community in Wales, Ireland, Cornwall and even France. It's not official and never provable, but the leads and information our contacts have given us over the years have never been wrong." He shifted in his seat. "Nees and I generally keep our contacts separate so we can double check the veracity of any information we're given. Both of us received information from sources late yesterday and today that we've corroborated..."

"Even as we rode down on the train" Nees interrupted.

"Callaghan has called an urgent Gorsedd of all Druid leaders, in Wales. It will be in the next few days."

"The trouble is," Nees continued, "we still don't know where. Or when."

"So we felt it imperative to get this to you as quickly as possible. We came ourselves knowing you'd be up to your necks in the Hyde Park massacre."

"You old fox! Simple phone call or email would have been sufficient. You just wanted to be in on the action."

Greyfell had the grace to look humbled before the four of them got down to business and reviewed and dissected all the information they had each gathered over the past days trying to find a pattern and to predict Callaghan's next actions and location.

"There's something else which may or may not be significant." Greyfell pulled more papers from his pocket. "For the last little while, I've been getting bits and pieces of information about Callaghan's brother Declan. He's paralyzed and apparently is sinking into depression. Apparently he's had raging battles with Diarmuid, battling over methods the Dragon Master is using to propagate the Druid faith. Declan wants to return to the quiet, nature-fixed aspect of Druidry. And Declan was always popular with the younger Druids; very charismatic until he was wounded. Now apparently he abhors the killings and violence Diarmuid has unleashed."

"How do you know this?"

"Declan has his own small group of friends and followers, some of whom were with him in France and saw the wastefulness and savagery of the Druids there. It shocked a lot of them and made them question the path they were on. Declan's injuries and his rejection of violence has influenced them."

Nees picked up the story. "Declan is apparently a virtual prisoner in the house. But he's made friends with some of the day help. He's not allowed a phone or internet connection of any kind, but he's been able to convince the cleaner and his nurse to pass messages along to one of his friends, a woman, who's moved to Neath to be close to him."

"Yes," added Lord Greyfell, "and that woman has twice been stopped at the entrance to the property and refused admission. The last time, she was threatened with her life. She's now become a quiet link between Declan and his friends."

Significant information, they all agreed. But how it fit and how it would help baffled them at the moment. After more time working and reworking the information they agreed to reconvene early Tuesday morning,

When Lord and Lady Greyfell left for a hotel, Sir Giles and Freddy hunkered down on flimsy cots at the office. Through the night they received continuing reports that Mandy was still in a coma. So far all the other casualties at St. Mary's and the other hospitals were holding their own with no further deaths reported.

Tuesday morning brought rain. Persistent showers interspersed with drizzle and low grey cloud blotted out many of the towers and skyscrapers that now dotted the London skyline. Not that it matters, Sir Giles grumbled to himself. Can't see much beyond the Palace from my windows anyway.

Freddy produced a time line in both written and chart form from the time they believed Callaghan had been named Dragon Master. They traced the movements and actions of all parties, friend and foe alike, seeking insight to the Dragon Master's thought processes and mindset.

Sir Giles was disgruntled to find that all trace of the Challenger had disappeared. "Either crashed into the Atlantic, which I don't bloody believe for one minute. Or somehow changed identity and landed in Ireland or the UK."

Stumped, he look at his three companions. "Missing something. Got to find it."

**Vale of Neath, Wales**

In the blackness of night, Diarmuid Callaghan returned home.

From the moment his plane landed at the Druid's private airfield near Carmarthen, his every movement and contact was done surreptitiously. Nothing, but nothing must draw attention to him. Even his flight was done in the shadows; his pilot covertly changed his registration and flight plan during the stop at Goose Bay. Then, halfway across the Atlantic, they changed their flight path and altitude, dropping to ten thousand feet and turning south. They followed that course, sucking fuel at much higher rates at the lower altitude, and then turned east again, allowing them to pass well south of Ireland and fly in almost a direct line to the Carmarthen field.

They landed at dusk. As soon as Callaghan and his precious package were off, the Challenger took off once again, turning west towards a disused former IRA secret airfield near Wexford.

He was bundled into a black Peugeot crossover with dark tinted windows. The driver took a long, circular route, doubling back on himself several times to check for unwanted tails. He avoided the A48 and M4 motorways, opting instead for lesser used back roads, skirting Ammanford and Pontardulais before sweeping around the north edges of Neath itself and then north toward Resolven.

In the back of the car, Callaghan seethed with anger and hatred. He said nothing to the driver or the companion beside him. He and he alone clutched the silver tube. His mind writhed with rage. On board the plane he'd heard reports of the attack in London. He heard too that young Quinn was dead, killed in the hotel room at the moment of the attack. How had they found him? And who?

All he'd learned was that Quinn secured the girl in the room while he conducted the assassination. Then he was to kill her and escape. Instead, he himself was killed. Just before the plane landed he found out the girl had somehow survived but was near death in a London hospital. He smiled at that news. Perhaps he could use that information to pull both Griffiths and Wallace together for their execution. One thing was certain. Their deaths would be at his hands alone. He would trust no one else to complete the act of revenge. The girl was insignificant in comparison.

At the same time, he thought of his brother; the brother he loved but who now opposed him. Declan's submissiveness didn't fool him. He knew his twin too well. Declan objected to Diarmuid's bold offensive moves. The injuries had softened his brother's resolve; he was now weak and a threat rather than support. He claimed to reject the concept of killing and destruction. Yes, Declan was a problem that also needed to be solved.

He tried to calm himself. Nothing really mattered now. He had the Scroll and the means to finding the sacred Lance itself. Visions of power swept through him. Now he could avenge himself on Griffiths and Wallace. A sudden bolt of fear shot through him as he thought of the old man. Somehow he had to deflect the old man from his search. It was a deadly game he was about to play, but once he had his hands on the Lance it would not matter. He would be supreme.

At Resolven, the driver took a little used side road off the Glyn Neath Road and headed up the mountain. A short time later, he stopped briefly while his passengers got out and slipped into the depths of the forest, then left immediately. Clouds rolled up the valley and began to obscure the quarter moon. Callaghan knew that rain was forecast for the next day but so far there was no hint of it.

For the first time since landing, Callaghan spoke. "You lead. Follow the path up and across this mountain. When we're above the house, I want to wait until the middle of the night. While I wait, you circle around and see if there are any watchers. If so, take them out. Absolute silence from here on."

It was a long, hard slug up and over the mountain, pushing their way through the dark forest with only a small flashlight to guide them, and that only once in a while. It was after midnight when Callaghan finally peered through the trees and saw the outside security lights on the driveway of the house. He stopped and sat down on an old stump, placing the silver tube on the ground beside him. His eyes, adjusted to the limited light, could see nothing moving. No hint of police or security people watching the house. But he would wait until his man cleared the area.

He signaled his companion who silently slipped off and disappeared into the woods.

Callaghan found a better, more sheltered spot and settled down for the long wait. His mind raced, chasing thoughts and seeking a plan. An hour later it came to him. Like a spider he would draw Griffiths and Wallace into his lair. All he had to do was identify the girl's hospital.

While the anger and lust for revenge still churned inside him, a sense of triumph and victory also surged in him.

He was close. So very, very close.

### Crown Security offices, London

The imperative now was to find Callaghan and retrieve the Scroll.

Colin was still tied up with the post-attack investigation. Although he'd given them as much detail as he could, M15 still wanted him kept around to help them. Freddy, Stone and the other Crown Security agents involved were also questioned thoroughly and repeatedly. The investigators now accepted the very real threat posed by the Druids and finally realized Sir Giles was right all along; the attack on Winchester Cathedral and the other churches were indeed linked. Remembering last fall's foiled attack on the Queen, however, the Home Secretary insisted that Crown Security stick to its own remit and ensure no further attacks were attempted against the Royal Family. Colin, meanwhile, was to remain attached to them and act as liaison.

By late Tuesday afternoon, little had changed. Mandy was still fighting for her life. Callaghan and the Scroll had disappeared. Frustration was beginning to set in once again. Working their sources hard produced no further information for Lord Greyfell and Nees. All they got was confirmation of the planned Druid council, but no hint as to time or location.

They were still ruminating the information when Huw and Stone looking grim, suddenly walked in. Everyone looked as Huw silently placed a letter on the desk in front of Sir Giles. He looked curiously at Huw and

Stone, then picked the letter up and read it. His face didn't change or show emotion as he put the letter down.

"What do you want to do?" Sir Giles posed the question directly at Huw without attempting to explain the letter or its content to the others.

"Go, of course. With Stone."

Sir Giles sighed and turned to his companions. "The note claims to be from Declan Callaghan and was delivered to St. Mary's hospital. It denounces Diarmuid and the Druids and says he, Declan, now realizes how horrific things have become under his brother's leadership. He says he wants to end all the violence by turning Diarmuid in. He wants to do this quietly and without what he calls 'fuss', so that Callaghan's supporters won't know and create more chaos and killing in revenge. He wants to make Diarmuid disappear like Damien Wyndham and Liam Murphy disappeared. He asks Huw and Stone to be there as witnesses that he was not involved in the attacks. They can bring agents with them."

"Bollocks! And double bollocks!" Greyfell's bellow resounded around the office. "It's a trap plain and simple. You'd be a fool to proceed with this, Huw." He turned to Sir Giles. "Stop this insanity Giles. Make him listen."

The argument raged amongst all of them. Between the shouting and fist banging on the desk, neither side was swaying the other. Finally, Sir Giles called a halt to the disagreement. "No one wants an end to Callaghan more than me. But the letter was addressed to Huw. What reasons for agreeing to this Huw?"

Huw thought carefully. The argument had been raging in his mind since he opened the letter. "I know full well this could be a trap. I know that Callaghan is a blood thirsty killer and that he wants revenge on me for Excalibur." He paused for a moment. "But I also hear that you Lord Greyfell, agree that young Declan feels this way. So this could indeed be a sincere attempt to end all this bloodshed." He threw up his hands. "All I know is that Diarmuid Callaghan must be stopped. If I don't go, we have very little to go on that would help us stop him. He could disappear at any moment and go find the Sacred Lance. He now has the Scroll it seems. It is vital that we get it back or at least prevent him from using it. But we can't even track his air travels to and from this country!" He said this with a direct look at Sir Giles, who nodded glumly in agreement.

"So yes it's perilous and perhaps deadly. But if I go and Declan is indeed behind this? Well…" He left the sentence unfinished.

"And you Stone. What do you feel?" Sir Giles directed the question right at the American. He didn't answer right away, his own feelings conflicted greatly. He wanted to stay and be with Mandy while—if—she recovered. But he owed so much to Huw. He could not let his friend, mentor and surrogate father go alone. After a few moments he shared these thoughts with the group. "So it seems to me, if Huw goes, someone must go with him and I will be that someone."

Quietness pervaded the office. The Guvnor looked from one to the other. "Send some men with you as well. Colin is not available. Freddy is not a field agent," he smiled at his assistant, "no matter how much he fantasizes."

"I'm going too." Greyfell blurted. He perceived the puzzled looks around him. "Not just a pretty face, you know. Retired Major in the Parachute Regiment. I served as a Captain during the Falklands campaign and was in the slog across the island from San Carlos right to Port Stanley. Had some hard fighting with the Argentines along the way and lost some good people, but we did it. We surprised them and we won." He glared at Nees. "Don't say a word, dear. If they're going I am. My mind's made up."

Sir Giles sighed in acceptance. "Freddy. Get a special arms permit for Stone." He turned to Stone. "Understand you resented the fact you didn't have a gun at the hotel."

Stone shook his head. "Thanks any way Sir Giles, but I'm better without. Only fired a gun once in my life when we were under attack in Canada. I might have wanted one at the hotel, I was so angry at what they'd done to Mandy, but frankly if I had one I'd be more dangerous to my friends than my enemies."

The argument over, all of them began working on how, when and where they would meet with Declan. Sooner rather than later, they decided, aware of the very tight time frame involved. More of the planning revolved around backup for Huw and Stone inside the house. "Give me command of six or seven men, Giles. I'll sort that out."

Finally, they agreed to head down to Wales immediately Greyfell had the men he needed briefed and equipped. Freddy was directed to organize transportation and supplies. Huw and Stone were ordered to eat a hearty meal and rest. Abbot was told to find detailed Ordnance Survey maps of the area around Resolven. Sir Giles called his MI6 friend and requested some further help, including the most up to the minute satellite photos of the

Neath house. Better yet, if he could arrange quickly for a satellite pass over the house and get one, even better.

"I know you'll have to pull a lot of strings Reggie, but this is tied in with the assassination of the Archbishops. It comes from the top, but needs absolute secrecy. You can do it? Fine, Reggie, fine. Let me know the minute you have something."

It was midnight before all the pieces came together. Greyfell briefed the six men assigned to him and when he was finished the whole group gathered around the conference table in an office adjacent to Sir Giles' domain. There they carefully scrutinized the maps and satellite photos the team had assembled.

"It's half way up a bloody mountain, man!" Greyfell barked. "Hard to get part of the team behind the place unless we stomp through the woods." Again and again they examined the information, finally coming up with a plan that, while it had holes, was the best that could be pulled together especially since, as Greyfell pointed out, "we have no idea whatsoever what we're going to face. Never mind what Huw and Stone will have to deal with."

Freddy arranged a helicopter to drop them off at a golf course near Bridgend. Vehicles would meet them there and transport them the twenty miles or so to the target. Freddy assured them all that secrecy was imperative which was why he chose the golf course. "It's the only real flat land available around that part of South Wales. We can't get much closer because of the mountains and valleys." Plus he added, the vehicles would be driven by two Crown Security agents already posted in South Wales to keep an eye on the old Druid compound around Careg Cennen Castle. "You can brief them as you drive, Lord Greyfell."

A telephone rang in the outer office. Seconds later Abbot appeared at the door. "That was Susan at the hospital. Miss Griffiths is still comatose, but her vital signs are beginning to improve. She said to tell Professor Griffiths that the doctors are now encouraged and cautiously optimistic."

Huw, Stone and the group smiled at that, clapping and delighted that the news finally was turning good. Maybe, as Nees pointed out, that was a good portent for their expedition.

They began assembling their equipment and started to head down the stairs to the large passenger van Freddy had allocated to take them to the RAF base where the helicopter was already set to launch.

"Take care gentlemen," Sir Giles said gruffly to Huw and Stone "I've become quite fond of you both. Even though you did cost the crown one of its jewels when you gave Excalibur away," he gently teased Stone. "Make sure you come back alive. Don't care about Callaghan."

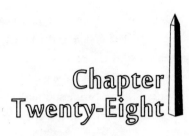

# Chapter Twenty-Eight

**Vale of Neath, Wales**

They walked slowly up the winding driveway towards the house. It was almost four in the morning. Behind them, they knew, some of the men in black camouflage and blacked faces and hands, would wait for a few minutes then follow them up the drive. Three others were already working their way up the sides of the property. Others were trying to work around the back of the house and two more waited down on the road.

The satellite shots plus their own on-site surveillance showed no guards, no patrols, no security huts. A sophisticated sweep by the team upon arrival an hour ago showed no trip wires, no laser light traps.

A quick discussion behind the trees a couple of hundred yards from the driveway had confirmed the decision to move forward even though the absence of any visible or even invisible security worried Greyfell. "Not like Callaghan at all. In my bones Huw, I am convinced this is a trap. Don't go up there. Let's wait and call in reinforcements and rethink this."

Huw uttered a very curt "No." He was deeply worried, he admitted. "But I have a real sense of peace about this. I believe that God is with me and that this is what he wants me to do." Stone simply nodded and added "What he said."

"Thought you might say that. There's been a slight change of plans. I discussed this with Sir Giles and the boys we have with us. I will be going up there with you. Neither of you is armed. I am. Discussion over."

It was too late to make a fuss or insist on anything, and both Huw and Stone saw the wisdom in Greyfell's words.

Now they were almost at the house itself. Huw stopped. The silence was overwhelming. Can you truly feel silence, he wondered, because it certainly feels so. Nothing moved. They could not even sense the men they knew were moving in and around them. No alarms had triggered, unless they were silent alarms in the house. The inside of the house was dark and the house itself silent. They stood just outside the reach of the one security light illuminating the main door and the path to the garage.

"Great time to think about this Huw," Stone suddenly whispered, "but what do we do? Just go up to the door and knock and this hour of the morning."

Huw nodded. "Yes. Lord Greyfell told me that both Callaghans sleep lightly anyway and are often up and working in the early morning." Stone saw Greyfell nod in agreement.

As if to prove it, an interior light suddenly snapped on, then a second.

"Bedroom and hall most likely," Greyfell murmured.

Stone straightened himself up and walked into the light and up to the door. Huw and Greyfell were only steps behind him. He stopped a moment, took a deep breath, and banged on the door.

As the door flung suddenly open, Stone braced himself for a blast of gunfire. Instead there was only silence and darkness. A voice penetrated the gloom.

"Come in. Lock the door behind you. Then step into the middle of the room."

They did as they were told. Walking slowly, hands at their sides to avoid threatening gestures, they moved into the center of what Stone surmised was the living room. At a command they stopped. Lights flicked on. They saw a man automatic pistol in hand poised behind and slightly to the left of the door, his weapon aimed unwaveringly at them. Again, a one word command to sit was barked at them. They obeyed. Stone and Huw sat on the sofa. Greyfell found a small side chair. All faced their captor.

His back to the wall, the man stepped forward into the light.

The Irish brogue was unmistakable. "Professor Griffiths. Mr. Wallace. We finally meet. I don't believe I know this third gentleman"

Before Huw could speak, Greyfell answered for himself.

"Ah. The shadowy Lord Greyfell who lurks around trying to find out about us and our ways. I wish I could say welcome, but I won't"

Stone's heart fell. He knew he was facing Diarmuid Callaghan. It was indeed a trap. He looked over at Huw who calmly eyed Callaghan. Greyfell sat impassive watching Callaghan like a hawk. There was no chance, Stone realized. Even though Greyfell was armed, he could not use his weapon in sufficient time to save them. It was over.

"Thank you for accepting my invitation." Callaghan was obviously enjoying the moment and, for some reason, delaying the inevitable. "Sorry I had to tell a bit of a fib and use my poor brother as a stooge for this charade, but honestly, would you have come so willingly if I had sent the letter?"

He paused. "Cat got your tongue? Ah well, it doesn't matter." He kept moving slowly, circling around past the main door and avoiding the windows until he was standing beside a table on which stood an ornament draped in a white sheet. A dark hallway stretched out behind him, leading to what Stone surmised were the bedrooms.

"I asked you here Professor, for two reasons. First, I want you and Mr. Wallace to know how much I hate you and how very much I am glad that you survived all my previous efforts to destroy you. I now realize how much more pleasant my revenge will be as I see you die before my own eyes. Lord Greyfell? Let's just say you are a welcome bonus."

He ranted on, rationalizing his loathing and laying the blame for Declan's injuries, the failure of the Samhein plot and a myriad of other setbacks at Huw's feet. Spittle collected and began to foam at the corners of his mouth as his voice rose and anger increased. He stopped and took a deep breath, wiping the spit away with his free hand.

"But I also want to thank you Professor. Without you we would never have known about the Scroll. Nor the hiding place of the Sacred Lance. Thanks to you we now know where to find it. And it will finally be in our hands and give us the key to all dominion over this world.'

His left hand moved again and slowly pulled the sheet off the ornament. The silver tube rested in its glory on the table. A flick of a switch and light bathed the glistening, shimmering object.

For the first time, Huw showed emotion on his face as he looked at the Scroll tube. His body stiffened, torn between the need to keep calm and the historian's desire to cradle his discovery in his hands.

"Thanks to your work and discoveries, Norris was able to get the original inventory list and documents from that old collector in Koblenz. His death alone was worth getting hands on this." His hand caressed the tube but his eyes remained fixed on his three prisoners.

Just as quickly as he'd adopted the calmer conciliatory tone, his voice changed again, deepening in anger.

"But this cost me the life of my dear friend Anson Quinn. He died obeying my orders when I should have just stayed an executed all those Americans myself!"

The tone changed again as he began to reminisce. "You probably don't realize this gentlemen but Anson and his son Norris were descended from a long line of Druids. Anson's own father played a pivotal role. Your British security people knew him as Mick O'Flaherty. They killed him on the Ulster border. But during the war he actually served as our Druid emissary to the German government. The Germans knew him as Hans Ostermann and he was the SS Major instrumental in guiding Hitler's search for the Lance. I'm willing to bet you didn't know that."

He was continuing his monologue, varying from foaming anger to quiet reflection. Stone glanced across at Huw and saw his lips moving. He heard his quiet words; "Thy will be done on earth as it is in heaven."

Suddenly there was banging on the two glass doors that led to the back patio. Callaghan automatically dropped into a firing position but waited. The knocking happened again. Cautiously, Callaghan made his way towards the doors, scrutinizing carefully. Then he straightened and purposefully walked over and opened it.

An old man, dressed totally in black and covered in a thigh length black cloak stepped in.

"Master."

Callaghan stepped back towards his former spot beside the Scroll, weapon fixed firmly on his victims. The man slowly surveyed the room, noted the three seated men. Then almost glided across the floor to close in on Callaghan. Stone watched carefully but did not see his legs move and didn't hear steps on the polished hardwood floor. Yet the old man moved across. Greyfell's eyes widened in surprise then tightened, recognizing just who he was facing.

"You have been busy, Dragon Master." An icy cold voice flowed out of the old man. It seemed to permeate the room. Huw shivered suddenly.

"Things have moved quickly, Master. My men found the lead to get this ancient Scroll."

"It is not the Lance I asked you to find for me."

"No Master. But this will tell us the Lance's hiding place. With this information we will get it."

Callaghan began to sweat in spite of the cold. He had hoped not to encounter the old man until he had his own hands firmly on the Lance and therefore in control.

"No. I will take the Scroll with me. Your efforts in this matter are no longer required. You are needed no longer."

Callaghan blanched. His face drained of blood as he saw his hopes and dreams disappear into the old man's claws. He was frozen into silence by the sudden change of fortunes, then stammered and stuttered.

"But...but...Master....It is my right as Dragon Master..."

"You have no rights, no power as Dragon Master. Only what I bestow," the old man bellowed.

Stone heard two whispers or hisses and was shocked to see both Callaghan and the Old Man suddenly drop to the floor.

"You three. Do not move."

An equally Irish brogue croaked out the command. Stone peered into the shadows of the hallway and saw a mirror-image Callaghan seated in an electric wheelchair. A strange looking gun was fixed firmly on the three of them.

"Declan!" Stone unconsciously uttered the name out loud.

"Correct. And I know who you are." He looked down at the two figures on the floor, eyes wide open but unmoving. He took a deep breath. "It's a drug. Zemuron. Paralyzes the body but keeps the mind clear and alert and does not interfere with the ability to hear. They won't move for hours. Diarmuid arranged for me to have it, to help counter my pain."

"But he's a Sidhe," Greyfell blurted, pointing to the prostrate old man.

"Yes. Not a human. Yet a human." Declan filled his agonizing lungs again. "But they are vulnerable to certain things like drugs. I made sure of that. And death."

While he struggled for another breath, Stone and Greyfell began to rise.

"Stop. Don't move." They resumed their seats as Declan wheeled his chair into the light. As he sat back down, Stone noticed a strong smell wafting through the air.

"Used a dart gun Quinn bought for me. Adapted some of the darts to carry the drugs and stuff."

Greyfell suddenly began muttering:

*By the turn of one*
*The curse is done*
*By turn of two*
*Its power is through*
*By turn of three*
*It ceases to be*

"Very good, sir, Lord Greyfell is it? You know the ancient Druidic curse removal chant." He thought for a moment, then laughed amusedly. "And used it against the Druids themselves." He was silent for a moment. "Perhaps it's as well," he said suddenly serious again. "It's time to end the curse. All the curses."

The odor grew stronger. "Declan. I smell gas. Let's get everyone out of here."

"Stay where you are. I have one last act to fulfill." He turned his chair slightly so that he faced back into the hall. "I turned the kitchen gas on. This must all end now. After this, no more deaths. No more murders. No more violence."

His hand abruptly moved to the gun as he reloaded. He raised it slightly and fired into the hallway.

The blast was instantaneous. The tiny flare mechanism adapted onto the last dart ignited the gas. Flames shot out of the kitchen and into the halls. The blast knocked the Scroll tube off the table. It rolled on the floor, landing against Diarmuid's immobile body.

Even as he fired, Greyfell noticed he reloaded yet again.

"Get out. Now." Declan aimed the gun at them and pointed to the main door just as the closest Crown Security men began trying to burst the door down.

"Come with us Declan. Let us save you." Huw moved toward him while Stone and Greyfell ran towards the door, Stone tugging on Huw's sleeve. A wall of flame burst out of the hallway and blocked them from the door. Another flash of fire crackled between Declan and his would-be savior.

Flames sucked the very air out of Huw's lungs and he partially collapsed against both Stone and Greyfell. Stone was desperately struggling to breathe himself as the former army major struggled to get them to the door.

Even as the front door burst open the inferno gained strength and engulfed the room. Greyfell staggered out, dragging Huw and Stone behind him. Welcome hands grabbed them all even as Greyfell heard the calls to fall back.

The last sight Stone had was flames licking around a serene Declan, waiting as flames engulfed the living room. Of the Sidhe and Diarmuid he saw nothing. There was one last glint of silver as the flames licked at the tube.

All three were bodily hauled away but had only gone a few yards when an enormous explosion wracked the building. They were flung to the ground by the force of the blast. Flames shot a hundred feet into the night sky and sparks and debris began to fall on them. More hands suddenly grabbed them and dragged them across the ground in a desperate attempt to get away from the hellhole that was the funeral pyre for both Callaghan twins.

Stone glanced back one more time.

It's over, he thought.

Then he blacked out.

# Epilogue

The return to London was quiet.

By the time emergency services arrived, the Callaghan house was a blazing, smoking, crumpled shell. Arriving fire engines aimed their hoses at the flames, adding to the sights and sounds that morning as the water turned to rising columns of white steam contrasting with the black burning smoke from the fire.

Ambulance attendants tried to persuade the three men to go to hospital for further checkups and tests. All refused. When he regained consciousness, all Stone could think of was the horror of the past twenty minutes, the shock of seeing Declan calmly accepting his own death while ensuring his brother's. His mind could not grapple with the vivid contradiction of brotherly love culminating in murder-suicide.

Huw sat slumped on the grass as the dawn light began to reveal more and more of the destruction and chaos around them. Greyfell, reverting to his military persona took charge of the Crown Security personnel on site, identifying himself and all of them to the local police who showed up shocked by the enormity of the disaster that had hit their tiny community.

The need for surprise no longer necessary, Greyfell quickly arranged for the helicopter to land at a small roundabout on the Glyn Neath Road, a mile and a half from the scene. Reluctantly and only after a long mobile phone discussion with Sir Giles, the police agreed to allow the three of them to leave on the chopper. The other agents would remain on scene to assist the investigation, manage the disaster site and recover the bodies.

The silence on board the helicopter was broken when word came through that Mandy was beginning to come out of her coma. Smiles creased all their faces as they contemplated what might have been.

Huw turned to Stone. "Bradstone, my boy. You see now don't you, that God was in this with us. All the way through. He would not allow such evil to continue or to go unpunished." He gripped Stone's arm firmly. "I told you before. He is using you. He has a plan for you, for me and for Mandy. He will not force us to follow his will. But he will make it obvious. This has been my prayer all along. That and asking for forgiveness for my own pride, my desire to gain acclaim for my work and my own stubbornness and lack of faith at times."

Stone thought for a moment. "I want to believe. I've struggled with this for months. And today, when I thought I really was going to finally die, I felt ready to accept the inevitable."

He put his own hand over Huw's. You've shown me what faith really looks like. But I still don't know what to do. Where do I go from here," he asked plaintively.

"Start with simple steps, my boy." Huw looked deep into Stone's eyes. "Go to Mandy. Be with her. Help her through her recovery. She loves you. More than even she realizes. Forgive her for letting her head get turned by that charlatan."

"I love her too Huw. But our lives and careers seem so at odds with it all."

"Wait. Pray about it, but wait. God will guide." He dropped his hand. "Now, if you don't mind, let me just close my eyes for a bit. I need a nap. I'm totally knackered. I'm an old man and don't need all this tiring excitement and stress. Two bloody fires I've been through in the past few weeks. It's as if the fires of hell were trying to consume us!" he grumped. "Probably won't wake up for a fortnight."

Stone smiled. He looked out the window of the craft as it flew across the countryside. He saw they were just crossing just north of the Severn Bridge. Time enough for him to get a bit of a nap in as well. He closed his eyes and settled back into the uncomfortable but very welcome seat.

ð

The young boy found the metal piece first. Their parents had forbidden them to play in the area where everyone, including the Israeli authorities, knew were unexplored shafts and shaky cellars belonging to the ramshackle houses above.

Supposedly, professors from some university were going to come and explore these underground labyrinths. But so many places in Jerusalem and the West Bank were under the same promises and plans. Lack of funding, personnel and especially sectarian violence and clashes meant the reality was that these places lingered on, unexcavated and uncared for.

Despite the parental missives, the children still used the area as a playground. The boy was scrambling around in the dirt, trying to pull away part of what seemed like an old wall. He found the metal object sticking out of the sandy soil. He pulled it out while the other children crowded around him.

"What is it," they clamored as he pulled it out, pushing and shoving to see the heavily rusted iron piece. He held it in his hand, turning it over and over, looking at it. It was pointed at one end, looking somewhat like a large arrow head, as one of the children commented.

"What will you do with it?" several shouted.

"It's just an old piece of metal. I'll to take it to Mustafah the metal dealer. He'll give me some shekels for it, I'm sure." As he played with it, it suddenly broke in two at a heavily rusted section. "Won't be worth as much now," he said dejectedly. "I'm just going to put it in the garbage" he said, walking dissonantly towards a rubbish heap at the end of the street. He was just in time as the sanitation workers tossed everything into the truck.

None of the children noticed the old Roman coin partially hidden by the sand, right next to the place they'd found the lance tip.

**THE END**

# About The Author

Barrie Doyle is an award-winning storyteller. For much of his writing career, he has told stories as a journalist and public relations professional. He has taught PR at a major Canadian college and also trained corporate and non-profit leaders in how to utilize media to tell their own stories. His awards reflect his success in helping real people tell real stories.

Storytelling, whether fiction or non-fiction, is a reflection of the human condition in all its glory and depravity. Barrie has covered the triumphant moon landings and also told heart-wrenching stories of returned POWs who were tortured at the infamous Hanoi Hilton in Vietnam. He's also covered everything from tragic plane crashes to Royal visits.

As a PR consultant, his clients have ranged from General Motors to Kids Help Phone, from the Christian and Missionary Alliance in Canada to Huronia Cruise Lines. He has also founded successful magazines and taught writing at various conferences and workshops, including the famous Billy Graham Schools of Writing in both Canada and the United States.

Taking real-world experiences and people and putting them into different situations is part of the excitement and challenge for him in writing fiction.

Although he was born in Wales, Barrie has lived in various parts of the United States, including Washington D.C., where he was assistant news editor of *Christianity Today*. He now lives in Canada on the beautiful blue water shores of Georgian Bay just north of Toronto. An avid traveller, he brings his travel experience to his novels, providing exotic and sometimes unfamiliar locales.

He is married and has two daughters, two sons, and two wonderful grandsons.

ExcaliburNation is the fan club for those who enjoyed *The Excalibur Parchment* and its succeeding stories in The Oak Grove Conspiracies trilogy.

View the trailers for both *The Excalibur Parchment* and *The Lucifer Scroll*. Enter contests (one of the characters in *The Lucifer Scroll* was named after a previous contest winner). Read more of the back story of Excalibur and learn about the real Druids and their religion. Find out interesting facts about the city known as Byzantium, or Constantinople before it became Istanbul as well as viewing photos of many key locations used in the books.

At www.excaliburparchment.com you will also find the latest news, reviews and speaking schedule as well as links to the fan club. The website is also packed with background information on life in the middle ages and even a pronunciation guide for those brave souls willing to tackle the tongue-twisting Welsh place names. A number of readers have already expressed appreciation that I did not include the name of this Welsh village in the book: Llanfairpwyllgwyngyllgogerychwyndrobwllllantysiliogogogoch. Look it up, it's on the island of Anglesey (Yns Mons, the holy island, to the ancient Druids) in North Wales.

You will also find information specific to *The Lucifer Scroll*, including articles about archaeology and Istanbul, as well as more photos and videos and links to various interesting websites.

You can also check us out or join our group on Facebook or follow Barrie on Twitter or simply email Barrie at excaliburparchment@gmail.com.